MW00950652

THE SCHOLAR

Rachel D. Moore

Chapter One

What is it with these bloody Brits and their fondness for gloomy lighting?

Anna Miller blinked in the softly glowing light that was emanating from the wall sconces evenly spaced around the large room. The text she was currently studying was already difficult enough to read in normal lighting, the handwriting tiny and cramped. In the soft, ambient lighting that the British seemed to prefer over the bright, fluorescent tubing that she was accustomed to, the writing on the page seemed little more than squiggles, even when Anna squinted.

With a sigh, she pushed her chair away from her desk and rubbed her tired eyes, silently cursing whomever had designed her office. The comfortable reading room down the hall --- with its wide cubicles, cushioned chairs, and electric fireplace --- had state-of-the-art reading lamps that could be adjusted to various intensities of light. *That* room had been designed to entice people into reading. It was her *job* to read, and all she had was an old banker's lamp.

Tomorrow, she told herself firmly. *Tomorrow I will acquire one of those lamps for myself, even it means I have to steal one.*

But it could wait. The lack of natural sunlight coming through her office's lone window told her that it was getting late. Despite the fact that London was on a completely different time zone than her native state of Tennessee --- a change that she had yet to adapt to, even after being in England for several months --- the long hours of attempting to decipher a fifteenth-century monk's journal had made her weary.

Yes, the lamp could wait. Right now she just wanted to go home and take a long, hot shower.

Anna got to her feet and stretched, wincing as several joints cracked in protest. The Bradley Library --- or The Stacks, as it was more commonly known --- was a drafty Victorian mansion that had been converted into a library in the early 20th century. Even though the library was climate controlled to better preserve the books housed within, London's constant *dampness* seemed to seep into everything. The hot shower would help to drive away the chill that seemed to always be clinging to her.

As luck would have it, however, Anna was going to have to put the shower on hold. Just as she was gathering up the monk's journal and a few other texts she had been working on, a knock came at her door. "Excuse me," called out a smooth tenor, its accent precisely clipped British colored with the accent of a native Londoner. "I know that the library is getting ready to close up, but I am hoping that you can help me. I am looking for a Ms. Anna Miller?"

She let out a mental groan as she plastered a polite smile to her face and set her books back down on the desk. *Looks as though there will be no rest --- or shower --- for the weary.* "Then you are in luck, for I am she."

The door swung open, and Anna blinked in surprise at the figure that stepped through.

It was a young man, perhaps only a few years older than she. He was tall and lean, dressed in dark jeans, a light-colored t-shirt, and a fashionably-cut sports coat. His face sported a strong jaw, an aquiline nose, enviously high cheekbones, and eyes the color of the palest green she had ever seen. His hair was dark, and fell around his ears in soft curls.

He looks as though he just left a photo shoot, she thought, watching his approach with an arched brow. *Which makes it all the more curiouser as to why he is in my office. Or in a library, for that matter. Men who look like that rarely crack books.*

Her visitor stopped on the other side of her desk, a sheepish grin making him look incredibly boyish. "Ms. Miller. It's an honor. I've heard quite a bit about you. Though I must say I was expecting someone a bit, ah, *older*." He flushed and raked a hand through his hair, making it stick out.

Meaning he was expecting a bespectacled, gray-haired librarian with a cardigan and loafers. Anna's brow lifted higher, and the edge of her lips curled up.

The man's blush deepened as he stuck out a hand. "Before my faculties fail and I forget my manners altogether, my name is Rhys. Rhys Blackwood."

She took his hand with a firm grip. His own grip was strong, but not crushing, and his hand was rough with callouses. *A working man, then.* "A pleasure, Mr. Blackwood. What can I help you with today?"

He gave her a full grin, and she was suddenly sure that the photo shoot he must have just come from was for a toothpaste ad as she caught sight of bright, perfect teeth. Her heart did a strange little flop in her chest. "Please, call me Rhys. And I am here about a book."

This time, she didn't bother to suppress her sigh. While this guy was undeniably gorgeous, she was *tired*. "This is a library, Mr. Blackwood. We have many books here. Perhaps you could be more specific?" She didn't bother to hide the sharpness in her voice, either.

He had the good graces to duck his head as his face turned an interesting shade of red. "Please excuse me. I tend to get flustered around women." He cleared his throat. "The book I am looking for is very old. We are unsure of the author. *Tractatu de Magicis Doctrinam* I believe is the title."

Anna's eyebrows nearly disappeared into her hairline, both in surprise at the ease with which the Latin rolled off of his tongue, and in wonderment as to why someone who looked as though he belonged in a magazine instead of in a library would even *know* of such a rare book. "*The Treatise on Magical Learnings.* I am somewhat familiar with that title. Though I am almost certain that we do not have a copy of it here."

The smile he gave her this time was neither boyish nor dazzling, but the slow smile of one who knew something she did not. "Ah, but you may be wrong. We have recently uncovered evidence that shows that a copy was sent to the Stacks in 1947."

Anna sucked in her breath through her teeth. She knew that there were only three known copies of the book in existence, and one of them had disappeared from London during the 1940s. Most scholars had believed the text to be a casualty of the Blitz, but this man was now saying it could be here. In her library.

2

She suddenly frowned. Wait. He had said that *we* had uncovered evidence. Who was 'we'?

She peered closer at him. He wasn't wearing a tweed jacket, nor was he covered in chalk --- two of the things she had come to associate with literary academics in London's universities --- so she doubted he was a professor. His clothes were well-tailored and looked expensive. She ruled out student. A journalist, then? Or a treasure hunter who had been taken up by the recent popularity of discovering 'lost' manuscripts by the great writers of early British history?

Anna shook her head, clearing her thoughts. It didn't matter who he was. "Mr. Blackwood, inventory is very well-documented here. Also, the *Treatise* would be a crown jewel in our collection, and we would proudly display it. I'm sorry, but I just don't believe it is here."

Rhys Blackwood, it would seem, was not used to hearing the word 'no'. Instead of admitting defeat, he placed both hands on her desk, leaned forward, and met her gaze head-on.

Anna felt her insides twist in a not-unpleasant way, and she had to drop her gaze as her cheeks warmed.

"Could you look?" he asked softly. "Please?" He suddenly flashed her his toothpaste-commercial grin. "If it is an inconvenience, I'll find a way to make it up to you. I promise."

She let out a sigh and reached for her computer mouse. *What the hell.* It's not like she had anything better to do. "Very well, Mr. Blackwood. But don't get your hopes up. There is very little chance that the *Tractatu* is here. Even if it is, I'm afraid that ---"

She stopped as the sound of shouts arose from down the hall. Frowning, she looked through the bars of the locked cage that housed the Stack's oldest texts to see that the light in the adjoining office was on. Abraham Clark, the Bradley's curator and head librarian, was still at work.

She turned back to her computer, pulling up the library's internal search engine. Abraham was in spectacular health for a man of seventy-two, but his hearing was infamously bad. This wouldn't be the first time he had been watching a television program with the volume up loud enough to be heard throughout the entire library.

Before she could type in her request, more shouting came from the other office. This time, she was able to make out words.

"*What is the meaning of this?*" That was Abraham, his voice angry. "*You cannot simply burst in here like that!*"

Another voice, this one also shouting. But it was muffled, and Anna couldn't understand what was being said.

"*That is preposterous! It isn't here. It never has been!*"

More muffled words.

"*I don't care what information you have. I have been at this library for nearly fifty years, and I know that ---*"

Anna never found out what knowledge Abraham had, for his words were suddenly interrupted by the unmistakable sound of gunshots.

Before she even had time to register what that meant, Rhys was diving across her desk. He pulled open the top drawer and snatched up a small, silver key before hooking an arm around her waist and propelling her towards the cage. Without hesitation, he unlocked the gate, pushed her through, then shut it and relocked it behind him. Then his arm was back around her waist, and he was pulling her into the deepest shadows of the room, positioning them behind a bookshelf and in a corner, dragging her to the floor.

Anna decided now would be a good time to scream.

Before she could, however, Rhys draped his own body over hers, slapped a hand across her mouth, and lowered his head towards hers.

Her eyes widened at the first thrill of fear went through her. *Oh, God. He's going to rape me!*

But he did not try to kiss her, as she had feared. Instead, he placed his mouth directly by her ear. "Don't make a sound," he murmured, his breath washing over the nape of her neck. "I am not here to hurt you. I want to help you. I swear. But you must not make a sound."

While speaking, he had been carefully reaching behind him. When his hand reemerged, he was holding a gun. A *large* gun.

Anna let out an involuntary whimper against his hand. *Ohgodohgodohgodohgod.*

"Shh. Not a sound." Rhys lifted his hand from her mouth and stared down at her, his green eyes glittering, mouth set in a hard line. She immediately pressed her lips together as tight as she could.

He gave her a nod, then lifted his head just enough to look through the narrow gap between the wall and the bookshelf they were squeezed behind towards her desk.

All she could hear was the steady *thump thump* of her pounding heart. After a moment, however, she realized that it couldn't be her heartbeat, which was racing at a much higher speed than the sound in her ears. Instead, she was hearing footsteps created by someone in heavy boots. And they were coming into her office.

She wanted to look, to see what was happening. But she couldn't. Rhys was on top of her, his weight pinning her to the floor. Even if she tilted her head back, the only thing she would be able to see was the ceiling. So she settled for keeping her eyes focused on Rhys's face.

A second later, she heard voices arise from the direction of her desk. "It better be here," came a low growl.

"If it is in the Bradley, this is the room it will be in," came a second, quieter voice.

A loud crash reverberated through the room as someone attempted to force their way into the cage. Anna squeezed her eyes shut and bit down on her tongue to keep from crying out in fear.

"What the fuck is this?" came the first, rough voice. "Who the hell locks books up in a cage?"

A sigh was audible over the sound of clicking computer keys. *Are they trying to find a book??* was the thought that came to Anna's mind as she realized she had left the search engine pulled up. "They are valuable. I know this may be difficult for your primitive brain to comprehend, but the collective worth of all of the books in that cage is greater than that of some countries."

Another crash sounded as the first speaker --- Growly Voice --- launched another kick at the cage. "Then put them in a vault or a safe or something. How the hell are we supposed to get in there? I didn't bring any cutters."

"No need for those." The clicking of the keyboard continued. "There should be a key in this desk. If the old man had it, this door wouldn't have been open."

Anna's eyes flew back open, and she pressed a hand to her mouth. *The key!* If they found the key, there would be nothing stopping the two of them from coming into the cage. With her.

Above her, Rhys flicked his eyes to hers and slightly shook his head. Then a fierce grin, more wolf than man, stretched across his lips, and he patted the breast of his sports coat.

She blinked, and the tiny portion of her brain that seemed to have retained its function primly pointed out that *they* had gotten into the cage. And there was only one key. The two men couldn't possibly get in.

She felt her whole body sag in relief. Rhys, who was resting his weight on her, had to place his free hand on the floor to steady himself. *We just have to wait until they leave. Then we can get out of here. I'll call the police and ---*

A sound of frustration came from behind her. "I don't understand," came the voice of the second speaker, his voice colored with a hint of anger. "It's not listed in their database."

"What? Are you saying they don't have it?"

"No. They *must* have it. Perhaps the old man didn't want to have proof that it was here. But without a call number I have no idea where it will be."

"So? We just get in there and start going through these books until we find it."

"Will you just use what brain you do have for once?" snapped the other speaker. "We don't know what it looks like. We could damage it by accident. And there are hundreds of books in there. It could take hours. We don't have time."

Growly Voice rattled the cage once more. "Well, then. What do we do now? The coppers will be swarming all over this place tomorrow. You shouldn't have killed the old man. We won't be able to get back in here for days."

You shouldn't have killed... Abraham! Anna had to bite down on her hand to keep from screaming. *No. Please don't let him be dead!*

5

Above her, she felt Rhys give a little jerk. Looking up at him, she saw his mouth tighten and his eyes flash.

She heard the sound of a desk drawer being opened. Then a loud snarl sounded, followed by a crash that sent the floor shaking as her desk was knocked to the ground. "The key is gone! The old man *must* have it. Or one of the other librarians."

"Why would they have it?"

"I don't know. But it's not here."

A nasty chuckle floated back to them. "He's not going to be pleased, you know. You told him ---"

"Shut up." The second speaker, the one who had been looking for whatever book they had been hoping to steal, let out another snarl. "Let's get out of here. Even if it is here, we have no way of finding it. He'll have to deal with it."

"Suit yourself". There was one last rattling of the cage, then those heavy footsteps sounded again as the two men began to leave.

For a long moment, Anna just lay there, heart pounding. Then she was shoving at Rhys, desperate to get up. "Let me go!" she whispered frantically. "Take whatever you want. I don't care. Just let me go check on Abraham. I have to see if he's still alive. I won't even tell the police that ---"

"Anna!" The gun had disappeared, and Rhys was gripping both of her wrists, staring down at her with a grim expression. "I told you, I'm not here to hurt you. And I'm not here to steal anything. I'm going to get you to safety, okay? Those two might decide to come back, and I'll be dead before I let them hurt you. I *swear* it. But you have to do *exactly* as I say. Do you understand?"

She could only nod. What choice did she have? He had a gun, and was currently holding her down. But ... "We have to check on Abraham. I won't leave until I know... Until I see him."

He blew out a breath. "I'm going to stand up," he said, not answering her. "The first thing we need to do is get anything of yours out of your desk. Do you have a purse? A bag? A wallet? Anything that has anything personal in it?"

"Yes. It's in my desk."

"Okay. You need to get it. If those two come back, they might realize there was another librarian in here and decide to track you down. I'd rather not make it easier for them by leaving all of your information behind."

Anna felt all of the color drain from her face. In all the chaos of the past few minutes --- *Has it only been minutes? It seems like hours!* --- she never thought that they might want to come after her personally. She had assumed it was just a robbery. Why would they want to come after *her*?

Before she could process that thought, Rhys was climbing to his feet. He held out his hand to help her get to hers. Once she was standing, however, he did not release his grip on her hand. "Stay right behind me," he murmured. "Don't leave my side for anything, understand? We're going to get your things, then I'm getting you out of here."

She nodded, gripping his hand as tight as she possibly could. She could feel her whole body trembling with both fear and adrenaline. *You're okay. You're going to be fine. Just do what he says. Everything is going to be fine...*

Rhys reached back to the waistband of his jeans and pulled out his gun once again. Anna closed her eyes and took a deep breath. *You're okay. You're okay.*

Wait a minute. Now that her brain had begun to regain some of its functions, a few thoughts were whirling through her head. Such as...

"You were in here looking for a book just before those two showed up," she hissed at him. "And you have a *gun*. No one comes into a library with a gun! Who are you? Are you working with them? I swear to God, if you ---"

"Anna, stop!" He turned so that he was fully facing her, and peered into her eyes. She would have taken a step back from the intensity of his gaze if she hadn't been so scared. "Listen to me. I am *not* working with them. I came here looking for a book... and for you." He offered her a half-hearted grin. "Abraham said you were sharp. He wasn't kidding."

She narrowed her eyes at him. "You know Abraham? How?"

"Later. I promise. I will answer as many of your questions as I can. But first, we have to get you out of here and to somewhere safe."

The two slowly inched their way through the cage back towards Anna's desk. She strained her ears for any sounds that might indicate the two men returning, but was unable to hear anything over her pounding heartbeat. When the gate was opened, she couldn't help but wince at the squeaking sound it made. *I'll have to look into getting that oiled.*

For a moment, the two stood perfectly still, holding their breaths. When nothing happened, Rhys nudged her forward. "Go," he whispered. "Get your things. I'll guard the door."

The second speaker had tipped her desk onto its back. Everything that had been on the top --- her computer, books and pens --- now lay scattered on the floor. Thankfully, the drawers had remained closed, and she was able to retrieve her purse from the bottom right drawer. As she went to rejoin Rhys by the door, she couldn't stop herself from leaning down to retrieve the monk's journal and shoving it into her bag.

"Ready?" he murmured. "It looks as though they are gone. Still, we need to get out of here as soon as we can. My car is in the side lot. We can go out through the ---"

"Not until we've checked on Abraham," she hissed.

He sighed. "Anna, we really should ---"

She pressed her lips together and didn't move.

7

He shook his head, and she couldn't help but notice the way his jaw tightened. "Right. Stick close to the wall. If you see or hear anything out of the ordinary, I want you to scream as loud as you can and get the hell out of here. There is a Met station two blocks from here. You go there, and you tell them what happened. You run, and you don't look back. Promise me, or I'll throw you over my shoulder and carry you out of here right now."

She lifted her right hand, palm outward. "Promise."

Rhys held out his hand again, and she took it. After checking once more that no one was in the hallway, he pulled her out of her office and towards Abraham's. They hugged the wall, with Rhys holding his gun at the ready.

Once they reached the entrance to Abraham's office, Rhys stopped. "Stay here and let me go in first," he murmured. He released her hand and, gripping his gun tight, stepped around the frame and through the doorway.

For a long moment, there was nothing. Anna stood where he had left her, one hand on her chest, the other clutching at the edge of the doorframe. *He's going to be okay. Abraham hasn't even taken a sick day since I've been here.* She had to believe that he was going to come walking out of his office, maybe with some help from Rhys. But he was going to be okay. He had to be!

Another moment passed. No sound was coming from within the office. Her heart, if possible, began to pound even faster. *What if the two men are in there? What if they got Rhys, too? What do I ---*

Before true panic could finally set in, Rhys reappeared through the door. She didn't have to ask him if Abraham was okay. The look on his face told her everything she needed to know.

"No," she moaned. "Oh, no. No no no. Abraham!" She tried to push past Rhys, to go into Abraham's office and see for herself, but he held out an arm, blocking her path.

"You don't want to go in there," he said in a tight voice, his eyes holding an emotion she couldn't place. "He's gone, Anna. There is nothing you can do for him." His voice grew thick, and he looked away from her. But not before she saw a tear leak from the corner of one eye.

"No. I have to go in there. I have to see him. I *have* to!" Anna finally ducked under his arm before he could stop her. Once she was past the barrier of his arm and in the room, she felt her whole body go cold, and a hand was raised to her mouth without her consent.

Rhys had been right. Abraham was beyond her aid. He lay sprawled out on the floor, a pool of blood spreading out underneath him. His glasses were askew, but they would no longer do him any good, as his eyes were staring sightlessly up at the ceiling. Two holes punctured the chest of his white shirt, red stains spreading across the fabric.

He's dead. Oh, God. Abraham is dead.

She suddenly felt the urge to be very violently ill.

"Not here." Rhys was by her side again, wrapping an arm around her shoulders and pulling her along. "Let's get outside first. Come on."

She couldn't have protested, even if she wanted to. She was no longer in control over her body. She was trembling so hard that she doubted she would have been able to walk on her own. She also found that she was having a hard time breathing. She thought that she might actually shake apart if she couldn't get herself under control soon.

"Almost there." Rhys pushed open a door, and Anna felt a welcoming blast of cool air on her face. Before she could do anything, he was helping her over to the side of the building and behind a row of bushes. As soon as he let go of her, her knees hit the ground, and everything she had eaten within the last few hours was coming back up. Her shaking intensified, and she was crying and hiccupping uncontrollably as she retched.

She stayed like that for a long moment, emptying the contents of her stomach, before her body could no longer support her. She slumped against the wall and did the most logical thing she could do in her current situation.

She fainted.

Chapter Two

When she woke up, her head was pounding, her mouth felt like cotton, and her stomach was empty.

Anna let out a groan and lifted a hand to her head. Sure, it wasn't the first time she'd woken up with a hangover. She was a notorious lightweight. But it had been a long time since she had felt *this* bad. And why on earth had she been drinking, anyways? Didn't she have to go to work?

"Well, hello there," came a soft, decidedly female voice from somewhere off to her right. "Welcome back."

Anna let out a yelp and sat straight up, wincing as the pounding in her head increased. She was about to ask a question --- such as one normally would when faced with finding a stranger in their room upon waking --- but she stopped when she realized something else.

She was naked. She wasn't even wearing a bra or panties.

With another cry, she slid back down onto the bed, pulling the blanket up to her chin as her face burned. *Just what did I do last night??*

A chuckle floated from the same direction that the voice had come from. "Sorry. I, ah, didn't think you'd want to sleep in clothes that had vomit on them. So I laundered them for you. Don't worry. No one saw you but me. I made sure Rhys stayed outside, though he was very anxious to make sure you were all right."

Rhys? Why did she know that name? Maybe that was ---

Then she remembered. The library, the handsome stranger, the gunshots, Abraham...

"Abraham!" she shouted. She sat back up, making sure she moved more slowly this time around, and to keep the blanket pulled up. "He..."

"I know." The voice sounded sad. "Rhys told me. I'm sorry. Abraham was a good man."

Anna squinted towards the sound of the voice, but could only make out a vague outline in the darkness. "Who are you?"

"Oh, I'm sorry. Here. Shield your eyes."

Anna did as she was told. A *click* sounded, then light blossomed from a small lamp by the bed. Blinking, she turned her gaze back towards the direction the voice had come from.

A woman was sitting in a chair just a few feet away. She looked to be a few years older than Anna, with long dark hair and an aquiline nose. Even with her foggy memories she could easily see the resemblance between this stranger and the man who had rescued her at the library.

The woman in question offered her a kind smile. "Hello, Anna. My name is Nicola. I'm Rhys's sister. You fainted at the library, and he thought it would be a good idea to bring you here until we can figure out what happened."

"So it wasn't a dream. Abraham really is dead." She had hoped…

"I'm afraid so." There was a pause, then a scraping sound as Nicola got to her feet. "I'm sure you want a few moments alone to process. There is a bathroom behind me if you would like to take a shower and get cleaned up. Your clothes are on the foot of the bed. When you are finished, just walk through the door and take a left. You'll be in the kitchen. We'll wait for you in there." Another pause. "Take all the time you need. I'll let Rhys know you're awake. He's been out there pacing ever since I shooed him away. I told him you would be fine, but he always worries too much."

"Thank you," was all Anna could think to say.

Nicola offered her a nod before leaving the room.

Anna sat there for a moment, the blanket clutched to her chest, her mind whirling. She was naked in a stranger's home. Two men had come into the library to… what? Rob it? But she had been saved by Rhys, the man who had come in with a gun, as though he had known something was going to happen. And Abraham…

At the thought of the kindly old man, she placed her face in her hands and began to sob.

Abraham Clark had been more than just a boss to Anna. He had been her mentor, the one who had convinced her to move to London. In the two years she had known him, he had become something of a father figure to her, encouraging her curiosity and her desire to learn.

She had first met him back in the States, when she had been working at a university library as a rare book curator. The university was hosting a series of lectures on literature throughout the centuries, and Abraham had been invited as a guest speaker. More importantly, he was allowing the library to borrow a small collection from the Bradley to display. Included in the collection were several pages of *Doctor Faustus* that had notes in the margins that had been handwritten by Marlowe himself. Anna had been chomping at the bits to have the chance to study them.

Abraham had barely walked through the library's doors when she first pounced on him. The head librarian was on his way to greet the Englishman, but Anna had beat him to it.

"Doctor Clark! It's an honor to meet you, sir. I've read all of your articles dealing with your interpretation of *Beowulf*. I have to say that your idea that Grendel was actually a ---"

"Miss Miller." That had been her boss, and he had been irritated. "Please excuse her, Doctor Clark. This is Anna Miller, our rare book librarian. She is in charge of the collection you have so kindly loaned us, and I'm afraid she is a bit… overeager about having such important documents under her care."

"Please. No need to apologize. There is no such thing as 'overeager' when it comes to the study of literature." Abraham had offered her his hand. "It is a pleasure, Miss Miller. And I would be lying if I did not say I am flattered that you are so familiar with my work. Are you a literature scholar as well?"

"Actually, I am. My undergrad is in early British Literature. I have a Masters in fifteenth- and sixteenth-century British Literature, as well as a Masters in Library Science. I wanted to actually *study* literature instead of teaching it. That's why I decided to be a librarian."

The head librarian cleared his throat, and Anna blushed. She had a tendency to ramble when she was excited.

But Abraham hadn't seemed to mind. Instead, he had laughed. "It is so refreshing to see someone who is enthusiastic about literature. Especially someone so young! Please, Miss Miller. You must allow me to take you out for dinner one night while I am here. I would love to hear about your studies."

That had been the beginning of a wonderful friendship. During the two weeks that Abraham had been at the university, the two of them had shared many conversations. He had been delighted when she had told him that she believed Shakespeare had actually been a woman --- and was able to argue her point --- and shared with her his own theories as to who the Bard had actually been. He had also granted her permission to study the Marlowe pages in the evenings after the exhibit had closed, which had cemented him as a hero in her eyes.

Even after returning to London, he had still kept in contact with her. He had even recommended one of her papers to a prestigious academic journal, and had been the first to call and congratulate her when it was published. Then, one day, he had called her out of the blue.

"What do you want to do, Anna?" he had asked without preamble. "With your career, I mean? I hope you don't plan to stay at the university library forever. Not that there is anything wrong with that, but that place is too small for you."

He was right. While she loved what she did, the university just did not have access to the texts that she wanted to study. Besides, her office was windowless and hot. "I want to go to the Folger. I could study Shakespeare all I wanted. Then maybe I could finally write that paper proving that he was in fact a she." She had often fantasized about getting lost in the famed Folger Shakespeare Library and accidently stumbling across a lost play, or a piece of solid proof of the Bard's true identity. Something that would re-write history and cement her career as a literary academic.

Abraham chuckled. "Yes, I have no doubt that you would do well there. However, I have another idea that I would like to run by you." He paused. "How would you feel about coming to work for me?"

Anna blinked. "Work for *you?* You mean, in *London??*"

Another chuckle. "Yes, in London. After all, this is where the material you want to study is *from,* correct? We may not be as big as the Folger, but we do have many original manuscripts here. And a lot of texts that you will not find within the States. I am in need of a librarian to handle the older texts we have in our collection, and I can't think of anyone more suited for the job."

There hadn't even been a need to think it over. She had accepted right then.

He had worked so hard to make sure she adjusted to her new life well. He encouraged her to get out of the library and meet others her own age instead of spending all of her time with 'ancient ghosts', as he had called the books under her care. Once a week he invited her over to his own home for dinner and conversation. He asked after manuscripts she was studying, or papers she was planning to write. He had told her many times how happy he was she had come to London, and that he hoped she was happy as well. During their last dinner, he had told her that great things awaited her. And that he was going to help her achieve them.

Now he was gone. Not only had she lost a friend and mentor, but the world had lost a brilliant man, whose collected knowledge was unmatched by anyone else. And all for what? A *book?*

Anna felt the flow of tears halt as a ball of anger formed in her chest. How *dare* someone come into *her* library and turn her whole world upside down? How dare they defy the sanctity of her haven and take away her friend? And how dare they decide that his life was less valuable than pieces of paper? She would find them. She would learn who they were and what they wanted. And she would make them explain to her why they had killed Abraham.

But first, she needed to get dressed.

Remembering that the other woman --- Nicola --- had told her there was a bathroom, Anna slid out from under the blanket and found her clothes lying on the end of the bed as promised. Picking them up, she headed towards the bathroom. First, she would shower. Then she would get answers.

After the shower, Anna felt almost human again. Her headache had subsided somewhat, and the stench of bile seemed to finally be out of her nose. She stood in front of the mirror for a moment, running her fingers through her hair in an attempt to make it look as though she was not a drowned rat before deciding she looked presentable. After all, Rhys had seen her throw up. And Nicola had seen her naked. She doubted she could look any worse.

"All right," she murmured to her reflection. "It's time to find out what the hell is going on."

Nicola had told her to make a left when she left the bedroom. Anna did as she was told, and found herself entering a brightly lit kitchen. As if her eyes were immediately drawn to him, the first thing she noticed was Rhys, who was standing by the sink and bouncing on his toes with a nervous energy. Vaguely, Anna remember that Nicola had said he'd been pacing. *"He always worries too much."*

Unexpectedly, she could feel her cheeks warm. He had been worried about *her*.

"Ah. Here she is!" That was Nicola, who was sitting at a bar stool situated at a large kitchen island. She turned a bright smile onto her brother. "See? I told you she was fine."

"Anna." There was a smile on Rhys's face as he came to stand next to her, but she could still see worry in his eyes. "You're all right?"

"Yes. I'm fine. Thanks to you." She nervously tugged on the end of her hair. "You probably saved my life back at the library. If you hadn't been there, if they had found me... I don't think saying 'thank you' is enough, but thank you."

His smile widened, and she could see the concern fade from his eyes. "I'm just happy I was there and able to help." He gestured towards the island where his sister sat. "Would you care to have a seat? I'm sure you must be starving. I'll grab you a sandwich and something to drink."

"Yes. Thank you." Anna took the stool next to Nicola, taking the opportunity to glance around the kitchen. It was large, with modern appliances and granite countertops. But the floor and the cabinetry were made from dark wood, which made it look more like a kitchen and less like a spaceship.

"Here you are." Rhys sat a plate in front of her that contained a large sandwich, accompanied by a large glass of water. "I'm not sure what you like, so tell me if you'd prefer something else."

Anna took one look at it, and her stomach let out a loud growl. She didn't care *what* was on it. She would have gladly eaten cardboard, she was so hungry. Without another word, she eagerly began to eat.

Rhys chuckled as he took a seat on a bar stool across the island from the two women. "I'm glad to see you up and moving. I have to admit that I panicked a bit when you fainted."

"That is putting it mildly," came Nicola's amused voice from Anna's right. "You should have seen the look on his face when he carried you in here. I thought you were dead."

Anna swallowed and stared across the island at her rescuer. "You carried me?' she asked. Then she immediately blushed. *Of course he carried you in here,* her brain said snidely. *How else do you think you got in here?* The thought of him doing something so intimate with her when she didn't even know him made her blush deepen.

However, his own cheeks had colored, and he raked his hand through his hair, making it stick out in several places. "I didn't know what to do," he said defensively. "It's not as though I have women fainting around me all of the time. And things were so crazy when we were in the library. I thought that maybe you had been hurt."

"Just my pride," she muttered quietly. She couldn't believe she had thrown up in front of him and then fainted. She had never fainted before in her life. Of course, she had never seen a real dead body before. Especially not one that had recently been a person she knew.

Speaking of which... "You said you knew Abraham. How?"

Rhys opened his mouth to answer, but was cut off by his sister lifting a hand. "We'll answer your questions soon. We promise. But first, you are going to eat. I would prefer it if you did not faint again. I'm not sure Rhys's heart could take it."

Rhys glared across the island at his sister, who simply smiled sweetly in return. Anna took another bite of her sandwich. "Can you at least tell me where I am?" she asked around a mouthful of meat, cheese and bread.

"Our home," Nicola replied, waving a hand in the air. "We're in West Dulwich, about half an hour from the Bradley. Rhys called the police as soon as the two of you arrived here and left an anonymous tip. I'm sure they've found Abraham by now." Her voice was sad.

Anna closed her eyes briefly and swallowed as the image of Abraham lying in the floor, his glasses askew rose unbidden into her mind. "You didn't tell them who you were? Or that you were there?"

"No." His voice was firm. "And I didn't tell them you were there, either. So when they call you to tell you that Abraham is dead, you must act surprised."

She nearly choked on her sandwich. "You lied to the *police?* You could get in a lot of trouble for that! What were you thinking?"

"Of you, keeping you safe. We don't know who those two men were who killed Abraham. They were after something, and they didn't seem too happy that they were unable to find it. If they are monitoring the police reports, they would find out that someone else was there. And they would have your name. I don't want them to have it if I can help it." His voice had dropped to a growl.

Anna dropped her eyes to her sandwich. Suddenly, she wasn't feeling so hungry any more.

"Rhys, stop it," Nicola chided softly. "You're scaring her. She has enough to deal with already. Let's handle one crisis at a time, shall we?"

He opened his mouth to reply, but stopped when another figure walked into the kitchen.

Anna let out an involuntary whimper and hunched down on her seat, trying to make herself as small as possible. Her mind immediately flashed back to the library, and the sound of the heavy footsteps that came into her office while she was wedged behind a bookshelf, lying underneath a strange man with a gun.

"Easy," Nicola said in a soothing tone of voice, lying a hand on Anna's arm. "I am sorry. I should have told you that someone else was here so that you wouldn't be frightened. This is David. He's a friend."

Heart pounding --- and chastising herself for jumping like a scared rabbit --- Anna let out a shaky breath and lifted her head to study the newcomer.

He was an older gentleman. Anna guessed him to be in his late sixties or seventies. He looked exactly like what Anna pictured when she thought of the stereotypical British professor, complete with a tweed jacket that had leather elbow patches. His graying hair curled tightly against his skull, and blue eyes peered at her curiously from behind a pair of glasses. He was even wearing brown loafers.

He frowned as he came closer. "I wasn't aware that you two were expecting company tonight. Where is Miss Miller?"

"David," Nicola said gently, "*this* is Anna Miller. Anna, this is David Albinson. He was also a very good friend of Abraham's, and a family friend of ours."

The older man blinked down at her in surprise. "*You're* the Anna that Abraham brought from the States? I am so sorry. I had thought you to be somewhat ---"

"Older?" she finished for him, her lips turning up wryly. "Don't worry. You're not the only one." She nodded at Rhys. "I think he was expecting me to have gray hair and be wearing a cardigan."

"Or at least be wearing glasses," he responded, grinning. Anna felt herself relax, and managed to return his grin with a smile of her own, small though it was. "I was rather surprised to find you. The way Abraham spoke of you, we were under the impression that you were around his age."

"I'm also sure that you don't find very many people my age working in dusty old libraries." She paused to take a drink of water. "Now. I have been very patient, considering the fact that I woke up naked in a strange bed just a few moments ago." Anna noticed that Nicola was smothering a grin, while Rhys's face was turning an interesting shade of red. David just lifted an eyebrow. "*You* three are going to answer my questions. Starting with how you know Abraham."

"Fair enough." David sat on the stool next to Rhys and rested his elbows on the table, steepling his fingers together. "Abraham and I are --- *were* --- both known as Scholars. We work to find and preserve knowledge that has been lost over time."

Anna frowned. That had not been what she was expecting to hear. "Work for whom?"

"An organization that strives to either protect the world from that knowledge, or stop unscrupulous people who would use that knowledge for evil purposes. He and I have known each other since we were young men in university together." His voice took on a sad tone, and Anna thought he suddenly looked much older. "I can't believe he is gone."

Nicola reached across the table and laid a hand over his. "David."

He blinked, then smiled and patted her hand. "I am all right, dear. Thank you." He cleared his throat. "Actually, Miss Miller, this is why Abraham wanted you to come to London. He was getting ready to retire from being a Scholar soon, and he was hoping that you would take his place."

Anna stared at him blankly. "I'm sorry. I don't... He hired me just to be a librarian."

"Mmm. Hardly." He turned a kind smile on to her, and she was suddenly struck by how much it reminded her of Abraham. "He's been talking about you for some time now. I can remember when he returned from his trip to the States when he first met you. He kept talking about how he had met a woman who had a deep passion for old literature, and had what he called an 'overabundance of curiosity'. He was so excited to have found you. He had been thinking about retiring for some time, but he didn't want to leave us short-handed. He had been looking for a replacement, but no one lived up to his standards. He said that, within the first five minutes of meeting you, he knew that you were the one."

"So... The job at the library. Are you saying that was all a lie?" She felt as though she had just been punched in the gut. Had it all been a ruse? And for what? What had he wanted her to do? When had he planned on telling her? Why hadn't he bothered to tell her from the beginning? Was he afraid she would say no? Is that why he had lied to her?

She felt the unexpected prick of hot, angry tears form behind her eyes, and she ducked her head before any of the others could see them.

"Absolutely not." David's voice was stern. "Abraham would never have manipulated you. He needed a librarian. And you were indeed the best candidate for the job. He thought it would be much easier for you to work under him as a librarian while he taught you about his other duties. And he wouldn't have forced it on you. It would have been your choice to join us or not. Of course, he was fairly certain that you would say yes. If he wasn't, he never would have asked you to come all the way to London. Abraham was many things, but he was *not* a liar."

Feeling somewhat mollified, Anna nodded and took another drink of water. "So why didn't he tell me any of this?"

"He wanted you to get acclimated to being here first. He thought that moving to another country where you didn't know anyone and starting a new job was stressful enough. He wanted you to get settled in before he dropped this on you. I'm also sure that he was afraid to tell you upfront in case you decided not to come to London at all. At least this way, he would still have you as a librarian. And, if you were here and said no, he could always try and change your mind. He was a stubborn old man."

Anna felt her lips curl up into a smile. *Yes. Yes, he was.* "So what exactly does this entail? Being a... what did you say? A Scholar?"

"A Scholar, yes." He gave a slight shrug. "It's really not much more than what you are already doing: studying old texts and manuscripts, looking for Lost Knowledge. Then, when you do find something, you would tell someone who was a part of the organization that we work with so that they would investigate further and decide what, if anything, needed to be done."

She could feel the pounding in her head increasing once more, and she reached up to rub at her temples. "What exactly do you mean by 'Lost Knowledge'?" Something about his tone of voice told her these words came with capital letters. "And what is this 'organization' that you keep talking about? Who would I tell?"

David opened his mouth to answer, but was interrupted by Rhys getting to his feet. "I think that is enough for tonight," he said firmly. "We don't want to overwhelm her, and she's already been through enough for one day."

David gave the younger man a surprised look, then nodded. "Yes, of course. You're right. My apologies." He turned his kindly smile back onto Anna. "I am sorry, dear. I have been wanting to meet you for some time now. I tend to get carried away when I am excited, and Rhys is right. You've had a trying day."

"Wait a minute! I still have a lot of questions!"

"Tomorrow." Rhys walked around the table and offered her a hand. "Come on. If you're finished eating, let me take you to your flat to pick up some clothes. You'll need to stay here until we can figure out what happened tonight."

She frowned at him. "You really think those two men are going to come after me? You told me that the reason you didn't tell the police that we were there is so that they wouldn't know about me."

"No. I said that I didn't tell the police that you were there so that whoever did this wouldn't know you were there while *they* were. If they thought you might be a witness, I doubt they would hesitate to kill you. They've already killed Abraham without much thought. They will know about you if they've done any research about the library employees. And one of them already knew that there was supposed to be

17

a key in your desk that opened the cage. It would be stupid to think that they don't know you are the librarian in charge of that section."

Anna felt the color drain from her face at his words. What he was saying made sense. The two men who had come into her office *had* known about the key. And they had known how to use the database. They had to know that she worked at the library, and that she was the one who was most likely to have the key that they had been unable to find. Which meant that there were two killers out there who knew who she was and had a reason to look for her.

She started to feel faint again.

"Easy." Rhys's voice was soothing, and she felt a large, warm hand land on the back of her neck. He crouched down beside her so that he could look her in the eye. "I told you at the library that I was going to protect you, and I intend to keep that promise. It will be much easier to look after you here than if you were at your place. I'll take you over there, and I'll be with you the whole time. And I seriously doubt they are going to try anything else tonight. You heard them at the library. They have already screwed up. Okay?"

"Okay." Her voice sounded small, even to her. She took a deep breath and placed her hand in his, letting him help her slide off of the stool. "And, umm. Thanks. All of you. I..." Those damned tears were back, and she flapped her hand in the air in a useless gesture.

"We're happy to do what we can." Nicola hopped off of her own stool and came over to take Anna's hands in hers. "And I don't know about these two, but *I* am happy that you are not an old lady. It's been a long time since I've had any girl time. We can stay up and gossip and paint each other's nails. It'll be like a sleepover!"

Anna gave her a weak smile. "Thanks."

"Absolutely." The other woman gave her a wink. "Rhys, don't keep her out too long. She looks like she could use some more rest."

"Yes, Mother." Grinning at his sister, he dropped his hand from the back of Anna's neck to rest at the small of her back. It was a comforting gesture, and Anna was extremely grateful for it, especially as she was still not feeling very steady on her feet. "Come on, Anna. I'll drive you over."

When they got into Rhys's car, Anna could still make out the faint smell of vomit lingering in the upholstery. She was glad it was dark so that he couldn't see her furious blushing. She wondered if she should volunteer to have it cleaned so they smell wouldn't linger.

The first part of their drive was quiet, Anna staring out the window as she tried to sort through the information that she had just been given. The part that she was having the most difficulty with was the idea that Abraham had been a member of some sort of secret society, and that he had wanted her to be a part of it as well. While she didn't know exactly what being a Scholar entailed, it seemed as though it was something that she would enjoy doing. It was this 'organization' that David had kept referring to that was bothering her.

Finally, she stirred. "Can I ask you a question?"

"Haven't you learned enough for one day?" Rhys's voice was gentle, with a hint of amusement. "I was serious about not overwhelming you. You're still in shock over what happened earlier. Once that wears off, you may have trouble dealing with it all at once. And, as I have already demonstrated, I'm not good in handling that sort of thing."

 Anna ignored him and asked anyway. "Why were you at the library with a gun? You said you had come to find a book *and* me. I already know that you thought I was an old lady. Were you expecting the book to have teeth? Or were you expecting trouble? Did you already know something was going to happen? Did Abraham?"

He risked taking his eyes off of the road long enough to glance over at her. She returned his gaze with one of her own. She wasn't about to let him ignore her under the pretense of coddling. She *hated* being coddled. And she was involved in whatever this was whether she wanted to be or not. She had a right to know. Knowledge, Abraham had always said, was the best defense.

"Very well." He paused. "I didn't know for certain that something was going to happen. And I certainly didn't know that it would be happening *tonight*. But there have been... *rumors* that there was information that had been recently uncovered that someone was willing to gain by any means necessary, information that mentioned the Bradley, and the book I was asking after. Abraham had asked me to come by and introduce myself to you as a library patron so that you could get used to me being around. That way I could keep an eye out without being conspicuous until he could gently break all of this in to you."

"I see. So you and your sister are *not* Scholars like David and Abraham?"

"No."

"That means you must be members of this organization that David was referring to."

"Yes."

Anna fell quiet at this information. *He knew,* she thought, feeling that ball of anger returning. Only this time it was aimed at Abraham and not the nameless men who had killed him. *He knew that something could happen, and he never told me. He should have warned me instead of sending me a babysitter. I had a right to* know!

"We never dreamed that something like *this* would happen." Rhys spoke as though he had read her mind, his voice apologetic. "Usually the people we deal with are more... subtle."

"He still should have told me. I could have *done* something. If he thought it was serious enough for me to have a babysitter, then he should have warned me. Your friend David said that it would have been my choice to become a Scholar, to join this little club of yours. But it looks to me as though Abraham was determined to make sure I got involved no matter what!"

"He was only doing what he thought was best for you." Rhys's voice was beginning to grow defensive. "He cared for you very much. I could tell just by speaking to him. I had thought that maybe he was in love with you. Now that I know you're not older, I think he looked upon you like a daughter. My guess is that he wanted you to only do the work you loved, the research and discovery. He wanted to shield you from the uglier aspects." He offered a humorless smile. "The aspects that *I* deal with."

"Yes, well. *That* worked out well for him, didn't it?" She knew she was being unfair. Abraham wasn't here to defend himself, and it wasn't Rhys's fault that Abraham hadn't told her anything about being a Scholar. But Rhys was here, and she needed to yell at someone. And after today, she felt she had a right to a tantrum. *"Maybe* he would still be here if he had told me. I'm not some damsel in distress. I *can* take care of myself. Just because I'm a *woman* doesn't mean I'm *helpless!"*

Rhys didn't respond.

Anna let out a frustrated sigh and crossed her arms over her chest, her gaze going back out the window. "Just what is this organization that you are a part of anyways? Or is it just called The Organization? Or some other ridiculous, unimaginative name?"

Rhys sighed. "No. But we'll get to that later. It's a long and complicated story. Let's just say that it is a family legacy, that Nicola and I *didn't* have a choice in the matter. Not like you do." He didn't bother trying to hide the bitterness in his voice. "We mostly protect people. That is why I swore to you in the library that I would keep you safe. It is my *job.* And I take it very seriously."

Anna couldn't help it. He had her curiosity piqued. "Is it one of the not-so-secret secret organizations? How long as your family been a part of it? What kind of people do you protect? And what did David mean about you deciding what to do about Lost Knowledge? What exactly did he mean by 'Lost Knowledge'?"

"Later. I promise. But first thing is first." He reached over to turn the car off, startling Anna with the sudden silence. "We're here."

Blinking out of her window, she saw that they had indeed arrived at her apartment. *Flat,* she reminded herself. Frowning slightly, she turned to Rhys, who was staring at her expectedly. "You know where I *live?"*

He shrugged. "Abraham told us where your flat was. I don't know what number, if that makes you feel any better. He only told me the name of the building."

Anna wasn't sure how she felt about the fact that these strangers knew where she lived, but then she decided it didn't matter. They knew, and there was nothing she could do about it now. "Let's just go in and get my things."

No one was waiting for them when they walked in through her door, though Rhys insisted that he enter first and make sure the apartment was clear before she entered. Once inside, she threw T-shirts, jeans, socks, and several pairs of underwear into her battered duffel bag. From the bathroom she gathered her toothbrush and other toiletries. Then, because she didn't know how long she would be gone, she grabbed the old quilt her grandmother had made for her when she left for college and folded it up over her arm. She knew it would make her feel better to have something familiar with her.

The last stop was her desk, tucked away in the small area that was meant to be used as a dining room.

Sitting on top was an odd contraption: an adjustable desk lamp that also had a large square magnifying glass clipped to it. This was also placed, reverently, on top of the pile of clothing in her bag. She also added a thick notebook as well as several pens.

Rhys watched her with a look of bemusement on his face. "What on earth is that thing?"

"My work light," she responded, turning in a slow circle to see if there was anything else that she needed to take with her. "It helps to keep me from going blind before I'm forty."

His brow creased. "You're planning on working?"

Having completed her circle, Anna placed her hands on her hips and pursed her lips at him. "What else am I supposed to do? The library is going to be closed. It *is* a crime scene after all, and there is no head librarian." Her voice stuck in her throat, and she quickly hurried on before she could let herself get sad. "If I am going to be under house arrest, I need to have *something* to do. Oh! That reminds me." She turned and walked back to her desk, unplugged her laptop, and held both computer and cord under her arm. "Okay. I think I have everything."

Still looking bemused, Rhys held the door open for her. She locked the door behind her, and the two walked back to his car in silence.

Chapter Three

As expected, the police called Anna's cell phone the next morning to inform her of Abraham's murder. She didn't have to fake the tears that fell as they gently but efficiently broke the news to her. The library, as she had suspected, would be closed for the duration of the investigation. No, she did not need to call anyone. They had already informed the library's board of directors, who would be contacting Anna with further information as to the library's functions. Abraham's next of kin --- a younger sister who lived in Scotland --- had also been informed. And would Anna please come in to give a statement?

When she ended the conversation, she felt exhausted, even though she had only been awake for a few hours. She wearily scrubbed at her eyes --- would she *ever* stop crying? --- and slid off of the kitchen barstool to head back into the room the Blackwoods had given her. "I'm going to go get dressed," she announced. "The police want me to come in to answer some questions."

The Blackwood siblings, both leaning against the counters in the kitchen, exchanged worried glances.

Anna sighed and waved a hand in the air. "I know, I know. I wasn't there. I left before the time they think the killers came in. I have no idea as to who would have wanted to hurt Abraham. Yes, I'll be happy to let them know if I think anything was stolen." Rhys had drilled her during the ride home last night as to what to say to the police, and he and Nicola had picked it back up that morning over breakfast. They had made her repeat it so many time that, if she hadn't been awake all night due to the image of Abraham's body lying on the floor, his glasses askew, showing itself every time she closed her eyes, she might actually believe it to be the truth.

She took her time getting ready, going over everything she was supposed to say in her head. She had always been a terrible liar. Sure, she could recite the story that Rhys and Nicola had come up with, but she wasn't sure about her body language. And these were the police. They were trained in detecting lies. What if they decided she wasn't telling the truth? What if they pushed her? Would she be able to keep up the façade? And what if she did break and told them what had really happened? What would happen to her?

By the time she stepped out of her room, her stomach was knotted with fear, the piece of toast she had managed to eat threatening to make a reappearance.

She found Rhys in the entryway, leaning against the door, arms crossed over his chest. "Are you all right?" he asked, standing up at her approach.

She must look worse than she thought, if the worried look in his eyes was anything to go by. For some reason, that infuriated her. "I'm on my way to lie to the police about the murder of my friend," she snapped. "I couldn't sleep last night because I kept having nightmares. I'm in a stranger's house because there are a pair of killers out there who *might* be looking for me. I'm just peachy. How are you?"

He let out a sigh and raked his hand through his hair. Anna may have only met him yesterday, but she had already picked up that this was his nervous habit. "Look, I know that you ---"

"I don't want to hear it. I just want to go get this over with." She reached for the door.

But he beat her to it, opening it and stepping out of the way. He then followed her out of the door and went ahead of her to where his car was parked. He then opened the passenger door and held it open, looking at her expectantly.

She glared at him. Under normal circumstances, she would have been thrilled that a man was opening doors for her. Today, however, she was not feeling very charitable. "What is this, the 1960s? I'll take the Underground, thank you."

Rhys didn't move, just continued to hold the door. "I'm an old-fashioned kind of guy," he responded amiably, not seeming the least bit put-off by her aggressive attitude. "I believe in holding doors for women, even if they don't want me to. And I'm going to be your chauffer today. The tube is too public. Besides, there isn't a direct route from here to the station by the library. It will take you over an hour to get there via the Underground. I can have you there in half that time. Maybe less, if the traffic gods smile down on us."

Anna's glare intensified. He met her glare with a cool expression of his own. Neither of them blinked.

Finally, she let out a snarl and stalked to the car, sliding in to the passenger seat. She tried to yank the door out of his hand so that she could slam it, but he held on to it until she was in before shutting it --- gently --- behind her. As he walked around to the other side of the car, she crossed her arms over her chest and stared out of the window.

In the back of her mind she knew she was being childish. Rhys had done nothing wrong. But she was upset, she was tired, and --- she had to admit --- she was *scared*. And when she was scared, her defense was to get angry. Rhys just happened to be a convenient target.

To his credit, Rhys didn't try to chat with her. He simply drove in silence, keeping his eyes on the road in front of him.

Anna was scared, yes. But she was also curious. It was the trait that often got her into the most trouble, and the trait that Abraham had admired the most in her. Even scared, she still needed to *know*. As Rhys navigated through the winding streets that lead to the section of the city where the Bradley sat, she couldn't help but ask the question that had been the most prevalent on her mind since the previous evening when she had awoken in the Blackwoods' home. "Why are you helping me?"

He turned to her and offered his toothpaste-ad grin. "Maybe I have a thing for damsels in distress."

A hot retort sprang to Anna's mind, and she opened her mouth to let him have it. *He* may think she was in distress, and maybe she was. But she was certainly no *damsel*.

Before she could unleash her scathing reply, however, he raised his hand. "I'm sorry," he said, although his dancing eyes and amused voice told her he was anything but. "That was uncalled for. You made sure to tell me last night that you were as far from a damsel in distress as one could get." The car came to a stop as they waited for a traffic light, and he fell silent for a moment. When he spoke next, his tone was firm.

"Abraham was more than a friend. We didn't just work with him. I've known him my whole life. When my parents died, he stepped up and adopted me, practically raised me. I would have never been able to pay him back, even if he'd lived to be a thousand. I know you were important to him. Like I said last night, he talked about you a lot. I can't help him anymore. But I *can* help you."

"Oh, Rhys." Immediately, she felt ashamed for taking out her frustrations on him. She had lost a mentor. He had lost a second father. "I'm so sorry. I didn't know. He... he had never mentioned you before."

He waved a hand in a dismissive gesture. "We'll mourn him properly when we can. Right now, the best thing I can do for him is to keep you safe and help track down the bastards who did this to him." His eyes glittered.

The rest of the trip was occupied by amiable chatter. Rhys told her about how he had never been to the States, but he loved the sport of baseball, and wanted to one day go to Boston to watch the Red Sox play and see the famous Green Monster of Fenway Park. She in turn confessed to her terror of heights, and how she had never been on a plane before she moved to London. His favorite color was green, and he hated chocolate. She was an only child, and had never broken a bone in her body. When they pulled into the parking lot of the police station, she was beginning to feel relaxed.

As soon as she realized where they were, however, the sick feeling in her stomach came back with a vengeance. She sat in the car for a long moment, leaning her forehead against her window and praying that she didn't throw up. Rhys just sat in his seat, not moving, not speaking, for which she was grateful. If he had tried to soothe her, she would have forgone her earlier vow not to use him as her emotional punching bag.

Finally, she felt as though she was stable enough to get out of the car. With a deep breath, she opened the door and climbed out. She still felt shaky, but at least she was standing.

Rhys got out of the car and came to stand by her. "I have a friend who works here," he told her softly. "He's worked with us quite a bit. I called him last night and told him what had really happened, and why we felt it was best if we weren't entirely truthful at this stage. Hopefully, he'll be one of the officers who questions you. His name is Finn."

She let out a whoosh of air. She supposed she should be surprised by this revelation, but her capacity for being surprised had diminished greatly since yesterday evening. Besides, a secret society who had a member imbedded in the police department really shouldn't count as a surprise. "It would have been nice to know a bit sooner," she admitted a bit sharply. "My nerves could have used a break."

"I'm sorry," he said, and his eyes told her that he meant it. "But I needed you to be on edge so that you didn't relax and slip up. Nicola told me not to even mention Finn, but that's not fair. None of this is your fault. You shouldn't have to be punished for it."

Had that been a hint of anger she'd heard in his voice? She felt the knot of fear in her stomach relax as a warm feeling tried to settle there. If she had known him better, she would have reached out and given his hand a squeeze. "Thank you," she said softly. "It does help to know that there is someone else who knows. And I understand." She didn't *like* it. But she understood.

The smile he gave her was one of relief. "Come on," he said, gesturing her forward. "Let's go get this over with, shall we?"

She swallowed hard and nodded, running her damp palms over her jeans to smooth them out --- one of her own nervous habits --- before moving forward. Rhys placed a hand in the small of her back as he fell into step beside her. It made her feel oddly comforted, as if she was drawing strength from him through the contact.

Anna had not had any reason to visit a police station since arriving in London, and was surprised by the difference in this station and the ones she had been in back in the States. It wasn't stark and sterile like the stations she was accustomed to. The walls were made from some dark wood, and, just like her office, sconces were spaced evenly along the walls. Large, comfortable-looking couches were huddled around a large, flat screen TV in what she guessed was the waiting area.

Across from the waiting area was a large, glass window. She could see someone sitting behind it, talking on the phone. Deciding that was where she needed to go check in, she began to walk in that direction. Rhys walked with her, his hand still on her back.

Before they had taken more than a few steps, however, they could hear the sound of someone calling out Rhys's name.

Anna stopped and turned to view the newcomer. He was tall and skinny, wearing a suit that was ill-fitting and made him look like an awkward teenager. He had bright blue eyes and a shock of dark hair.

"Finn." Rhys's voice held more than a note of relief, and he reached out to shake the other man's hand. "I was hoping you would be here. Finn Elliot, this is Anna Miller. Anna, meet Detective Inspector Finn Elliot. He's a member of the Criminal Investigation Department."

"Ma'am." The young policeman reached up to tip an imaginary hat at her, and Anna wondered if all British men were as polite as these two. "It's a pleasure to meet you. I wish it was under better circumstances. I'm sorry about Abraham. He was a good man."

She swallowed hard. "Yes, he was." Damn it, she needed to get better control of herself. It wouldn't do her any good to break down every time someone mentioned Abraham's name.

"Thank you for coming down to give us a statement," Finn continued. "It shouldn't take long. They are just going to ask you a few simple questions. They'll want to know if Abraham had any enemies, if you've noticed anyone unusual hanging around the library lately, if there was anything valuable enough worth taking. Those sort of things."

"Will you be questioning her?" Rhys asked in a soft voice.

The other man sighed and shook his head. "No. I'm not on the case. I'm sorry."

"We understand." The hand on her back seemed to press down a little harder, offering her more comfort. "Have they found anything at the crime scene?"

"Not that I've heard. But the CSU is still out there. It's a big place." He glanced sharply at Anna. "Are they going to find anything that will indict that she was there?"

Anna tried desperately to think if she had left anything behind, but the previous night's events were still hazy. "I don't think so. I have my purse, so that wasn't still there. I usually don't bring anything else with me, except maybe some work." She thought of the monk's journal, which was still in her bag, and clutched it closer to her.

Finn gave a nod. "Good. As long as you don't say anything that will contradict what they find at the Stacks, you should be fine. If something doesn't quite match, they'll think it's due to shock. You and Rhys go have a seat. I'll get you signed in."

"Thanks, Finn," said Rhys, using his free hand to clasp his friend in the shoulder. "I owe you one."

The other man waved his hand in the air. "Don't thank me yet. And since when have we bothered to keep a tally?" He walked off towards the glass window before Rhys could reply, and Rhys gently guided Anna over to one of the sofas that was situated around the big screen TV.

Anna sat on the edge of the seat, absently picking at the hem of her shirt. One leg was bouncing rapidly. Now that she was here, she was so nervous she couldn't sit still. Her stomach was completely in knots, and her heart was pounding hard enough that she feared for her ribs.

"It's going to be okay," Rhys said soothingly. His hand had moved up and now rested in the middle of her back, rubbing small, soothing circles. "You heard Finn. They have no reason to suspect you were there, or that this is anything more than a robbery gone bad. They only want to know if you can think of any reason why someone would want to hurt Abraham. You'll be fine. And I'll be out here the whole time. If anything happens, Finn can come and fetch me."

Part of Anna wanted to laugh at this. If things were different, she would have made sure to let Rhys know that she was completely capable of taking care of herself, and would be just fine without his help. However, in a strange country where the only person she trusted had just been murdered, knowing that there was someone there for her if she needed him was a huge relief. Even if he was little more than a stranger.

"Miss Miller?" Finn was back, standing in front of her and holding out a plastic clip-on badge. "They are ready for you. Come on. I'll walk you back."

While the foyer of the police station had been warm and inviting, the room that Finn led her to was anything but. There was a table with three chairs, a ceiling fan, security cameras, and nothing else. The walls were white and bare of any decoration. Finn had shown her in, then given her an encouraging smile as he left.

Two of the chairs were already occupied by men who both rose to their feet as she entered, affirming her theory that all British men had been taught to be chivalrous. "Miss Miller," said the one closest to her. "Thank you for coming to speak with us. I'm Detective Inspector Howard. This is Detective Inspector Pelley. Please, have a seat."

Anna did as she was told, sitting up as straight as she could, clutching her hands in her lap so that the two men wouldn't see them shaking. "I don't know what I can do to help, but anything that will catch whoever did this to Abraham…" She pressed her lips together as tears formed in her eyes. She blinked rapidly before they could fall.

The man who had spoken, Inspector Howard, gave her a sympathetic look. "We know this is difficult for you. But you were the last person to see Dr. Clark alive, so you have the best chance of giving us a lead." He paused and looked down at a notebook that was laid out on the table in front of him. "First of all is the obvious question: were you aware of any enemies that Dr. Clark may have had?"

She shook her head. "No, sir. I only moved to London a few months ago. My relationship with Dr. Clark --- Abraham --- was mostly based around academics, so I'm afraid I don't know much about his personal life."

"Did he have any academic rivals that you were aware of?"

"No, sir. Everyone I knew highly respected Abraham. I'm sure he had his critics. Every scholar does. But I am not aware of any that were especially hostile towards him."

The second inspector scribbled something onto his own notebook.

"Is there anything at the library that someone might want to steal?"

She gave a shrug. "We have many valuable texts, but I don't think a common thief would be aware of their monetary value. We have a few items that once belonged to Mr. Bradley himself, but their value comes from their provenance, not their material wealth. So yes, we have things that someone may want to steal. But it would have to be someone who was acquainted with the library and knew the history of the items and the texts. Without that knowledge, they wouldn't know what to take and what would be worthless."

"How many librarians work there?"

"Four total. Abraham, myself, and two others." She frowned, following the inspector's line of thinking. "I don't know the other two librarians very well. They work upstairs with the modern collections. We've never really spoken beyond introductions. But if they had wanted to steal something, they could have come in at any time and taken it. We all have keys. And I don't think they would have killed Abraham." One of them was a woman, and the other a young man fresh out of university. It was two men who had killed Abraham, and neither of them had sounded young enough to be Ellis.

"But you don't know what kind of relationship they had with Dr. Clark? Both professionally and personally?"

She shook her head. "No, sir. Abraham and I never discussed them in our own conversations."

He nodded, as if she had answered a suspicion, and wrote something down. The second inspector was still writing furiously in his own notebook.

"Was Dr. Clark involved in any organizations that you are aware of? Any clubs or civic groups?"

She felt her heart skip a beat as she remembered the revelation of Abraham's identity as a Scholar the night before. "No, sir. At least, not that I am aware of. Though I would have to say that it is highly unlikely. Academics were Abraham's life. He has never taken a sick day since I started working there. The only time he left was to attend conferences at universities. Again, it was never something that we discussed in our conversations."

"I see." He paused. "Would there be any reason someone would be after *you*?"

She blinked, surprised at the sudden shift in the line of questioning. "Excuse me? I-I'm not sure I understand."

Inspector Howard tapped his pen on his notebook. Inspector Pelley has stopped writing and was looking at her intensely. "Dr. Clark's body was found in his office. The only other disturbance we found was in *your* office. Your desk had been turned over. We are still checking, but there doesn't appear to be any damage in any other part of the library. Even the pieces you have displayed in museum cases were untouched."

She swallowed hard, feeling her meager breakfast threaten to come back. "I don't know why anyone would be after me for anything," she said, her voice hoarse. "I only moved here three months ago. I don't do anything besides work. I don't really know anyone in this country other than Abraham."

"What about academically?"

She gave a helpless shrug. "I am not well-established in the academic world yet. I have only had a few papers published, and nothing that could be considered earth-shattering. I had a few good reviews, a few so-so reviews, but nothing scathing or mean."

"No former boyfriends or jilted lovers left behind in America? No one that you think would have a reason to hurt you?"

She shivered. "No, sir."

The tapping became faster. Anna was suddenly reminded of a shark that smelled blood in the water.

"So why do you think someone would go into your office and overturn your desk? They didn't even bother Dr. Clark's desk. It seems as though he got up --- maybe to confront them --- and they shot him. Nothing seems to be out of place or missing. Except for your desk." His eyes were glittering.

She found herself fighting back the urge to flee in a blind panic. "Well, there are some valuable texts in my office. I am in charge of the oldest collection of books that the Bradley has. That is why we have the cage, and why my office is climate-controlled. We don't even let those books leave the library."

"The cage was still locked. As far as we could tell, nothing was out of place or missing. Would they have even be able to get in the cage?"

"There is a key. In my desk. It's the only key that can unlock the gate."

"Was this key in your desk when you left yesterday evening?"

"Yes. It was in the top drawer. That's where I always have it, in case I am not there and one of the other librarians needs to get a book."

Howard brought a hand up to his mouth, and Anna knew he was covering up a frown. If he had the notes from the crime scene, as she suspected he did, he would know that no key had been found in her desk. Rhys still had it. Which meant that Howard would have to think that perhaps the thieves had taken it with plans to return later. And that this was nothing more than a simple robbery.

"Tell me about the young man you came in with." That was Inspector Pelley.

Anna blinked at him. She had been so focused on Howard that she had almost forgotten the other man was there. "I'm sorry?"

His eyes were dark and his gaze intense. It made her uncomfortable, and she dropped her eyes so she wouldn't have to meet it.

"You said that you didn't know anyone in England besides Abraham. Yet you came into the station with a young man. And he seemed to be quite friendly with you."

She felt her wave of panic rise up from her belly and threaten to engulf her. She hadn't thought that they would ask about *her*, much less ask about Rhys. How would they even know about him? Unless Finn told them, or Pelley had been in the other room.

So she took a deep breath, pushed the panic back down, and lied. "He is --- *was* --- an acquaintance of Abraham's. His adopted son, actually. Abraham introduced us a few weeks ago. He was worried about me spending all of my time at the library, and wanted me to get out and meet other people my age."

"What is his name? This young man?"

"Rhys. Rhys Blackwood. Like I said, I've only met him once before this morning. He came by my apartment this morning after hearing about Abraham to check on me and offered to drive me here."

Pelley fell silent and wrote some more into his notebook. Howard was looking at him out of the corner of his eye, as though he was also trying to figure out his partner's line of questioning. "So," he said slowly. "This couldn't have been some romantic entanglement gone wrong? Perhaps your young man thought that Dr. Clark was taking advantage of you and was trying to... *save* you?"

Anna just stared. "Romantic...?" Then her face heated up. "No, sir. There was no romantic involvement between Abraham and myself, and there is certainly no romantic involvement between Rhys and I."

The three of them were silent for a long moment, the only sound coming from Pelley's scratching pen. Anna thought she was going to have to scream to relieve the tension that she was sure was radiating off of her.

Finally, Howard let out a sigh and stood, his chair scraping on the floor. "I believe we have all we need for the moment, Miss Miller. We'll contact you if we have any more questions. Here. Let me walk you back out."

Rhys stood as Howard walked Anna over to where he waited. "Mr. Blackwood?" the DI asked softly. When Rhys nodded, Howard offered a hand. "I think Miss Miller could do with a good deal of rest."

Rhys shook hands with the inspector as the other hand went to its now-familiar place on Anna's back. "I'll make sure she gets it."

He didn't say anything as the two of them walked out of the police station. It wasn't until they were in the car that he turned to her and asked in a very soft voice "What's wrong?"

Anna buried her head in her hands. Normally, she hated to let people see her cry, especially strangers. Tears were often viewed as a sign of weakness, and she never wanted any one to think her weak. At the moment, however, she didn't care.

Much to Rhys's credit, he didn't 'freak out' as he had threatened to do the night before. Instead, he simply sat there and let her cry. And when her sobs began to die down, he simply leaned across her, opened his glove box, and handed her a package of tissues.

Once she had stopped crying, and had wiped as much of the snot and tears away as she could, she told him everything that had happened while she was being questioned. Including Inspector Pelley's questions about him.

She could see a muscle jump in his jaw as he took this in. "This inspector. The one who asked you about me. What was his name?"

"Pelley. It wasn't the one who walked me out. And they didn't give me a first name."

He nodded, but didn't reply. They lapsed back into silence again, Rhys staring out of the windshield thoughtfully, and Anna leaning her head back against the head rest with her eyes closed.

After a moment, Rhys let out a sigh and turned to face her with a reassuring smile. "You did great," he said softly. "I know that had to be hard. And don't worry about them asking about me. I'm sure it's nothing." He reached over to start the car. "What do you say we go and grab some lunch? It's almost noon, and I know you didn't eat much for breakfast. It will be my treat."

Anna shook her head. Now that the questioning was over, all she wanted to do was go back to the Blackwoods's, crawl into bed, and sleep for the next hundred years. "I just want to go back to the house," she whispered.

Rhys didn't reply. He put the car in gear, backed out of the parking lot, and headed back the way they had come.

When they returned, Anna went immediately to her room. Her first stop was the bathroom, where her nerves and stress sent her toast back up. After scrubbing her face and rinsing out her mouth, she all but crawled back to the bed. She didn't even bother to pull the quilt over her. She laid her head on the pillow, closed her eyes, and fell into a deep, exhausted sleep.

She hadn't moved an hour later when the door slowly opened and Rhys took a step in. He stood there for a moment, watching her, a look of concern over his face. Then he walked over to the bed and very gently pulled the blanket up to her shoulders.

When he walked out of her room, he found his sister leaning against the wall, arms folded, and a grin on her face. "You know, going into a lady's room and watching her sleep could be considered right creepy."

Rhys flushed. "I was just checking on her," he muttered. "She said she didn't sleep much last night because of nightmares. And she had a rough go this morning at the Met station. I just wanted to make sure she was okay."

Nicola lifted an eyebrow, but all she said was "Mmmm."

Her brother glared at her. "Do you have a problem with that?" he snapped.

She stood and held out her hands in self-defense, but she was grinning broadly. "Hey, no need to bite *my* head off." She paused, pursing her lips. "You know, *some* women don't want a knight in shining armor."

He huffed. "What on earth are you talking about?"

"Oh, please. You are the most over-protective person I know." Nicola gestured at Anna's closed door. "She needs help, and you can't resist someone in need. *Especially* if that someone is a woman. And a beautiful one to boot. But your 'help' often means acting like they can't defend themselves."

He opened his mouth to hotly reply that Anna *hadn't* been able to defend herself, but his sister continued speaking before he could interject. "I know you want to help her. But she doesn't seem the type of girl to roll over and cower when trouble comes to call. And if you treat her like one, she's going to end up resenting you." She reached up to tweak the end of her brother's nose. "Just think about it," she said softly before disappearing down the hallway.

Rhys watched her go before turning a frown onto Anna's door. He *did* want to help Anna. She had experienced a lot of trauma in less than twenty-four-hours. Her whole world had been turned upside down in a rather violent manner. Why wouldn't he want to help her?

But Nicola, as much as he hated to admit it, was right. From the few conversations they had shared, Anna did seem like the type of woman who could take care of herself. Or at least wanted everyone to think she could. He remembered how she had reacted to his damsel in distress comment, and how she had balked at him holding doors for her.

The desire to help came to him just as naturally as breathing. But he didn't want Anna to hate him. Not until they had this all figured out. Not until he knew she was safe. Not even then.

With a sigh, he turned from Anna's door and headed for the stairs that lead to his own room. He wasn't going to be helping *anyone* by standing around brooding, and there was research to be done.

Chapter Four

The faint amount of light coming in through the window told Anna that she had been asleep for quite some time. Her eyes were dry and swollen from her earlier bout of crying, and the feeling of cotton balls was back in her mouth. Worse, her bladder was demanding to be emptied, and her stomach was begging --- loudly --- to be fed.

She made a hasty trip to the bathroom, where the matter of her bladder was quickly resolved. She splashed water on her face, hoping to hide as much of the damage her tears had done as possible. She then ran her fingers through her hair before giving it up for lost and pulling it back into a ponytail. With all of the more immediate problems dealt with, it was time to pay attention to the matter of food.

While both Nicola and Rhys had encouraged her to 'make herself at home', Anna was not about to go raiding the kitchen of people she had only just met. She could order takeout, or maybe have someone take her to get food. She didn't have a car. Abraham had told her there would be no need for one in London, not when both her apartment --- *flat* --- and the library were in the same borough, and the Underground ran all over the city.

As soon as she left the bedroom, however, she realized that she wasn't going to have to worry about finding food. She could easily make out the delicious aroma of pizza, and it was coming from the direction of the kitchen.

Anna felt as though she could float into the kitchen, much like in the old-school cartoons. The smell grew stronger the closer she got, and her stomach's growls grew louder as well. By the time she reached the kitchen, she was nearly drooling.

Rhys was sitting at the kitchen island, staring intently at the laptop in front of him. Next to him were three pizza boxes, a stack of paper plates, and a roll of paper towels. As she watched, he absently picked up a slice of pizza from a plate to his right and took a bite, chewing thoughtfully, eyes never leaving the screen.

Anna took a step into the kitchen, her hands already reaching for a plate. "I hope you plan on sharing. I'm so hungry I could eat a horse. If I don't eat something, I might start snacking on you." She opened the top to the first box without waiting for his reply. Olives. Yuck.

Rhys swallowed his bite of pizza and blinked at her. "Anna! I didn't realize that you were awake, else I would have told you to come and eat. Of course you can have some. It's just you and me at the moment, so you can have as much as you want."

She opened the next box. Pepperoni. Her favorite. "Where are David and your sister?" she asked as she piled several slices onto her plate.

Rhys was watching her with amusement. "David is at home. He said he might stop by later so you can ask more questions. Nic is at yoga. She won't be home for several hours. Can I get you a drink? Water? Fizzy drink? Beer?"

Anna plopped her plate down on the island opposite of Rhys and hopped up on the bar stool. "A Coke --- sorry, fizzy drink --- would be great, thanks." She bit down on the tip of the first pizza slice and closed her eyes in bliss. She couldn't be sure, but she thought she may have let out a small moan.

Her companion let out a chuckle as he slid off of his stool and moved to the refrigerator. "You haven't eaten more than a few bites all day. It is a wonder you didn't start to gnaw on your own arm while you were asleep." He returned with a frosty glass and a bottle of soda.

"Thank you," she murmured around a mouthful of pizza. She was nearly finished with the first slice. As she reached for the bottle, she nodded towards the laptop. "What are you looking at? Porn? Or is it some of your secret club stuff?"

"You mean the kind of stuff that I could only tell you if I was going to kill you?" He grinned to let her know he was teasing. "No. Nothing like that. And no porn, either. I've been trying to find out more information about your friend, Inspector Pelley."

"The one who was at my questioning today?" She almost said 'interrogation'.

"The very same. I find it curious that he was so interested in who I was. And if he wants to know more about me, then I want to know more about him."

Anna fell silent, concentrating on her pizza.

The two sat in comfortable silence, both eating, Rhys occasionally 'hmmm'ing as he read something interesting. Somewhere in the house, a clock ticked, marking the time. Anna wondered what time it was back in Tennessee, and wondered what her parents were doing at that moment. She had briefly thought about calling them to tell them what had happened, but then thought better of it. They would be on the first plane to London, then demand that she return to the States with them. She did not want to go back, not until she knew what was going on. Not even then. She loved living in England, and even Abraham's murder could not diminish that.

After another long moment, Anna decided that her stomach was, at last, satisfied. All three slices were gone. She pushed her plate away with a sigh. "I think, just maybe, I might actually live."

Rhys waved absently at the boxes. "Like I said, there is plenty. Get more if you want."

She watched curiously as he sat his current slice down --- nibbled all the way down to the crust --- and pick up a second slice. "You don't eat the crusts?"

He looked up and met her eyes briefly over the top of his computer before looking down, a faint blush spreading over his cheeks. "Don't laugh. It's... My father never ate the crusts. When I was younger, I idolized him, wanted to be just like him. So I never ate the crusts, either. And old habits, as they say, die hard."

"That's right," she said softly, remembering something he had said earlier. "Your parents passed away, didn't they? I'm sorry."

He flapped his hand in the air in a dismissive gesture. "Nothing for you to be sorry for. It was a long time ago." He paused. "Can you describe Pelley to me? Was he tall? Short? Dark?"

"Let me think." Anna leaned forward so that she could rest her elbows on the island. "I am not sure about his height. He only stood for a moment, and I was looking at the other inspector. But if I had to guess, I would say he was on the taller side. He had dark hair. And I remember he was rather skinny. Not as bad as your friend Finn, but still small."

"Don't let Finn's size fool you. He is as quick as a snake, and has managed to knock me on my arse more than once. Would you say Pelley was older?"

"Mmmm. A bit past middle-aged, I'd say. But I was terrified the whole time I was in there, so my memory may not be the best."

"It's the best that we've got." Rhys wiped his hands on a paper towel before picking up his laptop and turning it to face her. "Are any of these men the one you saw today?"

On the screen were four different photos. They looked like passport or ID photos, all four men. Three of them were youngish, perhaps no older than forty, and white. The fourth was also younger, and had the extremely dark skin that she always associated with native Africans. "No. None of those are Inspector Pelley. I know that much."

Rhys let out a sigh and turned the computer back around, a grim look on his face. "That is what I was afraid you would say. Your Inspector Pelley, it would seem, is an imposter."

Anna frowned. "What do you mean?"

"After we came home and you fell asleep, I decided to do a little research. As I said, if there is someone interested in me, I want to know as much about them as I can. So I used some of my --- what did you call it? --- 'secret club' powers and began to track down the good inspector. Thankfully, there are only a few hundred families with the name Pelley living in the London area. Then I narrowed down how many of them professed to be police officers of any kind. I only came up with these four. And, as you just said, none of them was the man who introduced himself to you as Inspector Pelley."

"Wait a minute." Anna held up a hand. "Are you saying that the man I talked to today was *not* a police officer?"

"Oh, I think he was a police officer. I just don't think his name was Pelley. Which begs the question of why would someone join the Met under an assumed name? And why would he be interested in who I was?" He stood, closing the laptop as he did. "I'm going to go call Finn and see what he can tell me about your inspector. I'll be back shortly." He left the kitchen, laptop tucked under his arm.

Anna watched him go, a frown on her face. A man who was not who he said he was asking about Rhys while questioning her about Abraham's murder couldn't be a coincidence. Not that Anna much believed in coincidences. If it walked like a duck and talked like a duck... But the main question was why. *Why* would he want to know who Rhys was? And what would he do ---

Anna suddenly let out a gasp, a hand flying to her mouth as a thought twisted her gut.

She had told the inspector Rhys's name.

"Rhys!" She jumped off of her stool and hurried after him. "Rhys, wait!"

He stopped in the hallway and turned to look at her with a raised eyebrow.

"I told him your name. Pelley. The fake inspector. I told him your name. Your *full* name. And he saw you at the station. What if... Do you think he'll come after you? Or try to hurt you?" She wouldn't be able to live with herself if someone got hurt because of her.

He gave her a smile, the same wolfish smile that she had seen on his face last night when he was shielding her in the library. "I'm counting on it."

After her long nap and the added worry that she may have inadvertently painted a target on Rhys's back, Anna couldn't even think about sleep. So she dug out her work light, the monk's journal, and her notebook and pens and took them all to the small desk located in the corner of the bedroom she had been given. If she couldn't sleep, she might as well get some work done. Plus it would help her calm down and relax. Solving problems had always done that for her.

So it was that a few hours later, when a knock came at her door, Anna was furiously scribbling in her notebook. *The monk recorded a visitor at his monastery. He hasn't named the visitor, but if his description of the entourage is anything to go by...* "Come in!" she called, not bothering to look up from her task.

The door opened, and Nicola stepped through. "Here you are!" she said cheerfully. "Rhys said you disappeared on him. I told him you probably just wanted a break from his ever-present hovering."

"Hmmm?" Anna looked up and blinked, the end of her pen stuck between her teeth. "Oh. No. He wasn't hovering. He had to make a phone call, and I thought I'd get some work done. How was yoga?"

Nicola let out a dramatic sigh and threw herself across the bed. "Grueling, as always. Who would have thought that a bunch of *stretches* could hurt so much? Personally, I think it was designed as some kind of secret torture technique. If it wasn't for the absolutely dishy yoga instructor I would not go. But it is totally worth it to watch her sweat. It makes her... 'Sexy' doesn't even start to cover it."

"Her?" Anna blinked. *Her?* Then... "Oh." She blushed.

Nicola looked up from her sprawl. "Rhys didn't tell you?" A note of worry crept into her voice. "It's not going to be a problem is it? I don't want you to feel uncomfortable."

"No, Rhys didn't tell me. Not that it was any of my business. And no, it's not going to be a problem. Not at all." She couldn't help but smile. "So... Dishy?"

Her companion grinned, a look of relief on her face. "Yes. Dishy. Her name is Fallon. That name alone screams sexy, don't you agree? She is very dark skinned, almost Indian. And her hair is white-blonde, and she wears it in dreadlocks. She is absolutely *fit*. You should see her ab muscles. When we do yoga, she wears yoga pants and a sports bra. Nothing else." She let out a happy sigh.

Anna felt her face split into a grin. "You're right. Even *I* think that sounds dishy, and I prefer sweaty men to sweaty women."

"That means more for me," Nicola replied. "I am happy just to ogle while I am torturing my body."

Anna couldn't help but laugh. She liked the other woman, even if she had not had more than one conversation with her. She was humor and light where her brother was serious and dark. She had no doubt that Nicola could be just as serious as Rhys when need be, but it was refreshing to know that she chose to laugh instead.

Nicola propped herself up on her elbows. "So. What are you working on?"

Anna waved in the direction of the journal. "It's... Well, you will probably think it's boring. Most people do."

"Try me."

"It's a journal written by a monk in the late 15th century. It really offers a glimpse into the life of the monasteries at that time. You know, the clergy were the only ones who knew how to read and write for a very long time. They were basically the keepers of all knowledge. There is no telling what I can learn. In fact, I just found out that the monastery had a visitor. It was a pretty remote monastery, so it was odd enough that the monk recorded it. Normally, we would think it was a visiting monk, or maybe a pilgrim. But this monk records that the visitor had an entourage. And that suggests that ---"

Anna bit her lip, feeling her face warm. "Sorry. I tend to ramble when I'm excited."

Nicola chuckled. "You're right, though. It *does* sound boring. Monks are a little bit much for me, unless there is sex involved." She swung her legs over the side of the bed and sat up. "Tell you what. Let me take a shower and then we can do something girly. Maybe pop some popcorn and watch a movie. Rhys isn't here, so we can watch a chick flick and not have to hear him complain."

"Rhys is gone?" He hadn't told her he was leaving. Not, she told herself sternly, that it mattered. He didn't have to tell her everything he did.

"I think he was going to see Finn. I believe you met him this morning. The skinny bobbie? Anyways, he left just a few minutes ago, right after I got home. I told him to take as long as he wanted. I thought you might like a break from all of the testosterone." She got to her feet. "Well, I'm going to go shower. Go back to your monk. I'll come and fetch you when I'm done."

The two were sitting on the couch, wrapped up in blankets with a large bowl of popcorn between them, when they heard the front door open and close. "Nic?" Rhys's voice rang throughout the house.

"In here!" his sister called out. Then, with a wink at Anna, added "I'm having a hanky panky with Anna. You might want to keep your eyes covered for a bit."

Anna covered her mouth in an attempt to stifle her giggle. When Rhys hurried into the room a moment later, she couldn't help but burst out laughing. "I'm sorry," she said, eyes dancing. "But the look on your face is priceless."

Nicola leaned over and, in an exaggerated whisper, said "I do believe he was jealous!"

Rhys let out a huff of air as he walked over to the couch. "I wish you would believe me when I say that you are not funny."

She beamed at him. "It's because it's a lie. I'm hilarious. You just don't have a sense of humor."

"If you say so." Rhys picked up the popcorn bowl and waved Anna over. "Scoot."

She obliged, and he sat down in between the two girls, placing the bowl in his lap for easy reach.

"See?" Nicola said, leaning around her brother so that she could grin at Anna. "He's going to play chaperone and make sure I keep my hands off of you."

"That's right," he said easily, stuffing a handful of popcorn into his mouth. "It's not polite to grope our guests."

As the three of them sat on the couch, watching a movie and exchanging banter, Anna felt herself beginning to relax for the first time since her ordeal began twenty-four hours previously. Yesterday, these two had been strangers. Now they were friends. They took her in without a second thought, and were making sure that not only was she safe, but that she was a part of something. Abraham had wanted that for her. They were making sure she got it.

An elbow in her ribs brought her back to the present. Blinking, she saw that Rhys was looking at her with a raised eyebrow. "What are you smiling about?"

She opened her mouth to answer, but was interrupted by Nicola, in an airy voice, answering for her. "She's probably imagining me naked."

Rhys rolled his eyes. Anna laughed.

Chapter Five

The next few days passed by rather uneventfully. Anna received a phone call from a member of the Bradley's board of directors, telling her how very sorry they were about the loss of Abraham. He had been a wonderful man and a superb scholar. The board knew that she and Abraham had been very close, and that his loss was no doubt devastating to her. But they hoped that she would remain at the library, as she had been highly recommended, and they knew that they would not be able to find anyone like her to take her place. She happily told them that she very much wanted to stay. The woman on the phone had sounded relieved.

They also promised her that they had already begun the search for Abraham's replacement, and were hoping to have someone ready to go by the time the police finished their investigation. Until that time, however, the library would remain closed. They would let her know when a replacement had been selected, and when she could return to work.

David informed them that he had received word from Abraham's sister in regards to funeral arrangements. She would be flying in from Scotland and was hoping they could have a small memorial service. She did not think her brother would want a big extravagant send-off, but would prefer to give friends and colleagues a chance to gather and celebrate his life. The memorial service would take place the upcoming weekend.

In the meantime, Anna continued to decipher the monk's cramped journal. She had finally learned, much to her delight, that the visitor who had come to the monastery had been a member of the royal family. This had been before Henry VIII had broken with the Catholic Church in order to divorce his first wife, and the monasteries had flourished. The monk never revealed the visitor's name, but just the fact that she had found a record of such a visit was exciting for Anna.

When she wasn't working, the Blackwoods were occupying her time with sightseeing trips around London and the surrounding boroughs. Nicola took her shopping. Rhys took her out for coffee and a walk along the Thames. She would be lying if she said she wasn't enjoying herself.

The only time she was reminded that she was possibly in danger is when she would overhear the two discussing their schedules to make sure that one of them was with her at all times. It was frustrating to feel as though she was under house arrest. She knew they were trying to keep her safe, but the lack of freedom was beginning to become cloying.

She was currently in her room, working on the journal. Nicola had left for yoga --- "What I do to myself in the name of eye candy" --- and Rhys was watching some sporting event on television. As her knowledge of sports was vastly limited, she had left him to it. She had just begun working on a March day in 1489 when a knock came at her door. "Come in!" she called absently, chewing on the end of her pen.

The door opened, and Rhys stepped through. "Hey," he said softly. "I was just wondering where you had disappeared to." He nodded at the journal. "Is that the monk's diary? The one you've been working on?"

"Yeah." She clasped her hands over her head and stretched, wincing as her joints popped in protest. "I thought I would get some work down while you were watching the, ah... I have no idea what it was."

"Rugby match," he replied with a grin. "And don't worry. You're not missing much. It's terrible." He paused. "You can come back out here if you want. I can turn it."

She offered him a smile. "Thanks, but I think I'll just work for a bit. I'm not a big TV watcher."

"Okay. Well, do you mind if I stay in here with you for a bit then? I'm getting lonely out there by myself."

She blinked at him in surprise. "Umm, sure. I mean, all I do is read and then scribble. The only time it gets exciting is when I can't figure something out and start cursing. I don't know if you would find that as entertaining as a rugby match, but I've been told it's a pretty powerful sight."

He chuckled. "I don't mind. And I'll try not to bother you."

She let out a sigh and put down her pen. "Rhys, I am perfectly safe in here. You don't have to always have your eyes on me. I mean, I am fairly certain there are a lot of things worth watching other than me. You can stay in there and watch TV. I promise I won't climb out of the window. And if anyone climbs *in* the window, I'll be sure to yell."

He shrugged. "I just wanted to sit with you. It has nothing to do with watching you. I'm not a creeper." His voice held a note of amusement. "Although my sister has informed me that I may come across that way sometimes. If you don't want me in here while you work that is fine. Just tell me. It won't hurt my feelings."

"No no. You can stay. I don't mind it at all. I just don't know why you would want to."

Rhys turned on his toothpaste-ad grin. Anna hated it when he did that. It made her forget to breathe, and her brain turned to mush. She couldn't help but wonder if he knew the effect it had on her, and did it on purpose. "Great! I'm going to go grab a drink first. Would you like anything?"

"No, thank you."

As he left the room, Anna let out a whoosh of air and stared down at her book, which was illuminated by her work light. But her eyes were not focused on it.

Part of her felt bad for monopolizing all of Rhys's time. He was incredibly good-looking and had a charming personality. She was plain and boring. He liked people. She preferred the company of books. He needed to be out around other people, not stuck in his home with someone who was as interesting as a rock. She knew that he took the responsibility of protecting her very seriously. Nicola had warned her several times that Rhys could be extremely single-minded when it came to someone's safety. But that didn't mean he had to enjoy it. Anna hoped that all of this would be over soon so that he could go back to his normal life.

She lifted her head as he returned, carrying a glass in his hand. "So," he said cheerfully as he sat on the edge of her bed. "Tell me about this monk that occupies your waking hours."

She arched an eyebrow at him. "Surely you can't be that interested in him?"

"I'm interested if you are," he said simply.

For some reason, his words made her blush. She ducked her head, hoping he wouldn't notice. "Well, I don't know much about him personally. He started this journal in 1465, and it gives no clues as to his age. But, if he was writing, I am going to assume that he was either older, or he had grown up in the monastery. The clergy were the only ones who knew how to read and write at this time. Well, except for the exceptionally wealthy. But *they* mostly kept books as a status symbol, because books were expensive. It was the monks who wrote and copied most of those books. The printing press had only been invented eighteen years previously, and the only books being printed en masse were Bibles and other church books. If it wasn't for the clergy, we would have lost a lot of history."

"What does he write about?"

"What most people would write about in their journals." Her eyes glittered. Once she got going, it was hard for her to stop. And the fact that she had a willing audience was just adding fuel to her passion. "But this man was writing less than a hundred years after the Black Death swept through Europe. So many things had changed. The population was still rebuilding. There were whole towns that had been wiped from the map, and many of the wealthy had to turn to farming. This was when we started to see the rise of the middle class and the beginnings of the Renaissance. There is so much *history* to be found in here. I feel like I'm an archeologist every time I open this book."

She paused to take a breath, and Rhys burst into laughter.

Anna stared at him, startled. Then she began to feel her cheeks burn, and a sense of hurt settled into her a chest. "Well, you asked," she said sharply. "I told you that it was boring."

He reached out to squeeze one of her hands, his eyes dancing merrily. "I'm not laughing at you," he promised. "Not at all. You should see how you look when you're talking about this. You light up. It looks good on you."

Her blush deepened further. "Sorry," she murmured, nervously tucking a stand of hair behind an ear. "I'm just not used to people actually caring about this stuff. I usually get blank stares. Or outright boredom. That's why I could never teach."

"So why did you choose to study this? Why not, say, American writers?"

She snorted. "Please. Have you ever had to read Faulkner? I would rather dig out my own eye with a dull spoon than read Faulkner. American writers are so boring. This…" She gestured at the journal. "*This* is our history. America wasn't even a country at the time this monk was alive. He saw so much in his lifetime. And there is so much that we don't know. For instance, there is a member of the royal family visiting the monastery at the moment." She tapped the journal. "I still don't know who it is, but it is a significant piece of history. What if someone at this monastery makes a suggestion to this royal that later becomes a law? What if this royal learns something from the monks that he or she takes back to court? This could teach us so much that we don't already know. *Much* more interesting than reading about old women sleeping next to dead bodies." Although that had been the only Faulkner story that she had actually enjoyed.

He was still watching her with a half-grin on his face. "You know," he said softly, "I may not be a Scholar myself. But Abraham was right in choosing you as his successor. You are going to be an excellent Scholar."

"Do you really think so? Abraham left some awfully big shoes to fill."

Now it was his turn to snort. "I've known Abraham a long time. I can guarantee you that he never intended you to fill his shoes. He wouldn't have expected that of anyone. What he wanted was someone who had the same passion as he did. And passion is something that you obviously have no shortage of. The rest will be a piece of cake for you."

She paused for a moment. "Will you tell me about him?" she asked quietly. "Abraham, I mean. I've only known him for a few years, not nearly enough time to really get to know him. And our relationship was more academic than personal, though he was my friend. I would like to know what he was like as a person. If you don't mind."

"He was a fantastic person," he said without hesitation. "As I told you before, I'd known him my whole life. He has been a Scholar for a very long time, and my family has been in London since before there was a London. And though I knew who and what he was, it wasn't until my parents died that I really got to know him."

"What happened?" she asked, then pressed her lips together, wishing she hadn't.

But Rhys only gave her a smile. "It's all right," he assured her, although she could see the sadness that flittered across his face. She didn't like it. It didn't sit well on him at all. "I was thirteen when they died. The police told us it was a car accident, but other members of our organization thought it was murder. My parents had been working on something major, though no one was quite sure what it was. There had apparently been some threats --- notes and a few phone calls --- but nothing violent. There was an investigation, but no one could ever prove anything."

Anna reached out and placed a hand on his knee. "That's horrible," she said softly. No one should ever have to go through anything like that, but she couldn't imagine losing her parents when she was a teenager. She didn't think she would have been able to survive it.

He placed a hand over hers and left it there as he continued speaking. "It was worse for Nicola, I think. She felt as though it was her responsibility to raise me. But she was only eighteen. And she was grieving herself. There is no way she could have tried to take care of herself and a traumatized thirteen-year-old. Not if she wanted to stay sane.

"David and Abraham convinced her to stay at university. She had won a prestigious scholarship, and they told her --- rightfully so --- that our parents would be devastated if she didn't take advantage of it. Abraham swore to Nicola and myself that he would take care of me, that he would raise me as if I was his own. And he did. He was were already older, and had never had children of his own. But he took care of me. That is just the kind of man he was. It was as much a part of Abraham as his love for *Beowulf*."

Anna felt her heart swell for the man that she hadn't gotten the chance to know as well as she would have liked, and for the thirteen-year-old that he had sworn to protect. "Sounds to me as though

Abraham might have passed some of that white-knight complex on to you," she murmured.

Rhys laughed, and the sadness faded from his face. "Nic says it's because I couldn't protect our parents, so I'm always looking for substitutes. She is a therapist, so she's always saying things like that. But I agree with you. I think it was being around Abraham and seeing how he worked to look after me that made me that way."

Both of them lapsed into silence. He kept his hand over hers, and she was content to leave it there.

"Well, enough about me," he finally said, his voice cheerful. "What about you? Why did you decide to move to London? Did you leave a broken-hearted boyfriend behind in America? I bet you did. Maybe more than one."

Anna laughed, a full laugh that brought tears to her eyes. She couldn't help it. The idea that anyone would put her name and the word 'boyfriend' in the same sentence was preposterous. "If you're trying to flatter me, it's not working. In case you haven't noticed, I prefer the company of books over the company of people. People tend to let you down. Books don't."

Rhys lifted an eyebrow. "I take it this is something you've learned from experience?"

She sighed and looked down at her shoes. "I'm... plain. Boring. Most of my life has been spent with my nose in a book. I never got invited to parties, was never a popular kid. So when any man shows me any kind of attention, I always fall in love. Hard and fast. It's my curse. And I end up getting my heart broken every time." She gave him a humorless smile. "Pretty pathetic, huh? Anyways. I'd always wanted to come to London. After reading the stories of Arthur and Guinevere and Beowulf and everything ever written by Shakespeare I was dying to see the places where these people walked, both in real life and in legend. When Abraham asked, I didn't even have to think about it. As soon as I got off the phone with him I put in my two-week's notice at work, went home and started packing." She hadn't even called her parents until Abraham had called her back saying he had secured her a place to live. She knew that they would try to talk her out of it, and she didn't want them to.

Silence greeted her. She was beginning to worry that she'd said too much when she felt cool fingers brush her cheek. She sucked in a breath and looked up, eyes going wide.

Rhys was looking at her with an expression she couldn't read, his eyes roaming over her face. "What a ridiculous idea," he murmured softly. "You are far from 'plain', Anna. You are beautiful. Anyone who says otherwise is obviously blind."

She held very still, not even daring to breathe as he continued to study her. Then he sighed and dropped his fingers from her face. "Well, I'll let you get back to your monk. I've taken up enough of your time with chitchat. I'm sorry. I said I wouldn't bother you, and that's all I've done." He stood, his untouched drink in his hand. "I'll be back out in the living room. I'm sure I can find something to entertain myself with until Nicola gets home. If you haven't emerged by dinner, I'll come and fetch you." With a last grin, he walked out of the room.

Anna watched him go, her hand absently rising to touch the spot on her cheek where his fingers had been.

It had been a long time since she had felt a man's touch. It had been nice to have that skin-to-skin contact again, both from the hand that he had held hers with, and the quick brush across her cheek. She knew it couldn't mean anything to Rhys. It was just another aspect of his chivalrous nature. But it made her realize just how much she had missed it.

She let out a sigh and looked at the journal. She had been telling the truth when she said she wasn't much of a people person. She'd always had a difficult time connecting with those around her. The move to England was supposed to be a fresh start for her. Not just for her career, but for her life in general. This time, she had vowed, things would be different.

Abraham had wanted that for her, too. He had encouraged her to find friends who were her own age. She didn't need to spend all of her time with old men and old ghosts. He had planned for her to meet the Blackwoods. To meet Rhys, whom he had raised as his own son.

At that thought, she felt the corners of her mouth turn up in a smile. *You sneaky old bastard. You were trying to play matchmaker, weren't you? That's why you didn't tell them I was young. That's why you asked Rhys to come to the library and see me, not Nicola.*

She could almost hear his chuckle. *"Abraham said you were sharp,"* she remembered Rhys saying. She wondered if Rhys had reached the same conclusion. And, if he had, what he thought of it.

Still smiling, she reached over, turned off of her work lamp, and followed Rhys into the living room.

He looked up at her, startled, when she plopped down on the couch next to him. "Anna. Are you all right? I didn't upset you, did I? I didn't mean to."

She turned to him and offered a grin. It wasn't as breathtaking as his, but it was the best she could manage. "That monk has waited for over six hundred years for someone to read his story," she said. "He can wait a little longer."

He had found another rugby match on TV and, after a few minutes of her coaxing, was eagerly explaining the rules to her. He had wanted to know more about her interests, she pointed out. It was only fair that he share his.

She thought she was beginning to finally understand how the scoring system worked when a knock came at the door.

Instantly, Rhys was on his feet, moving to stand between her and the foyer. "I'm not expecting anyone," he said in a soft tone. "And neither Nicola nor David would knock."

They waited with baited breaths. After another moment, the doorbell rang, deep chimes sounding throughout the house.

"Coming!" Rhys shouted as he moved towards a large cabinet. As Anna watched, he removed the handgun she had seen in the library. "I need to you to go back to your room," he told her quietly, placing the gun in the back of his jeans before pulling his shirt down to conceal it. "Shut the door. Don't open it for anyone except for me, Nicola or David. There is a baseball bat in the closet. Get it. If you hear shooting, climb out of the window and go to the Met station in Gipsy Hill. Ask for Finn. They'll know how to get in touch with him."

The doorbell rang again.

"I said I was coming!" Rhys didn't take his eyes off of her, urgently waving at her to go. As she disappeared down the hallways, she saw him striding towards the front door.

She quickly hurried into the bedroom, shutting the door softly behind her. Her heart was pounding as she moved to the closet. As promised, there was a Louisville Slugger just inside the doorway.

A bat, she thought, feeling a sense of hysteria rise within her. *Rhys answers the door with a gun and expects me to be able to protect myself with a* bat!

Still, the feel of the smooth wood in her hands made her feel better.

She didn't know how long she waited in the dark, clutching the bat hard enough to turn her knuckles white, her ears strained for the slightest noise. Rhys's instructions be damned, if she heard the sounds of a struggle, she would go and help. She didn't know if she would be able to do anything, but she couldn't just leave him if there was even a small chance that she could help. He'd risked his life to save hers. She would be a coward if she simply ran away.

Minutes ticked by. To Anna it felt like hours. Her hands were beginning to cramp from her death grip on the bat, and her heart was pounding loud enough that it filled her ears, blocking out any sounds that might alert her to a struggle.

When a knock finally came at her bedroom door, she couldn't stop a yelp of fear from escaping.

"Anna?" a familiar voice called out from the other side. "It's Rhys. I'm coming in."

The door swung open, and Anna felt herself squinting in the sudden light that came pouring in. She blinked furiously, trying to get her eyes to adjust, and didn't drop the bat. Even when his cool fingers slid over hers she still wouldn't let it go.

"It's okay." Rhys's voice was soothing, and he squeezed her hands reassuringly. "He's gone now. You can let go."

She swallowed, then slowly loosened her fingers until Rhys held the bat and her arms hung limply at her sides. "Who was it?" she asked, hoping that he would tell her it was a neighbor or a friend stopping in for an unannounced visit and they could laugh at their paranoia.

But the grim look that her newly-adjusted eyes could see on his face told her that that wasn't the case. "It was our friendly neighborhood imposter, Inspector Pelley."

The kitchen had taken on the air of a war room. David, Nicola, and Rhys were all huddled around the table with laptops, talking about things that Anna didn't understand. Finn arrived sometime later that night with a box full of papers. He thunked it down on the table in front of Rhys, who began pulling out files and passing them around. Finn joined them at the table. Anna, who was sitting on the countertop, started to feel claustrophobic.

She hopped down and began to walk out of the kitchen. Everyone was so lost in his or her own work that she doubted anyone was even paying attention to her. But she should have known better.

"Where are you going?" Rhys's voice was sharp. The visit from the fake Pelley had spooked him because he didn't want the man to know that Anna was with him. Nicola had warned Anna that, if she thought Rhys had been hovering before, then he wasn't going to let Anna out of his sight now. Apparently, she had not been lying.

"I'm going out on the deck," Anna said in a small voice, hunching her shoulders in and not looking at him. "I need some air." Then, without waiting for a response, she hurried out of the room.

Nicola had shown her the deck and swimming pool a few days ago, much to Anna's delight. She loved sitting outside in the sunshine. And, Nicola had told her with a grin, it gave her a place to escape when she started to feel crowded.

As she slipped through the sliding glass door and into the cool night air, Anna didn't bother to turn on the lights. There were already a few lights that stayed on all the time, casting a soft glow over the pool. Besides, Rhys would probably have a fit if she lit the whole deck, telling her she was drawing attention to herself. And she didn't want to cause him any more trouble than she already had.

She walked to the edge of the pool before sitting, rolling up the legs of her jeans, and dangling her feet in the water. She looked out over the wooden fence surrounding the pool area at the bright lights of London, but her thought were elsewhere.

She had put someone else in danger. Worse, she had put *Rhys* in danger.

She shivered and hugged herself, although it had nothing to do with being cold. Pelley had only come to ask a few questions, according to Rhys. He had only wanted to know about Rhys's relationship with Abraham, and if he might possibly know of anything that could have gotten the older man killed. He also wanted to know more about Rhys's relationship with Anna. Rhys assured her that the police would have come to him eventually, as Abraham had once been his legal guardian.

That didn't help Anna's conscious. *She* had told the man about Rhys. If anything had happened to him, she would be responsible. The thought that he could have been hurt *because of her* made her want to run as far away as she possibly could and hide in a cave.

Instead, she lowered her head into her hands and cried. She had thought she was through crying. After all, she had cried enough in the past week to last her a lifetime. But it seemed as though she still had plenty of tears left. And she no longer cared who saw her cry. At this point, it felt as though everyone in London had seen her cry.

When she finally lifted her head, she realized that she was no longer alone. Rhys was sitting next to her, his feet also in the pool. She had been so lost in her own guilt and misery that she hadn't heard him approach.

"What are you doing out here?" she sniffed, scrubbing at her eyes. "Don't you have a war council to lead?"

"David is much more qualified to lead a war council than I am. You know, the whole 'with age comes wisdom' thing."

He was making a joke. She didn't feel much like laughing.

He sighed. "Anna..."

"Don't," she said sharply. "Don't even say it."

"It's not your fault," he said anyway.

She turned so that she could glare at him. "How is this *not* my fault?" she snarled. "Rhys, what if he had walked through that door and shot you? He could have hurt you. He could have *killed* you. And it would have been *my fault*. I can't handle that. I just *can't*." She could feel more tears threatening to spill. She turned her head away angrily before he could see them.

Much to her surprise, he began to chuckle. "I'm glad you think it's funny," she snapped, angrily swiping at her eyes.

"I'm not laughing at you, Anna. I told you earlier that I would never laugh at you, and I meant it. It's just..." He paused. "I've always been the protector. I'm not used to having someone worry about looking after *me*. It's... nice."

Under normal circumstances, she would have blushed. Instead, she just lowered her head. "You wouldn't need protecting if it wasn't for me," she whispered.

"Anna." He reached out to gently grasp her chin and turn her face towards his. She let him, but refused to meet his eyes. "I've been doing this for a long time. This... *this* is what I've been trained to do since I was a child. I know how to defend myself. Pelley wouldn't have gotten the jump on me. I promise." He moved his hand up so that he could cup her cheek.

Anna's eyes went to meet his, and she felt that little pitter-patter her heart always seemed to do when he was near.

He was smiling at her. "I don't want you to worry about me," he murmured. "Let's just worry about you, okay? You don't know how to protect yourself. That's what I'm for." His smile faded, and his face turned serious. "I told you that night in the library that I would die to protect you. And I will if I have to."

She felt her lip quake, and guilt flooded over her. "Rhys..."

"That doesn't mean I *plan* on dying. I would rather not, thank you very much." Then he was grinning. "Besides, if I died, who would be around to protect you? Or, as Nicola says, to smother you?"

Anna managed a weak smile.

He peered into her eyes, hand still on her cheek. "All right, now?"

She let out a breath and nodded. "I... I think so."

"That's my girl." He leaned forward slowly and pressed his lips against her forehead. Anna closed her eyes, relishing the contact. "I'll let you be now. I just wanted to check on you. Let me know when you come back in, all right?"

"Okay."

He gave her another grin, then got to his feet and headed back inside to the rejoin the others.

Anna watched him go, then let out a sigh and lay back against the wooden planks of the deck, throwing one arm across her eyes.

Her whole body was quivering, and her mind was whirling with thoughts and feelings. Rhys's touch --- both earlier and just now --- had sparked something in her, something that she never thought she would feel, or that she even *wanted* to feel. That was problematic. Was it simply that she had been touched by another human being in an intimate manner that was causing the warm feeling in her stomach? Or was it because she had been touched by *him*? And if it was Rhys, did she really *care* for him? She had known him for less than a week. And if it turned out that she did have romantic feelings towards him --- and she wasn't ready to commit to that thought just yet --- then what? Every time she had allowed herself to have those feeling towards another human being, she'd ended up hurt. She didn't want to go through the pain of yet another heartbreak just because she *thought* she cared for him.

She felt her lips curl up in a wry smile. *Only I,* she thought dryly, *could have bad guys coming after me and still be worried about romance. Get it together, Miller. You have more important things to worry about right now.*

Besides, Rhys might already have a lover. He hadn't mentioned one, but that didn't mean anything. And the more she thought about it, the harder she found it to believe that he *didn't* have one. With his good looks and that devastating smile, she had no doubt that many women would happily throw themselves at his feet.

That thought sobered her up. With a sigh, she pulled herself back up to sitting a position. She'd spent enough time wallowing. She still felt guilty over drawing Pelley's attention to Rhys. But sitting around moping wasn't going to do anything to fix the problem. And if there was one thing she was good at, it was solving problems.

She got to her feet, cast one last look out at the London skyline, then walked back inside the house.

Everyone was still in the kitchen, just as she had left them. They all looked up at her entrance, but only Finn acknowledged her. "All right there, Miss Miller?" he asked politely.

She offered him a smile. "Please, call me Anna. And I am fine, thank you." She nodded at the piles of paper that all but covered the table. "What can I do to help?"

The smile that Rhys gave her was fierce and proud. "I was hoping you would offer your services. We need a researcher, and you are the best one we've got."

David cleared his throat.

"Well, next to David, of course. But he's working on something else. So you are the best researcher we have *available*." He lifted an eyebrow. "Think you're up to it?"

She snorted as she came to stand by his side. "Please. Just tell me what you need and I'll ferret it out."

He handed her a stack of files from the box that Finn had brought in. "These are all Pelley's files. His personal files, case notes, records, all of it. We need anything, *anything* that will give us a clue as to who he really is and why he felt the need to join the Met under an assumed name. And why he might have an unhealthy interest in me."

"I can do that." Anna took the files and turned back to Finn. "How long has he been with the police?"

The young DI let out a sigh. "He transferred to the Stoke Newington station about three months ago. But I know he's been with the Met for longer than that."

"Three months, huh?" That was when she had moved to London. That thought sent a shiver down her back, though she told herself there was no way it could be connected. Probably. "So are these only three months-worth of files?"

"No. I went to our headquarters at New Scotland Yard and pulled stuff from there, too. I don't know if it's complete, but I got as much as I could."

"It'll be enough," she told him firmly. Then she walked back over to the counter, hopped back up, and opened the first file.

As she always did when researching, Anna lost all sense of time. She was aware of the other people moving around her, but had tuned out all conversations and anything else that could be a distraction. All of her focus was on the papers in front of her.

She didn't know how long she had been sitting there --- though it had been some time, if her stiff neck and numb bottom were anything to go by --- when she found the first oddity. "Finn," she called out softly. "Can you come here for a moment?"

There was a scraping of stool legs against the floor, and then a shadow fell across the pages she was studying. "What is it?"

"What did you find?" That was Rhys, who had come to stand on Anna's other side.

She bit her lip. "I'm not sure yet." She turned to face Finn. "I know that police cars in the States have computers that track everywhere the car goes. Is that the same way here?"

He nodded. "It sends updates to the dispatchers every five minutes so that someone always knows where the officers are in case of trouble."

"And this is for all police vehicles?"

"Yes."

Anna pointed to a notation on the page in front of her. "This was a little over a week ago. This is the address for the library."

Finn took the file from Anna's hand and glanced at the spot she had indicated. "According to this, his car was there for an hour and a half." He glanced up at Anna. "Was there any reason that the police would have been called to the library at that time?"

She shook her head. "Not to my knowledge. I've never seen an on-duty police officer at the library since I started three months ago."

Finn's eye swung to Rhys's. "We need to look at his case files from that time to see if there is anything that was noted. Anything that would explain why he would have been there for nearly two hours."

Rhys nodded grimly and went back to his seat. Finn handed the file back to Anna with a smile. "Good eyes. Let us know if you find anything else, or if you see he was at the library any other time recently."

For another hour Anna flipped through pages, looking for anything else unusual. When she did find the next clue, she blinked. She flipped back a few pages to check, just to be sure. When she knew for certain that she was right, she felt her whole body go numb.

"Rhys." Her voice was barely more than a whisper, but he was by her side in an instant. She pointed at the spot on the page that had caught her attention. "Do you see this?"

She raised her eyes to his face. By the angry set of his jaw, she knew that he realized what she was pointing at... and what the implications were.

"This was the day Abraham was murdered," he said grimly. "Pelley was there."

Chapter Seven

Anna had never considered herself to be paranoid. She had never done much of anything in her life to cause her to be paranoid. There had never been any jealous ex-girlfriends or even jilted ex-boyfriends. No one had ever been out to harm or kill her before.

At least, not before *now*.

Knowing that Pelley had been at the library for an hour prior to Abraham's murder was making her jump at shadows. She was bone weary and wanted nothing more than to crawl into bed and sleep, but she was sitting on the couch in the living room, her knees pulled up to her chin and her quilt draped over her. She didn't want to be alone. Not tonight. Not after Pelley had just been there that afternoon.

As soon as they had realized that Pelley had been at the library just prior to the murder, Anna's guilt came flooding back. "What if he saw you come in?" she had urgently said to Rhys. "He'll know you were there. And if he had anything to do with Abraham's murder…"

He had tried his best to reassure her. If the inspector had wanted to kill Rhys, he could have attempted it when he stopped by the Blackwood's home earlier that afternoon. And while they had to assume that Pelley was involved with Abraham's murder, they didn't know how. Until they did, it did them no good to worry.

"I'm more concerned with the fact that he was at the library a week before the murder happened," Rhys had told her. "That, with the connections he has as a Met officer, has me worried that he may be looking for more information about *you*."

That was when she had decided she was going to stay in the living room. Images of Pelley crawling through her bedroom window made her go into her room with Nicola only long enough to get her quilt before going to sit on the couch. For once she was glad of the constant bodyguards.

Next to her, Rhys and Finn were quietly talking. Nicola had gone to bed some time ago, and David was still in the kitchen. Anna could feel her eyes burning, and her eyelids felt as though they weighed a hundred pounds each. But she stubbornly fought to keep them open. She didn't want to go to sleep. She was too scared.

On the TV, some hyped-up man with slicked-back hair was cheerfully detailing the benefits of a stick-on light bulb. Anna knew it had to be late --- or early --- if infomercials were playing. She wondered if the British had the same stupid products that the Americans did, or if they were more interesting. If the stick-on light bulb was anything to go by, it was the same boring stuff advertised to the same kind of lazy people.

"Anna."

She blinked and turned to Rhys, who was now sitting alone. Finn was gone. Anna wondered if he had left, or if he had just found somewhere to pass out. "You look exhausted, and it's late. Go to bed."

"No. *You're* still awake, and you don't look any better." She was right. His eyes were bloodshot, and he had run his hand through his hair so much that every inch was sticking out. "Besides, I don't want to go to bed. I don't want to be by myself. I'm going to stay right here. You can go to bed. I'll be fine."

He let out a sigh and leaned back against the couch, closing his eyes. "I'm too tired to argue," he told her, his voice rough with fatigue. Before she could enjoy her victory, however, he reached out and pulled her against him, guiding her head to rest against his chest, his hand settling in her hair.

Her eyes went wide, and she didn't dare breathe for fear of moving. "What are you doing?"

"You don't want to be alone, and I'm too tired to move. Maybe this way we'll both at least get some sleep." He paused. "Is this a problem? Are you uncomfortable?"

"No!" she answered quickly. "No. I just... I'm fine. Are you fine? I mean, okay?"

"Mmmm." As her cheek was resting against his chest, she could feel his breath begin to slow. After only a moment, she knew he was asleep.

She lay there for a moment, basking in the warmth that radiated from his body, from the gentle hand that rested on her head. She listened to the steady *thump thump* of his heartbeat, and couldn't help but notice that her own synced with his. She thought back to earlier worries about the feelings that he elicited in her.

I don't care, she told herself. *I'll worry about that later. Right now, I just want to enjoy this.*

So she let out a sigh, closed her eyes, and quickly fell asleep.

When she next awoke, bright sunlight was coming in through the windows. She was also alone.

She was lying stretched out on the couch. A pillow had been placed under her head, and her quilt was pulled up to her shoulders. That had been Rhys's doing, no doubt.

She pulled the quilt off of her and stretched, letting out a yawn as she did so. She didn't know what time it was, but the unmistakable smell of bacon was wafting in from the direction of the kitchen. She decided to go and investigate before taking a shower.

She found Nicola standing over the stove, flipping strips of bacon. The other woman's head came up the sound of Anna's entrance, and she grinned, waving her spatula in greeting. "There's our Sleeping Beauty. Good morning. Or, rather good afternoon. Would you like some bacon?"

"Yes, please." Anna sat on one of the bar stools and snagged a piece of bacon off of the plate Nicola brought over before the other woman had a chance to set it down. "Where is everyone else?"

"David is still sleeping. I think he was the last one of us to actually go to bed, so he may be out for a while longer. Finn and Rhys left about an hour ago. They said they were going to go talk to some other people, see what more they could find out about Pelley. Now that we're fairly certain he is somehow connected to Abraham's murder, the boys wanted to see if they could learn more about the how of that connection." She offered Anna a bright grin, her eyes twinkling. "You and Rhys looked cute, by the way, all snuggled up on the couch together. I wish I had taken a photo so you could have seen it."

Anna blushed, nibbling on the end of her bacon. "I tried to get him to go to bed, but he wouldn't do it. He said that way we'd both get some sleep."

"I'm sure that was all he was thinking about." Nicola's smile would have done the Cheshire Cat proud. "Rhys may be an old-fashioned guy, but he *is* still a guy. That means he'll just ask your permission before he charms the pants off of you. Literally."

Speaking of which... "I was actually hoping I could ask you about that."

Nicola cocked an eyebrow. "Has he already asked your permission? Wow. That was quick."

Anna's blush deepened, and she waved her hand in the air. "No no. No pants are coming off. At least, not to my knowledge."

Her companion let out a dramatic sigh. "Pity. I was hoping to get a vicarious thrill. Lord know no one is asking to take *my* pants off." She went back to the stove to check her bacon. "Any ways. You were saying?"

"Well..." How did she say this? She wasn't used to gossiping about boys. She didn't want Nicola getting the wrong idea. Especially when she herself wasn't sure of her feelings. Or even if her feelings were real.

Nicola let out a snort. "I'm not blind or stupid, Anna. You care for him. And he cares for you. If he didn't, he wouldn't have pulled that stunt last night. He would go out of his way to make sure you didn't get the wrong impression. Trust me, he would rather keep his distance than lead you on only to break your heart later on down the road. That's just the kind of guy he is."

"So he doesn't, you know, have someone?" Anna could feel her face warm. God, she sounded like a schoolgirl with a crush.

A brief shadow passed over Nicola's face. "No," she said softly. "He hasn't for a very, very long time." She turned a kind smile onto her companion. "Which is how I know he's got something for you. He wouldn't even let you touch him if he didn't. Trust me."

She would be lying if she didn't admit Nicola's words gave her a sense of relief. "I do have feelings for him," she said softly, studying a piece of bacon as though it held all of the answers. "That much I know for certain."

"But..."

Anna sighed again. "But I don't know! I don't know if it's feelings for Rhys himself, or if it's feelings for the man who rescued me. If it's the latter, then it would be wrong of me to do anything with them. Because once he was no longer my protector, those feelings would go away. And I don't want to hurt him." She took a bite of bacon and chewed for a moment before swallowing. "And I don't want to hurt *me*. I've been hurt before. A *lot*. I will *not* open myself up for that kind of pain again unless I know it will be worth it. And right now, I just don't know. Besides, I've known him for less than a week. I don't know *what* to do."

The two women were quiet for a long moment. Anna had begun to wonder if she'd said too much, or if Nicola was trying not to laugh at her. At least she had finally gotten it off of her chest. That, at least, was a relief.

Finally, Nicola turned to face Anna and put her hands on her hips. "You want my advice, both as his sister *and* as a professional? Don't try to figure it out. Just let things play out. You already have enough to worry about without adding this to the pile. And *this* isn't life-threatening. I think that when the time comes you will know if it's real or not. *Then* you can deal with it. In the meantime, let's work on the problem we already have. Your feelings for Rhys will work themselves out."

"Do you really think so?"

"I do. I also *know* that Rhys won't do anything until *you* are certain of your feelings." Her lips twisted into a grimace. "You're not the only one who has been hurt. If he thinks you are worth it, he will wait forever."

It wasn't the answer that she had been hoping for, but Anna did feel a lot better. "Thanks, Nicola."

"Don't thank me yet. You haven't seen my bill." She winked. "And don't worry. I won't tell my brother about any of this. Counselor-client confidentiality and all of that."

Afterwards, Anna went to shower before reemerging into the living room with her laptop. She wasn't even going to bother with the monk today. She had much more important things to worry about, and she knew she wouldn't be able to focus enough to get any real work done.

She didn't have Finn's police connections or the Blackwoods' 'secret club' connections, but she *was* a good researcher. So she pulled up a search engine, typed in the name Henry Pelley, and hit search.

She hadn't been expecting much. Rhys and the others had been pouring over every bit of information they could find on the man who had been going by that name. She was just going in a direction that no one else had thought to go. And when she saw what her search results were, she realized that their direction had been the wrong one.

Henry Pelley, she learned, had been a character from a serial that had been written in early 20th century Scotland. He had been an inspector, too. But the original Henry Pelley had been a monster. He was a serial killer, a rapist, and committed numerous other crimes throughout the serial. He had become a police inspector so that he could help to cover up his own crimes, and because no one would ever suspect a police officer of murder. Worse still, he was often hailed as a hero by his superiors. And when he successfully 'solved' one of his own crimes and had an innocent man sentenced to death, he was given a promotion.

It could be a coincidence that the inspector shared the same name as the fictional policeman, but Anna seriously doubted it. She had never believed in coincidences.

She was on the third scholarly text when the front door opened and Rhys appeared. "Hey," he said, coming over to her. "How are you? Did you sleep well?"

Anna looked up at him, and frowned.

There were dark circles under his eyes. He was smiling, but it was a tired smile. And he was wearing the same clothes he had been wearing the day before.

"You look terrible," she said softly. "You need to go back to sleep."

He chuckled as he took a seat next to her. "Well. It's good to see you, too."

"I'm serious, Rhys. You look like you could fall over at any moment. And you won't be doing anyone any good if that happens." Her lips twisted. "I happen to know that you spent the night sitting up on the couch with a lump lying on top of you. I doubt that it was conducive to a good night's sleep."

"At least the lump didn't drool." He met her gaze. "You're not going to go anywhere, are you?" His voice was soft, almost pleading. "I don't want you to go anywhere without me. Please."

Her heart gave a little thump, and she raised her right hand. "I swear I won't step foot outside of this house. I'm actually working on something right now. I may have found something about Pelley, but I want to look at a few more things before I'm ready to say that it is important. I'll probably still be sitting here when you wake up."

He didn't seem reassured. "I need you to promise me."

"I promise." She gave him a gentle push. "Now go. Rest. The world won't fall apart while you sleep."

"Let's not tempt fate, shall we?" He stood and stretched. "All right, I'm going to sleep. But if anyone asked, tell them I put up a fight against you. I'd hate for people to think I was a pushover."

"Hmmmm."

David had a thoughtful look on his face as he leaned back away from the computer screen. His eyes flickered over to Anna, and he offered her a smile. "This is good work, Anna. I never would have thought to look at this from an academic standpoint."

She gave a pleased blush. "That's the only way I know how to research. Besides, the rest of you have been working on trying to figure out what his real name is. I thought I might look into why he chose the name that he did." She paused. "So do you think that this is connected?"

"I think there are too many similarities for it *not* to be connected." He let out a sigh and rubbed his face. "Now the question is what is he trying to tell us? That he is the one who killed Abraham?"

"No. I know that's not the case. I heard the voices of both of the men who were in the library that night. So did Rhys. We would have known if Pelley was one of them. Neither Rhys nor I recognized his voice."

"So then he's working with them?"

"That would seem the most likely scenario." She pointed to one of the articles she had found on the Internet. "The original Henry Pelley joined the police so that he could mislead them. He wanted to cover up his own crimes, make someone else take the blame for it. Maybe that is what our Henry Pelley is doing. Only he's covering up someone *else's* crimes."

"Which gives us the idea that this is not the first time something like this has happened. I doubt he would join the Met simply to cover up one crime." He paused. "Have you told Rhys about this yet?"

She shook her head. "I sent him to bed as soon as he got home. He looked as though he was about to fall over. And I wanted to be sure before we went down a rabbit hole. Just because they have the same name doesn't mean anything. But now... "

"Now we would be foolish to *not* think they are connected." He passed her laptop back to her and pulled out a cell phone. "A few of the other Scholars I know are more versed in that period of history. I'm going to call around and see if I can find out any more information about the original character, see if there is anything else linking the two." He raised an eyebrow. "Do I need to inform them that you have accepted the position as Scholar? With Abraham gone, they will be wanting to know if you plan on replacing him."

"Of course," she answered before she had even thought about it. She hadn't been planning on accepting so readily, especially not with everything that was currently going on around her. But she remembered Rhys talking to her yesterday evening while she had been reading the monk's journal. *"You're going to make a great Scholar."* She wanted to prove him right. Besides, wasn't she already acting as a Scholar?

"Excellent. I'll let them know, and I'll be sure to tell them that I'll be your teacher since Abraham can no longer complete that duty. Keep researching. I'll let you know if I find out anything different." He stood, offered her nod and then strode away, phone pressed against his ear.

Anna signed and leaned back into the couch. She felt... happy. Vindicated. She had done something to help. She wasn't useless. She wasn't just sitting back and letting others take care of her. She could be a productive member of this group. And that was a huge weight off of her shoulders.

She continued to scroll through the academic articles about Henry Pelley, but found nothing else new. One article contested that the Pelley serial was a rip-off of the Dr. Jekyll and Mr. Hyde story. Anna's favorite was the article that claimed that the author was trying to take ownership of the Jack the Ripper murders, and was trying to tell the readers that the reason he was never caught was that he was a policeman and had moved to Scotland. She had told David that maybe they should go back through Pelley's files and see if there were any other murders or crimes that had gone unsolved while he was on the case. He had thought that was a good idea.

After finding nothing new, she made her way back into the now-empty kitchen and found the box that Finn had brought containing all of the fake Henry Pelley's records. She wasn't sure that they were in any kind of order, so she pulled out the first folder and began to flip through it.

She was halfway through the third folder --- and cursing whatever filing system the British police used --- when Rhys walked into the kitchen. He had obviously showered, and the dark circles under his eyes had faded, even if they hadn't vanished completely. Anna couldn't help but smile at him. "I do believe you'll pass for a human now."

He chuckled. "Glad to know it." He walked to fridge and pulled out a beer. He offered her one, but she shook her head. "Were you able to find out anything?"

"Actually, I *did* find something." She told him the story of the fictional Henry Pelley, and that she and David thought their Henry Pelley had chosen that name on purpose. She told him about her theory that he and the two men from the library must be working together, and repeated David's concern that there must have been other crimes covered up.

By the time she was done, his beer was pushed to the side and he was looking at her with an expression she couldn't quite make out. "Amazing," he murmured. "Abraham was an academic. And those two men were after a book. We should have at least considered a connection when we began looking into this." He tipped an imaginary hat to her.

Rhys's praise meant more to her than David's had, and she ducked her head to hide her blush. "David is calling some of the other Scholars who deal more with that time period to see if he can find anything new."

"Well, if he can't, we can ask around tomorrow."

She frowned. "Ask who? Around where?"

"Abraham's memorial. I'm sure most of the Scholars will be there."

Chapter Eight

In all the excitement, Anna had nearly forgotten that Abraham's memorial service was to take place the next morning. As she had not planned on attending any funerals after moving to England, she had nothing to wear. So Nicola volunteered to take her shopping.

Rhys had looked disappointed when his sister cheerfully tugged Anna towards the door. Anna had given him an apologetic look, but Nicola had informed him that he wouldn't know good fashion if it bit him in the nose. Anna needed something that was respectful and mournful, not a Little Black Dress. If it were up to him, the elder Blackwood sibling declared, poor Anna would be wearing a mesh, see-through dress. By the time they were out of the door, Rhys's face was crimson, and Anna had tears of laughter in her eyes.

Much to Anna's surprise --- and relief --- Nicola *did* have a good fashion sense. It didn't take them long to find a black dress that would be proper for a funeral, but that Nicola readily assured her --- with a wink --- could be dressed up for a date night. They also found a pair of shoes, a wrap, and some silver jewelry.

"Not that it matters," Nicola said smugly, "but you're going to be the best-looking woman there tomorrow. Well, except for me, of course."

It seemed as though all of London and half of Scotland had turned out to give Abraham Clark a proper send off. Colleagues and former students from universities he had taught at were there, as was the entire Board of Directors for the Bradley Library. Anna had been passed around to every single one of them, having her hand shook, her shoulder patted, and being told how happy they were she was staying. She couldn't remember a single name, and her brain was swirling by the time she was able to escape.

Many of his fellow Scholars were there as well. David introduced her to several of them. There were more names that Anna forgot, more handshaking, and more gratitude. She was contemplating running out of the large church and catching the Underground back to the Blackwoods' home when Rhys came to the rescue.

"Pardon me, ladies, gentlemen," he said, bowing slightly as he tucked Anna's arm into his. "I'm afraid I must steal your newest colleague. Abraham's sister has asked after her."

There were mutterings of sympathy, and then she was being led away.

She let out a breath that she hadn't realized she was holding. "Thanks for the save," she muttered. "I felt like I was in a pool of sharks."

He chuckled. "You have to remember that they are Scholars. Like you, they deal mostly with the past. When anything new comes along, they all want to study it and learn as much about it as they can. Even if the 'it' in question happens to be a person." He paused for a moment. "This may be entirely inappropriate, but you look very nice in that dress."

She made a pleased noise. "Thank you. I'm glad you like it."

There was a long line of people stretching from the front of the church, but Rhys steered her around them. As they neared the beginning of the line, she saw that they were heading for a woman who, despite her gray hair and wrinkled skin, looked ageless. This, Anna decided, must be Abraham's sister.

She swallowed and gripped Rhys's arm tighter. This was one of the reasons she hated funerals. She never knew what to say to someone who was grieving. 'I'm sorry' had always sounded lame to her, and she didn't know this woman at all. She had hoped to avoid the unpleasant task altogether, but Rhys had said she was asking for Anna. Anna couldn't say no without being rude.

Rhys came to a stop just to the side of the woman, who was currently in a conversation with an elderly gentleman who was walking with the aid of a cane. Once the conversation was over and the man had given her a hug and moved on, the woman's eyes fell on Rhys.

"There you are," she said with a smile. Then her eyes moved to Anna, and the smile widened. "Ah. This must be your Anna. I am so glad to meet you, my dear." She held her hands out

Anna didn't bother to point out that she was not Rhys's, nor anyone else's, as she grasped both of the other woman's hands in hers and accepted air kisses on both cheeks.

"I am so pleased to meet you," the older woman murmured. "Abraham spoke very highly of you. He had promised me that he would bring you around the next time I came for a visit. It was so good to hear the excitement in his voice once again. It had been a long time since anyone had caused him to sound like that."

Anna tried to offer her a smile. "It really is a delight to meet you, Ms...."

Her companion laughed. "Please. Abraham saw you as more of a daughter than a prodigy. I had not heard him fret over another person like he did you since he became Rhys's guardian. That means we are family. You must call me Katherine."

"Katherine. I wish we could have met under different circumstances."

Katherine's smile never wavered, but she suddenly looked much older. "Aye. I will miss that old man. And I know you will, too. You've only just moved here, and then to have *this* happen. But at least you have Rhys. He will take good care of you."

"He already has," Anna answered truthfully.

The two hugged, which Anna found wasn't as awkward as she had thought it would be. Katherine made her promise to keep in touch --- the Blackwoods had her information --- and then Rhys was leading her away once more.

"See? That wasn't so bad." There was a hint of amusement in Rhys's voice.

"Maybe. It was still better than being passed around the directors and Scholars like some shiny thing."

He chuckled. "Well, you are a shiny thing. Maybe they thought you looked good in that dress, too."

She tried to scowl at him, but she could feel his arm tightening around hers as he said it. He was jealous, and that revelation made it hard not to smile.

"Come on. Let's find our seats."

The memorial service was simple and light. Much, Anna thought, like Abraham himself. Instead of crying, the speakers invited the mourners to laugh. There were stories told that would have embarrassed Abraham had he been there to hear them, favorite songs played, and a listing of his many achievements.

Katherine spoke of how he had stepped in to help take care of a thirteen-year-old boy who had just lost his parents without a second thought. Abraham, she stated, had never had children of his own. But he had been a father when it was needed of him. And that had been his proudest accomplishment.

Anna glanced over at Rhys, to see that he was blinking furiously, but that a few tears had already escaped and were trailing down his cheeks. She reached out to take his hand, threading her fingers through his and squeezing. He offered her a smile, brought her hand up to brush his lips across her knuckles, and then placed their joined hands in his lap. They stayed there for the rest of the service. One time, when Anna happened to glance over, she noticed that Nicola was looking at their linked fingers with a smug grin.

Chapter Nine

"Let's go out."

Anna looked up from the monk's journal, pen stuck between her teeth. "Come again?"

Rhys stood in the doorway of her bedroom, hands in his pockets. He was bouncing on his toes, looking for all the world like a young boy.

"You've been stuck in the house for days without complaining. And you've been by yourself for most of the time. I feel bad, and want to make it up to you."

It had been three days since Abraham's memorial service. Rhys, Nicola, David, and Finn had all been popping in and out of the house the whole time. There was always someone in the house with her, but they were usually going back through Henry Pelley's files, or doing something else important. She had exiled herself to her room and worked on the journal. Other than seeing someone in passing, or having the bodyguard of the hour stick their head in to say hello or goodbye, she'd hardly seen anyone since the service. Anna had been feeling left out, but she didn't complain. They knew what they were doing, and she didn't want to get in their way.

"You don't have to make it up to me," she said softly. "I know you all are busy. Besides, I've been able to get some more work done. I don't mind."

"Well, *I'm* starting to go stir crazy. There is a street fair going on in Shepherd's Bush. I thought I'd go check it out, and I'd rather you come with me than anyone else." He held out his hand. "Come on. It'll be fun."

She let out a sigh, but she quickly pushed her chair back and got to her feet. There was no reason to argue. Besides, she hadn't seen him much at all over the past three days. So she took his offered hand and let him pull her out of her room.

Something had changed between them. Their relationship had evolved past friendship to something else. What that 'something else' was Anna didn't know, but she liked it. They had an easy way with each other that she had never had with anyone else. He didn't demand anything of her, which was fine by her. She was still sorting out her feelings for him, and was thankful for the room he was giving her to do so, even if he didn't realize he was doing it.

No one had said anything to them about their holding hands after the service. Nicola, however, had been going out of her way to make sure the two of them were alone together every chance she got. When Anna had informed her she had all the subtlety of a bomb going off, Nicola had only laughed and redoubled her efforts.

When they were outside, Anna headed for Rhys's car, but he tugged her in a different direction. "Not today," he said, eyes dancing. "It's beautiful out, and the roads are going to be packed. I have a better way for us to get around."

He led her around the side of the house and into the detached garage. He unlocked the door, turned on the light, and led her to the back corner.

She recognized the shape that lay beneath the blue-colored tarp. "You have a *motorcycle?*"

He nodded, grinning like a kid on Christmas, as he removed the tarp. "This is my pride and joy. I built it myself from the ground up. Took me two years, but it was worth it. I know where everything is, and I don't have to worry about paying a fortune to someone else if anything goes wrong." He patted the gas tank affectionately.

She thought about the callouses on his hands, and now understood where they had come from. "She's beautiful," she said softly. "I've always wanted to ride on a motorcycle."

"Well then. Allow me to grant you your wish. I warn you, though. Once you do, you'll never want to ride in a car again. There is nothing like it." He came to stand next to her, a helmet in his hands. "This is Nic's helmet. Here. It should fit you."

Anna stood very still as he strapped the helmet onto her head, trying not to shiver every time his fingers brushed her skin. Once he was satisfied, he donned his own helmet, then helped her onto the bike.

"You're going to have to put your arms around me," he said over his shoulder, that wolfish smile on his lips. "And make sure you hold on *tight.*" Without waiting for her response, he started the engine.

The bike didn't rumble so much as purr. She didn't know much about motorcycles, but she had spent her fair amount of time stuck in traffic next to bikes that rattled hard and loud enough to shake her car. This engine wasn't nearly that loud, but it still managed to somehow convey power.

As instructed, she leaned into Rhys's back and wrapped her arms around his waist. Through the fabric of his T-shirt, she could feel the muscles of his abdomen. *Hard* muscles. She tightened her grip.

"Here we go!" he shouted over the noise of the engine. Then he was slowly propelling the bike out of the garage and onto the road beyond.

Anna gasped and squeezed even tighter as the full power of the bike threatened to jerk her out of her seat. She ducked her head down so that Rhys would be a shield between her and the worst of the wind. But as Rhys pushed the bike up to the speed limit, she felt herself began to relax.

He had been right. There *was* nothing like riding on a motorcycle. The wind was making her eyes water, and every now and then she would feel a zing on her face as a bug slammed into her, but oh, what a *rush!* The rumble of the bike underneath her and the rush of the wind around her made her feel as though she were actually flying. If she knew it wouldn't knock her off of the bike, she would have held her arms out to both sides

Instead, feeling giddy, she let out a laugh, only to have it snatched away by the wind.

As they approached the area where the street festival was being held, Anna could see why Rhys had opted for the motorcycle instead of his car. Many of the streets had been blocked off, and the cars were at a near standstill. Rhys deftly weaved between them, causing Anna to yelp and hold on tighter. After another few moments, he was pulling into a small area between two other cars and killing the engine.

After the rumbling of the bike and the roar of the wind, the normal sounds of cars and people seemed nearly inaudible to her. She almost missed hearing Rhys telling her that she could let go of him now.

"What? Oh! Sorry." She dropped her arms and shook them, trying to get rid of the tingling that ran all the way from her fingertips to her shoulders. "I wasn't crushing your ribs, was I?"

He chuckled as he slid off of the bike and held out a hand to help her do the same. "I told you to grip tight, remember? Besides, you're better than Nic. She holds on like a vise. She may not crush any bones, but she certainly leaves bruises." He was grinning. "What did you think?"

She let out a whoosh of breath as he reached up to unstrap her helmet. "That was *amazing!* I can see now why people are so dedicated to their bikes. I could do that every day."

"You didn't eat any bugs, did you?"

She made a face. "Ewww. No, I don't think so."

"Good. I meant to tell you to keep your mouth closed before we left. Nothing like choking on a bug when you're riding down a highway." He stowed their helmets into the saddlebags that lay across the back of the bike and lead her forward.

Anna hadn't been sure what to expect out of a London street fair. Street fairs in Tennessee consisted mainly of a lot of fried foods, kiddie games, and someone who thought they could sing belting out country music. She hoped that this fair would be somewhat better.

The first thing she noticed was the smell. Like Tennessee, there were a number of food vendors set up along the side street they had parked on. But unlike Tennessee, it wasn't a jumble of hot grease and deep fried dough. She could make out all sorts of heavenly smells, with the strong odor of fried fish being the most prevalent, followed by the smell of fries.

Her stomach let out a grumble. "Mmmm. I smell fish and chips!"

"We'll stop by and grab something to eat first, then we'll go check everything out. I read on the Internet that there is a knife-throwing booth around here."

She raised her eyebrow. "Knife-throwing booth?"

"You know, one of those booths where you can win a prize if you do something? I used to be pretty good at it. I'd like to see if I still am."

Anna just shook her head. She didn't want to know why he was good at throwing knives.

They stopped at the first fish and chips stand they came across. Anna happily dug in, licking the grease from her fingers when she was finished. Rhys just laughed and handed her a napkin.

Stomachs full, they wandered down the side streets looking at everything that the vendors had sat up. Rhys didn't try to hold her hand, but he stayed close enough to her that they would occasionally brush against one another. She bought a T-shirt that bore the Union Jack, then bought a large, felt hat to match. They found the knife-throwing booth, and Rhys proved that his skills were not rusty at all. He was awarded a large, stuffed frog for his troubles, which he gallantly presented to Anna with a bow. She kissed him on the cheek in delight, and he grinned.

They were currently sitting at a small group of tables that had been set up close to a stage. A band was warming up, and they had decided to stick around so that they could listen to the music. Rhys was in the middle of telling her about building his motorcycle when Anna's ears picked up on a conversation coming from nearby.

"I don't know why we're here," growled a deep, surly voice. "There's too many people. *Someone* will be bound to see us. We should just snatch her from those people she's staying with. There's a lot less of them."

"The boss wants us here so we're here," replied a second voice. "And this would be an ideal place to take the girl. No one will pay any attention to us, and we just have to get her someplace quiet before we hit her with the chloroform. It will be easier here than if we did it someplace people were more likely to pay attention to us. And you know who those people are that she's staying with. We'd never be able to get to her with all of them around."

Anna felt her whole body go numb, and her heart came to a crashing halt.

She *knew* those voices.

Rhys must have noticed something was wrong, because he let his voice trail off. "Anna?" he asked quietly, reaching over to touch her hand. "What is it?"

She turned terror-filled eyes to him. "They're here," she whispered frantically. "The men from the library. Both of them. I heard them." She would never forget the sound of their voices as long as she lived.

Rhys's expression didn't change, but he was suddenly crushing her hand. "Where?"

"Behind me and to the left. They must be close, because I didn't have any trouble making out what they were saying."

Rhys's eyes moved. Anna didn't dare turn around, but she saw when his eyes narrowed, and knew he must have spotted them. "I've got them," he said in a low voice. "Two men. Both of them are tall, one has a ponytail. What were they saying?"

She had to swallow. Suddenly, she was regretting the fish and chips she had eaten earlier. "They... They are supposed to get me away from the crowds and chloroform me. They thought that it would be easier to do it here where no one would notice them. The one who killed Abraham said he knew who you were."

Rhys swore. Loudly. She wanted to tell him to be quiet, to not draw attention to himself, but the sheer anger that she suddenly saw spring into his eyes held her mouth shut. "Okay. I'm going to get you out of here. Do you understand me? They're not going to get you. But we have to find a way to lose them in this crowd. First, take your hat off. That thing is better than a beacon light."

She did as she was told, removing the felt monstrosity from her head and crushing it against her chest. Her hands were shaking.

Rhys was muttering to himself. "Stupid, stupid, stupid. I should have known better. What the hell was I thinking, bringing you here?" His eyes swept around, looking for the best escape route. "They've already

63

marked us, and we'll never outrun them in this crowd. And if they've brought guns there could be innocent people hurt. Or hostages. We need to find a way to give them the slip."

Anna felt a hysterical giggle rise up in her throat. 'Give them the slip' made it sound as though they were part of a bad spy movie. Or Saturday morning cartoon.

"Just act normal, okay?" He stood up and offered her his hand. "Come on," he said in his normal tone of voice. "Let's go see what else is going on."

"O-okay." She took his hand and let him pull her to his feet. Once standing, he slung an arm around her shoulders and pulled her tight against him. She clutched the shopping bag containing her shirt, hat and frog to her chest as they began to push their way through the crowd that was beginning to stream in towards the stage.

She was shaking so hard that she wasn't sure she could walk straight. Hearing Growly Voice had brought the memories of that night in the library back into sharp focus. She remembered the terror, the feel of Rhys's weight pinning her down behind a bookcase as Growly Voice kicked at the cage. She remembered the sounds of the gunshots and of her desk crashing to the ground. And she remembered Abraham lying in a pool of his own blood.

The shaking intensified. Rhys's grip on her tightened, and he murmured comforting words and apologizes to her.

She didn't know how long they walked before Rhys angled her over to a small fountain area. He quickly dodged behind a large family with a stroller and then pulled her to the corner behind the fountain. He pushed her against the wall and leaned forward like he was going to kiss her. "Do you see them?" he whispered in her ear.

She glanced over his shoulder, and let out a whimper as she saw the two men he had described earlier. "Yes. They are on the other side of the fountain. But they are looking around. I don't think they've seen us yet. Rhys..."

He moved so that his face was once again in front of hers, blocking her view of the men, but blocking their view of her face in turn. Before she could say anything else, Rhys had placed a hand on her cheek, leaned forward, and kissed her.

Chapter Ten

Anna forgot how to breathe.

She stood there, body stiff, eyes wide, as Rhys pressed his lips to hers. He had taken her completely by surprise, and she found herself unable to react.

But then she realized just what was happening.

Rhys was *kissing* her.

As though her body had been waiting for that conformation from her brain, she found herself moving. Her eyes fluttered closed, and her shopping bag fell to the ground, forgotten. One hand came up to tangle in his hair, pulling him closer to her. The other hand reached up to clutch at his arm. She was so lost in the moment that she never noticed Rhys slide his hand from her cheek to cradle the back of her head, and wrap his other arm around her waist, pulling her body tighter against his.

She had found herself wondering what it would feel like to kiss him. Would there be fireworks, as she had always heard? Would her knees turn weak? Would her body tingle?

No, she thought faintly. *It's not like that at all.*

It was much, much better.

A taste exploded in her mouth that she could not describe. It was musky and earthy, and oh so unmistakably *him.* Goosebumps had appeared on every inch of her skin at the same time fire raced through her veins. Her knees had turned to water, and only his strong arm around her waist kept her upright. And forget fireworks. Anna was certain a nuclear bomb had exploded just over their heads.

When he pulled away a moment later, both of them were panting slightly. He leaned his forehead against hers, murmuring her name. Then, much to her own surprise, she was kissing *him.*

All of her doubts about how she felt for him faded away at that moment. The feelings she had were for *him,* for Rhys. She cared for him. Deeply. This moment, this kiss, had shown her that---

Suddenly, he was shoving her away from him. Already dizzy from the sudden kiss and lack of oxygen, she stumbled and would have fallen had it not been for the wall at her back to support her. She blinked at him, heart pounding, wondering if the two men had found them.

But he was standing alone, a few feet away, staring at her with a look of horror on his face. One hand rested on his stomach as though he were about to be sick, and the other was clenched into a fist. "Anna," he rasped out. "I am... Oh, God. I am so sorry. That shouldn't have happened. I shouldn't have done that."

She stared at him. "What?" was all she could manage.

"I shouldn't have kissed you. That was a mistake. I am so sorry. Please."

"A... mistake?" Her heart, which had just been soaring somewhere high in the clouds, came crashing down to the ground. Rhys had finally kissed her. And now he was saying it was a *mistake?*

He sighed and raked a hand through his hair, looking absolutely miserable. "It won't happen again. I swear to you."

But I want *it to happen again!* she thought desperately. She could feel a knot beginning to form in her chest, and she was suddenly having a hard time catching her breath. What had just happened?

Rhys spun on his heel, putting his back to her and looking out through the crowd. "I don't see them anymore," he said, and she could hear a note of anger in his voice. When Rhys strode over to her, she winced away from him.

But all he did was reach down, scoop up her shopping bag and hand it to her. "Come on," he said roughly. He didn't try to take her hand or put an arm around as he had earlier. Instead, he took her by the elbow --- looking as though he'd rather not touch her at all --- and tugged her forward. "Let's get out of here while we can."

Anna let him pull her along, her brain finally coming out of its fog and trying to process what had just happened.

Nicola had told her that Rhys wouldn't have been acting the way he had with her if he didn't have feelings of some kind. That he would never lead her on or do anything that might unintentionally hurt her.

Then why had he said the kiss was a mistake? Had she been so wrong about all of the touches and words that had passed between them? Had Nicola been mistaken about her brother's intentions? And if it was such a bad idea, why had Rhys kissed her in the first place?

You know why, she told herself angrily. He had wanted to lose their pursuers in the crowd. If the two men had lost sight of them as they ducked behind the fountain, they might not pay attention to a couple were who were kissing in the corner. They would assume that they had tried to get as far away as possible. He hadn't kissed her because he wanted to. He had kissed her simply as a way to avoid detection from her would-be kidnappers, and now he was sorry for it. Because she would take it to mean something else. And he had no feelings for her.

By the time they reached the motorcycle, she could feel the hot prick of angry tears forming behind her eyes. But she swallowed them down before they could have a chance to spill. She would be *damned* if she let Rhys see how much he had hurt her. She would not cry in front of him. Not again.

The idea of touching him --- something she had craved just moments ago --- now nauseated her, but she knew he would never let her take the bus or the train. So while he was stowing her bag in his saddlebags, she jerked her helmet on and climbed onto the bike without his assistance. When he started the engine, she gripped the saddlebags instead of holding on to him.

As soon as they returned to the Blackwoods' home, she was going to lock herself in her room and let herself cry out all of the tears that she would allow herself to shed over Rhys Blackwood. Now that she knew how he felt for her, she could easily work on ridding herself of her feelings for him. She had been betrayed before. She knew how to handle a broken heart. Then she would wait for her chance to leave him behind forever.

Nicola's car was in the driveway when Rhys pulled up, so he merely idled his bike at the curb and jerked his head, indicating for her to get off. She did so, retrieving her bag from the saddlebags and stuffing the helmet in its place. As she strode to the front door, he roared off down the street.

Thankfully, Nicola was not in the living room, so Anna was able to make it to her room without having to explain why Rhys had left and why she was blinking back tears. As soon as she entered the comforting darkness of the bedroom, she locked the door, threw herself on the bed, and wept. At some point in time, she reached out for her shopping bag and pulled out the stuffed frog Rhys had won for her. She thought about throwing it across the room, but hugged it to her chest instead. She curled her body into as small of a shape as possible, buried her face into the frog's soft fur, and continued sobbing.

The worst of the tears and the hiccupping had died down when a soft knock came at the door. She tensed, thinking it was Rhys, but relaxed when she heard Nicola's voice call out "Anna? Are you all right? Can I come in?" She sounded worried.

Anna got to her feet, unlocked the door, then headed to the bathroom so that she could blow her nose and splash water on her face before Nicola could get a good look at her.

Nicola followed her, brows pinched together. "Are you all right? Rhys called to tell me the two men from the library were at the fair. He feels like he needlessly put you in danger, and he's taking it pretty hard."

I'm sure he is, Anna thought nastily. Instead, she offered a weak smile. "I'm fine. It just... When I heard their voices, it was like I was back at the library, you know? It caught me off guard. And then I heard them talking about wanting to kidnap me, and it just..." She sighed heavily. "It was a shock. That's all. I didn't realize how much it would upset me."

"Well, who can blame you? I'd be upset, too." She paused. "Can I get you anything? Water? Tea? Beer? Maybe something stronger?"

"No. I'm fine, really. I feel a lot better now that I've cried it out."

"That usually is the best thing to do." Nicola patter her hand. "You just stay in here and rest. I'll come to get you when dinner is ready."

Rhys was absent at dinner. When Anna emerged from her room the next morning, Nicola informed her that he still hadn't come home. That was fine with her. If he wanted to sulk, he could go right ahead. She would be the bigger person and go on as though nothing had happened.

She didn't see him for two whole days. When she politely asked after him, Nicola told her that he had returned home but had been busy working with Finn on discovering the identities of the two men. Anna had made some noncommittal noise before returning to her room and her monk.

On the third day, she received a phone call.

"Is this Miss Anna Miller?" asked a cultured female voice. Anna assured her it was. "My name is Maggie Romilly. I am calling to inform you that I am the new head librarian of the Bradley, and that we will be re-opening tomorrow. Would you mind coming in an hour early just so I can introduce myself and discuss matters with you?"

Of course Anna would be happy to. She was very happy that she would be going back to work, and she looked forward to meeting the other woman.

Anna felt like skipping when she left her room to go find Nicola. *Finally!* she thought happily. *Finally I can get out of here and away from Rhys. I can get back to my own life and forget all about this nonsense.*

She found both Blackwood siblings in the kitchen in the midst of a low, heated discussion. They both fell silent as she entered, and she couldn't help but notice that Rhys lowered his eyes so he wouldn't have to look at her.

"Anna?" She couldn't be sure, but she thought Nicola looked angry. "Is everything all right?"

"Yes." She took a deep breath. "I wanted to say thank you for all of the help you have given me over these past two weeks. You have saved my life more than once and given me hospitality and shelter. I'll never be able to thank you enough. You, and David, and Finn. But I am returning to my apartment this evening. The library will be re-opening tomorrow, and I am going back to work."

Rhys had gotten to his feet as soon as she said the words 'I am returning'. "No," he growled. "I'll not let you."

She coolly met his gaze, and had to fight a smile when he dropped his eyes first. "I have to return to work. The new head librarian just rang me, and she wants me to come in early for introductions. We have been closed for nearly two weeks. There will be a lot of work to do. I can't just hide here forever. And even you said that there is no direct route from here to the library on the Underground. Do you expect me to walk to and from work every day?"

"I'll drive you." Rhys's jaw was tight, and his hands were clenched into fists. "I'll take you to work and pick you up. But I will *not* let you be alone. Do you understand me?"

Anna set her own jaw and glared at him. He glared back. Nicola must have realized something else was going on because she wisely took a few steps back so that she was standing across the kitchen from them. "You are not my father," she spat out. "You are not my brother. And you are *certainly* not my lover. You have *no* claim to me and, therefore, no right to tell me what I can or can't do. I am going home and returning to work. That is all there is to it."

She watched as a muscle in his cheek twitched and his face slowly turned red. She honestly was expecting to see steam come out of his ears. Instead, he spun on his heel and stalked out of the room, his back stiff with anger.

Nicola watched her brother go with concern before turning to Anna. "Are you sure that's a good idea? I mean, Abraham's killers just tried to kidnap you a few days ago, and now you want to be alone?"

Anna sighed and reached up to massage the bridge of her nose. "I have to," she said tiredly. "I really can't thank you enough for all that you have done. But I have to get back to my life. Besides, I'll be in public most of the time. I won't stay late at work, and I'll be on the bus or train. And there are a lot of apartments with mine. No one will be able to do anything without at least a hundred people hearing. I'll be as safe as I can be."

Nicola nodded, though she still looked troubled. "Can I at least come to visit from time to time? You're the only real girlfriend I have, and I need to have someone to gossip with."

Anna couldn't help but grin. "Of course you can!" she said, striding forward to hug the other woman. "Besides, you're my *only* friend here. We have to stick together, don't we?"

By the time she had packed up everything, Rhys had left again. So Nicola offered to drive her back to her apartment. They spent the entire trip chatting about normal girl things, planning their next shopping trip, and Nicola offering to take Anna to one of her yoga classes so that she could see the dishy Fallon for herself. Nicola didn't ask about Rhys, for which Anna was thankful. She didn't want to tell the other woman how wrong she had been, and how deep Rhys's rejection had cut her.

When she walked through the door of her apartment, Anna was relieved to find everything was just as she had left it. After everything that had happened, she had half expected to find someone had come in and ransacked it. Nicola checked everything just to be sure, then, with a final hug, left.

Anna let out a sigh and fell back onto her couch, throwing an arm over her eyes. After having been around other people for the past two weeks she couldn't help but feel a sense of loneliness at being by herself. However, she had always enjoyed being on her own, and knew that she would return to her normal ways after a day or two.

At least I don't have to worry about always having a babysitter, she thought sourly. While she had understood and appreciated their desire to keep an eye on her, she had chafed at the idea of having a guardian. Being able to move without having to worry about someone not being able to find her was going to be magnificent.

She was also angry. No matter what had happened between them, she had still wanted to be friends with Rhys. But he hadn't even bothered to tell her goodbye or ask her to call him if she needed anything. He had just left. She supposed that meant that he didn't want anything to do with her at all. Very well, then. If that was how he felt, she wasn't going to waste her time on a friendship that would be entirely one-sided. If she never saw Rhys Blackwood again, she would die a happy woman. *Good riddance.*

She had, she finally decided, spent altogether too much time worrying about that man.

Chapter Eleven

Anna knew within the first five minutes of meeting Maggie Romilly that she was going to like the other woman. Maggie was tall, with iron gray hair that she wore pulled back into a tight bun. She immediately set to work asking Anna about the day-to-day operations of the library and what she would expect to have to do on a daily basis. They walked around the lower floor, including the reading room, with Anna pointing out all of the things she thought the new librarian would need to know. Best of all, when Anna wistfully stated that she wished she could get a reading lamp like those in the reading room for her own desk, Maggie had marched straight to the supply closet and retuned with one of the high-tech lamps in her hands. Yes, Anna was going to like her very much.

Maggie was also, as she said in a whisper, a Scholar as well. She had known Abraham, and had even met Anna briefly at the memorial service.

The younger woman blushed at this news. "I'm sorry," she murmured. "I met so many people that day. Everyone started to blur together after a while."

Maggie laughed. "Don't worry, dear. I understand. I don't think you were able to turn around without one of us old biddies wanting to introduce ourselves to you. Most of us Scholars have known each other for a long time. When there is a new face, we tend to get... excited. Especially as you are so young."

The library had barely been open for ten minutes before people began pouring in. There were a few academics who were needing texts for their research, but the vast majority of them were simply curious about seeing the scene of a murder. Anna left Maggie to deal with the latter as she headed to her own office to track down the texts that were being requested.

She had just managed to sit down and open another text that she was working on --- this one a household ledger kept by a noblewoman in the early 1500s --- when someone came striding into her office. "Hello," came a pleasant voice. "I am needing some assistance, and I was directed to come in here."

Anna looked up from her book to see a young man standing in front of her desk. He wore a messenger bag slung across his shoulders, and she could see brown loafers peeking out from under the hem of his jeans. This, she decided, was an academic, not a curiosity seeker.

She smiled and rose to her feet. "I shall do what I can. How can I help you?"

"My professor told me that you have a first-edition copy of Dante here. Do you?"

She could feel herself perk up at this. She had always enjoyed Dante, and she was curious to see what his interest in the Italian poet was. "We do indeed."

He let out a sigh as his shoulders sagged in relief. "Thank God. I've been trying to get in here for days, but you've been closed. I was afraid that I wasn't going to be able to have a look at it in time."

Anna brought up the search engine so that she could locate the call number. "I'm afraid you won't be able to take it out of the library."

"I thought as much. I'll probably have to come in for several days in order to get everything I need. Will you be able to keep the book on hold for me until I'm finished?"

"Not a problem. We don't have very many people come in asking after Dante. Which is a shame." She wrote down the call number and slipped the silver key from her pocket and headed to the cage. Rhys had left the key with his sister to return to Anna before he had disappeared the night before. She supposed she should just be grateful that he had thought to return it at all in his haste to get away from her. "Here we are," she said a moment later, reemerging with the thick volume in her hands. "Might I ask what you are working on?"

His eyes lit up as she relocked the gate behind her. "Sure! I'm a Ph.D. candidate. For my thesis, I want to compare the imagery of Hell from both the Bible and the *Inferno*. Then I want to randomly sample different religious leaders about their views of Hell. Then I will compare them to both the Bible and Dante. I want to try and prove that the vast majority of Christianity's views of Hell come from Dante and *not* the Bible."

"That is…" She shook her head in amazement. "That is going to be an *amazing* thesis."

He looked at her shyly. "Do you really think so?"

"I absolutely do. You'll have to bring it by when you're finished so that I can read it. I'll be eager to see what you find. Let me walk you down to the reading room so I can get your cubicle number."

They walked down the hallway to the reading room, chatting about Dante and his graphic version of Hell. The young man, who introduced himself as Graham, told her that he had learned Italian for the sole purpose of being able to read the original version of the *Inferno*. He didn't want to take the chance on a mistranslation. One mistake could undermine his whole thesis, and he had worked too hard and too long for that to happen.

As promised, he returned the next day. And the day after that. By the fourth day, she didn't even bother walking him to the reading room. He simply came into her office to pick up the book himself.

"Here," he said, placing a Styrofoam cup on her desk. "I thought I'd bring you some tea. Good, English tea. I know you said you haven't been in London very long, and I didn't know if anyone had taken the time to properly introduce you to our beverage of choice. That coffee you Americans like to drink tastes like burnt asphalt."

Anna laughed as she picked up the cup. "I have to say that I agree with you. I never have liked coffee." She deeply inhaled. "This smells amazing. What kind of tea is it?"

"Early Grey, the best. And it really does work better than coffee to help keep you awake. Doesn't make you twitch like a junkie the way coffee does."

"Thank you, Graham. This was very kind of you." She blew across the lid, trying to cool it down before taking a sip.

He stood there for a moment, resting one hand on the copy of the *Inferno*, looking uncomfortable. When Anna raised her eyebrows at him, he let out a sigh and rubbed the back of his neck. "I was wondering… Don't take this the wrong way, but would you… Maybe we can go for drinks when you get off of work? Not the alcoholic kind," he hastily added. "I know better than to ask a woman to go out for alcohol with a man she hardly knows. But I know this great coffee shop --- and they have *lots* of tea --- that's just a block from here. I thought maybe we could go. Together. After you get off of work." He blushed furiously and rubbed his face. "That sounded a lot better when I practiced it in my head."

Anna sat there for a moment, studying him as she waited for her tea to cool. He looked to be a few years older than her, and he was working on his doctorate. At Oxford, no less. He had been nothing but polite to her every time he had come to the library. And going out sounded like fun. She hadn't gone anywhere except to work and the market since returning to her flat. Nothing had happened to her, and she was beginning to grow bored. She hadn't heard from Nicola once, and she found that she missed having someone to talk to. Besides, it was just drinks. She could do drinks.

She gave him her most charming smile. "Sure," she said. "That sounds like fun."

"Hey, Maggie." Anna stuck her head around the door to the head librarian's office. "I'm going to go out for lunch today. Would you like me to bring you anything?"

"Hmm?" The older woman looked over the top of her glasses at Anna. "Oh. No, dear. I'll be all right." She smiled. "Are you going out with your young man?"

Anna let out a sigh and rolled her eyes, but she was smiling. "He's *not* my young man. He's just a friend."

"Oh?" Maggie raised an eyebrow. "This is, what? The fifth time he's taken you out? I think that means something, don't you?"

Anna blushed. Maggie had a point. Graham had been at the library every weekday for the past two weeks now. Even when he finished with Dante, he found a reason to come by the library, even if it was just for a few moments. Up until now, they had only gone out for drinks. But yesterday he had asked her out to lunch.

Still, he hadn't made any kind of move to make their relationship more than platonic, which she was extremely thankful for. She liked him, sure. He was charming, and smart. He could hold a conversation about Shakespeare. But there were no... sparks. He didn't take her breath away or twist up her insides.

Not like Rhys had.

She gave herself a mental shake, sternly telling that thought to go back to where it had come from. "Friends, Maggie. We're just friends. And I'll be back in an hour. Call my cell if you decide you want me to bring you something."

Maggie laughed. "Go have fun, dear. Let me know when you're back."

Anna waved, then walked to where Graham was waiting for her by the front doors of the library. "What is it?" he asked when he saw her face. "Did she say you couldn't go?"

Anna shook her head, grinning. "No, she's fine with me going. But I swear, she's worse than my mother."

He raised an eyebrow, but didn't ask any more. She only chuckled and walked out the door he was holding open for her.

They had planned to walk the two blocks to a small fish and chip shop --- or a 'chippy', as she had learned they were commonly called --- that Graham promised had the best chips in the whole city. When she had told him of her love for the greasy food, he had laughed and said that he would take her one day. It was a small place, really nothing more than a hole-in-the-wall. It wasn't a place that tourists knew about, and was usually pretty quiet at lunch. It would be perfect.

Once outside, he offered her his arm. After a moment, she took it, and he steered them down a narrow alley that ran past the library and between two old Victorians that were now businesses. "This is the best way to get there," he confessed. "If we take the main road, we'll have to hit at least four crosswalks. And I don't know if you've noticed this or not, but we British aren't the best at obeying traffic laws. This may not exactly be the scenic route, but it will get us there quicker. And probably safer."

This was fine by her. She still didn't know her way around very well. And she *had* tried to cross a few crosswalks since her arrival. She was amazed that she had managed to survive four months without being mowed down.

At the end of the alley, he turned her down another one. Trash littered the ground, and the smell of garbage was strong. Suddenly, she wasn't so sure about this. "This doesn't look like a very nice place," she said uneasily. "Are you sure we shouldn't just take the main road?"

He smiled and squeezed her arm reassuringly. "Trust me. It won't be but just a bit longer. I'm not going to hurt you, Anna. I promise."

She gave him a small smile and tried to relax. He knew where he was going, and she didn't.

Suddenly, a van came to a screeching halt just in front of them, where a delivery service road intersected with the alley they were currently in. Before Anna's mind could register what was happening, two men jumped out and raced towards them.

She let out a shriek and tried to run, but Graham held fast to her arm. "Let me go!" she shouted "*Let me go! What are you doing?*"

But Graham didn't let her go. Instead, he looped his other arm around her chest, effectively pinning both of her arms in place. "Grab her legs," he said roughly to the two men who had come out of the van. Belatedly, she realized that they were the two men she had seen at the street fair. Abraham's killers.

She let out another scream, this one full of pure terror.

Graham let go of her arm so that he could place a hand over her mouth. "Quiet," he snarled in her ear. "I told you I'm not going to hurt you, and I won't. But only if you behave."

She tried to twist out of his grip, tried to remember the techniques that had been taught in the self-defense classes she had taken in college. But all she could think of was that she had to get away or they were going to kill her.

One of the other men grabbed her legs and, between the two of them, they carried her to the van. The third man had climbed back inside, and she could see that he was holding some kind of cloth in his hand.

Her eyes went wide. She remembered one of them saying that they were going to use chloroform on her when they were planning on kidnapping her from the street fair. She jerked her leg, and managed to

73

get one of them free from the other man's grasp. She lashed out, scoring a hit directly in his nose. He swore and brought both hands up to his nose, which was now spurting blood. Anna took the opportunity to twist in Graham's grasp, trying to yank her arm free. The movement made his hand slip off of her mouth, and she was able to bite him.

"Ouch!" he yelled, jerking his hand back. "You little *bitch.*"

"*Help!*" Anna screamed, still trying to pull her arms free. "Someone, *please!* Help ---"

The man whom she had kicked in the nose let out a snarl, raised a fist, and hit her.

She gasped, feeling the wind knocked out of her as bright lights danced before her eyes, the taste of blood suddenly filling her mouth.

"That's enough!" Graham said sternly, readjusting his grip and pulling her into the van while she was momentarily stunned. "If you strike Miss Miller again, I will put a bullet between your eyes. Do you understand me?"

'Sorry, boss," replied the other man, and Anna immediately recognized him as Growly Voice. "But I think she broke my nose."

"You'll live," was the crisp reply. "Mr. Sanderson, if you would please?" Graham removed his hand, and Anna could feel a cloth cover her nose and mouth. She could also smell a strong, sickly sweet odor.

She had been right. It was chloroform.

She thrashed, kicking out with her legs and struggling to turn her head away. But a hand was holding the cloth firmly over her face, and she could feel a weight press down on her legs. *No! I have to get away! I have to ---*

But she was running out of air. She couldn't hold her breath any longer. She tried to only take in a small amount of air through her mouth, but as soon as she inhaled the chloroform, she no longer had control over her body. Her limbs suddenly felt as though they weighed a ton a piece, and her vision began to swim.

Just pretend to pass out, she told herself. *Maybe they'll leave you alone and you can get away.*

As though he could read her mind, Graham said "Don't let go, Mr. Sanderson. Our Anna is very smart. She could be playing opossum." So the cloth stayed on her face.

She was growing frantic. She was being kidnapped by three man, two of whom had killed Abraham. She hadn't been able to stay safe.

Unexpectedly, she could feel tears form in the corners of her eyes. *Rhys. I am so sorry. I tried.*

Then she was out of air again. Another breath, and she could no longer keep her eyes open. A moment later, the world around her ceased to exist.

Chapter Twelve

Nicola had to carefully balance one of the greasy brown bags in the crook of her elbow so that she could unlock the front door and push it open. Once inside, she took the bag back in her free hand and made her way into the kitchen.

Which is where she was greeted by the sight of her brother at the island, head bowed and a beer in his hand.

"Rhys!" she exclaimed, blinking in surprise. That surprise quickly turned to anger, and she stalked forward to place her bags on the island and glare at him. "Where the *hell* have you been?? No one has seen you for days! All I've gotten are some random text messages and a vague voicemail. Are you *trying* to give me a heart attack? And what are you doing drinking beer this early in the day?"

He looked up, and she was shocked by how bad he looked. "You're not my mother," he grumbled as he took a swig of his beer. "And I am a grown man."

"You could have fooled me. Jesus, Rhys. Are you *drunk?* When was the last time you ate?" She wrinkled her nose. "Or took a shower, for that matter. You look like a homeless person. Smell like one, too."

And that, she thought, was being kind. It was obvious that he had not shaved in days, and an untamed beard covered the lower half of his face. His hair was greasy and hung in lank strands around his face. His clothes were hanging off of him and did nothing to disguise the fact that he was much thinner than he had been when she had last seen him. She could also see the dark circles under his eyes, and wondered if he had been sleeping at all.

"Here." She reached into one of the brown bags she had brought in with her and handed him a cheeseburger, pulling the beer out of his hand and moving it out of his reach. He opened his mouth to protest, but after one look at his sister's face, he wisely closed it and began to unwrap the cheeseburger she had given him.

While Rhys was eating, Nicola walked over to the fridge and busied herself pouring him a glass of water. When she brought it to him, she noticed that one third of the cheeseburger was already gone. "Now," she said. "You want to tell me why you've been gone for several days only to show back up looking like this?"

He let out a sigh and rubbed his face. "It's Anna. She's ... *seeing* someone." He looked like he had swallowed something unpleasant when he said that.

Nicola lifted an eyebrow. "Have you been *stalking* her? Rhys, we talked about this. Remember?"

He glared across the island at her. "I haven't been stalking her, thank you very much. I've only been checking up on her. Just making sure she gets from home to work and back again okay. That's all."

And probably sleeping in his car outside of her apartment at night. No wonder he looked like a street beggar. "Okay. So you've been checking up on her. And you say she's got a boyfriend?"

"Sure looks that way. He's been taking her out for drinks after work for about a week now. Today, he took her out to lunch." He angrily wiped his fingers on a napkin. "I guess she doesn't need *me* anymore. She's got someone else to look after her."

75

The pain in his voice was raw enough to make Nicola wince. She let out a sigh and settled on one of the stools, folding her arms on the island in front of her. "Rhys, what happened? With you and Anna, I mean? You've been moping ever since she left."

"Have not." His voice was sulky.

"No. You're right. *First* you got mad and stormed out when she said she was leaving. Then you vanished for a few days. When you came back is when you started moping." She glared across the table at him. "I know something happened when you two went to that street fair, and I don't think it was just the fact that Abraham's killers showed up. After you two got back, I found her crying in her room. When ---"

"Wait." Rhys's head had snapped up. "She was *crying?*"

Nicola nodded. "When I went in to check on her, she said that she was just upset because she had overheard them planning to kidnap her. I didn't think anything else about it. After all, I would have been upset, too. But that's when you two started acting weird. You were hardly ever in the same room as her, and when you were, the two of you barely spoke. You had been holding hands and being flirty just that morning. *Something* happened. Didn't it?"

He lowered his head so that his forehead was resting on the edge of the island. "I screwed up." His voice was so small she could barely hear him.

"Rhys." She reached across the table to place one of her hands on top of his. "I'm your sister. Talk to me. Tell me what happened."

For a moment, there was a silence. Then he let out a heavy sigh. "I kissed her."

She blinked. "I'm sorry. Did you say you *kissed* her?"

"Yes." He sounded miserable.

She reached up to massage the bridge of her nose with her free hand. "Okay, I'm confused. I was rather under the impression that you *wanted* to kiss her. So why would this be a problem?"

"Because I just *did* it. I forced it on her. I didn't give her a chance to say no or pull away or tell me to stop." He swallowed hard. "She's been hurt before. Several times. I didn't want to hurt her. I swore that I would *never* hurt her. And when I realized what I had done... It was a mistake."

"Oh, Rhys." She started to say something, then frowned. "Wait. You didn't tell *her* it was a mistake, did you?"

He looked up at her. "Of *course* I told her. I apologized and told her that it would never happen again. I didn't want her to think that I was trying to use her, or take advantage of her." He shuddered. "It almost made me sick when I realized what I had done."

"I don't suppose you told her *why* you thought it was a mistake, did you?"

He frowned. "I didn't have to. She was so angry after that, it was obvious that she thought it was a mistake, too."

Nicola removed her hand from his and walked around the island to stand by his side. "Rhys," she said softly, reaching out to touch his shoulder. "Look at me."

He did, his face full of misery and hurt.

She slapped him. Hard

For a moment, there was silence, the sound of her hand striking his cheek echoing throughout the room. Then he raised a hand to his face. "*Ow!* What the hell did you do *that* for?"

"Because, my dear brother, you are the biggest idiot in the history of all mankind. And that is saying something." Her voice was calm, but her eyes were snapping with anger. "Do you have *any* idea of what you've done?"

He just stared at her, anger, shock, hurt, and guilt all playing across his features in quick succession.

"You kissed a girl, a girl that you care for very much, and then told her it was a *mistake.* Worst of all, you did not *explain* to her why it was a mistake. You *assumed* that she knew."

He blinked at her. "But... She was so mad at me. I thought..."

"She was *mad* because you *kissed* her and then told her it was a *mistake* and that you'd never do it again! Can you blame her for being mad? Especially since she had feelings for you, too?"

He nearly choked. "W-what?"

"She *cares* about you, you big lummox. As more than a friend. At least, she *did.* She was talking to me about it one day because she was afraid of her feelings, and she wanted to make sure that what she was feeling was *true* before she acted on them." She reached over to pick up Rhys's beer and took a long swig. "I can't believe you were so thick. It's no wonder she was crying that night."

Rhys placed his head in his hands and started to shake. For a moment, Nicola thought that he was angry. Then she realized he was crying. "This is all my fault," he whispered. "I didn't want to hurt her. I *promised* her I wouldn't hurt her. But I did it anyways. Now she hates me, and it's all my fault."

Nicola walked back around the island, leaving him with his emotions for a moment. She poured herself a glass of water, before returning to the stool and pulling out a second cheeseburger and unwrapping it. "Rhys," she said in her counselor voice. "You need to talk to her, tell her what happened. You might still have a chance to fix things between you two."

"How?" He lifted his head, rubbing at his eyes. Nicola was sharply reminded of the way he had looked when they had lost their parents, and she had to fight not to go hug him and tell him she would take care of everything. "How on earth can I possibly fix this? I doubt she would even want to talk to me. Besides, she's got *him* now."

"Anna's crazy about you, Rhys. Enough to consider opening herself up to you and risk being hurt again. You need to talk to her. I can't guarantee that she'll fall in your arms and you'll live happily ever after or anything like that, but Anna doesn't strike me as the type to hold grudges. You need to explain what happened. Then I would suggest begging. Or, better yet, groveling. Maybe buy her lots of flowers. And chocolate. Chocolate helps a lot."

Rhys looked at her. And there, deep in his eyes, she saw the faintest spark of hope. "Do you really think so?" Even his voice sounded like the thirteen-year-old who wanted to know what was going to happen to him now that their parents were dead.

77

She offered him a smile. "I do. And I'll even drive you over to the library so you can talk to her today. But first thing's first. You need to take a shower. I'm not going to let you in my car when you smell like you've been lying in a ditch for two weeks."

Rhys bowed his head and let the water run over his shoulders and back, closing his eyes and enjoying the feel of the water on his skin. He wasn't exactly sure when he had last taken a shower. He guessed it had been the last time he was home, but he couldn't quite remember when that had been, either.

He wanted to go to the library right that moment. He knew without a doubt that he could have easily ran the distance if it meant he might have another chance with Anna. But Nicola, as usual, was right. He looked like a refugee from a zombie film. Besides, the beard was itchy. It was going to have to go.

He couldn't believe how stupid he had been. He had simply thought that Anna was mad at him for forcing himself on her, especially since she had told him about her previous attempts at relationships. Even if he was trying to protect her that had *not* been the way to do it. He had been so angry with himself. He had vowed that he would be gentle in his pursuit of her. He would do everything in his power to not hurt her, to prove to her that he cared for her, that he wanted nothing more than what she was willing to give. And then, when he thought the time was right, he would ask her to be his. Because he did, in fact, want her.

He *loved* her, damn it. The idea that he had lost her had nearly been more than he could bear. And when he had seen her today with that other man, walking arm-in-arm...

He stayed in the shower until the water ran cold. Then he spent another twenty minutes in front of the mirror, trying not to cut himself as he sheared away all of the facial hair he had managed to accumulate over the past few days. Or had it been weeks?

When he finally emerged from the bathroom, he both looked and felt like a new man. Now that he knew he might --- *might* --- have another chance with Anna, he felt like he was looking up over the fog that had surrounded him since she had left. He only hoped that she would listen, and that she could at least find some way to forgive him. If he had to claw his way back into her good graces, then so be it. She was worth it.

"Rhys."

He turned to find Nicola walking towards him. She held the phone in one hand, her face grim.

He felt something heavy sink into the pit of his stomach. "What is it? What's wrong?"

"Maggie just called." She took a deep breath. "It's Anna. She's gone missing."

Chapter Thirteen

The first thing that she became aware of was her headache. She could it feel it pulsating against her temple with each heartbeat, sending sharp waves of pain over her entire skull.

The second thing that she became aware of was the fact that she couldn't move.

She was lying on her back. She wasn't sure what she was lying on, but it was cool and smooth. She could feel something rough wrapped around her wrists and ankles, holding her in place. When she tried to move a wrist, a dull pain spread across the area that rubbed against her restraint, followed by something wet running down her hand. If she had to guess, it was rope. Thick rope, from the feel of it.

This isn't happening, she whimpered to herself. *This only happens in the movies and books. Real people don't get kidnapped and tied up. Especially not me. I'm a* librarian!

But she knew that she had, in fact, been kidnapped and tied up. The next question was why. And by whom

That thought lead her back to the young man who had come into the library to study Dante. The young man who had shyly asked her out for tea, then lunch. The same young man who had dragged her into the van and held her while his companion had drugged her.

Graham.

She must have made a noise, because she could suddenly hear movement somewhere off to her left. "Ah, Miss Miller." That was Graham's voice, sounding much deeper and rougher than she remembered. He must have been acting the whole time he was trying to get her to gain his trust. She felt sick. Once again, she had been fooled by someone she thought cared for her. "I see you've decided to rejoin us."

She slowly cracked open one eye, then blinked both open when she was not immediately blinded by a searing light. "Where am I?" she croaked. At least they hadn't gagged her. She wasn't sure if she should be relieved by this, or should be frightened even more.

"Somewhere private. I need to have a chat with you, and it wouldn't do to have anyone poking around while I'm doing so. Don't worry. I'm not going to hurt you. Not unless I need to."

His last words sent a shiver down her spine. "You killed Abraham."

He *tsked.* "I did not, in fact, kill Dr. Clark. Nor did I instruct my associates to kill him. I'm afraid Mr. Sanderson can be somewhat… trigger happy. When they confronted Dr. Clark, he moved towards them, and Mr. Sanderson acted on pure reflex. It was nothing more than an unfortunate accident."

She growled at him and twisted in her bonds.

"Now, now. If you behave and tell me what I need to know, I'll return you to your precious Stacks no worse for wear."

She gritted her teeth. "What do you want?" She knew she should be afraid. And she was. But anger had always been her defense mechanism.

"I'm so very glad you asked." There was a scraping sound. Turning her head to the left, Anna could just make out a figure sitting in the darkness. There was a click, and she quickly shut her eyes and turned her head before the lamplight could sear her eyes and blind her completely. "You see, I am looking for the Key. And I think that *you* know where it is."

Her heart pounded faster, which made the pounding in her head even worse. "What key are you talking about? The one that opens the cage in my office?"

"Ah, so you *did* take it. I told them that you had probably removed it from your desk before they went in to your office. You were there, weren't you? When they shot Dr. Clark? My good Inspector Pelley had told me he saw the young knight's car, and when Mr. Sanderson reported back that the key had been missing, I assumed that the knight had found you and hid you away. No matter." He sighed. "No. I am not talking about *a* key. I am talking about *the* key."

"I have no idea what you are talking about. They key to what?"

"Solomon's Key. The *Tractatu de Magicis Doctrinam.*"

Anna froze at the familiar Latin phrase. She knew *that* book. It was the book that Rhys had been looking for the night she met him. The night Abraham was murdered.

It suddenly felt as though an icy fist had gripped her heart. "Is Rhys working for you, too?" She had to know. "Was he just another ploy to try and get me to spill some information to you?" *He couldn't be. Not Rhys.*

"Rhys? I don't... Oh! No." He chuckled. "Imagine, one of the knights working for *me*. No. Your young man and I are very much on opposite sides in this little tug-of-war."

"He's not my anything," she said hotly, but she couldn't deny the overwhelming relief she felt at knowing he hadn't tricked her as well. At least beyond making her think he cared for her. "And why do you keep calling him a knight?"

"They have not told you yet? Well, perhaps I will enlighten you while I have you under my care. It seems that there is much Dr. Clark neglected to tell you before inviting you to London." There was another scraping sound, and out of the corner of her eye she saw him stand and begin to pace. "We have met before, your Rhys and I. It was in Prague, I believe. Or was it Berlin? Prague. Yes, it was Prague. We were both after the same thing then. He is a tenacious young man, I shall give him that. I had almost forgotten that he survived our encounter. The fact that you are someone important to him only sweetens the fact I stole you away from under his nose."

"I hate to break it to you, but I am *not* important to him. So if you were hoping to use me to hurt him, you can forget it. He'll probably thank you." She didn't bother to keep the bitterness out of her voice. Even weeks later, his rejection still stung.

"Is that so? From what my associates told me, I was under a different impression. I suppose we shall see." Suddenly he was at her side, hands on her arm, squeezing. She couldn't bite back a yelp of fear as he leaned over, staring at her intensely. "Let's cut the chitchat, shall we? Where is the *Tractau?*"

She swallowed the sudden sense of panic that arose at his nearness. "I don't know. We don't have it. I've never even seen it. I've only read about it. I swear!"

He was suddenly gone. Anna looked around wildly, but her movements were limited and she couldn't see him. Then he was there again, this time on her right. And he had a knife, a knife that he plunged down into her bicep.

She screamed, her whole back rising up off of whatever she was lying on. The pain that was suddenly shooting up through her arm was like nothing she had ever felt before. She writhed, trying to somehow get the offending knife out of her. But Graham just held it there and looked at her coolly. "I think," he said softly, "that you are lying."

"I'm not lying," she sobbed, feeling hysteria threaten to overwhelm her. Jesus Christ, had she just been *stabbed??* "I swear to you I am not lying. Please." She was going to be sick.

"Begging will not help you, Miss Miller." His voices was stern. "You know where that book is. You were Dr. Clark's prodigy. He would have told you where it was. The Scholars have been trying to hide that book for decades. He would have passed that knowledge to you first thing."

"He didn't. He never had the chance to tell me anything about being a Scholar. I didn't even know he wanted me to take his place until after he died. Another Scholar told me. I don't know *anything* about that book. You have to believe me. I would tell you if I knew." She let out a choking sob. "Please. Don't hurt me."

He removed the knife from her arm, and she could feel the blood pouring from the wound. Before she could do more than whimper, he was running it along the outside of her arm, slicing it open from her shoulder to her elbow. She let out another cry and tried to pull away.

"I told you that I would hurt you if I had to." He sounded apologetic, as though he really didn't want to harm her. Anna knew better. The gushing wound in her arm told her otherwise. "I *need* that book. And you are going to tell me where it is. Even if that means I have to cut it out of you."

She moaned at his threat. "Please. I don't know where it is. I know Rhys was looking for it, too. I told him the same thing that I'm telling you now. If we had it, we would have put it on display. I swear to you. It is not at the Bradley. If it is, I don't know where. Abraham didn't tell me. You have to believe me!"

Graham paused thoughtfully. "So the knights are looking for it, are they? Tell me what he said when he asked for it. Tell me *everything.*"

Anna tried to sort through the pain to remember what exactly Rhys had said that night when he had asked after it. "When I told him we didn't have it, he said that we had uncovered evidence that a copy was sent to the Bradley in 1947. I thought it was odd because he had said 'we' and I wondered who 'we' was. That was it. Right after that is when we heard Abraham arguing with the two men who killed him." She said it in a hurry, the words tumbling out one after another.

"And that was all he said about the book?"

"Yes. That was it. I told him I would look in our database, but I didn't think we had it."

Graham smiled. It reminded her of a shark. "Liar."

This time, he sank the knife into her side and carved a line around her navel. She let out another wail and tried to twist away. But he held her down with his other arm, prohibiting her from moving. He kept moving the knife till it was on her other side, leaving a deep gash across her abdomen and soaking her shirt and jeans with blood.

He stood up and looked down at her with cold eyes as she turned her head to the side so that she could throw up, her sobs turning into panicked, hiccupping cries. "Miss Miller, I do believe that you and I are going to become very well-acquainted with one another. Very well-acquainted indeed."

The ride from the Blackwoods' home to the library was held in grim silence. Nicola had firmly stated she was driving, so Rhys was staring out of his window, clutching his arm rest tightly enough to turn his knuckles white. He wished his sister had let him drive. Without anything to concentrate on, it was too easy for his mind to wander in directions that he would prefer they didn't.

In the few terse minutes the siblings had spent leaving the house, Nicola had explained that Maggie had not given many details. She had simply called and said that Anna was gone, and that they needed to come quick. She had sounded worried.

When they pulled into the Bradley's parking lot, Rhys was jumping out of the car before it had even come to a halt. He didn't bother waiting for Nicola before striding through the doors of the library and into Maggie's office. "What happened?" he asked before she had even acknowledged his presence.

She blinked up at him, a look of deep concern on her face. "Rhys," she said, visibly relaxing when she saw who her guest was. "Thank God you're here. Is your sister with you?"

"I'm here," Nicola replied, coming to stand beside her brother. "Can you tell us what happened?"

The older woman sighed. Rhys noticed she was tapping a pen in a steady beat against her desk, no doubt a nervous tic. "Well, Anna came by to tell me that she was going out to lunch. She was going out with the young man who has been coming to see her for the past few weeks, so I told her just to let me know when she had returned." The tapping increased. "That was three hours ago. She hasn't returned. I haven't received a phone call either. That isn't like Anna. She is a very dependable girl."

Rhys and Nicola exchanged frowns. They both knew that Anna wouldn't vanish for that long without telling anyone. Especially not at work. Something had to have happened.

"Did you call the police?" Rhys asked, feeling his insides begin to twist. He hadn't been able to protect her. He had watched her walk away just a few hours ago and had left because he was feeling sorry for himself. Now she was gone. He shouldn't have let her go. He should have followed her. He could have saved her.

Maggie glared at him. "Of course I did. I called them an hour ago. They said that they were very sorry, but that they couldn't do anything at this point. They told me that she had probably just left for a 'romantic entanglement' with her young man and would show back up some time later today. They said that I should call them back in the morning if she still hadn't shown up."

Rhys let out a growl. Nicola placed a hand on his arm. They both knew that they couldn't wait until morning. "Do you know who the young man is that she left with?" Nicola's voice was soft.

"No. But I have his picture." Maggie beckoned them to come around the desk before turning to her computer to tap a few keys. "After Abraham's murder, the board of directors thought it would be a good idea to install a security system. So I pulled up the footage from the front door and went through it until I found a good shot of him." She tapped a few more keys before sitting back. "Here. This is him."

Rhys leaned over Maggie's shoulder to peer closely at the image on the screen. It was a side profile, but it gave him a good look at the man's face. Once he saw it, however, he felt his heart drop to his feet.

"God *damn* it!"

Maggie gasped and looked up at him with wide eyes. "Rhys! Watch your language!"

But he ignored her, staring over her head to meet his sister's eyes. "It's Graham Thurston," he said, his tone furious.

Nicola sucked in her breath. "Are you sure?"

"It's been a few years, but yeah. It's him."

"God damn it." Nicola's curse was much quieter but no less fierce.

Maggie was looking at them warily. "I take it you know this man?"

"Unfortunately." Rhys's lips curled up into a snarl. "He's a monster. That's the best word for him. He...*acquires* Lost Knowledge and sells it to the highest bidder. He's murdered several people that we know of, and probably more that we *don't* know of. He bombed the home of a Scholar in Prague a few years ago. That's how I met him." Rhys didn't bother to explain that he had barely come out of that exchange alive. "If he's here, then I have no doubt that he is the one behind Abraham's murder. And now he's got Anna." He felt sick. *I shouldn't have let you leave. I should have made you stay. Anna...*

"We don't know that yet. She may have gotten away from him and doesn't have any way to contact us." Nicola let out a breath. "Maggie, can you print this off? We have a friend in the police who might be able to move this along. I can give him this photo and see if we can't at least go ask around and see if anyone saw anything. Do you know where they were going for lunch?"

"No. She didn't say, and I didn't ask."

"Rhys? You said you saw them leave. What direction where they going?"

"Back towards the alleyway," he replied, ignoring Maggie's frown. He knew she was wanting to ask him why he'd been there watching, but he didn't feel like explaining anything to her at the moment. *I should have followed you.* "I left before I saw anything else."

"Okay. Why don't you go into her office and see if she maybe wrote down where they were going. That would at least give us an idea as to where to start looking. Then you can call David and tell him what happened. I'll call Finn and see what he thinks we should do."

He nodded and walked out of Maggie's office, turning right and walking briskly down the hallway towards Anna's office. Part of him was hoping that he would walk in there and find her hard at work. She would be embarrassed that they had all fussed over her, and that she had forgot to tell Maggie that she was back. Rhys would kiss her, his sense of honor be damned. He would kiss her *right* and tell her how he felt. How he was the biggest idiot on the planet and that he would never be able to apologize enough for hurting her. And would she please give him a second chance.

But her office was empty. He had to stand there for a moment and let the sense of crushing disappointment wash over him before moving to her desk.

She had a large calendar spread across her desk with each day denoted with a square. Anna had marked through each day with a red pen as it had passed. Peering at today's square, Rhys saw that she had written in her flowing script the words 'Lunch with Graham'. That was it. There was no record of where they were planning on going.

He sat down heavily on her chair and leaned forward until his forehead was resting on her desk. One hand reached into his pocket for his cell phone while the other hand reached out to gently touch the now-familiar bindings of the monk's journal that lay on her desk. *Anna...* If something had happened to her, if Graham had hurt her, he would never forgive himself. Never.

"Rhys?" David's voice buzzed through his cell phone. "What's going on?"

"It's Anna," he replied thickly. "She's missing. David, Graham Thurston is here. He has her."

There was silence on the other end of the phone. "David?"

"Where are you?" There was a note of anger in the older man's voice that Rhys had never heard before. When he answered that he was at the library, David told him tersely to "Stay there. I'm on my way" before hanging up.

Rhys stayed where he was, surrounding himself with all things Anna. The seat had still been warm form her body heat, and he could detect faint traces of the floral perfume that she wore. Her notebook containing her translations lay open to one side, with the current text she was working on resting on a small wooden podium in the middle of the desk. Everything was so unequivocally Anna: tidy and in its place. He could still remember seeing her standing here on that night they first met and being shocked that she was his age instead of Abraham's. And being shocked at her fragile beauty that had turned out to not be so fragile after all.

He closed his eyes and took a deep breath, inhaling the smell of old books, ink, and perfume. Anna's scent. *I will find you,* he thought fiercely. *I promise.*

"Rhys?"

He lifted his head to find his sister standing in the door to the office. When his eyes met hers, she gave him an encouraging smile. "Finn said he'll come by as soon as he can. He's working on a case in King's Park right now. Did you get in touch with David?"

"Yes. He told us to stay put. He's coming over."

She nodded, then let out a sigh. "I guess we're going to need a place where we can strategize. I doubt Anna's office is the best place to do that. Let me talk to Maggie and see if there is a conference room we can use."

Rhys knew that he should be paying attention to what was going on around him, and that he should at least try to participate. But all he could do was stare at his cell phone and will it to light up. Maybe Nicola was right and Anna had gotten away. Maybe she would call him to come to her rescue, just like the white knight she had once professed him to be. He had never been good at sitting and planning. His mind kept thinking about all of the things that could have happened to her, that *were* happening to her. He had seen Graham's work before. None of the images were pleasant.

"Rhys? Hello?"

"Hmmm?" He blinked, pulling his mind back to the present. "I'm sorry. What did you say?"

They were all looking at him expectantly. "I said," Nicola repeated softly, "could you tell us about Graham Thurston? It might be a good idea to see if there are any habits of his that we can use to find him."

He sighed and rubbed his face wearily. Now that his adrenaline had died down, he could feel the lack of sleep pressing in on him. Finn had brought him a large cup of coffee --- no doubt Nicola's idea --- but it sat mostly untouched. His stomach was already in knots.

"Graham is a mercenary of sorts. He goes after Lost Knowledge and sells it to the highest bidder. Or sometimes he is hired to retrieve certain artifacts by whatever means necessary. Now that we know he is here, it's almost certain he is the one behind Abraham's murder." He paused. "Abraham wouldn't be the first Scholar he's murdered."

Across from him, David's jaw clenched.

"What is he after?" That was Maggie, sitting at the head of the conference table like a reigning monarch. She had called in one of the other librarians to take charge and locked up her office so that she could join them in one of the basement conference rooms. "And why would he take Anna? She only just became a Scholar."

Rhys glanced at David. When the older man gave a sharp nod, he let out another sigh. "We're not certain, because this is the first we've heard of him being back in London. But we have a pretty good guess." He took a deep breath. "There is a book that the Scholars have talked about for years, a book that was supposedly lost during World War II. A Scholar in Turkey recently found a letter stating that the book was sent to Mr. Bradley's son for protection in 1947. The letter writer had apparently spirited it out of London and hid it in Istanbul because Hitler had expressed interest in it. Now that the war was over, he thought it was a good idea to send it to a new hiding place. And he thought that a library that was going to be run by a Scholar would be as good a hiding place as any."

Maggie sucked in her breath. "Abraham."

"Right. Mr. Bradley's son was getting ready to retire soon and had already appointed Abraham as his successor." He spread his hands. "The problem is, this letter is the only indication we have that the book was actually sent here. The night of Abraham's murder I had come here at Abraham's request to meet Anna. He had heard about this new information and was worried someone might come looking for it, and he wanted me to look after her. I asked her about the book, just out of curiosity, because Abraham never said if it was actually here or not."

"Is it here?" Finn's voice was sharp. "If I've got some bastard murdering people over a bloody book I need to know about it."

"We don't know. Anna said she wasn't aware of a copy being in the library. She never got a chance to actually look it up before Abraham was shot and we were hiding. But we could hear the two men trying to look something up on her computer. If they were looking for the same book, they couldn't find it."

Maggie was writing furiously on a yellow legal pad. "What is the name of this book?"

"The *Tractatu de Magicis Doctrinam*." David's Latin was much better than Rhys's.

Maggie's pen hit the pad with a thump. Looking up, Rhys saw that her eyes had gone wide. "Oh," she said in a small voice. "*That* book."

"If I had to guess, he took Anna because he thinks she knows where it is. We heard Abraham tell the two who killed him that whatever they were looking for wasn't here and never had been. Since they killed him, Graham himself can't ask about it. He knew that Anna was in charge of the older books, which is where it would be if it were here. He may also know that she was Abraham's replacement in the Scholars." He felt his hands clench into fists. "The one positive thing about this is if he does think she knows something he's going to need to keep her alive." *Hopefully.*

"How would he know that she was a Scholar?" Finn again. He was also keeping notes. "How would he know about *any* of this, for that matter? You guys are fairly hush-hush."

Rhys and Nicola both turned to David. His looked as though he had aged thirty years since Rhys had last seen him. He knew this was a difficult topic for the older man, but Anna was in trouble. They needed all of the information they could get.

David was silent for a moment. When he finally spoke, his voice was quiet, and he had a faraway look in his eyes. ""Graham Thurston was once a Scholar himself. Twenty years ago, I began training him. He had been one of my students at university. He was bright and inquisitive. And, much like Anna, he was full of curiosity. However, unlike Anna, he did not see the position of Scholar as a chance to learn and make discoveries that could change the world. He saw it as a way to make money."

He let out a heavy sigh, his shoulders sagging as he dropped his face into his hands. "I didn't realize it until it was too late," he said, his voice muffled. "Or maybe I was just in denial. When he would make a discovery, he wouldn't report it. He would find a black market art dealer or look around for someone who might be interested in whatever he had found and sell it to them for an astronomical amount of money." He shrank in even more. "It wasn't until he killed Bella and almost killed Rhys that I finally realized just what a monster he was."

Silence fell over the room at that. Rhys had met Bella a few times before he had nearly died trying to pull her out of her burning home. She had had bright eyes and an infectious laugh. She and David had been sweethearts for many years. David still hadn't forgiven himself for her death.

"So is he from London?" Finn's eyes were focused on David now. "And is that his real name?"

David shrugged. "As far as I know. He had that name when he was my student. And his accent would mark him as a Londoner."

"All right. I'll look him up in the system, see if I can find anything." He scribbled something down. "I'll also see if I can track down any personal information on him. Friends, family, known addresses. Hopefully I can find some people who will be willing to talk to me about him."

"What about Pelley's files? Do you still have those?" That was Nicola. "We already decided that he was working with the men who killed Abraham. If they were working for Graham, it's a sure bet he is, too. We could go back through his files and cross-reference any case notes he has with crimes that would fit Graham."

"Might not be a bad idea. And I can look through all of our files for cases that fit him. Which would be what, exactly?"

"Art theft, rare book theft, museum robberies, artifacts being stolen... Sometimes people simply pay him to steal a piece that they want. And, as you've seen, he usually gets someone else to do the actual stealing for him." Rhys let out a growl. "He doesn't get his hands dirty unless he had no other choice."

"Good. If I can find a few folks who have been in lockup for that kind of stuff, it may turn out they are associates of his." He pushed his chair back and stood up, gathering his notebook and pen. "I'll go back to the station and get started on this. I'll bring those files back by your place this afternoon." He leveled a stern finger at Rhys. "Don't do anything stupid, Blackwood. I know you're worried about Anna. We all are. But if you run off half-cocked, you're not going to be helping her at all. And you'll cause more trouble for me. I swear to you that we will do everything we possibly can to find her. But we've got to be smart about this. Hear me?"

Rhys nodded. "I promise." He wouldn't even know where to start at this point. And even he knew better than to go running off into what could very well be a dangerous situation when he was this tired. Especially if Anna was involved. He didn't want to cause her any more harm than he already had.

"Good." Finn paused. "This book that you were talking about. I don't suppose you could tell me what it is?"

Rhys shook his head. "No. Graham isn't the only one who has killed to find it. The less you know about it, the less likely you are to be a target."

"Understood. Now, go home and get some rest. You look absolutely knackered. I'll call you if I find anything before stopping by this afternoon. Nicola, if he tries anything, sit on him and call me. I've got a pair of handcuffs we can use if we have to."

Chapter Fourteen

When they returned home, Rhys didn't even need Nicola's urging to go to bed. She tried to help him up the stairs to his own bedroom, but he refused. Instead, he went into the guest room that had been Anna's and fell onto the bed, asleep before his head even hit the pillow. Nicola pulled off of his shoes and covered him with a blanket before turning off the light and shutting the door.

He had no idea how long he had slept, but there was no sun coming in through the window when he awoke, and his stomach was growling. He threw off the blanket and padded into the kitchen. Hopefully the others would have discovered something while he had been sleeping.

He found Finn, Maggie, and Nicola all seated around the kitchen island, paper covering every available surface. David, they explained, had left to do his own research. Talking about Graham had left him agitated, and they had had to send him away before he drove all of them insane.

Rhys pulled a soda out of the fridge and cleared a small space on the counter for him to perch on. "Have you found anything yet?"

"Nothing we could bank on," Finn answered, looking pointedly at the glass in Rhys's hand. Rhys gave him a half-hearted grin and went back to the fridge to pull out another one. "But we have found a few different robberies and such like you were talking about. I'm going to write down all of the case numbers so that I can look them up in the morning when I go into work."

Rhys frowned. "In the morning? We can't wait that long, not if he has her! What if she's hurt? What if she's…" He wouldn't let himself think the word, much less speak it.

"Rhys." Nicola's voice was sharp. "Finn is doing everything he can to help Anna. Okay? Besides, if he went in on his off time to look this up Pelley may notice it. We don't know if he knows about Finn yet, but we have to hope he doesn't. If he finds out Finn is looking this information up for us, he may tip Graham off. Anna's tough, remember? She's made sure to tell you that on numerous occasions. Let's give her some credit and trust that she can hold out until we find her."

Nicola was right. He *knew* Nicola was right. But his heart was screaming at him to do something. Anna, *his* Anna, was in danger. And he was just sitting here. So he took a deep breath and held it for three seconds before letting it out. "Okay. What can I do to help?"

It was after midnight when Nicola finally went to bed and Finn, David and Maggie left to return to their own homes. If Anna had not shown up by the time the library opened in a few hours, Maggie could officially file a missing persons report with the police. Finn would see if he couldn't make sure he got the case. If not, he would be sure to get all of the notes from those who did. He would look up the case numbers he had written down and call Rhys if it looked like anything panned out. In the meantime, Rhys could work on cross-referencing Pelley's files. If he was indeed covering up crimes like his namesake had, the official record might not tell them anything. But his notes might provide a clue. If Rhys found anything, he was to call Finn immediately and wait for the policeman. If he didn't, Finn promised that he would have the other man arrested for interfering with a police investigation and leave him in a cell while they looked for Anna.

88

Not for the first time in his life, Rhys was thankful that he hadn't decided to go into law enforcement. The filing system took a degree in engineering to figure out, and he had yet to meet a police officer who had legible handwriting. At least Finn had given him an idea of what to look for and a starting point.

Inspector Pelley was a meticulous note-taker. Each official report had several pages of notes stapled to it, along with diagrams and witness statements. If Rhys wasn't looking for information about his missing friend, he would have found some of them amusing. *Accusing your neighbor of stealing your fence indeed. Do the police really have to respond to these crack calls?* Pelley had attached five whole pages of notes to that one.

It wasn't until he was on the third case file that he found his first clue. The case had all of the hallmarks of a robbery that Graham would have executed. A wealthy art collector had returned from vacation to find three of his paintings missing. He suspected his lawn keeper, one Ollie Wyman. But Wyman had been cleared of all charges, and another man had been charged with the theft. However, the paintings had never been recovered.

He read through four more case files before he found another clue. This had taken place nearly a year after the first one. It wasn't a case that Rhys would have associated with Graham and would have just skimmed over it if a certain name hadn't caught his attention.

Ollie Wyman, it seemed, had been arrested for stealing pills from one of his employers. It could have been a different Ollie Wyman, but somehow Rhys doubted it. Especially when he saw that the employer ran a rare book shop.

By the time they sky outside had begun to lighten, Rhys had found two more cases that involved a man named Ollie Wyman. He had been arrested again, this time for cashing forged checks. The man whose name was on the checks owned an art gallery. In another, he had been interviewed as a potential suspect when a museum had had several artifacts stolen, but had been let go when no evidence could be found tying him to the scene.

He closed the last of Pelley's case files with a sigh before standing up to stretch. He had written down several names in connection with Wyman's. He decided that he would make a cup of tea before taking his list into the living room and using his laptop to find out what he could about all of them. Now that he had names, he wanted to hop on his bike and go chase them down and make them talk, using whatever means necessary. But he knew that could potentially tip Thurston off. So he would make sure he had as much information as he could before talking to Finn later that morning.

This was where Nicola found him when she emerged from her bedroom a few hours later. His laptop was at one end of the couch while he sat the other end, writing furiously. "What are you doing?" she asked, noting the large amount of paper he had used to take notes with. "Did you find something?"

He looked up at her, eyes bright and cheeks flushed. "I think so," he said excitedly. "Sit down and take a look at this."

"Give me a minute. Let me go grab a cup of tea and I'll be right back."

By the time Rhys had gone over everything he had discovered during the night, Nicola had to admit she was feeling pretty hopeful, too. "So you think this Ollie Wyman guy is connected to Graham?"

"I think that there is a very good chance that he is. Think about what we know about Graham. He's a manipulator. He gets others to do his dirty work for him. I'm willing to bet that the only reason he came after Anna himself is because she was familiar enough with all of the other players that he was the only one left. She had met Pelley and had both seen and heard Abraham's killers. She had no idea who he was. Maggie said that he was pretending to be a Ph.D. student studying Dante. I mean, that's pure Anna bait. She wouldn't have been able to resist that. And after what happened with me... I'm sure she was excited to find a guy who wasn't a total ass."

"You're probably right." Nicola took a sip of her tea and scanned over her brother's notes. "Have you called Finn with this yet?"

He shook his head. "Not yet. He didn't leave until late last night, and he has to go into work this morning. I'm going to wait until after I know he's at work before I ring him." He gave her a small smile. "No need to sit on me and get the handcuffs. I'm not going to do anything."

She leaned over to kiss his cheek. "You know this isn't your fault," she said softly. "I told you when we first met Anna that you couldn't just lock her up or she'd hate you. You had to let her go, no matter how much you wanted her to stay."

He sighed and ran a hand through his hair. "Yeah, but she would have been *safe*. I would rather her hate me and be safe than hurt any day."

"Liar. You would rather chop off your own arm than have her hate you. I'm your sister. I know these things." She smiled. "We're going to get her back. You'll see. Then you can grovel and tell her how much of an ass you are and that she really shouldn't forgive you but you hope she will. Then I'll have to cover my eyes all the time so I don't have to see the two of you making hanky panky."

He chuckled. "You're being a bit optimistic, aren't you? I mean, I haven't even apologized yet. She may slap me and tell me she never wants to see me again."

"I doubt that's going to happen. Call it women's intuition." She finished her tea in a last gulp. "Let me go take a shower. Then we can call Finn together and tell him about your amazing detective work."

Sometime during the day Rhys fell asleep again. He remembered sitting on the couch and clutching his cell phone, hoping either Anna or Finn would call. She had now been missing for twenty-four hours, and anxiety had his stomach twisted into knots. He knew that he was doing the right thing by giving his information to Finn, who would be able to do something with it. But if something didn't happen soon, he was going to go crazy. The longer he waited, the worse the images his imagination came up with were.

He awoke to the sound of low voices talking urgently. Blinking open his eyes, he saw Finn and Nicola having what appeared to be an animated conversation across the room.

He was instantly on his feet, wide awake. "What is it? Did you find her?"

They turned to face him, both of their faces grim. Rhys's heart gave a lurch, and he had to place a hand on the end of the couch to keep from falling over. "No...." *She's not dead. She's not dead!*

"We haven't found her yet." Finn's voice was soft. Rhys sagged in relief and fell back onto the couch, putting his face in his hands, which were shaking. "But I did some digging on Mr. Ollie Wyman. I think you've got something, Rhys. Both times he was arrested, the people he stole from reported having items stolen from them several months later... while he was in prison."

This brought Rhys's head back up. "So you think he was... what?"

"I think it's damned convenient that he was already in prison both times they were robbed the second time. Both of the second robberies were of things that this Graham fellow seems like he would want. And it *must* be coincidence that Mr. Wyman was released from prison shortly after both of the second robberies."

"So Wyman steals information, which he passes off to someone else, who then goes *back* in and uses that information to steal what they are really after. Wyman is in jail, so it can't be him." Nicola rubbed the bridge of her nose. "And is our Mr. Wyman currently incarcerated?"

"No. And we don't know where he is exactly." Finn gave Rhys a sharp look. "We've got people out looking for him. As soon as someone on patrol picks him up, he and I are going to have a nice long chat."

Rhys glared back. This was just too much. He couldn't sit still any longer. "Finn, she has been missing for a day. A *day!* He is our only lead to her. And you have a dirty copper! Do you really expect me to sit here and patiently *wait* and *hope* you find him and *hope* he tells you something that *might* lead to her?" His voice was growing louder with every word. "She is out there somewhere. Possibly hurt. Because of *me*. I will *not* sit by and do nothing! Not anymore."

"You will do as I say." Finn's voice had dropped into a growl. "You forget, I am an *officer.* I am sticking my neck out for you as it is. My job, my *only* job, is to find Anna. If you get in my way, I can't help you. What will you do if you get arrested, hmm? Better yet, what if you get your dumb ass *killed?* What's that accomplish? How does that help Anna?"

"I don't care!" Rhys had gotten to his feet and the two men were now only inches apart. Both of them had curled fists and clenched jaws. "But I am *done* sitting. I don't care if you want to arrest me or whatever. I am going to go find this man, and I am going to make him tell me where she is. If you don't want me to do that, then you might as well kill me right now and get it over with. Because that is ---"

"Enough!"

Nicola would never be accused of being tall or intimidating. But when she stepped between the two men and roared that one word, both of them fell silent and took an instinctive step back. "You can both just go ahead and put your willys away. This isn't a pissing contest." She turned to her brother and put a finger under his nose. "*You* are awfully close to being a total ass again. Finn is on your side. On *Anna's* side. You need to remember that before you push *him* away, too. He doesn't have to tell us anything, you know. He could get in trouble for even telling us that they are looking for Wyman. He could leave you here to stew while they work. So quite acting like a child and *listen* to him."

Rhys crossed his arms and glared down at his sister. But he bit down on his tongue and didn't say anything else.

"Now then." She turned back to Finn. "I believe that you were going to tell me something before my great lump of a brother decided his brain no longer worked?"

The young inspector shot Rhys a smug look. Nicola punched him in the shoulder, causing him to wince. "Right. What I was saying is that we have people out looking for Wyman, but that Inspector Pelley is one of those people. And Rhys is right. He's a dirty copper. So what I was *not* going to tell you is that Pelley and Howard are supposed to be looking down by the docks. I'm also *not* telling you that Wyman's last job that we know of was dockworker. And I will most certainly *not* tell you that a man matching his description was seen down there sometime in the last few weeks."

Rhys blinked at him, uncrossing his arms. "Wait. Are you..."

Finn shook his head before the other man could finish. "No. I'm not. The only thing I am saying is that we are looking for him, and you better stay out of my way. I mean it, Rhys. Stay out of my way."

Understanding dawned in Rhys's eyes, and he felt ashamed for yelling at the other man. Finn knew that it was likely Ollie Wyman would be at the docks on the Thames, the same area that Pelley had been sent to look for him. And Finn knew that Pelley couldn't be trusted. Finn was telling Rhys that he should go look himself because Finn couldn't. As long as Rhys didn't involve Finn in whatever he did to find Wyman, Finn wouldn't stop him.

He let out a grunt and reached a hand out around his sister. "Sorry for being an ass. I'm apparently very good at it."

Finn grinned and shook his hand. "I'll forgive you this time. You've been under a lot of stress. You might not be so lucky next time." He nodded at Nicola. "I've got to go. I'm due to start my patrol in twenty minutes. I'll call you if I find him." He didn't say the rest, but Rhys understood him perfectly. *Don't call me if you find him.*

"Thanks," Rhys said, his voice soft. "For everything. You've been a huge help. We --- *I* --- couldn't have managed without you."

Finn rubbed the back of his neck, spots of color appearing on his cheeks. "Hey, what are friends for? Besides, there's a pretty girl in trouble. I wouldn't be much of a man if I didn't do something to help her."

Chapter Fifteen

Nicola wanted to wait until after nightfall before heading out to the docks. But Rhys reminded her that they weren't very familiar with the area, and they had nothing but a grainy black and white mug shot of Ollie Wyman to go by. Besides, they wanted to try and find him before Pelley was able to tip him off that the police were looking for him. If he disappeared, so did their only chance of finding Anna. While Nicola didn't like it, she couldn't help but agree.

By the time they made their way to the docks and had found what they hoped to be an inconspicuous place to park, the sun had begun to sink over the horizon. Rhys held a pair of field glasses to his eyes, squinting through them at the large group of men who were unloading large crates from a ship. "What if he's already left for the day? I mean, surely they don't work all night."

Nicola had laid her seat all the way back and was reclining, her eyes closed. "I've seen the lights on here all night before. I'm sure they have people who work at night, too. We could ask the security guard on duty, you know. I'm sure he's liable to have a roster of who works when."

But her brother shook his head. "Not yet. If he's not here now, the guard may tell him someone was looking for him when he starts his shift. . We can't afford for him to bolt or hide. We *need* him. If we don't see him soon, then we'll ask."

Nicola sighed but didn't say anything else. She could think of better ways to help Anna than sit in her car in a seedy part of town, but she hadn't dared to let Rhys go by himself. She had watched him tuck his gun into the back of his jeans before leaving the house.

The next hour passed in silence, with the two of them passing the glasses back and forth when their eyes began to get tired. The sun sank behind the horizon, leaving only streaks of golden light across the sky. The lights above the docks came on, washing everything in a harsh blue glow.

Finally, Rhys let out a sigh and rubbed his eyes. "All right. Let's go ask around and see if we can find him." He turned a frown on his sister. "Actually, you might want to stay here."

Nicola glared at him. "I'm not letting you go by yourself. Just because you have a gun doesn't mean you're invincible. He may have mates. You need backup."

"Yeah, but you're a woman. I doubt that they have very many of *those* on the docks. You're going to stick out worse than a flashing neon sign. And I can't call Finn."

Nicola didn't answer. Instead, she reached across her brother to open her glove compartment and pull out a dark baseball cap. She twisted her ponytail into a knot before placing the cap on her head and turning to Rhys with a raised eyebrow.

He sighed but offered her a half-hearted grin. "Aye. In the dark, it'll do. Just try not to talk. And walk hunched over."

The two got out of the car and began walking towards the entrance to the docks. Nicola shoved her hands in her pockets and kept her head low as they approached a small guard station. "Excuse me!" Rhys called, tapping on the glass.

The guard, a heavyset black man, looked up from his magazine. "Yeah?" he said in a bored tone of voice.

"What do you want? If you're looking for work, you'll have to---"

"We're not here for work," Rhys interrupted. "We're here looking for someone. Ollie Wyman. Know him?"

The other man frowned, his eyes suddenly turning sharp. "Wyman? You with the police, too? I told that other bobbie that he is still on shift for another few hours. He's already gone in there looking for Wyman."

Rhys and Nicola exchanged glances. 'The other bobbie' had to be Pelley. They could already be too late. "There shouldn't have been another cop," Rhys said, playing off of the guard's assumption that they were police officers. "My partner and I just got the call to come in and talk to Mr. Wyman. That other cop must be an imposter." That part, at least, was true.

The guard looked alarmed at this. "Are you sure? Maybe one of your Met buddies decided to save you the trip. I mean, he sure *looked* like a cop. Had a badge and everything. What did Wyman do, anyways?"

"We simply want to ask him some questions." Rhys fixed him with the best imitation of the 'cop stare'. He had seen Finn use it dozens of times, often on him. "Are you going to let us in? We could have you arrested for interfering with a police investigation. And if this other cop isn't really a cop at all..."

"No need for all of that," the guard replied hastily. He pushed a button and a deep buzz sounded, followed by a click. "Gate's open. Let me know if there is anything else I can do."

"Can you tell us where we might find Wyman?"

"He should be helping with the unload." He waved a hand in the direction of the group of dockworkers the Blackwoods had seen from their car. "Gonna take most of the night. If he's not sneaking a smoke, that's where he'll be. That's what I told that other bloke, too."

"Thanks. We appreciate your assistance." Rhys offered a nod as he followed his sister through the gate and into the dockyard.

The two of them tried to stick to the shadows as much as possible. While the guard may have simply wanted to avoid a problem, these men would be different. Many of the dockworkers had been in trouble with the police before. They wouldn't take very kindly to strangers poking around as it was. If they thought Rhys and Nicola were with the Met, they would have more trouble than they could deal with. Rhys may have brought his gun, but he didn't want to have to use it if he didn't have to.

They could hear shouts and rough voices calling out insults to one another as they approached the area where the ship was being unloaded. They tried to look at every face that they passed, hoping one of them would be familiar. But they saw neither Inspector Pelley nor anyone who resembled the photo they had of Ollie Wyman. Rhys was beginning to think they would have to actually try and talk to some of the men when a faint noise from his right caught his attention. He grasped Nicola's elbow and tugged her in that direction.

They edged slowly down a narrow aisle that had been formed by several large shipping containers. At first Rhys thought he had been mistaken and that there hadn't been anything. But then they both heard loud shouts coming from close by. And these weren't the jovial shouts of the workers they had heard earlier. These were angry shouts. As they got closer, they could begin to make out words.

"You will do as you are told." Rhys felt a shiver go down his spine as he recognized the voice of Inspector Pelley. "He has requested it of you."

"No." The second voice was unfamiliar and clearly agitated. "This wasn't part of the deal. I'm *not* taking the blame for this, no matter how much he's willing to pay me. Find some other sod to set up. That's your job, isn't it?"

"My job," came the cool reply, "is to make sure that his plans get carried out. This was an unexpected hitch. I did not realize that they would connect you to Mr. Thurston so soon. Our usual agreement stands. Except that your usual compensation will be greater for your added troubles."

"No! I will *not* be arrested for a kidnapping. I don't mind doing time for petty shit. But I'm not going to have a kidnapping on my record. Especially not the kidnapping of a *woman*. And an American to boot! You can tell Thurston just where he can stick it."

Rhys pressed himself against the last of the shipping containers, pushing Nicola behind him, and peered around the corner. He found himself looking at a small area formed by the containers. This was clearly where the workers came for their breaks. There were several ashtrays, a few chairs, and a large amount of cigarette butts. The man whose back was to Rhys was standing in a relaxed position, but Rhys could make out the tell-tell bulge of a hip holster, clearly marking him as the false inspector.

The man who was facing Rhys matched the photo they had been given of Ollie Wyman. He was pacing back and forth, smoke curling above his head from a cigarette. He would stop every few steps, glare at the other man, take a deep drag, and return to pacing.

Pelley let out a sigh. "I am sorry to hear that, Mr. Wyman. I know that Mr. Thurston will be as well. I also regret to inform you that we will no longer be in need of your services." While he had been speaking, his hand had slowly been moving towards his holster.

Rhys made sure he never reached it. Pressing Nicola back against the container, Rhys drew his own gun and moved. But he didn't point it and pull the trigger. Instead he raised it high and, moving as swiftly as possible, brought the butt of the gun down hard on the back of the man's head.

Pelley crumpled to the ground without a sound.

For a moment, there was silence. Wyman was staring down at the unconscious inspector, mouth agape. His cigarette dropped from his fingers, forgotten. Rhys stood where he was, chest heaving, staring down at the man he had just struck. Nicola came out from around the corner and walked up behind her brother, reaching out to place a hand on his shoulder.

"Holy fuck." Wyman's voice was quiet. "What the fuck was *that*?" He lifted his head and seemed to notice the Blackwoods for the first time. "And who the fuck are *you*?"

Rhys raised his gun and pointed it at the other man. "We," he growled, "are here about the girl."

Ollie had lit up another cigarette and resumed his pacing. Once he had realized that Rhys wasn't going to shoot him --- at least, not yet --- he had picked right up where he left off when Rhys had stuck Pelley.

"Look," he said in between puffs, "I didn't sign up for this shit. It was just supposed to be another job, right? All Thurston told me was to pick up two other blokes and have them and the van at a certain place at a certain time. That was it. He didn't tell me that he was going to be *kidnapping* anyone! If I had known that, I wouldn't have done it. I mean, the petty shit wasn't a big problem. I did some time, nothing major --- a few months at a time --- and Thurston paid me very well."

"So the plan wasn't for you to take the fall for the kidnapping?" Rhys was still keeping the gun pointed at the other man.

"I don't know what the plan was for *any* of this. Like I said, I didn't know anything about this until they were dragging that girl into the van. I swear!"

"Did he hurt her?" Though his aim was rock steady, his voice was rough. Ollie had admitted to kidnapping Anna, and Rhys wanted to punish him for it. He was having a hard time keeping his anger in check.

"No. One of his cronies slapped her. You know, 'cause she was putting up a fight? And Thurston told him that if he touched her again he would be a dead man. They knocked her out with something, smelled sweet. But that was all they did while I was with them."

"Where did you take them?"

"Some new development down in Westminster. You know, one of those super ritzy areas? Lots of empty houses. Thurston made me drop them off at the entrance, so I don't know where he took her. I can tell you where the subdivision is, though."

Even Nicola didn't see Rhys move. But suddenly he had Ollie pinned up against the side of one of the containers, gun pressed against his forehead. "Why," Rhys growled, "should I believe you?"

"Hey, man! I'm telling you the truth! Thurston's a bastard. You heard that other guy. He was just going to throw me to the wolves like that. Do you know how much time I'd have to do for a kidnapping? And if he finds out I disobeyed him, he'll kill me. As long as he's alive, I'm fucked. I want someone to take him *down.*"

Rhys pulled the hammer back on his gun. "If you're lying to me, so help me God..."

"I'm not! Geez, man. I have no *reason* to lie to you!"

"Rhys." Nicola's voice was calm, soothing as she put placed a hand on his gun arm. "Put the gun down. I don't think he's lying. He's helping us. Besides." She bared her teeth at the other man. "If it turns out he's lying, we can find him again. Then you can kill him. I'll even help."

Ollie's eyes went wide. "You're both fucking *bonkers!*"

They stood that way for a long moment in a frozen tableau. Then Rhys put the safety back on his gun and stepped back, letting Wyman sink to the ground. "You better hope I find her alive," he said in a low, dangerous voice. Then he spun on his heel and walked away.

"Wait!" Wyman pulled himself back to his feet. "What do I do about him?" He nodded at Pelley, who was still unconscious.

"We'll call the police," Nicola said. "Annonomous tip and all. I'm sure they'll come and get him. Until then, he's yours."

Wyman grinned as he lit another cigarette. "Good."

Chapter Sixteen

The two siblings returned to their car in silence. The guard waved at them cheerfully from his small office. Rhys didn't even bother to nod.

Once they were both in the car, Nicola let out a deep sigh and finally spoke the words that neither of them wanted to hear. "Rhys, we have to call in Finn." Her voice was soft. "We can't go after her by ourselves."

He growled in response.

She let out a frustrated sigh and yanked the cap off of her head. "I know. I don't like it either. But it's our best chance of finding her. If we ---"

"I can't sit here and do nothing! We *know* where she is! We just have to go and get her."

"*Think* about this, Rhys! It's a subdivision, which means it's most likely gated and patroled. Somehow Graham was able to get in. If we try to go in there, we're more than likely going to end up arrested ourselves. If that happens, Graham will be tipped off and we'll be in jail. By the time we get everything sorted out, he'll be gone, and we'll be back at square one. Or he'll kill her. We *have* to play this smart."

Rhys didn't say anything for a long moment. He simply sat and stared out of the window.

Nicola nearly jumped out of her skin when he let out a howl and smashed his fist into the dashboard as hard as he could. She couldn't be sure in the dark, but she was fairly certain he had dented it. But she could make out the blood on his hand, glinting in the moonlight that was streaming in through the car windows.

Rhys slumped in his seat, eyes closed while Nicola started the car. He wasn't even paying any attention when she called Finn.

"He said he'll see about getting us a warrant," she said softly after she had hung up. "They're on the way to pick up Pelley. Now that Anna is officially a missing person, he can use police resources to help us find her. He also said that if Ollie will at least say on the record that he knows where Anna was taken, they can bring an army of cops in to search. He's going to see if he can talk Ollie into coming to the station as soon as his shift ends at eleven. He'll put in the request for the warrant as soon as he can, but he doubts they'll be able to get it before morning."

Rhys didn't respond.

Nicola reached over and put her hand on his knee. "Rhys --- "

"Don't," he said roughly, pulling himself away from her. "Just... don't."

"We're doing all we can. *You're* doing everything you can."

He was silent, but his mind was whirling with a million thoughts, all of them guilt-laden. *I'm leaving her there. I could have been looking for her right now, but I'm going home. And who knows what Graham is doing to her? What if he hurts her? What if he kills her? And I could have stopped it. I could have saved her...*

His stomach clenched, and he drew his knees towards his chest. He wanted to curl into a small ball and just cry. *Useless. Useless.*

Nicola didn't try to say anything else for the rest of the ride home.

It didn't turn out to be quite as easy as they had hoped. Ollie did come to the station and gave a statement, saying that Pelley had come to the docks to threaten him. He told them where he had been told the girl was being held, making sure to not say that he himself had been involved with the kidnapping. But Ollie was a known criminal, and Pelley was a police inspector. Worse, Pelley was still unconscious and in the hospital, thanks to the beating he had mysteriously sustained. They had learned, however, that Pelley was not his real name. And it was that information, more than anything else that gave Finn the edge he needed to get permission to search the subdivision.

But it had taken longer than planned. It was after noon when everything had been hammered out. By the time Finn pulled up to the Blackwood household in his police car, Rhys had chewed off nearly all of his fingernails, and had resorted to pulling out his hair.

The first thing that Rhys noticed was that Finn looked as though he had gotten a full night's sleep. Rhys knew that he hadn't. Neither had Rhys, except he had the dark circles under his eyes and grouchy temper to prove it. When he said something about it, Finn just laughed. "Met coffee," he explained. "I'm fairly certain they spike it with the confiscated drugs they keep in Evidence. Here. I thought you might need some." He handed Rhys a large Styrofoam cup.

Rhys took a large gulp, then nearly spewed it out again. "God, this is *awful,*" he exclaimed, making a face.

Finn laughed again. "I never said it tasted good. I only said that it was potent."

Rhys eyed the cup warily, but took another drink. This time, it was a cautious sip, and he was able to swallow it.

"I called the developer of the subdivision as soon as I could. He agreed to go ahead and let us in without seeing the paperwork, so I've already got boots on the ground. He told me only a small section of the subdivision is being lived in right now, with about two hundred empty homes. He's going to meet us there. He said he lives there himself, and hasn't noticed any suspicious activity. He said none of the other residents have reported any, either." His eyes met Nicola's in the rearview mirror. "And you were right. It *is* gated."

"Does he know how Thurston got the gate code?" Nicola asked from the back.

Finn shook his head. "He didn't say, and I didn't ask. If Thurston knows the gate code, then these two may know each other. And I don't want to tip Thurston off if I can help it. Not until we find Anna." He looked at Rhys out of the corner of his eye. "We *could* ask Pelley, but he still hasn't woken up. The docs say his worse injury looks to be a blow to the back of the head with a blunt object."

Rhys shrugged as he continued to sip his coffee. "Let's just be glad they decided to hit him instead of shoot him."

Finn sighed and reached over to turn on his siren.

When they reached the subdivision, the gate was wide open. A police cruiser identical to Finn's sat just inside the entrance, along with a sleek Mercedes. Finn pulled up next to the Mercedes and killed his siren, but left the car running. "Stay here," he told Rhys and Nicola sternly. "Let me talk to him first." Then he climbed out of the car before either of them could answer.

Even though Finn had directed the Blackwoods to stay in the car, he had left his door open, allowing their voices to drift back to the siblings. "... last section, section G," the man from the Mercedes was saying. "The neighborhood is set up in a grid pattern, so the other officers have been going over it square by square. They started in the front, so no one is looking in the back."

"And those homes are still under construction?"

"Some of them are. There are a few that have already been completed." The man wrung his hands and looked worried. "If what you're saying is true, if there is a kidnapped girl being held here, will I be in any trouble?"

"That depends," Finn replied. "Let's find her first, then we can worry about that. But you have been very helpful. Will you please stay with this officer until we finish our search? Just in case we need you?"

"Certainly. I'll do whatever you need me to, Inspector."

"Thank you." Finn turned and climbed back into his cruiser. "All right. The other officers have started working in the front. Let's head towards the back and start there. Mr. Quincy informed me that there is still construction going on, so no one would pay attention to a few men coming and going. The others have instructions to call me if they find anything."

The homes in the subdivision were what Rhys liked to call 'cookie-cutter' houses. For the most part, they all looked the same, except for different color paint and different yard decorations. Many of them were large and opulent, some with Greek columns and others with garages larger than his own home. The only thing that Rhys cared about, however, was which one – if any --- held Anna.

The insides were just as opulent. One held a marble staircase, one an indoor swimming pool. Some of them had bathrooms bigger than Rhys's bedroom. One even had a pair of marble statues that were replicas of famous Italian sculptures.

By the fifth house, Rhys was beginning to grow worried. No one had called Finn to report anything, and there were only a few homes left. Maybe Graham had learned they were coming and had disappeared, taking Anna with him. Maybe he had killed her and dumped her body, leaving no clues behind at all. Maybe Ollie had lied and she was never there at all.

But when they walked into the fifth house, Rhys knew they had found it. "Do you smell that?" he asked Finn, reaching behind him to pull out his gun. "I smell cigarette smoke."

"Aye," Finn replied. "And food. I smell... grease. Someone has been eating in here." He looked at Rhys grimly. "I'll go ahead and look around here. You'll..."

"Check the basement," Rhys replied. Every single one of these homes had a basement. The developer had explained that to Finn earlier. Rhys had been checking them at every house they had gone to. "I'll yell if I find anything. Or I'll shoot something."

"Let's hope it doesn't come to that. Be careful."

"You, too."

As Finn crept slowly towards the living room, Rhys opened side doors until he found the one that led to the basement. He went down a small flight of steps before opening another door.

As soon as he opened that one, he knew he had found the right place. The strong odor of unwashed bodies, stale urine, and sick rolled over him. Under normal circumstances, he would have gagged. Instead, he lifted his gun and slowly walked in, trying to give himself as small of a profile as possible.

There was another short flight of steps. A small light was glowing somewhere in front of him. Heart pounding, he stepped closer and closer to the light. He didn't dare try to find an overhead light. If Thurston or one of his men were in here, they would have the advantage over him. They knew the layout of the room while he didn't. So he stood in the darkness for a long moment, waiting for his eyes to adjust.

The first thing he noticed in the dim light was a dark, rectangular shape in the middle of the room. *A table,* he thought. This was where the odor seemed to be coming from. He took a step closer. Two steps. And then...

He was close enough now to see that there was something on the table. Something that was human-shaped. Something that had long, blond hair.

"Anna!"

He didn't care if Thurston or any of his men were still there and could hear him. He would kill them with his bare hands if necessary. Anna was here. And, even over the other smells, he could make out the sharp tang of blood. She was hurt.

He jammed the gun back into the waistband of his jeans and sprang forward, his hands immediately reaching for Anna's neck. "Anna," he breathed, desperately searching for a pulse. "Please be okay. Please be okay."

His fingers found the side of her neck. For a long, terrifying moment, he thought that there was no pulse. But then he found it. It was faint and weak, like a butterfly. But it was there.

He nearly fell to the floor in relief. *She's alive!* But then he realized something else: she hadn't responded to his words. Or his touch.

He ran back to the stairs. *"Finn"* he roared. *"Finn, I found her!"* Without waiting for a reply, he ran back to where Anna lay. "Anna," he murmured, smoothing hair away from her face. "Anna, wake up. Please, sweetheart. Open your eyes."

She moved. He held his breath. Then...

"Rhys?" Her voice was so faint that he had to lean over in order to make out what she was saying. "Is that you?"

"Yeah." He had to swallow the lump that had suddenly formed in his throat. "It's me."

He felt her breath wash across his cheek, and he could see one corner of her mouth turn up. "I knew you would come."

Unexpectedly, tears sprang to his eyes. "I am so sorry I took so long," he whispered. "I should have been here sooner."

"S' okay. You're here now."

He reached out to touch her face, and let out a sharp hiss. "You're burning up!"

"Mmmm. Fever. At least a day. Cold."

Now that his own heart had started to calm down, he could feel her trembling underneath his hand. He had thought it was his own hand that had been shaking.

He quickly pulled off his jacket and gently tucked it around her. "I'm going to get you out of here," he said, leaning down to kiss her burning forehead. "I promise."

He moved to go yell again. The house was big, perhaps Finn hadn't heard him. But he stopped when she whispered his name again.

"It's okay," he said. He went to squeeze her hand, and found the rope around her wrist. He let out a growl. "I'm not leaving you. I'm right here."

"Rhys." Her voice was growing even fainter. "Rhys, I have to tell you something."

"Wait until we're out of here. Then we'll have a nice, long talk. Okay? I have things I need to tell you, too."

"No. I need to tell you now." She let out a sigh. "I love you, Rhys."

His heart stopped. His breathing stopped. For a moment, time stopped. All he could do was stare down at her stupidly. His brain was screaming at him to find Finn, to find a light, to do *something*. But his feet might as well have been bolted to the floor.

She loves me?

That one thought electrocuted him, causing his heart to beat once more, and his lungs to remember how to work. *She loves me!*

Suddenly, he was laughing. And crying. He leaned over so that his forehead was touching hers. "Anna," he croaked. "Can you hear me?"

She didn't answer. She had passed out again.

He kissed her forehead again and moved his lips to her ear. "I love you, too," he whispered, feeling as though he could jump and start soaring around the ceiling.

But he didn't. Instead, he took a deep breath and moved away from her, going back to the steps. *"Finn!"*

Rhys found the light switch while Finn was thundering down the steps. In the harsh, fluorescent light, things looked even worse.

There was blood all over the table. When Rhys moved his jacket so that they could begin sawing at the ropes that held Anna down, they saw that she too was covered in blood. And when Rhys moved to the other side, he saw the jagged hole that was in her upper arm. Her shirt and jeans also had several holes in them that looked as though they had been formed by a knife blade. Rhys had to fight back the tidal wave of rage that rolled over him at the sight.

When Rhys re-covered Anna with his jacket and lifted her gently in his arms, she let out a cry of pain. But then she fell silent once again, her head pillowed against his shoulder. He could feel the heat of her fever radiating off her body. He could also feel her violent shivering. He held her tightly against him, hoping to God he wasn't causing her any more pain than she was already in, and desperately willed his own body heat to warm her.

Finn was already on the phone as they re-emerged into the daylight. His first call was to the other officer at the front of the neighborhood, letting him know that they had found Anna and to call off the search. He also instructed his partner to get the developer's phone number and to tell him not to leave town. The second call was to the hospital, warning them that they were coming.

Nicola, who had stayed outside to monitor the radio, saw the battered bundle in her brother's arms and turned white, a hand flying to her face. "Is she…"

"She's alive," Rhys said grimly. Nicola held open the back door of the cruiser so that he could carefully slide in. She climbed in to the front seat, while Finn slid behind the wheel. Without a word, he turned on his sirens and roared down the street.

Rhys cradled Anna against his chest, resting his head on top of hers as he rocked her gently back and forth. "Everything is going to be okay," he said softly. "I've got you now."

He only hoped that he hadn't been too late.

Chapter Seventeen

The lights were dimmed, but the sudden brightness still stabbed into her eyes, causing her to blink rapidly. There were quiet beeps somewhere off to her side, machines that were monitoring her vital signs and letting the world know that she was still alive.

And... another sound, somewhere close by. It was faint, a buzzing sound that she struggled to understand. *Is that... Is someone talking?*

"Anna?" The buzz was slowly resolving itself into words. "Are you awake? Anna?"

She turned her head towards the voice, blinking hard against the fluorescent lights. There was a shadow there, a dark shape standing in stark contrast to the light. "Rhys?" she murmured.

Silence. Then...

"Oh! Oh, thank the gods you are awake!" Her hand was lifted, and warm lips were pressed to her palm before that palm was pressed tightly against a cheek covered in stubble. Another hand was brushing her hair away from her face. "I've been so worried. I thought... I was terrified that..." There was a pause, followed by a sharp intake of breath. "Oh, Anna."

At that moment, despite the fuzziness in her head, despite the heaviness of her limbs, she very much wanted to wrap her arms around him, hold him close, and do everything she could to make the naked pain in his voice go away.

The thought dredged up a half-memory of softly spoken words. Had she said them? Or had it all been a dream?

She had to know.

She licked her lips, her mouth feeling incredibly dry. "Rhys," she murmured again.

The hand holding hers against his cheek squeezed. "I'm here. I'm not going anywhere. I promise."

"Did I... say something to you? Earlier?"

The fingers that were stroking her hair stopped. Anna's heart thudded so hard in her chest that she was certain no one needed the machines to hear it beating.

There was silence. Her heart beat again. Then again. *Maybe I dreamt it after all.*

Then a sigh drifted down to her, and Rhys placed his hand on her cheek. "Yes," he said softly. "You told me you loved me."

Anna closed her eyes as a cold pit formed in her stomach. This was not what she had wanted. The last time she had allowed herself to convey her feelings for him, when they had kissed, he had been mortified. He had told her it was a mistake, apologized, and promised that it would never happen again.

Now that he knew how she felt, she could only imagine what would happen next. He would wait until she was out of the hospital before passing her care off to someone else. She had no doubt that he would continue to look after her, but it would be from a distance. He would never come into contact with her again, lest she be hurt even worse by his rejection.

Tears began to slide down her cheeks, and her chest heaved with a sob.

"Anna!" Rhys's voice became panicked, and he dropped her hand so that he could lean down closer to her. "Anna, what's wrong? Are you in pain? Why are you crying?"

She couldn't answer him. All she could do was lie there and sob. She wished her body did not feel like a lead weight so that she could curl into a tiny ball. As it was, she could only turn her head away from him.

There was a loud *clack* as the railing on the side of her hospital bed was lowered. Then, much to her surprise, Rhys very gingerly climbed onto the bed next to her. Moving as carefully and gently as he possibly could, he wrapped both arms around her and pulled her against his chest.

"Anna," he murmured, using a thumb to wipe her tears away. "I'm not going anywhere. Not now. Not *ever*. I swear it to you."

She blinked in surprise at this.

"I know you think that I don't have feelings for you." She heard more than saw him smile. "My sister has informed me about what a total idiot I was to you, and I hope you can forgive me for it." He paused. "When I told you that I was sorry that I had kissed you, that it never should have happened, it didn't come across quite the way I had intended. I very much wanted to kiss you. I had for some time, in fact."

Anna was confused. She sniffed, her sobs having quieted, though tears were still falling. "Then... Then why ---"

"Because I felt like I had forced it on you. That I had not asked for your permission. Or at least given you the chance to turn away if it was not what you wanted." She could feel him shudder. "I would never hurt you, Anna. *Never*. Even if it meant never being with you. And the idea that I had forced something on you that you didn't want horrified me."

Again Anna found herself wishing she could make the pain in his voice vanish.

"I am so sorry that I drove you away. I am so sorry that I made you feel like I didn't care. Because I *do*. Very much." He gently grasped her chin and titled her face up to meet his. "I *love* you, Anna Miller."

She gasped at his words, eyes going wide. Her heart was hammering against her ribs and some part of her lazily wondered if the machine was going to explode. "Are... Are you sure?"

He gave her his most magnificent smile, the one she thought belonged in toothpaste ads, as he brushed another strand of hair away from her face. "I've never been as sure of anything in my life."

Still holding her chin in his hand, Rhys began to lower his face towards hers, moving slowly, giving her the opportunity to move away if she wished.

But she didn't. She had wanted this for so long.

Anna knew that there were no words to describe the feeling that came over her at the contact. Her hand, moving entirely on its own, reached up and found its way into Rhys's hair at the nape of his neck.

He gently pulled away, much to her disappointment, and rested his forehead against hers. "That," he murmured, "was how it should have been done the first time."

More tears were streaming down her face. He used both thumbs to wipe them away. "No more. I will not let you shed another tear because of me. If you don't want me..."

"You *are* an idiot," she whispered. But she was smiling. "These are happy tears, not sad ones."

He sucked in a breath, eyes searching her face. "So... Will you give me another chance? Even though I screwed up? Even though I caused you to be hurt?"

"It wasn't your fault," she told him firmly. "And yes. I *love* you, Rhys."

He could have flown to the moon. He could have run around the hospital a million times without ever stopping or tiring. He wanted to laugh. He wanted to cry.

Instead, he grinned. Then he kissed her again.

Rhys had reluctantly climbed out of the bed and called the nurse to alert them that Anna was now awake. A few moments later, the doctor entered the room. "Why, hello there, Miss Miller," he said, a smile stretching across his face. "Welcome back. You gave us all quite a scare there."

She opened her eyes to stare at the doctor and offered a weak smile. "I'm sorry."

"That's all right. You're here with us now, and that's all that matters." He nodded at Rhys. "Would you mind stepping out for a moment? Now that Miss Miller is awake, I can do a more thorough exam."

Rhys frowned. "Are you kidding? I'm not leaving her. Not for a second."

The doctor stared at him hard. "I know that you are concerned for Miss Miller, and that you are very happy that she is awake. But I am under no obligation to you. My only concern is for the well-being of my patient. Now, you can either step outside while I exam her, or I can call security and have you removed from the hospital. It is up to you."

Rhys opened his mouth to answer hotly, but was stopped by Anna squeezing the hand Rhys had placed in hers. "Rhys." He looked down, and she offered him a smile. "It'll be okay. Just wait outside. I don't want you to get kicked out of the hospital. I want you here."

His face softened. "Are you sure?"

"I'll be fine. Promise."

He gave a sigh and bent over to kiss her once more on the forehead. "I'll just be outside if you need me." Then, with a glare at the doctor, he walked out, shutting the door softly behind him.

The doctor let out a sigh, but was still smiling as he came around to the side of the bed Rhys had just vacated. "I must say that your young man is quite overprotective of you. We nearly had to pry you out of his arms when he brought you in to the emergency room."

Anna couldn't help but smile. She liked how the doctor had called Rhys her young man.

"Tell me, Miss Miller. How are you feeling?"

"Thirsty," she replied hoarsely.

He laughed. "I would imagine so! Nurse, would you be so kind as to step out and ask Mr. Blackwood to fetch a glass of water for Miss Miller? It might help to let him feel useful, and she would be very grateful."

The nurse nodded and stepped out of the room to pass on the doctor's message as he picked up Anna's chart from the end of her bed. "What about physically? How are you feeling?"

She quickly took a mental survey of her body. "I feel... heavy. Like I can't lift anything. And my arm is throbbing." She frowned. "What happened to me?"

"That I can't tell you. You'll have to ask your young friend about that. But I will tell you what I *do* know." He sighed and pulled the room's lone chair to the side of her bed and pulled out a penlight. "You were brought here three days ago. You were dehydrated and had lost a lot of blood. You also had several wounds, most of them knife wounds, some of which had begun to become infected. This led to a fever. Your body had basically shut down and was using what resources it had left to fight the fever and keep you alive. You've been unconscious ever since. We were beginning to worry that you might not wake up." He shone the light in one of her eyes, then the other. "Thankfully, many of your wounds didn't require stiches. The worst injuries are the one on your arm, and one on your leg. Both of those required stiches, as did the one across your stomach. You've got about seventy-five stiches all together." He stared at her over the top of his glasses. "You are a very lucky woman."

Anna swallowed hard. *I almost died...*

"We've been giving you blood and fluids, which has pain medication mixed in. That's why you feel heavy. But..." He looked at one of the monitors and then back at her chart. "It looks as though your fever has gone done substantially. Hopefully, that means that your wounds are no longer infected." He nodded at the nurse, who drew a curtain around Anna's bed. "Let's take a look and see how we're healing up, shall we?"

Rhys had taken to pacing outside of Anna's door, the cup of ice water he clutched in his hand threatening to slosh over with each angry step. When her door finally opened, he nearly tipped it over.

The doctor gave him a kind smile as he and the nurse stepped out. "She is healing very well. I want to keep her for a few more days just to make sure there are no complications, but I'm confident she's going to make a full recovery."

Rhys blew out a long breath, his body sagging in relief. "Thank you," he said, holding out a hand.

The doctor chuckled as he shook Rhys's hand. "Don't think me! She's a strong young woman."

"Yes," Rhys agreed strongly. "Yes, she is."

"Don't strain her too much. She's been through a lot. And we're going to give her pain medication every six to eight hours, which will probably make her sleep. If she needs anything else, just have her press the call button. Also, if she needs to use the bedpan, have her press the call button. I don't want her putting any weight on that leg if she can help it."

Rhys nodded. "I'll make sure to call a nurse in if she needs to use the bathroom or needs anything else."

"Good!" The doctor put a hand on Rhys's shoulder. "If all goes well, I'll see you in a few days to discharge her."

Rhys nodded again, then slipped back in to Anna's room.

Part of him had thought that maybe it had been a dream, that he would wake up and find Anna was still unconscious. Or worse, still in the clutches of Graham Thurston. But when he walked into the room and saw her lying there, eyes open, he had to stop and collect himself.

Anna turned her head and gave him a soft smile. "Hi," she croaked. Then her eyes fell on the cup in his hands. "Please tell me that's for me."

"It certainly is. Here." He sat the water down and reached for the bed controls. He pushed a button, and the head of the bed began to rise, putting Anna into a sitting position. "I'd rather not drown you right after you wake up." He held the cup in front of her and pulled the straw towards her.

She leaned forward and took a sip through the straw. He watched as she closed her eyes and let out a moan as she took another sip. After a third, she opened her eyes and fell back against the pillow. "Thank you. My mouth felt like a desert."

"I can only imagine. Let me know when you want more." He sat in the chair by her bed and lowered the rail so that he could take her hand in his. "I am so happy you're awake." His voice grew thick, and he had to swallow a lump in his throat.

She smiled up at him. "Me, too." Then she nodded at the water cup. "More, please."

He laughed as he brought it back up for her to drink.

When Nicola arrived a short time later, she found her brother sitting next to Anna on the bed. Anna was asleep, thanks to the pain medication a nurse had inserted into her IV, but one hand lay firmly tucked in Rhys's. Her head was lying against his shoulder. And he was using his free hand to gently stroke her hair.

Nicola couldn't keep a grin off of her face. "Well. It would be childish of me to say I told you so, but... I told you so."

Rhys just smiled in answer. Even though his face looked tired, Nicola didn't think she had ever seen her brother look as happy as he did in that moment. "You did. And I am so glad that you were right." He looked down at Anna, and Nicola would have been able to see the love that shown in his eyes even if she were blind. "She's going to give me a second chance. And she didn't even make me beg."

"She's a bigger woman than I am, then. I would have made you crawl on your hands and knees for at least a week." Nicola held out a bag to her brother. "Why don't you go and change, hmm? And maybe take a shower?"

Rhys took the bag, but didn't move. "It's... hard to move. I feel like I'm in a dream, and if I move, it'll all shatter."

Nicola sighed. "Rhys, you're starting to smell ripe. You've been wearing the same clothes for days, and you haven't shaved. You're starting to resemble a homeless person again." She jerked a thumb at the bathroom. "Go. She's not going anywhere, and I'll stay here with her. If she wakes up again and still sees you looking like that, she might change her mind."

Rhys made a face at his sister, but he slowly pulled his arm from around Anna and gently eased off of the bed. "I'll be right back," he whispered, kissing the top of her head. Then he took the bag Nicola had brought him and disappeared into the bathroom.

Nicola watched him go before turning back to face Anna, who hadn't so much as twitched when Rhys moved. Anna reminded Nicola of photos she had seen of Holocaust victims. She was thin, painfully so, with her collarbones sticking out prominently, and her hospital gown seemingly only draped around her. She was pale, her skin nearly the same color as the sheets of her bed. Her cheeks were sunken in, and the circles under her eyes were the color of bruises. And what skin wasn't covered by the hospital gown seemed to be covered by bandages.

Nicola could feel a knot of anger begin to form in her chest. Anna was her *friend*. And she had done nothing more than be asked to work at a library. She had not asked for any of this. She hadn't done anything to anyone. And yet Graham had hurt her. Graham had hurt a lot of people that Nicola cared about. She would find him. She would find him, and make him pay for everything he'd done.

She was still letting her imagination think of all of the creative things she could do to the former Scholar when Rhys reemerged some time later. He had shaved, and, much to Nicola's relief, smelled clean. He had also lost a lot of weight, both from his moping after Anna had left, and then from the stress of her being kidnapped and injured. He had dark circles under his eyes as well, but, for the first time since the disastrous street fair incident, she could see a spark in her brother's eyes. "What now?" she asked softly.

Rhys sighed and raked a hand through his hair, slicking it back. "We need to find where Graham has gone to ground," he said quietly, his eyes never leaving the small form in the hospital bed. "We can't sit around and wait for him to come to us. Not again. We need to find him first and take him out."

Nicola looked at him out of the corner of her eye. "I was talking about Anna, not Graham. He's the least of our worries right now." When she saw him clench his jaw, she turned to face him fully. "Rhys. You are *not* planning on charging after Graham. Not now!"

"*Someone* needs to," he growled. "*Look* at her, Nicola. He *tortured* her. And I doubt he even blinked at it. He's proven that he is willing to do whatever he needs to get the information he wants. What is he going to do next, hmm? I was supposed to be looking after her, and she still got hurt. What if he decides to go after innocents? People that we know nothing about? We need to stop him before he starts to rack up a body count. And we both know he'll do it."

"And just how do you plan on finding him? Finn said they couldn't find anything in that house that could lead them to Graham or his two cronies. Anna might know something, but no one is going to question her until she's better. Maybe Graham was able to get the information he needed. Maybe he didn't, and decided to leave London for a while and let things cool down. You forget. He's lost his police insider and one of this lackeys. I doubt he's just going to make a flashing neon sign advertising where he is."

Rhys flashed her a smile, showing all of his teeth. "I can draw him out. I have something that he needs."

Nicola placed her hands on hips. "And what might that be?"

"Me. Abraham is dead, so he can't ask him about the book. Anna didn't know anything about the book, either. He doesn't have what he needs. The next logical choice would be to come after me. And if he is desperate, he'll be making mistakes. So I just need to make myself a nice, available target. He won't be able to resist."

"You will do no such thing."

The siblings turned at the sound of the tired, yet firm, voice. They had both been so caught up in the heat of their argument that neither one had realized Anna was awake. She was sitting on the edge of the bed, feet dangling over the side, grimacing as she tried to get to a standing position.

Rhys was at her side almost immediately, his face softening. "What are you doing? You shouldn't be up."

"I need to use the bathroom, and I refuse to use the bedpan." She gave him a tired grin. "I'd like to retain what little dignity I have left. Here. Can you help me stand?"

Rhys looked like he wanted to argue. But when she tried to slide forward and let out a hiss of pain, he picked her up with as little trouble as if he were lifting a child and set her on her feet.

She leaned hard against him, the movement costing her what little energy she had. "Thanks," she murmured. "Nicola, do you mind giving me a hand? I know it's not glamorous..."

The other woman grinned. "I'd be happy to. This way, I can see your ass through your johnny." She wiggled her eyebrows.

Anna laughed, then winced. "Oooh. No laughing. That hurts."

Rhys's eyes grew even more worried as his sister came to grasp Anna gently by the arm. "Are you sure about this? I don't want you to injure yourself any more. I can step outside."

But she shook her head stubbornly. "No. No bedpan." She looked at him, and he could easily make out the sharp glint in her eyes. The medication had done nothing to dull that. "And, when I get back, we're going to chat about this crazy idea of yours."

"Anna..."

She held up a hand, silencing him. "Bathroom first."

Rhys watched as his sister helped her hobble to the bathroom, pulling her IV pole with her, a worried look on his face. When they came back out several moments later, he strode over to the bathroom door and, moving very gently, gathered her in his arms and carried her back to the bed. She let out a sigh as he pulled her blanket up to her chest, but she gave him a smile. "Thanks," she said, squeezing his hand. Then her eyes narrowed. "Now, about this using yourself as bait nonsense."

He sat in the chair by the edge of the bed. "Look, I know---"

"No. You look. You will not be doing any such thing. Do you understand me?" Her eyes grew worried, and she tugged on his hand until he was leaning over close enough for her to place her free hand on his cheek. "It's not just you anymore," she murmured. "I love you, Rhys. And if we are going to make this work between us, we have to remember that we are partners. That means that you can't run off willy-nilly and play hero. We are going to have to make decisions *together*. And I refuse to let you use yourself to call him out. If you can't agree to that, then we need to end this relationship now."

He stared down at her. She stared back. Neither of them looked away.

Finally, Rhys let out a sigh and turned his head so that he could kiss the palm she had on his cheek. "You'll have to give me time," he said softly. "I'm not used to this. And we all already know that I can be... stupid when it comes to women. Especially you."

"As long as I am the only woman who makes you stupid, I'll let it slide." Anna was grinning. It was weak, but it was genuine. Rhys felt his heart warm at the sight of it. "I'm not perfect either, you know. I have no clue how this works. But we'll find out together. We'll make our mistakes together. And we'll *learn* together." She lifted an eyebrow. "Do you think you can handle it?"

He grinned in response. "Aye. I think I can." He leaned forward to kiss her softly on the mouth.

Nicola let out a dramatic sigh, but she was beaming. "Get a room already!"

Chapter Eighteen

Anna continued to heal and, as promised, was discharged into Rhys's care a few days later. "Don't let her put too much weight on that leg," the doctor told him sternly. "I want her resting as much as possible. She's coming along nicely, and I would prefer it if none of those stiches were ripped out. Make sure she takes her medicine as instructed. No skipping because she's feeling better. If you have any questions, don't hesitate to call me. If you do not, then I want to see her again in a week. Until then, no work, lots of rest, and the least amount of walking she can get away with. Understood?"

Rhys understood. He didn't bother to mention that he didn't plan on letting Anna out of his sight until the man who had hurt her was dead. He took the written prescriptions for Anna's medication and wheeled her out to Nicola's waiting car. She had protested the wheelchair, but the nurse walking along with them had sternly told her that she could either leave in a wheelchair or stay in the hospital, so Anna had pressed her lips together and let Rhys lift her from the bed to the wheelchair.

She let out a huff as Rhys picked her up once again and placed her in the back of Nicola's car. "You're getting awfully comfortable with carrying me around," she grumbled.

He grinned as he slid in to the seat next to her, reaching over to buckle her in. "Admit it. You like it." He gently tugged on the seatbelt, trying to make sure it wasn't chafing against the stitches that ran across her stomach. "Is that all right?"

"It's fine," she assured him. She leaned her head back against the seat and closed her eyes with a sigh. "I just hate feeling helpless. I don't like having to depend on someone else for everything."

"Anna. You were kidnapped and tortured. You've been injured. *Badly.* I can't wave a magic wand and make you instantly better. But I can take care of you. So let me. Please."

She cracked an eye wide enough to look at him. "It sounds to me like you are blaming yourself for what happened to me. But that would be stupid. Only an idiot would think it was his fault."

Nicola snorted from the front seat. "Good luck with that," she said, looking in her rearview mirror. "I've already tried. He won't listen."

Anna opened both of her eyes so that she could watch him. "Rhys?"

He sighed and leaned sideways so that his head was resting on hers. He took one of her hands, lacing his fingers through hers. "I can't help it. It was my job to keep you safe. It was my *only* job. And I failed. I didn't just fail. I failed *miserably.* I sent you away due to my own stupidity, and I wasn't there when you needed me. So yes. I blame myself."

She closed her eyes again, leaning into him and soaking up his warmth. "I don't blame you," she murmured. "What if he had come after me while I was still with you? He might have just killed you outright. He might have killed *all* of you. Then who would have saved me? You were there when *I* needed you the most. You saved me from Graham. You were there when I woke up in the hospital. And you're here now. That's what matters."

He didn't respond. Instead, he took her hand and pressed it against his chest. Just being near her soothed him, but hearing her absolving him of guilt caused a warm glow to spread throughout his body.

112

He could never forgive himself, but knowing that she didn't blame him at all was a massive weight removed from his shoulders.

Nicola glanced at them once more in the rearview mirror, and was grinning broadly as she pulled out of the hospital parking lot.

There had never been any arguments as to where Anna would be going when she left the hospital. It had never even been discussed. So after stopping to fill Anna's medications, Nicola drove them to the Blackwoods' home.

This time, Anna didn't complain when Rhys lifted her into his arms. Instead, she wrapped her arms around his neck and pillowed her head against his shoulder. While she hated not being able to do on her own, she would be lying if she didn't admit, at least to herself, that she enjoyed having him carry her. His arms were strong, and she felt safe. And after the events of the past week, that was a feeling that she desperately craved.

He carried her into the bedroom that she had come to know as *hers* and laid her gently down on the bed. Nicola had been to her flat, because it was Anna's quilt that Rhys pulled up to her chin. "Do you need anything?" he asked softly, brushing a stray lock of hair away from her face.

"I don't think so."

He smiled. "All right, then. I'll leave you to get some rest. Yell if you need anything." He leaned forward, presumably to kiss her, but paused when she reached out to grab his wrist. "What is it?"

"Don't leave. Stay with me."

"Anna. You need to rest. You can barely keep your eyes open as it is."

"I know. It's just... I'll sleep better knowing you're here. Please." She licked her lips, and her next words were barely more than a whisper. "I don't want to be alone."

She watched his face crumple, and instantly wanted to kick herself. He blamed himself for her abduction, and it would stand to reason that he would blame himself for the fear that was in her voice as well. "Let me get a chair. I'll stay as long as you need me to."

"No." She tugged at his wrist. "I want you here. With me. You need sleep, too. The bed is big enough for both of us."

No." His voice was firm, and she could feel him try to pull his arm away from her. "I could hurt you."

"You won't. Please, Rhys." She paused. "I need you."

She could see her arrow strike home, and he let out a deep sigh, his shoulders slumping. "Do you really?" His voice was low.

"Yes," she replied firmly. "I do." She let go of his wrist so that she could pat the bed next to her and slowly inched over so that there was more room. "The sooner you lay down, the sooner we can both get some sleep."

He still didn't look very happy, but he leaned over and began removing his shoes. She let out a satisfied sigh and closed her eyes. When she felt the bed shift under his weight and his breath wash across her face, she reached out to find his arm. "Here," she said, guiding his arm across her stomach and placing his hand on her ribcage. "No stiches there."

"Are you sure about this?" He was lying on his side, but he was stiff, and he wasn't touching her aside from his arm.

She had never been so sure of anything in her life, and she told him so. "Come closer. I promise I'll tell you if you hurt me."

So he inched closer and closer until he was pressed against her, one arm lying across her torso. She let out a happy sigh and leaned her head to the side so that it was pressed against his chest. "There," she murmured, smiling as she listened to the sound of his heart beat in her ear. "That's better."

For a moment, he hardly dared to breath, afraid that he would bump her and cause her more pain. But when he realized that she wasn't going to fall apart, he gently slid his other arm under her head so that he could curl it around her shoulders. He laid his cheek against the top of her head, breathing in her scent and wondering at the feel of her body lying in his arms. When he finally allowed his eyes to close, he had a smile across his face.

The fact that she woke up in a familiar space did much to drive away Anna's fear. The fact that she woke up encircled in Rhys's arms sent it away completely. She wanted to simply lie where she was and soak it all in, bask in the warmth and safety that it all offered. But her bladder had other ideas, so she reluctantly shook Rhys awake so that he could help her limp to the bathroom.

"This," she groused when she reemerged a few moments later, "is going to get old very quickly."

Rhys chuckled. "Well, at least you can go to the bathroom by yourself now. And it won't be forever."

"True." It had been awkward having Nicola in the tiny hospital bathroom with her, even though the other woman had made sure to keep her back turned the whole time. Still, she couldn't wait until it didn't take her half an hour to get from the door to the toilet.

Rhys came to her side, but didn't pick her up as she had expected. Instead, he cupped her face in both of his hands and kissed her. She closed her eyes and leaned into him, wishing she could wrap herself around him and kiss him forever and ever. But when he pulled away and leaned his forehead against hers, she let him go with a sigh. "Now *that* is something I will never get tired of."

He laughed, and she smiled. She hadn't realized how much she'd missed that sound. "Me, either." He kissed her again, just because he could. This time, she reached around to tangle the hand of her good arm into his hair, pulling him down and deepening the kiss. She could feel his arms trembling with the need to crush her against him.

"Careful," he gasped when he broke away. "I can't... My control isn't too good right now. I don't want to hurt you."

She wanted to tell him that he wouldn't, that she knew he wouldn't. But the truth was that he probably would. And she would gladly let him. "Later," she growled, wishing her body would heal faster.

"Promise," he vowed. "But right now, let's go find some grub. I don't know about you, but I'm starving."

As if in answer, her stomach let out a loud growl. Laughing, he swung her up into his arms and carried her into the kitchen.

They found both Nicola and David in there, talking quietly. Both of them jumped up when Rhys entered the room. "There you are!" Nicola cried out, putting her hands on her hips. "I've been looking everywhere for you. You just disappeared on me when we got home."

"My fault," Anna said sheepishly. "I needed a nanny, and I volunteered Rhys for the job. He really didn't get a say-so in the matter."

Nicola squinted at her brother, then broke into a grin. "And I very much doubt that he put up a fight. Doesn't matter. At least I know you didn't run away again."

Anna lifted an eyebrow and turned her face up so that she could look at Rhys. "Run away? Again? What is she talking about?"

"Long story," he replied, his cheeks taking on a faint tinge. Before Anna could press any further, he gently sat her down onto the wooden chair he had asked Nicola to pull from his bedroom. "I'll grab us some food."

"There's spaghetti in the fridge," Nicola said, sitting back down on her stool. "There is also soup and some frozen dinners."

David smiled kindly at Anna while Rhys rummaged in the refrigerator. Anna recalled seeing him at the hospital once or twice, but her memories were still fuzzy from the pain medication "How are you feeling?" he asked her softly.

She smiled in return. "Seeing as how I have enough thread in me to sew a quilt, I feel pretty well. Of course, the medicine they gave me may have a lot to do with that."

The other Scholar chuckled. "Well, I'm glad you are feeling better. That's what matters. And I am glad you are back with us. I must admit. Things were a little... tense without you around."

Nicola snorted. "That's putting it mildly."

Anna knew there was a story in there somewhere, but she knew that it had to involve Rhys, and he would tell her when he was ready. If not, she would corner Nicola sometime and ask her. "Well. Since we're all here, how about you answer some questions for me? Like just who exactly Graham Thurston is, and what the hell he wanted with me. And don't give me the Cliff notes version either. I've shed blood. I think I have the right to know *everything*."

"I agree," David replied. "Especially as it seems you have a more... vested interest now."

He meant her and Rhys. She blushed.

He grinned at this and reached over to pat her hand. "I, for one, am very glad for it," he whispered. "You'll be good for him."

"I hope so," she whispered back.

He patted her hand again, the sat back as Rhys brought over a plate of spaghetti and a bottle of soda. "Where should we start?" he asked in a more conversational tone.

Anna shrugged. "I'm not sure. What is this book that Graham wants so much? How do you know about it? What does it have to do with me?"

Rhys chuckled and held up a hand, silencing her. "Let's start with the first question and go from there, shall we?" He turned to the older man. "David?"

The light glinted off of David's glasses as he shifted his attention to Anna. "Tell me, Anna. What do you know about King Solomon?"

She blinked. "King Solomon? As in from the Bible King Solomon?" At his nod she let out a breath, her eyebrows coming together. "Just the basics, I guess. Was a great wise man who built the Temple in Jerusalem. And, of course, I know the story about him threatening to cut the baby in half in order to discover who its real mother was." She gave an apologetic shrug. "Like I said. It's basic."

David made a noise, and Anna got the distinct impression that he was disappointed. "What about the Apocrypha? Surely you've heard of that."

"The books that were banned from the Bible? Sure, I know about..." She trailed off as a half-remembered memory tugged at her. "Wait. King Solomon had his own book, didn't he? One that didn't make it into the Bible. I remember seeing that on a TV program."

David *did* wince at the mention of the television, but simply pushed his glasses up and continued on. "Yes, well, you are correct. King Solomon does have his own book. And the reason it was kept out of the Bible is because it speaks of demons. More specifically, it tells of how Solomon used magic to *control* demons. It is even reported that he used demons to help in the construction of the Temple."

"And heaven forbid the Church give their stamp of approval to a text that basically says one of their most holy sites was built by demons," Rhys snickered.

"So... what? Graham is after a copy of the Testament of Solomon? I mean, he can just get on the Internet and find that."

"It's not the Testament that he's after." David leaned forward to place his elbows on the island, steepling his fingers together. "According to the Testament, Solomon gained his wisdom by traveling to the Far East and learning the magic of the Orient. It also tells us that he brought back three magical items with him. One was a ring that he used to control the demons. Another was a flying carpet." He smiled at the expression on her face. "Yes. *That* kind of flying carpet."

Anna lifted a skeptical eyebrow. "Okay. So he had a magic ring and a flying carpet. What was the third item?"

David shook his head, but his smile was growing. "The Testament doesn't say. Some of the text is missing. It could have simply crumbled with age. But my guess is that the Church didn't want *anyone* to know about it."

Anna's gaze went from David to Rhys and back again. "But *you* know, don't you? Or at least have a good guess."

"Oh, we know." The Scholar paused, his eyes shining. "It was a book. A book filled with all of the magic spells that Solomon learned while on his travels."

"Okay. So King Solomon had a flying carpet, a spell book, and a magic ring that let him control demons." Anna shrugged. "What does this have to do with the book Graham wants? Is it supposed to tell you where to find Solomon's stash or something?"

"No. Solomon's spell book *is* the book that Graham wants."

Anna blinked, waiting for David to explain further. When he didn't, she slowly shook her head. "I--- I'm sorry. I'm still feeling a bit fuzzy from the painkillers. I don't understand what you're saying."

"Solomon's book --- his spell book, as you said --- is the book that Graham is after, the one he thinks you have. It's not a book to tell you where to find it. It's *the* book itself."

Anna fell back against her chair, her breath coming out in a *whoosh.* "So he tried to kill me over some *spell book?*" she said weakly. "Magic isn't *real.* There are no such things as *demons.* I can't ---" She placed her hands over her eyes. "Cut up by a guy who thinks he can do magic. God, it's worse than those D&D guys in college. At least *they* knew it was all fake. *You* guys don't believe in this crap, do you?"

Silence greeted her. Suddenly feeling as though she was caught in some kind of madhouse, Anna peeked through her fingers.

All three of them were looking at her, and the expressions on their faces told her that yes, they *did* believe. And that this was no laughing matter.

"Oh, God," she breathed. "You're all mad!"

"Not quite," Rhys replied. "'There are more things in Heaven and Earth', after all."

Anna glowered at him. "Don't quote Shakespeare at *me,* sir."

"The book is real," Nicola interjected. "There are documents going back thousands of years that speak of it. We've found medieval alchemy texts that reference it, since the secret of alchemy is one of the spells rumored to be in the book. DaVinci speaks of it. And, despite what is in it, Graham believes it is real. And he's already proven that he is willing to kill for it."

Anna paused for a moment at that. Despite her disbelief in a book of magic spells, Nicola had a point. Graham believed in it enough to not only kill Abraham, but to kidnap and torture her as well. And that was all she needed to know.

"Okay. So this book is real. How do the Scholars know about it?"

David took off his glasses to clean them on his shirt. "The book was at the Temple until the Crusades. At that time it was given to the Templars to keep safe, along with several other items the people of Jerusalem wanted to keep out of the hands of the invaders."

Anna eyed the older man. "Wait. Don't tell me you're a Templar, too. Cause that would just be too much."

"No." That was Rhys, and Anna had to carefully turn in her chair so that she could see him. "David's not a Templar." He took a bite of his own spaghetti and nodded at his sister. "*We* are."

Chapter Nineteen

"What?" she asked stupidly.

Anna could only stare dumbly at the Blackwood siblings as what Rhys had just said sank in. She thought that it must be the medicine, making her foggy and confused. She must have misunderstood. "You can't be Templars," she finally said as her frantic thoughts began to coalesce. "They were disbanded, burned at the stake. By the French king and the Pope. That's where we get the legend of Friday the 13th from. Supposedly. They are all gone." She had seen that on TV as well.

Nicola chuckled. "Not quite. The arrest orders weren't as secret as King Phillip thought, and a lot of the knights were able to avoid being arrested. And there were knights all over Europe. It was mainly the French knights who were arrested and sent to the stake. More knights escaped than were arrested. They had to go underground, or join other organizations. But they survived. And, since the arrests were so sudden, they didn't have time to give the items back to their rightful owners. They had been sworn to protect it, and they would continue to do so. But they had to get creative, else they could be turned in to the local authorities, who could have them executed for heresy."

Anna reached up to massage her temples. She was pretty sure her head was going to explode. "So... what then? The Templars took their book and other stuff and went..."

"Everywhere. They spread out all over the world. They broke the treasure up and put it where they could best keep an eye on it. Some pieces went to museums to be put on display. Some were eventually given back to the descendants of their original owners. Some, like the book, were put away to be guarded very carefully.

"Over the years, some of the treasure has become lost. That is where you and the other Scholars come in. We need to find those items, as well as any other information that may be out there. It is our job to protect. It always has been."

"Lost Knowledge." Her voice was barely more than a whisper. "That's what you meant by Lost Knowledge. We find things that have been lost to time, and then let you know about it."

"Right. We then take that information to our superiors, who then decide what should be done about it. Is it something that can be made public? Or is it something that can't be destroyed but could cause widespread panic if the general public learned of its existence? Think about it. You may scoff at the idea that magic is real, but it's only 'magic' to you because you it's something you don't understand. Electricity was once considered magic. So was the telephone."

This, Anna thought weakly, *is madness.*

"Anna?" Rhys's voice cut across her thoughts, full of worry and dismay. He didn't say anything else, but she could almost hear his unspoken thoughts: he thought this would be her breaking point, and that she wouldn't want any more to do with him.

She blew out a breath, but still didn't lift her head. "That explains a lot, actually. Graham kept calling Rhys a knight. I asked him what he meant, but he never said anything else. Just kept asking about the book." At least, that's what she remembered of her time with him. "How does he know about all of this? If you've worked so hard to keep it a secret, then he must have a mole on the inside."

"Worse than that," David said grimly, and proceeded to tell Anna about Graham's history.

When he had finished, she had lifted her head and was looking at the older man with sympathy... and interest. "So why is he after this book *now?* If he knew about it --- since all Scholars seem to know about it --- why hasn't he gone after it before? And why would he think *I* knew anything about it?"

"That is a very good question." Rhys's voice was grim. "The real book was supposedly destroyed in the 1940s, right? Even the Scholars and the Templars thought the Germans' bombs took it out during the Blitz. But a Scholar found a letter in Turkey not long after you came to London that stated the book was sent to the Bradley after the war was over. From what we could tell, this Scholar had smuggled the book out of Europe when Hitler began to rise to power and kept it in Istanbul. But once Hitler was dead, he thought it would be safer in London, hidden in plain sight."

She offered a humorless smile. "No better place to hide a book than a library." Her smile faded. "But it's not there. At least, not to my knowledge. And you heard Abraham that night. He told them that it had never been there."

"I know. But what bothers me more is that Graham somehow had this knowledge almost at the same time we did." He raked a hand through his hair. "There had been rumors that there was something at the Bradley, a powerful piece of Lost Knowledge. That was why Abraham had me come to the library to be around you. I didn't know why he was so afraid. I mean... A turncoat? Amongst the Scholars? I know there have been others who have gone bad, like Graham. But do you really think there is someone feeding him this information?"

"He has deep pockets," David replied. "And we're still only human. We can be bribed just as easily as the next person." He looked angry.

"Okay. Wait. Slow down." Anna raised her hand. "Let me see if I got this: Graham had this information not long after the Templars were told about it, correct? Couldn't it have been a Templar who sold you out? Are there any Templars who would benefit from this?"

Nicola chuckled as Rhys shook his head. "It doesn't work like that," he said softly. "The Templars... We don't have a choice. This is in our blood." His lips twisted wryly. "Literally. It is who we *are.* If a Templar turned their back on their duty, if they allowed someone to get hurt on purpose... Let's just say we police our own, and our justice is swift and not very impersonal. It *could* be a Templar, but it is very doubtful. The last time we had a traitor was in the early 1800s, and his punishment was gruesome enough that it's still used to scare us into obeying."

Anna felt sick. She couldn't believe the Blackwoods would be a part of an organization like that. "Okay. Not a Templar, then. How many Scholars knew about that letter? And how many of them knew I was Abraham's replacement? Yes, Graham knew about that, too. That's why he thought I was lying, because he said it would have been the first thing Abraham told me when I became his apprentice." She shivered at the memory. That was right before he had driven the knife into her arm.

A low growl vibrated throughout the kitchen. At first she thought it was someone's cell phone. Then she realized it was Rhys, and she could see that his jaw was clenched. He must have been thinking about Graham, too.

David ignored him, rubbing his jaw thoughtfully. "I'm not sure how many knew about the letter.

Abraham had been notified, of course, as he was the current curator of the Bradley. And he told me. I don't know who else he may have told, or if anyone else was notified when Abraham was. But all of the Scholars know about you. Do you not remember how they were all flocking around you at Abraham's memorial?"

"Like I was something shiny," she replied, glancing at Rhys. He smiled at her in remembrance. "So is there no way we can find out who might have known both of those things? Is there... I dunno. A Headmaster or something?"

David chuckled. "No. We don't really have a leader. We have someone who kind of directs everyone and keeps up with who is where and whatnot, but we mostly take care of ourselves. I can ask around, see if anyone else might know of something that could help us."

"We need to find out soon," Nicola said. "Before anyone else gets hurt. Or worse."

Silence greeted that statement.

Finally, Rhys sighed. "Well, there is nothing we can do about it right now. Anna, are you finished? It's time for your medicine."

Neither of them spoke as he carried her back to her bedroom. She lay against the pillows, eyes closed as he busied himself with reading the instructions on the medicine bottles. The first time he spoke was when he handed her the two pills and a glass of water.

"Are you all right?" he asked softly as she swallowed them both with one gulp. She knew he wasn't asking her about her pain. She could feel the tension coming off of him in waves. He was worried about something else.

She handed him her empty glass and let out a sigh. She wanted to tell him that she was fine, that nothing had changed. And nothing had changed between *them*. She loved him, and she had gone through a lot to be able to call him hers. She wasn't about to just turn tail and run. But this was a lot deeper than she had originally thought.

"Why didn't you tell me any of this before?" she finally asked in a quiet voice.

She was picking at her quilt, but she didn't miss his wince. "You were in shock over what happened to Abraham. I was a stranger. I didn't want to overwhelm you. And when I saw you for the first time... My protective instincts went into overdrive. I thought that the less you knew, the less of a danger you would be to whomever had killed Abraham. I know, that was stupid. Knowledge is the best defense. Abraham taught me that, too. I knew I would have to tell you eventually, but I wanted to put it off as long as I could. You're a Scholar, through and through. The Templars are.... Well, we're not exactly nice people, and I guess I didn't want you to see it. Didn't want you to know that there was that side to *me.*"

She smiled at him. "Would've made a hell of a pick-up line, though. 'Hello. My name is Rhys Blackwood, and I literally am a knight. I left my shining armor back at home. Wanna come see it?' You'd have women throwing themselves at you all day long."

He threw back his head and laughed, and she relaxed at the relief she could hear in it. "I'm hardly Lancelot."

120

She made a face. "For which I am glad. I always thought Lancelot was a bastard. Cheating on his wife with his best friend's wife. I mean, he's the whole reason Camelot failed. I don't know why people romanticize him. All of Arthur's knights were fallible. Except for Gawain. But he was a prude."

Rhys was still grinning as he sat down next to her. "Only you could compliment someone by using the legends of Arthur. And I am glad that you are not running away screaming."

She sighed and reached out for him. "Rhys, I think it's safe to say at this point that it will take something *very* bad to send me running. I love you. *All* of you. The good, the bad, and the ugly. Although I have a feeling that what you and I classify as good, bad, and ugly are very different."

He paused, his eyes going down so that they wouldn't have to meet hers. "I've killed people, Anna," he said softly. "More than I can count. And even more people have died because of me."

She swallowed at his admission, but she would not be deterred. "You have to do not-so-nice things. I get that. But you do it to help people. You're a good man, Rhys Blackwood, with a good heart." She paused. "Do you really not have a choice?"

He shook his head. "No. It's expected of us. Our ancestor was one of the nine original knights that formed the order. He swore upon the Temple Mount that he and his descendants would always protect those who cannot protect themselves. Now, we can have careers. Like Nic, who is a counselor. But we *must* undergo training and we *must* answer any call that goes out for help. If I were to turn away from this, say that I didn't want to be a knight, I would have been disowned by all of my family and friends. That's why I said it would be very difficult for a Templar to be a traitor. One of my earliest memories is of my father taking me to a graveyard and showing me the dates on the tombstones. All of the ones he showed me were children. And he told me that my goal in life was to make sure that there weren't any more tombstones like that."

She winced. "That's pretty rough for a kid."

"Maybe. But I never forgot it. And he was right. Protecting others is who I am, *what* I am. I could never be anything else. It's as much a part of me as my eye color or height."

She shifted her body enough so that she could look up at him, reaching out to touch his face. He closed his eyes, leaning into her touch. She traced his cheek, then slid her fingers along the outline of his jaw. She could feel the stubble that was growing there.

Then her fingers were skimming across his lips, and she could feel his breath, warm against her skin. She let them rest there, memorizing the shape of his mouth, remembering the way it felt against hers. She couldn't help but wonder what it would feel like to have those lips on other parts of her body. She wished she didn't have all of the stiches so that she could find out right now. She knew he wouldn't touch her while she was still injured. At least, not like *that*.

She let out a sigh and dropped her hand, feeling her face flush. Rhys wasn't the only one whose control was in danger of coming undone.

He caught her hand before it hit the bed and pressed it back to his lips. "I am so sorry I screwed up," he murmured. "I never should have told you it was a mistake to kiss you. It wasn't a mistake. I never thought kissing you was a mistake. It was just the way I had kissed you that ---"

"Hush." She pinched his lower lip. "We've already established that you are an idiot, and I've forgiven you for it. It's over and done with. I don't want to hear about it anymore."

He sighed. "I know. I just hate that we missed all of this time together."

She couldn't help but grin. "Don't worry. I'll make sure you make it up to me. Several times over."

Her medicine must have been stronger than she thought, because he was still laughing when she fell asleep.

Chapter Twenty

As promised, David took up her tutelage as a Scholar, shooing Rhys out of the house for a few hours every day so that he could explain things to Anna. And, she was sure, to get Rhys out of the house before he drove them all insane. Finn came by one day, bringing her a bouquet of flowers which he shyly presented. She had been delighted. Rhys hadn't looked happy until Finn also said that he wanted to get a statement from her about her abduction. Rhys's jealousy had delighted her almost as much as the flowers. Maggie brought the monk's journal and the noblewoman's ledger for her to work on.

Her favorite parts of the day, however, were when it was just her and Rhys. He had finally realized that he wasn't going to break her, and would lie down next to her every time she would get ready to sleep. They would simply lie next to one another, his arms curled around her like a protective cage, and talk. He told her of how they had discovered she was missing, and how they had found her. She had let out a cheer when he told her that Pelley had been apprehended. When they weren't talking, they were kissing or touching, exploring one another as much as was possible. She could feel his muscles underneath his shirt, and fervently told her body to heal faster so that she could convince him to let her to take the shirt off and see what lay beneath.

Finally, after what seemed more like a year than a week, Anna returned to the hospital to have the doctor who had treated her check her over once more. She had already told Rhys that if he didn't remove her stiches and let her return to work, she was going to throttle him.

Thankfully, the doctor declared that she was healing very nicely, and when she finally left the hospital, she walked out with only a slight limp, stich free. She still had bandages covering her arm and leg, but she could deal with that. Bandages were better than stiches. She danced all the way to the car.

Rhys grinned as they got into his car. "Let's go celebrate. Fish and chips?"

She returned to work the next day, wearing a new sweater Nicola had bought for her so that she could hide the fading bruises that still encircled her wrists, left there by the ropes Graham had used as restraints. Rhys had driven her to the library, promising to be back to pick her up later that afternoon. After a lingering kiss that made her tingle in all the right places, she pulled herself out of his car and walked through the front door.

Maggie was waiting for her, a large smile plastered on her face. "Anna," she said, coming forward to embrace the younger woman. "It is *so* good to have you back!"

"Thank you," Anna replied. "It is good to be back."

Maggie laughed. "I wouldn't say that just yet. You haven't seen what I have waiting for you." With an apologetic smile, she led Anna down the hall into the younger woman's office.

Anna's eyes went wide as she stepped through the door. There were book totes stacked three high along one wall of her office. She wasn't sure how many there were. She lost count after fifteen. She was certain they hadn't been there when she had left for her ill-fated lunch date with Graham over a week ago.

She turned to her boss, one eyebrow arched in question.

Maggie let out a sigh. "We received a collection of books from a library in Edinburgh. Apparently, it was something that Abraham was working on at the time of his death. I didn't know anything about it until a few days ago, when the truck rolled up and started unloading the totes. These are all yours, apparently. The other library is closing, so their entire collection was sent to us."

Anna let out a sigh, hands on her hips, lips twisted in a wry grin. "You sure do know how to throw a welcome-back party."

Maggie patted Anna's arm. "I've already installed the inventory system on your computer, and you have the label printer as well. Do you know how to operate everything?"

"I do." It had been the first thing Abraham had taught her to do, so that she could get used to the Bradley's filing system.

"All right. I'll leave you to it, then." She grinned widely and gave Anna another hug. "It really is good to have you back. The library feels empty without you here." She turned and headed back towards her own office.

Anna sighed and eyed the numerous totes, ready for her to empty them of their contents. "Well, no use standing around waiting!"

By the end of the day, Anna was well and truly irritated. She was only on the third tote. The two other librarians had come by to chat, eating up much of her time. They claimed they only wanted to check on her, but she knew that they were chomping at the bits to find out what had happened to her. When she only responded with polite chatter instead of the gossip they had wanted, they just continued to talk. Between them and the researchers who had come in requesting texts, she did not get to devote much time to the totes.

The time she *did* get to spend on them did not fare much better. Many of the books were small, with cramped handwriting. By the time she deciphered the title and the author, entered it into the computer system and carefully placed the label containing the call number on the inside front cover, she was spending over an hour on each book.

When a shadow fell across her desk later in the evening, she had to force herself to put a smile on her face and not snap at whomever had entered her office. When she looked up, however, she found herself face-to-face with a large bouquet of flowers. She blinked, then followed the arm holding the flowers up to find Rhys's face smiling shyly down at her.

"Here," he said softly. "I thought you might like these. For your first day back at work."

She felt all of her irritation drain away as she took the flowers from him and brought them to her nose, breathing deeply. "Thank you, Rhys. These are beautiful." She paused. "How did you know daisies were my favorite?"

His smile widened, and the light that lit up his eyes made her heart sing. "I didn't. I just... They reminded me of you. Roses are so cliché, and I wanted something colorful."

The smile she had on her face was genuine as she rose and leaned forward to kiss him. "They are perfect. Let me see if I can find something to put them in."

"I, ah, took care of that, too." He held out a paper-wrapped package. "I didn't think you would have a vase lying around."

She felt her heart swell as she took it from him, unwrapping it to find a large, green vase. Green, she remembered, was his favorite color. "You know, I could get used to having you spoil me."

His eyes were shining. "Good. Because I plan on doing it a lot."

She left to go fill the vase --- he had told her jokingly that he had not brought any water --- and when she came back she found him eyeing the totes with curiosity. "What are all of these?" he asked.

She let out a sigh as she sat the vase on her desk and placed the flowers inside. "Apparently, Abraham had bought a collection from a library that was closing in Scotland. They all arrived the other day. I've been working on it all day and feel as though I haven't gotten a thing done." She made a face. "It's going to take me forever to get them all catalogued and put away."

Rhys made a sympathetic noise. "Well, at least you can't say that your job is boring."

She chuckled. "No. I suppose I can't."

Anna hadn't been happy upon learning that Rhys was planning on meeting with Finn. She was, she had confessed, still afraid that he was going to run off and play hero behind her back. He reminded her that he had promised not to, that they would do things together, just as she had asked. But he couldn't just sit back and do nothing, either. So he was going to find out what Finn had learned about her abductor.

When Rhys opened the door to let his friend in, Finn had immediately broke out into a smile. "Well," he said appreciatively, giving Rhys the once-over. "You are looking much better than you did the last few times I saw you."

Rhys shrugged, a grin spreading across his own face. "What can I say? Anna's okay. She went back to work a few days ago, her stiches are out, and she loves me. All is well in my world."

The policeman gave a firm nod. "Good. I'm glad someone has finally gotten a hold of you. It took long enough." He walked towards the kitchen. "Now, if we can just find her kidnapper, we can put this whole mess to bed."

Rhys pulled two beers from the fridge while Finn settled at the island, setting a stack of documents down in front of him. "I thought you would be interested to know that Pelley finally woke up and decided to talk." His tone was conversational as he took the bottle from Rhys, but his eyes were sharp.

"Oh?" Rhys's own tone was nonchalant as he sat on a stool across from the other man. "What did the good inspector have to say for himself?"

"Several things. Several *interesting* things. But the most important is that he never saw who hit him that night on the docks. And Ollie Wyman is claiming that whoever hit him was gone before he had time to realize what was going on."

"You're right. That is interesting. Imagine, someone who is running around knocking out bad guys before vanishing. Sounds like this person could be a menace. Is anyone making an effort to find this miscreant?"

Finn's lips twitched. "Not really. There are no leads, and my superiors feel as though our talents could best be used elsewhere. It is an open investigation, though."

"Mmm." Rhys took a swig of his beer.

The policeman couldn't stop a chuckle as he pulled out a small folder and handed it to the other man. "Well, since you have no insight into *that* particular crime, let me tell you what we've discovered about our man Pelley. His real name is Freddy Ingham. I was beginning to think we would never discover what his real name was. He managed to bury it under so many layers, our guys nearly gave up. It takes time, experience, and a lot of money to bury your real identity that deep. Near as we can tell, he's been living as Henry Pelley for fifteen years or so."

Rhys's eyes lit up in understanding. "That was about the time Thurston broke from the Scholars. It can't be a coincidence." He opened the folder Finn had given him to find a mug shot of the man he had known as Henry Pelley, though it had obviously been taken several years ago. "And I'm willing to bet it was Thurston's money that got him the new identity, as well as Thurston's idea to pick that name."

"That is what we are assuming as well. Pelley --- excuse me, Ingham --- won't name names. But he's answering enough for us to make educated guesses. He told us that he has been a con man his whole life. He had just done time for embezzlement when a man approached him asking him if he would like a job. He had to become a cop, but he would have a new identity, and he had to be willing to, and I quote, 'clean up the other man's messes'. He said the other man promised him he would pay him well for his services. He agreed, and he had all of the papers claiming him to be Henry Pelley less than a week later."

Finn's voice held a touch of anger, and Rhys couldn't blame him. He imagined it couldn't be easy, knowing that the police force had had a mole for over a decade without anyone ever suspecting him.

Rhys flipped a page in Ingham's folder, showing him a list of all the crimes the man had been arrested for before he became Henry Pelley. "What did he have to say about Abraham's death? About the book? About Anna?"

"He confirmed our suspicions that Thurston had him transfer to our station when Anna came to London. He said that his employer was concerned about her being the old man's replacement, so he wanted Pelley to be close by so he could keep an eye on things."

Rhys's eyes narrowed. "So he *was* watching her." His voice came out in a growl. The idea of Ingham stalking Anna made him wish he'd hit the other man harder.

Finn nodded. "Aye. But he was only there to watch, nothing else. Then, about a month ago, Thurston called him and said he wanted him to watch the library carefully. That something important had happened and he wanted to know if there was any extra activity at the library. You know, the same people coming every day, maybe staying late. I take it this was around the time you all found out there was a chance this book of yours had been sent to the Bradley?"

Rhys nodded, his frown deepening. It had been almost the *exact* time they had found out. That meant that Thurston's informant was someone close to Abraham, and that did not sit well with Rhys at all. "So if Thurston just had him watching the place, why the attempted robbery? What triggered that? And why did he have Abraham killed?"

"According to Ingham, Abraham's death was an accident, just like Anna said. As to why Thurston chose that day to try and find out about the book, Ingham said Thurston had called him and said something about knights being involved, and that they needed to try and find whatever it was they were looking for before the knights did."

Rhys blew out a breath. "This isn't good," he said grimly. "He's admitting that Thurston knew almost at the same time *we* did about the letter that was found in Turkey, *and* that he knew Abraham had asked me to keep an eye on Anna." He paused to raise his bottle to his lips. "I knew that Abraham was worried about something happening. He must have suspected a traitor amongst the ranks. That was why he had me come to meet Anna in the first place. I wonder if he realized how *close* the traitor was."

"Ingham claimed that he reported to Thurston that he saw a car --- I'm guessing it was *your* car --- at the library the night Abraham died, but he left when the two killers fled, so he never saw you or Anna leave. He said that made Thurston very angry, and that was when he began to arrange Anna's kidnapping. He said that he was furious with the other two men for killing Abraham, because now their best lead was gone, and the only other person who might know something was being guarded by two knights. Apparently, when Ingham came to your house as Pelley, he was supposed to try and grab Anna if he saw her here. When he didn't, Thurston had the other two men start tailing you in hopes they could somehow get Anna away from you long enough to snatch her."

Rhys gritted his teeth and clutched his bottle so hard his knuckles turned white. "And I almost handed her over to them gift-wrapped," he said. "I *never* should have taken her to that stupid street fair. If she hadn't heard them…"

Finn waved his hand dismissively. "That's in the past now. No sense worrying about it any longer. When they failed to grab her there, Ingham said Thurston nearly lost it. But then Anna returned to her flat without you, and that was when he decided to try and gain her trust until he could kidnap her himself. He said the last time he spoke to Thurston was when he called Thurston to let him know that we were looking for Ollie Wyman in connection with the kidnapping. Apparently, the plan had been for Thurston to keep Anna until the police started getting close, then he was going to leave her in some deserted area and have a junkie take the fall for her death."

The bottle broke in Rhys's hand. He didn't even seem to notice it. "So the plan *was* to kill her?" His voice was quiet. Only the violent light in his eyes betrayed his rage.

Finn looked at the glass shards and foaming beer that had spilled out over the island and moved his papers before they could become ruined. "Apparently so. As far as Ingham knew, the plan was for Thurston to keep her as long as he needed to. He figured that Thurston would be able to get all of the information he needed from her. Then he would kill her to both keep her from talking, and as a warning to the knights and the Scholars. When he told Thurston that we were already looking into Ollie Wyman, he told Ingham to have Wyman take the blame for it. He was going to kill Anna and set Ollie up as the murderer." He gave the other man a wolfish smile. "But then someone whacked him on the back of the head while he was talking to Wyman, and he has no idea what happened after that."

Rhys only grunted as he rose to find a towel to mop up the mess he had made. "Thurston probably thought Anna would die of her wounds before we could find her." *I'm going to kill him,* he thought savagely. *I am going to rip him to shreds so that there is no chance he can ever hurt her again.* "But she didn't. And now he's lost his police insider as well as one of his fall guys. I doubt he can be too happy about that."

"I would imagine not." Finn took another sip of beer. "You're bleeding, by the way."

Rhys blinked and looked down at the damp towel he held. Sure enough, there were dark red smears. And now that he was paying attention to it, his could feel his hand stinging. He held up the hand that had crushed the beer bottle and saw red streams pouring all over his palm. A few shards of glass were still embedded in his skin.

He swore and moved to the sink so he could run cold water over his hand and carefully pick out the shards. "What else did you find?" he asked, wincing as the stinging increased.

"I was also able to find out a few things about our good friend Graham Thurston." Finn didn't bother to mask the anger in his own voice. While he didn't have the same level of rage that Rhys did towards Anna's abductor, he still had hurt someone that Finn considered to be under his protection. And that was enough to rile the policeman. "From what I can tell, he's been a busy little bee."

Rhys had retrieved a first-aid kit from one of the kitchen cabinets and was pouring alcohol over his hand, hissing at the pain. "Busy how?'

"Ingham isn't the only one he's paid off to become someone else. And, according to the financial records I was able to obtain, he has made several large investments into several different companies." He gave a humorless smile. "Including an architectural firm that happens to be responsible for building the subdivision he took Anna to."

"So *that's* how he knew the gate code." Rhys wrapped a bandage around his injured hand. "All he would have to say is that he wanted to come and inspect his investment. Did the developer know him?" Deciding that he had done the best he could with his wound, he went to rejoin Finn at the island.

"Aye. When I showed him Thurston's photo he recognized him. But he had never formally met him, only knew that he was one of the investors. Didn't even know his name." Finn handed over another file. This one was thicker than Ingham's had been. Opening it, Rhys saw a list of companies and ventures Thurston had invested in.

He let out a long whistle. "There's not much in London he doesn't have his hand in." He flipped a page, and his eyes narrowed on one name in particular. "Including, it would seem, the Bradley Library."

"Mmm. I thought you might find that interesting." Finn's eyes were glittering. "We can be reasonably certain that Abraham was not your traitor. But seeing the library on that list makes me think that whoever it is could be connected that way. The library is run by a board of directors, right? Would they have been alerted that a very important book might possibly be at the Stacks?"

"I don't know. I'll have to ask Maggie. But I know several members of the board are Scholars." The connection between Thurston and the library made him uneasy. "That does seem to be the best bet, though. I can see the Scholar who discovered the letter alerting Scholars who were on the board of directors. I'll ask Maggie to get a list and send it to you."

Finn nodded. "Good." He picked up another file and thumbed through it. "I also managed to track down some of Thurston's known associates. People that he has *legally* worked with." His lip curled at the corner. "Did you know that he advertises himself as an antiquities dealer? Has a website and everything."

Rhys snorted and reached for the file. "'Antiquities dealer', my arse. The man is a snake."

"Agreed, but he is a very *clever* snake." Finn drained the last of his beer and sat the bottle down with a loud *thump*. "His whole business is very legal. And, I might add, very lucrative. The man has a lot of money to throw around. He has all of the proper documentation and licenses to do what he does. Of course, a lot of the people who buy from him probably don't ask where the pieces he has for sell come from. I worked a case a few years back where this collector paid someone more money than I will ever see in my lifetime for some 'authentic' military uniform. He never asked where the chap he bought it from had gotten it. Turns out, the 'dealer' had dug up several war graves in order to get all of the pieces needed to complete the uniform. And the wealthy bastard just wanted it so he could show it off to his pals."

Rhys could understand Finn's anger and disgust. That was what *he* was for. Well, the Templars. And the Scholars. If they had known about a man digging up graves for pieces of a uniform, they would have put a stop to it. Quickly and quietly. And they would have made sure that the wealthy collector understood that he would need to check his dealer's references more carefully in the future, or there would be consequences.

"So Thurston has his sticky little fingers in every aspect of London business so that he can find out through his contacts when something interesting comes along." Rhys began flipping through the last folder. "And then he acquires it by whatever means necessary and sells it to whomever will pay him the most money."

"And people pay him even *more* money to find them specific pieces, just like you said. Then he uses the money he earns to buy even more people off. You have to admit, its genius. Illegal and black-hearted, but genius."

"I've always heard most killers are geniuses." Rhys paused. "What about the two who killed Abraham? Do we have any idea who they are?"

Finn shook his head. "No. I used the descriptions you gave me along with the last name Sanderson that Anna got, but I haven't had any luck. My guess, from what the two of you have told me, is that they are mercenaries. Happens to a lot of guys who get discharged from the military. They still want to kill, but now they can't do it legally. Thurston probably just hired them as thugs."

"You're probably right, which doesn't help us much at all." Rhys paused. "Do we have any idea as to where Thurston is now?"

He tried to keep the eagerness out of his voice, but by the sharp gaze Finn leveled at him, he hadn't been successful. "I have a few different places I'm going to check out. He has a residence listed here in London, but when I looked into it, I found out that someone else has been living there for several years. Right now, we're looking into places owned by the companies he's invested in, but, as you saw, there are a lot." He shrugged. "Besides, if he was smart --- and he's proven that he is --- he'll have tucked his tail between his legs and left London in a hurry. But we're looking for him. I promise you that. In the meantime, you can sit back and *try* to relax."

Rhys sighed. "Yeah. I can try all I want, but there will be no relaxing until I know he's been dealt with." He looked at the clock above the kitchen sink and rose to his feet. "I hate to rush you, but Anna will be off of work in half an hour. If the traffic gods smile down on me, I can make it with five minutes to spare."

Rhys spent the whole trip trying to think of ways to tell Anna that she couldn't work at the library any more before giving it up for lost. He knew he couldn't do that to her, no matter how much it terrified him to know that Graham Thurston might have an insider on the board of directors. She loved her job, and it was so much of who she was. And he couldn't discount what Nicola had told him the day after he'd first met Anna: if he tried to lock her in a cage, she would hate him. Even if it meant keeping her safe, he couldn't do that to her. Or to himself.

It was that last bit that bothered him the most. He was a Templar Knight, a protector. That was who and what he was, what he had always been, what he always would be. He had been taught from birth that the lives of others were of higher value than his own. If he had to sacrifice himself to save the life of another, he would count it as an honor.

But that was before Anna. *"It's not just you anymore,"* she had told him in the hospital after overhearing his plan to lure Thurston out into the open. And she was right. If she had been anyone else, he would have gone through with his plan regardless of her protests. But he loved her, and the idea of hurting her made him grip his steering wheel hard enough to turn his knuckles white. If he died, it would most certainly hurt her. So he could no longer carry on the way he had done before. It was going to be hard.

"We'll figure it out together." The rest of her words made him smile and relax his grip. This was a new experience for him. He had never been in love before, never had found anyone who made his heart race the way Anna did. It changed everything he had ever known, everything that had been ingrained in him. But she was worth it, and he was willing to adjust as needed. And that included not locking her in her room while he ferreted out Thurston's informants.

When he pulled into the library's parking lot, he still had two minutes before the Bradley closed for the evening. He got out of his car and leaned against the hood. His eyes swept over the parking lot, taking in the few cars that were left in the lot. He found Maggie's, then focused on the other two. He didn't recognize either of them, but that didn't matter. That meant that there were at least two other people in the library with Anna that he didn't know.

Maybe they belong to the other librarians, he thought. He knew that Anna wasn't the only librarian who worked under Maggie, though he had yet to meet the others. He would have to ask Anna if she knew what they drove, or if they drove at all. He knew it would help to ease his mind.

He didn't know how long he stood there, evaluating his surroundings and gauging their threat level, when a sound made him turn his head. He watched as Anna breezed through the doors, talking with another, older woman that Rhys didn't recognize.

A smile stretched widely across his face as he watched her laugh at something the other woman had said. He couldn't help it. She just had that effect on him. He would go to the ends of the earth to hear her laugh.

She turned her head and caught sight of him, and he watched as her lips turned up into a shy smile. This made his own smile widen even more. He wasn't sure what amazed him more: the deep feelings that he felt for her, or the fact that she somehow had the same feelings for him. Knowing that he was the cause of that smile made him all the more determined to do whatever he had to do to make her happy.

She came down the stairs slowly. His sharp eyes noticed that she still limped, but it wasn't nearly as bad as it had been. The wound that Thurston had given her leg wasn't as severe as the one on her arm, but it still had been a bad one. When she had returned to work the other day, anyone would have noticed how heavily she favored her non-injured leg. Now, however, he doubted anyone who wasn't looking for it would have noticed.

At the bottom of the stairs, Anna said goodbye to her companion, who walked briskly to one of the other cars that were still in the parking lot. Anna came over to where Rhys was waiting, her smile growing wider with each step. "Hi."

"Hi, yourself." He nodded at the other woman's car. "New friend?"

Anna chuckled. "One of the other librarians. She is a gossip hound. She's never spoken more than a few words to me since I started working here, but she has been trying all week to find a way to get me to talk about what happened to me when I went missing. I've been trying to get her to leave me alone, but today she agreed to help me catalogue the rest of the books that I had in the totes. So I told her all of the gruesome details. I'm sure she's going to be calling everyone she's ever met tonight to tell them about it, but all of my books are inventoried and put away." From her smug tone, Anna felt she had gotten the better end of the bargain.

He couldn't help but laugh. *That's my girl,* he thought proudly. He brought his hand up to her face and leaned in for a kiss, but was stopped by her gasp. "What happened?" she asked, reaching up to remove his hand from her face so that she could examine it.

He blinked, confused, than realized she was holding his bandaged hand. "It's nothing," he told her. "A bottle broke in my hand. I have a lot of small cuts, nothing drastic." He grimaced. "Stung like hell, though."

She looked at him sympathetically, then brought his hand up to her lips so that she could gently kiss his fingers. A warm glow began to spread out from his belly. "At least it didn't require stiches. Those suck."

He chuckled as he took his hand back so that he could open the passenger side door for her. "So I've heard. Shall we go home?"

Chapter Twenty-One

Something was wrong.

Rhys couldn't put his finger on it, but he could feel it. He had just returned home, and there was a quiet, a *stillness*, that made goose bumps appear on his arms and the hair on the back of his neck stand up.

"Nicola?" he called out cautiously. "Anna? Where is everyone?"

No one answered him, and the feeling of *wrongness* intensified.

Rhys reached around to touch the butt of his gun, which was tucked into the waistband of his jeans. He didn't remember putting it there, but he rarely went anywhere without it anymore, not since Anna had been kidnapped. Reassuring himself that the gun was still there, he began to cautiously move through the house.

For some reason, he found himself walking slowly up the stairs to his bedroom. He had a feeling that he would find Anna there. Nicola had been trained to take care of herself. Anna had not. And he'd be damned if he lost her again.

As he approached his bedroom, however, his bad feeling grew even worse. *Don't open that door,* something whispered in the back of his mind. *You don't want to see what's there.*

But he *had* to find Anna. And she was there. He just *knew* it. So, swallowing the fear that just wouldn't go away, he pushed his bedroom door open.

The first thing he noticed was that Anna was, in fact, there. She was sitting on his bed, leaning back against the headboard.

Rhys stood in the doorway and sagged in relief. "Anna," he breathed. "My God, you gave me a scare. Did you not hear me calling for you?"

No answer.

Rhys frowned. *She must have fallen asleep.* "Anna?" he tried again, moving around to the side of the bed so he could see her. "Are you al---"

His words died away as he was finally able to face her, and he suddenly felt as though a giant had punched him square in the gut at the same time someone else was crushing his windpipe. He couldn't breathe. He had to clutch the headboard to keep from falling over.

Anna was wearing a flimsy white nightgown that he had never seen before, and some distant part of his brain wondered if she had meant to surprise him with a romantic evening.

But it would never happen now. For while Anna looked at him through half-lidded eyes, the wide gash across her throat ensured that she would never touch him again.

Rhys raised a trembling hand to his mouth, feeling as though he were about to be sick. Blood had soaked the front of her nightgown and was pooling around her on the bed. Her hair, which she had left down, was crusted with blood.

Rhys had no doubt that she was dead. But still, he had to check. He had to know for sure.

"Anna?" he whispered, gingerly reaching out to her. "Please, sweetheart. Say something. *Anything*. I ne---"

Her skin was cold. She had been dead for some time.

Rhys blinked, then threw his head back and let out a howl. "*No!*" he screamed as he pulled her lifeless body against him. "You can't *have* her! *Please!*" He began to rock her back and forth as hot tears started to fall. "Anna," he sobbed. "Don't leave me. *Please*. I'll do anything. I can't---"

Suddenly, the whole room started to shake. Startled, Rhys looked up, blinking the tears out of his eyes and he tried to determine what was happening.

"Rhys!"

He let out a gasp as he heard the voice faintly call his name. That had been *Anna's* voice! But she ---

He looked down and blanched.

Anna's body was gone. The blood was still there, but his arms were now empty.

"Anna!" he cried out, fear and panic taking over as the room began to shake even harder. "Where are you? *Anna!*"

"Rhys! Wake up! It's okay!"

With a gasp, Rhys sat straight up, his eyes flying open. He blinked, than began to struggle as he realized he was still in his bedroom. "Anna!" he called out, trying to climb out of his bed. "Anna, I ---"

"I'm right here, Rhys," came a voice from his left, full of alarm and concern. And oh so familiar.

He whipped his head around, and let out a gasp at what he saw there.

It was Anna, *his* Anna, alive and whole. Gone was the bloodied white nightgown, replaced by a t-shirt and a pair of shorts. Her hair was pulled back into a ponytail, and her eyes were open and full of worry.

Rhys felt a sob break in his chest. "Anna..."

"It's okay," she said softly, moving forward so that she could put her arms around him and pull him against her. "You were having a nightmare. It's over now."

He felt a shudder ripple through his body as he recalled the clarity of the blood and her empty, staring eyes. "I thought --- I thought ---"

"Shhh." She brushed his sweat-soaked hair away from his face. "I'm here. You're safe now. I'm not going anywhere. Oh, Rhys. You're shaking!"

He couldn't speak. He couldn't think, couldn't move, couldn't breathe. All he could do was desperately clutch at her has he tried to convince himself that it all had just been a nightmare, that she was real.

Anna reached out to gently wipe the tears from his face. "I could hear you screaming from downstairs," she said softly. "What can I do to make it better?"

133

You already have, he thought. Instead of speaking, however, he leaned up so that he could press his lips to hers. It was a desperate kiss, full of hunger and need. His mouth filled with her taste, and he could feel his body began to relax as he realized that she was, indeed, alive. It helped, but he needed more.

His arms snaked around her, crushing her against him. One hand went to cradle the back of her neck, tilting her head to give him better access to her mouth. The other hand slid under her t-shirt to rest on the small of her back. Her skin was warm and solid beneath his trembling fingers.

He released her mouth so that he could bury his nose into the side of her neck, breathing in her scent, letting it fill him. He tried to slide his fingers into her hair, but was stopped by her ponytail. With a growl, he pulled out the hair band so that her hair fell down around her shoulders. He fisted his hand in her hair, tugging gently so that her neck was exposed to him. Starting at her jaw, he began to run kisses down her neck.

Anna let out a gasp as she closed her eyes and leaned her head back further, giving him better access. When he got to her shoulder, he tugged savagely at the sleeve of her t-shirt to expose more skin. He moved his mouth to the hollow of her collarbone and delicately licked the skin there.

He could feel her shudder beneath him, and then her mouth was at his ear. "Rhys," she whispered, her warm breath washing across his neck. He could feel her hands at his waist, then she slipped them under the hem of his shirt.

Something in his mind screamed a warning, and even through the heady mix of relief and desire, he heeded it. He reached down to grasp her wrists and pull her hands away. "Wait," he gasped as he sat back. "Wait."

Her eyes were nearly his undoing. They were glittering with a need and hunger that nearly matched his own. She let out a growl, then leaned forward so that she could run the tip of her tongue around the outside of his ear. "If you stop now, Rhys Blackwood," she warned, "so help me God..."

He closed his eyes and took a deep breath to calm himself. "Anna, please. Stop. I need... There's something you should see first."

She let out a sigh, but she leaned back away from him. "What is it? Do you have a third nipple or something?"

He offered a small smile. "Not exactly. Just... Please don't leave. Even when you see, don't leave. I still need you here, no matter what." His voice was barely more than a whisper.

Her eyes softened, and she pulled one of her hands free of his to reach up and touch his face. "Of course I won't leave. Nothing could drag me away from you. You know that."

"Promise me."

She sighed. "I promise."

He gave her a curt nod, then blew out a long breath. Closing his eyes, he reached down, grasped the hem of his t-shirt, and pulled it up over his head.

He heard her gasp, but didn't open his eyes. He didn't want to see her reaction, too afraid that there would be a look of disgust on her face. Pity, he could deal with. He had learned to deal with that early on. But her disgust would break him.

He knew all too well what she was seeing. He had plenty of scars over his torso, many of them white and faded with age. But on his right side, beginning just under his armpit and running all the way down below the waistline of his pants, she would be seeing red, shiny skin. Some spots were puckered and angry-looking, while others were smooth. Even with several skin grafts, the massive burns he had suffered still left that side of his body little more than scar tissue.

There was silence. Rhys felt his body began to tremble once again, but he did nothing to hide it. He had never exposed himself to anyone who did not know him, who did not know what Graham Thurston had done to him in Prague. Would Anna see him as someone who was hideous and didn't deserve to be touched? He shouldn't have done it, shouldn't have revealed himself to her. The last time someone had seen him like this had been disastrous. But she needed to know. *He* needed her to know. If she wanted to ---

Cool fingers rested lightly on his side, right on the mass of scars, and he sucked in a breath.

"Sorry," he heard Anna apologize, and the fingers retreated. "Did that... Does it hurt?"

He couldn't tell what emotion colored her voice, and he was still too afraid to open his eyes. "No," he murmured. "Not anymore. I'm just... No one has touched me before. I'm not used to it."

"Do you mind if I touch you?"

His eyes flew open at her words, and he made himself look at her, steeling himself for what he would find there.

Her eyes were... He couldn't tell. But they were full of some emotion that were causing them to flash. Her mouth was set in a line. *Anger,* he thought. But no pity. And no disgust.

He could have wept with relief. Instead, he gave her a weak smile. "I think I'll be okay. As long as it's you."

Hesitantly, as if she were afraid she would damage him further, she reached out and gently placed her hand on his stomach, her fingers splayed over the mass of scars that the burns had left behind. He held his breath, his heart pounding, as she gently ran her hand up his torso, coming to a rest on his chest.

She lifted her eyes to his. "Who did this to you?" He had been right. Her voice was definitely angry.

He let out the breath that he'd been holding. "They don't bother you?" he asked, ignoring her question for his more important one.

"No. Well, yes. But not for the reason that you think." She brought her other hand up to also rest on his chest as she looked up into his eyes. "They bother me because it means someone hurt you. They don't make you... *ugly,* or anything." Her cheeks turned red. "They are a part of you, of who you are. They are beautiful in that sense. But they make me angry, because I can tell that ---"

Rhys didn't let her finish. His arms were back around her, and his mouth had claimed hers once more. This time, he pushed her back until she lay on the bed underneath him. "I love you," he murmured in her ear.

She reached up to wrap her arms around him, one hand going to the back of his head. "And I love you." Then she was pulling his mouth back to hers, using her body to ask him for things that her words could not. And he was happy to oblige.

135

His hands reached down to grasp the hem of her t-shirt and tugged upward. She obliging let go of him long enough to lift her arms so he could slide the shirt off. He immediately wrapped his arms around her once more, pulling her tight against him, pressing his chest to hers.

The feel of her skin against his was a balm to his soul. Something inside of him sighed, recognizing her as the other half to himself, the one that made him whole. She was warm and oh so soft.

His mouth left hers to trail kisses down her neck, down her chest, over the swell of her breasts. Then he gently ran his tongue across one of her nipples.

Her response was immediate. A gasp escaped her lips, and her back arched up off of the bed, pressing her breasts closer to him, giving him better access. He obliged, closing his mouth over the stiffened point and sucking gently. One of his hands came up to stroke the other nipple, gently rolling it between his fingers and tugging on it in time with his suctions until both of them were hard.

She let out a little moan and writhed underneath him. "Rhys." His name was a prayer upon her lips, and the hand that rested in his hair tightened painfully.

He left her breasts to return his mouth to hers, his tongue probing at her lips, seeking entrance. Her mouth opened beneath his, allowing him access, and the taste of her flooded him. He let out a moan of his own, letting it fill him. His hands moved down the length of her body to hook into the waistband of her shorts. She arched her hips, allowing him to slide both her shorts and her underwear off.

He pulled away to study her as she lay beneath him, and he had to suck in a breath at what he saw.

Anna blinked up at him, her eyes full of want. "Rhys? What is it?" When he didn't answer, she began to move her arms to cover herself.

"Stop," he said roughly, raising his head to meet her eyes. "Don't you *dare* try to hide your body." He leaned down so that his forehead rested against her stomach, running his nose along her own scar left by Thurston. "You are so beautiful," he whispered.

She let out a sigh and gently raked her nails over his shoulder muscles. "Rhys," she murmured, and her voice was so full of need that he was immediately back over her, his mouth pressed to hers.

He wanted nothing more than to plunge into her right then and there. He was so hard it hurt. But not yet. He was going to take his time. He had been dreaming of this moment for far too long.

His hands trailed down the length of her body, caressing her, skimming over the tops of her thighs to stop where they were pressed together. "Open for me," he whispered against her lips.

She obliged, her legs falling open to allow him access to her. His fingers gently circled her entrance, causing her to emit little gasps that nearly sent him over the edge.

One finger slid in. Both of them moaned against each other, her hips rising off of the bed to meet him. "Anna," he rasped. "My God, you're so wet."

"For you," she panted. "Only for you."

He slid another finger in to join the first. She gasped and fell back, eyes closed.

He gently slid his fingers in and out, moving his head back down to her stomach. He trailed kisses along her scar, still puckered and angry looking. He continued kissing her down her leg, moving to the inside of her thigh.

"Rhys." Her voice was little more than a whimper. "No. I want you. Inside me. Please."

He looked up, letting a smile creep over his face as he met her eyes. "And you'll have me. I promise. But I want to taste you first." He settled himself in between in her legs, placed his free hand on her hips to hold her down, and lowered his head.

While his fingers continued their exploration, he swept his tongue across the tight bud of her sex and was rewarded with a broken cry, her hands scrabbling at his shoulders. "Please," she moaned. "Stop. I---"

He didn't heed her pleas. Instead, he removed his fingers entirely, replacing them with his tongue.

She writhed underneath him, letting out little mewling cries interspersed with pleas for him to stop. He only delved deeper, holding her down so that she could not escape from his ministrations. He could feel her tense, feel her move closer and closer to the edge. And when she finally broke, he did not stop, not until her cries had died and her shuddering had ceased.

He rose back over her again, a smile on his face as he looked down at her.

Her face was flushed, her eyes glazed over. Her hair fanned out around her like a halo, and her chest was heaving with her pants.

He felt himself tighten even harder.

"Rhys," she whispered, but he didn't give her a chance to say anything else. He swooped down, pressing his mouth to hers once again. He felt her hands at his waist, pushing down the waistband of his pants until he was completely naked, hovering above her.

He wasted no time settling himself between her legs once more, his hardened length resting against her entrance. He paused, brushing a lock of hair away from her face so that he could peer into her eyes. "I love you, Anna." So much it hurt.

She smiled up at him, a smile so dazzling it took his breath away. "I love you, too," she murmured. She shifted and lifted her hips, causing him to gasp as he felt his tip slide into her. "Make love to me, Rhys."

He smiled in return. "It will be my pleasure."

She was so warm and slick. He couldn't hold back a groan as he slid into her, feeling her clutch at him as he entered. He pushed until he was fully sheathed in her, and had to stop as lights danced behind his eyes. If he didn't stop, didn't pull himself under control, he would not last a moment longer.

"Are you all right?" he murmured, brushing his nose along the shell of her ear. She was so tight. He didn't want to hurt her, didn't want to ruin the moment by causing her pain.

"Yes," she breathed in reply. Her legs twined around his, her calves resting atop his. "Christ, Rhys. You feel so good."

He let out a growl, buried his face into the side of her neck, and began to move.

It was a slow, almost agonizing pace. He wanted nothing more than to let his inner caveman take over and thrust and thrust until he found his release. But he wouldn't do that. Not with her. Not now. Now he was making her his, and he wanted it to last as long as possible. He wanted to remember this feeling of euphoria, the way he wanted to shout to the heavens that she was undoubtedly *his*. So he moved slowly, taking delight in every gasp that escaped her lips, every moan and whispered word that he elicited from her.

Anna, however, had other ideas. She moved her legs from where they rested on his, wrapping them around his waist instead. She dipped her head to his chest, and he felt her pinch one of his nipples between her teeth.

He let out a gasp and clutched at her as those light danced behind his eyes again. Suddenly, he was no longer in control of his body. His pace picked up, his hips thrusting against hers. He was so close, dangerously so, but he wouldn't let go. Not until ----

He heard her cry out his name as her body tightened around his. As she climaxed yet again, he felt her teeth sink into his shoulder.

That was all he needed.

With a shout he let himself go, feeling his body explode into a thousand sensations, losing himself completely. When he finally became aware again, he was draped over her, body limp. Both were panting.

"Rhys?" He could feel her body, slick with sweat, trembling beneath his. He wanted nothing more than to curl around her, hold her against him, and not let her out of his arms ever again.

He lifted his head to look down at her, feeling his breath catch in his throat at the sight of her. She was beautiful, the most beautiful creature he had ever laid eyes on.

And she was his.

"What was your nightmare about?" Anna asked softly, nuzzling his neck. "You were screaming. It must have been terrifying."

Rhys let out a shudder and tightened his grip on her.

He knew she was okay. She was warm and naked against his skin, her body draped over his. She was alive and as well as possible. But the memory of her blank, staring eyes and the blood staining her hair was still too close to the surface for him to relax completely. "Let's not talk about it," he murmured, pressing his lips to the top of her head. "You and I just made love for the first time. This is easily the happiest moment of my life. I'd rather not ruin it."

She reached up to touch his cheek. "Rhys, you couldn't ruin it even if you tried. I just want to make sure that you are okay. When I first woke you, you looked... I don't know. But it scared me."

I'm sure I looked as though my world had just ended. He reached up to take her hand, kissing her palm before placing it over his heart. "Later. Right now, I just want to hold you."

Anna let out a sigh. Rhys knew that she was still worried, and that she would be until he told her about the nightmare that had upset him so much. But it made him even all the more thankful when she didn't say any more about it. Instead, she pressed herself closer to him, trying to give him as much contact with her skin as she possibly could. "Just right now? I want you to hold me forever."

"Forever it is, then." He paused. "I love you, Anna." His voice was quiet, somber. "More than life. More than *anything*. I will *never* let you go. I promise."

Anna tucked her head under his chin, resting an ear against his chest so that she could listen to his heartbeat. "Good. Cause I'm never leaving. I'm afraid you're stuck with me."

He laughed as he reached down to pull his comforter up further, tucking it around her shoulders. "I think I might be able to live with that. Now. Get some sleep. You have to work tomorrow."

She let out another sigh as she closed her eyes. "Are you sure you're all right?" she asked softly.

"Anna, as long as you are here, nothing could be wrong. I promise."

He could feel the corners of her mouth turn up in a smile. "Good."

He should have been all right. Her arm was tucked around his waist, and one of her legs was wrapped around his. He could feel the rise and fall of her chest, slowing as she drifted off to sleep. His face was buried in her hair, and he had both his arms around her. She was okay. So why wasn't he?

He couldn't even close his eyes without seeing her sitting on his bed, the angry gash across her throat. The iron smell of blood still lingered in his nose, and he could remember the way her cold, dead skin had felt to his touch. His body had been satisfied that she was alive. His soul, however, had not.

Finally, he realized that he was not going to be able to sleep. With a sigh, he gently untangled himself from Anna. She let out a small noise when he slipped away from her, but otherwise didn't move. He brushed her hair away from her face and leaned over to gently place a kiss on her temple. "I'll be right back," he whispered, even though he knew she couldn't hear him.

He found his underwear and pants on the floor and pulled them on before quietly slipping out the door. He had decided to go the kitchen and get a glass of water. When he walked in, he was surprised to find his sister sitting at the island, eating a bowl of cereal.

When Nicola saw him walk in to the kitchen, she froze, her spoon halfway to her mouth. Milk dripped into the bowl, but she didn't seem to notice. Her eyes were fixed onto her brother's exposed chest. When she did lift her eyes to his, he could have sworn that he saw tears. "Rhys?" she said, her voice quiet. "Go back upstairs and marry that girl. *Now.*"

He laughed as he walked past her to the fridge. "I think it's a little soon for that, don't you think? Besides, we have more important things to worry about. Like catching a killer."

She turned on her stool so that she could watch him, her cereal forgotten as she folded her arms over her chest. "I don't care. If you don't want to marry her, just say so. *I* will. Whatever it takes to keep her here with you." She paused, and her voice was very soft when she spoke again. "You won't even let *me* see you shirtless. It has to be Anna."

"You're right. It was." He leaned against the counter, glass of water in hand. He was looking at Nicola, but his eyes had a faraway look to them. "Do you know what she said when she saw me? She wanted to know who had done it to me. Who had *hurt* me. That's all she cared about." He looked down at his glass and smiled. "She said my scars were beautiful. Because they were a part of me."

139

"Oh, Rhys." He could hear the thickness is his sister's voice, and took a drink of water so that he could pretend that he didn't see her wipe tears from the corner of her eye.

"Finn was here earlier today," he continued. "Pelley had talked, and Finn came over to tell me what he had learned. Pelley had confessed that the plan had been for Thurston to kill Anna. And that... I broke a bottle in my hand from squeezing it so hard." He looked down at his bandaged hand and flexed his fingers. "I had a nightmare tonight. It was... bad. And so *real*. I thought she was dead. Anna could hear me screaming from down here and came to check on me. I needed to know she was okay." He felt his face heat up. No matter what, Nicola was his older sister. Just the thought of discussing what had lead him to be shirtless with her made him squirm. But she only gave him a knowing grin, which made him blush even harder. "I still can't sleep. She's there, and I know she's okay. But every time I close my eyes, I still see the other her." He let out an involuntary shudder.

"You could try a glass of warm milk," she suggested. "I've always heard that works."

He shrugged. "I'm not going to get any sleep tonight. I already know that. I just thought I'd come and get a drink of water." He nodded at her bowl of cereal. "What about you? What are you doing in here eating at..." He glanced at the wall clock. "Two-thirty in the morning."

She shrugged as she turned back to her cereal. "I woke up and I was hungry. I came in here looking for a snack, and really couldn't find anything I wanted. I figured this would fill me up and not be too bad for me." She gave him a wide grin. "By the way, it is about damn time you took her to bed. I can't believe you waited so long!"

Rhys let out a groan and buried his face in his hand, feeling his ears heat up. "Nicola!"

"What? At least *someone* in this house is getting some action!" She pulled her bowl to her and took a happy bite of soggy cereal.

When Rhys was finally able to escape from his sister's interrogation and return to his bedroom --- his face a deep shade of crimson --- Anna was sitting up in bed. "There you are!" she exclaimed softly as he closed the door behind him. Relief was evident in her voice. "When I woke up, you were gone. And I didn't..."

He took two steps into the room and sat on the edge of the bed. "I'm sorry," he said, reaching out to touch her. "I was thirsty, so I decided to go downstairs and get a drink. Nicola was there, and she gave me the third degree about why I was walking around half-naked."

He could feel her smile. "I have no doubt that she did. And it's all right. I was just worried." She paused. "Have you gotten any sleep at all?"

He thought about lying to her, telling her that yes, he had slept. But he couldn't lie. Not to her. So he sighed and shook his head. "No. I haven't slept. I can't."

"Well." She pulled the blanket off of her and moved until she was straddling him. She wrapped her arms around his neck and wiggled her hips, causing him to gasp. He hardened immediately. "Let's see if I can't tucker you out, shall we?"

Anna was not well-versed in the art of sex. She had not had that much practice, and thinking about how long it had been since she had last been with someone was depressing. But her body seemed to meld with Rhys's perfectly, to know what he wanted. In return, he knew just where to touch, where to kiss, to drive her own desire higher and higher. When they finally lay next to one another, panting and trembling, she knew that she was going to be sore in the morning. But she didn't care. It was worth it. *He* was worth it.

Rhys groaned as he rolled over, pulling her to him so he could press his face into her chest. "You," he said earnestly, "are going to be the death of me."

She laughed as she put her arms around him, gently stroking his back. "At least you know you'll die happy."

He chuckled. "That I will."

His body was still trembling, but he could feel a lethargy settle in his limbs. He felt the blanket wrap around him --- Anna must have pulled it back over them --- but he didn't move. Her hands were gentle on his back, soothing, and he could hear her heart beating against his ear. He closed his eyes, let out a satisfied sigh, and was finally able to drift off to sleep.

Chapter Twenty-Two

Anna had been right. When she awoke the next morning, her legs protested at having to work after the unusual workout she had given them the night before. She told her muscles sternly that they were just going to have to deal with it, because she had to go to work.

If it had been up to her, she would have stayed in bed all day. And not just because her legs were as wobbly as a newborn foal's. Rhys lay sprawled on his back, one arm flung over his eyes, snoring softly. She simply sat on the edge of the bed for a long moment, watching him. A grin stretched across her face, and she could feel something break in her chest. She loved this man. Her heart, her soul, and now, her body, belonged to him. She could watch him all day.

But not today. She had to work. So, with a sigh, she headed to the bathroom.

When she finally made it to the kitchen several minutes later, she found Nicola there. The other woman was also dressed, and was leaning against the counter, drinking a glass of orange juice. When she saw Anna, she sat her glass down, walked over, and threw her arms around the younger woman in a tight embrace.

Anna squeaked at the unexpected gesture. "Um. Good morning to you, too," she said in amusement, returning the hug.

Nicola just hugged her tighter. "Thank you," she whispered, and Anna could hear the sound of tears in her voice.

For a moment, Anna was confused. But then she remembered that Rhys had told her Nicola had been down here last night when he had come for a glass of water, what she had said upon seeing her brother with no shirt on, and the older woman's actions suddenly made sense.

Anna hugged her back just as tightly. "I'm glad I was the one who could help," she replied earnestly. "I'm so happy that he let me."

Nicola let out a laugh as she pulled away, running a hand under her eyes. "I told him that he needed to marry you. And that if he didn't, I would. I think he thought I was joking."

Anna ducked her head, blushing. But she was pleased. "We'll just have to wait and see about that. Although, if you end up marrying me, I might make you wear the dress. Just because I want to see you in a dress." She moved past Nicola so she could pour her own glass of orange juice. "Since you are awake and dressed, do you mind taking me to work? Rhys didn't sleep much last night, and I don't want to wake him."

"Sure. I was going to offer anyways. I have a few patients scheduled for today, so I have to go into my office." She grinned. "I'll even take you out to breakfast. My treat. It's the least I can do for you. I haven't seen Rhys that happy in a very, very long time."

Anna smiled in return. "That sounds great. Let me just go leave him a note. I don't want him to panic when he wakes up and I'm gone."

The small café Nicola took her to was the closest thing Anna had ever found to Heaven on Earth, at least in London. The breakfast spread would have done her Southern family and friends proud. There were crepes, fresh fruit, bagels, cream cheese, bacon, and sausage. She ate with gusto, choosing to ignore the look of amusement on Nicola's face.

"So," Anna said, once she finally began to slow down. "I've been meaning to ask you something. When I came back from the hospital, you and David kept talking about Rhys running away. Something obviously happened while I was gone. What was it?"

Nicola looked thoughtful as she took a sip of her coffee. "When you two came back from the street fair, I didn't have a clue about what had happened between you two. I didn't know about the kiss, or what Rhys had said. When he left, I just thought that he was pouting. He felt like he had failed to keep you safe, and I figured he was just too embarrassed to face you. That would be just like Rhys. But then, when *you* left, I knew something was wrong. I didn't ask, because he was already moody."

"Then, after you were gone, he just... disappeared. He didn't tell anyone where he was going. Just vanished. I got a voicemail telling me he was okay, and a few text messages here and there. But I didn't see him for over a week. Neither did David. I called him every day. I begged him to come home. I yelled at him. But nothing."

Anna frowned. "What happened? Where did he go?"

Nicola smiled behind her mug. "I had no idea. Then, on the day you were kidnapped, I found him at home. He looked... awful. He hadn't shaved in days, had lost a lot of weight, and smelled like he hadn't seen a shower in a month. And he was drinking. Before noon. I knew it was bad. When I asked him what was wrong, do you know what he told me?" She took another drink of coffee, letting her companion stew for a moment. "He told me that you had a boyfriend. He said that you didn't need him anymore, so he had come home. And then I realized he had been watching you the whole time. I accused him of stalking you, but he just said he was watching out for you, making sure you were safe. I have no doubt that he was sleeping in his car outside of your apartment. He was with you the whole time. He only left when he saw you leave with Graham, because seeing you with another man broke his heart."

"Oh." Anna dropped her eyes. She felt ashamed, even though she knew she had nothing to be ashamed of. She hadn't known that Rhys was watching her. But she had hurt him, and it still made her heart ache. "I never knew."

Nicola chuckled. "Well, I would hope not. That would defeat the purpose. And, if you *had* seen him, it would mean that he was not doing a very good job. He didn't want you to know he was there." She sighed and leaned back in her chair. "I had just finished lecturing him on how stupid he was and sent him off to take a shower when Maggie called to tell us you were missing."

"No wonder he blamed himself." Anna could remember how upset she had been when she realized he had placed the blame of her kidnapping squarely on his shoulders. "Even though I told him it wasn't his fault."

"And we both know what a fat lot of good *that* did." Her companion sighed. "I've never... He *loves* you, Anna. I have never, *never* seen him look at *anyone* the way he looks at you. And last night, when I saw that he was shirtless... He told me what you said. About his scars. That you thought they were beautiful.

Because they were *his*."

Anna took an angry bite of a crepe. "He thinks he's ugly, doesn't he? That he doesn't deserve to be touched. He didn't *say* anything, but I could see it in his eyes." She stabbed a strawberry. "What happened to him? Who did that to him?" Her voice was a growl.

Nicola was silent, staring down at her coffee cup. The waiter came and filled it. Still she didn't say anything. Finally, she let out a sigh. "This is not the first time we've had a run in with Graham Thurston."

"I know," Anna said, much to Nicola's surprise. "Graham told me that they had met before. He said they were in... Prague. And that they had been after the same thing. I also think... Yes. He had said something about forgetting that Rhys had survived."

"It was seven years ago. There was a Scholar named Bella who lived in Prague. She and David had been lovers at one time, and were still very close. So when she found something interesting, she had called David to tell him." She paused to take another drink of coffee. "I was working on my Masters at the time, so David took Rhys with him and went to Prague to help her."

"What had she found?"

"To be honest, I don't remember. Like I said, I was preoccupied with school, so all I really registered was that they were going to Prague to help Bella. But whatever it was, Thurston had felt it was worth killing for. He threw a bomb into Bella's home. Rhys tried to save her. When I finally heard from David, all he could tell me was that Bella was dead and Rhys was in the hospital."

Anna dropped her fork. She suddenly felt sick. "Poor David," she whispered.

Nicola nodded, her eyes sad. "He took it hard. He felt that he and Rhys had drawn Thurston's attention, since David had once been his mentor. But David hadn't heard from Thurston in nearly ten years, so he hadn't even thought his old student would be a problem. The only reason we even knew Thurston was the one responsible is because they had clashed a few times before Bella's house was bombed. David said that if he hadn't of come, Thurston may have left Bella alone."

Yes, it was evident David and Rhys had spent quite a lot of time around each other. Anna mumbled something in that respect, causing Nicola to smile.

"Was Rhys in the house when it exploded?" was her next question.

"He and David were standing outside. They were getting ready to leave when they saw the car drive by and heard the glass breaking. Rhys ran towards the house. He said he didn't know what had been thrown, but he'd had a bad feeling. He had just reached the door when the bomb went off. The doctors said that is what saved his life. The door itself blew outward and shielded him from the worst of the blast. They said if he had been a split second faster and had managed to get the door open, he would have been dead." She closed her eyes and took a deep breath. She tried not to think about how close she had come to losing him, and it still surprised her how choked up she could get when she talked about it.

When she opened her eyes again, she couldn't miss the hard set of Anna's jaw, or the anger flashing in her blue eyes. "Thurston is dead," she snarled quietly. "I will rip his head off. No, I will rip *other* body parts off and feed them to him. *Then* I'll rip his head off."

144

Nicola laughed. She couldn't help it. The idea of mild-mannered, librarian Anna ripping someone's head off was ludicrous. But the fact that Anna meant it, and that she would do it to avenge a wrong that had been done to Rhys years before she had met him, warmed Nicola's heart. "Well, you're going to have to hope you beat Rhys to him. Because if Rhys gets there first, there won't be any pieces left big enough for you to rip. Especially after yesterday."

Anna paused, her own coffee cup halfway to her mouth. "What happened yesterday?"

"Apparently, Finn came over yesterday to talk about Pelley. I hear he's finally talked."

Anna nodded. "I knew he was coming over, but Rhys didn't mention anything about it when he picked me up from work. I just figured that Finn hadn't found out anything new."

"When Rhys talked to me last night --- or, this morning, rather --- he said that Pelley admitted to the police that the plan had been for Thurston to kill you."

Anna blanched, then swayed in her seat. For a moment, Nicola was afraid the younger woman was going to faint. But then she closed her eyes and began taking slow, deep breaths. After another moment, color began to return to her cheeks. "I thought ---"Her voice broke, and she swallowed. "I thought that was the plan. Thurston didn't seem interested in my well-being, only getting what he needed. Still, hearing Pelley admit to it is a bit... upsetting."

Nicola nodded sympathetically. "It upset Rhys pretty bad, too. He said he broke a bottle in his hand from squeezing it too hard."

"So *that's* what happened," Anna murmured. Then her eyes lit up in understanding. "His nightmare."

"Mmm. That's what I'm thinking, too. He didn't tell me what his nightmare was about, only that he thought you were dead. It must have been his subconscious playing off of what Finn had told him." She offered Anna a sheepish grin. "Sorry. Counselor talk."

"Do you think he's going to be okay?" Anna's voice was soft, her eyes worried.

Nicola's grin grew until is stretched all the way across her face. "If last night is any indication, I think Rhys is going to be *just* fine."

He felt... content. Satiated. He stretched languidly, like a cat, wincing slightly as his thigh muscles protested. That bit of pain brought back the memories of the night before, including his nightmare and the blind panic he had felt when he thought Anna was dead.

With that sobering thought he opened his eyes and turned towards the other side of the bed where Anna had lain the night before. It was empty, and when he placed a hand on the sheets, their coolness told him she had been gone for some time. He would have panicked, but the light streaming through his bedroom window told him that it was late morning. She would have left for work hours ago.

He let out a groan and rolled over, flinging out a hand to grasp her pillow. When he did, he heard a crinkle of paper. Lifting his head, he found a note that had been left on Anna's pillow, his name written across it in her familiar script. Feeling a goofy smile stretch across his face, he pulled it to him and opened it.

"Sorry for not telling you goodbye this morning," she had written. *"But I didn't want to wake you. You need rest. Nicola has agreed to take me to work, so don't worry about me being on the tube. Also, just so you know, my legs aren't working correctly this morning. I blame you."* He felt his face heat up, but he grinned, pleased. *"Last night was... magical. Amazing. A million other things that there are no words for. Thank you. I'll see you this afternoon. Get some rest. Anna."* At the bottom she had added *"Did you know you snore when you sleep on your back? I love you!"*

He laughed, pressing her letter to his lips. His sister had often accused him of snoring, but he chose not to believe her. Apparently, she had been right.

Feeling mollified, he rolled over again until he was sitting on the edge of the bed. Even though he was sad he had missed Anna leaving, he was glad for the extra sleep. She was right. He needed the rest. He had not fallen asleep until after three a.m., and he could be extra cranky when he didn't get enough sleep. And after his nightmare, he was going to be wound up enough as it was.

Except... he wasn't. He wasn't as restless as he had thought he would be. Anna had taken care of that when she had let him claim her, let him prove to himself that she was truly alive. And after both of their lovemaking sessions, his agitation was non-existent. He knew she was okay. Knew it in his head, in his heart, and in his soul.

He also knew that she was well and truly *his*. And he was hers. Last night had cemented that. And the fierce joy that sang through him at that knowledge was enough to drive away any lingering fears.

With a sigh of satisfaction, he pushed himself to his feet and headed to the shower, humming as he did.

Since it was Friday, it was a slow day at the Bradley. That was fine with Anna. All of the books from the Scottish library had been put away. The other female librarian had said hello to her, but avoided her for most of the day. Anna tried to hide her grin. The older woman had gotten what she wanted, and was now going to return to the way things had been before. So Anna was free to work on the monk's journal all afternoon.

Ten minutes before closing, she let out a sigh and looked sadly at the flowers that were still in the vase on her desk. They had already begun to wilt, and she knew that they would not last the weekend. So she made sure to throw them in the trash. But not before she removed a single daisy and placed it between two heavy books. Hopefully, when she came back in Monday, it would be perfectly pressed and preserved. That made her feel better about throwing the beautiful blossoms away.

When she walked out of her office, she found the other female librarian --- *Sarah,* her mind supplied the name --- waiting for her. She gave Anna a kind smile, then offered to walk her out. Apparently, Anna had sold the other woman short. She was pleased to find that she had been wrong.

Much to her delight, she found Rhys waiting for her. He had come on his motorcycle. When he saw her, he grinned and held up the extra helmet.

"Who is that?" she heard Sarah murmur, but Anna ignored her. Instead, she skipped down the stairs, ignoring the protest in her legs, and threw herself at Rhys, kissing him, not caring who saw her.

She heard him chuckle, but he was kissing her back, his arms going around her waist to pull her closer. He tasted of coffee and cinnamon, and she could smell the aftershave that he used. She wanted to bury herself in him.

He pulled away to rest his forehead against hers, gently rubbing his nose against hers. "What did I do to deserve that?" he rumbled.

"You're here," she replied simply. Then, to prove her point, she kissed him again.

The sound of laughter pulled them apart. Turning, they saw Maggie standing by her car. She was watching them with a grin on her face, hands on her hips. "Get a room already!" she called out cheerily. Sarah, Anna noticed, was at the bottom of the steps. She was staring at them openly, but when she noticed Anna was watching her, she flushed and hurried towards her own car.

Rhys laughed and turned to face the older woman, slinging one arm casually across Anna's shoulders. "I don't know if I can wait that long," he called back. "We could just go into the library." He waggled his eyebrows suggestively.

Anna blushed furiously, but Maggie just laughed again. "Be mindful of the cameras," she teased. Then, with a wave, she got into her car.

Rhys watched her go before turning back to face Anna. He leaned down so that he could run his nose down her neck, causing her to shiver pleasantly. "So," he said softly, his nose skimming across her collarbone. "Do you have any plans for this evening?"

"Mmm. Not that I'm aware of." At least, she didn't *think* she did. Then again, she was having a hard time thinking, what with her body singing out at Rhys's touches. "Should I?

"I was hoping that you would let me take you out." He was trailing kisses up the side of her neck, ending behind her ear. She tilted her head back for him.

"Out?" She was beginning to seriously consider taking him back into the library. They could go into the storage closet. Anna was certain there weren't any cameras in there. If she wanted to be honest with herself, she didn't even care about the cameras. They could go into her office. She could just sweep everything off of her desk and let him...

"Aye. It occurred to me that I have yet to take you out on a date. A proper one. So I've made reservations at this great place that's close to Big Ben. You can see the clock from the restaurant. Then I thought we could take a carriage ride back home. It's a full moon tonight, and it should be clear. We'll stay around other people, so Thurston will have to think twice about trying anything."

She opened her eyes to look at him. "Reservations? That sounds fancy."

He grinned at her. "I thought you could wear that black dress. You know, the one you wore to Abraham's memorial? Nicola is already at the house pulling out curling irons and bags of makeup. I'm afraid you may be subjected to her as soon as we get home. I'm sorry. I tried to tell her that you could take care of yourself, but..." He shrugged helplessly.

Anna laughed. Yes, she could imagine what Nicola had said when Rhys tried to curb her enthusiasm. "I don't mind. She'll do a better job than I would anyway. My idea of 'looking nice' is when my hair is down instead of up." She kissed him on the cheek. "You don't have to do this, you know. I don't want you to feel like you... *owe* me or anything for last night."

"Anna." He cupped her face in his hands, forcing her to look up into his eyes. She noticed that he had re-bandaged his hand, and she remembered Nicola telling her that he had broken a bottle when Finn had told him Thurston had planned on killing her. "This is *not* a repayment. Or anything of the sort. I told you the day after I met you that I am old-fashioned. Which means I want to court you. I want to take you out, to buy nice things for you." He reached up to tuck a stray lock of hair behind her ear. "You've already made me the happiest man in the world. I'd like to return the favor."

"Oh, Rhys," she sighed. "I *am* happy. Deliriously so." She kissed him.

"So," he murmured when they parted. "Is that a yes?"

Chapter Twenty-Three

Anna had thought that Rhys was exaggerating his sister's eagerness to make Anna up for their date. Apparently, she had been mistaken.

As soon as Anna walked through the door, Nicola pounced, pushing the other woman towards Anna's bedroom, calling over her shoulder for her brother to go get dressed. Once inside the bedroom, Nicola shut the door and pulled Anna towards the bathroom. "Come on. I only have an hour or so to get you ready. I've already got everything laid out and ready to go."

Anna sat on the toilet, bemused, as Nicola got to work. First, her hair. Nicola began placing hot curlers on Anna's head, expertly pinning them into place. Once she was satisfied with that, she began applying makeup. Anna simply closed her eyes and let Nicola have her way, sneezing once at as the powder the other woman was applying to her cheeks tickled her nose.

Forty-five minutes in, Nicola pulled Anna back into the bedroom, where her black dress lay out on the bed. Anna pulled off her regular clothes and stepped into the dress, letting Nicola zip up the back. Then it was back into the bathroom to finish up. The curlers came out, and Anna donned her jewelry while Nicola finished up her hair.

At long last, Nicola stepped back with a happy sigh. "Done!" she explained, pride evident in her voice. "Take a look and see what you think."

Anna stood to go look in the mirror, and gasped at what she saw.

The woman looking back at her was unrecognizable. Blond hair fell around her shoulders in soft curls that framed her face nicely. Her blue eyes stood out from the dark eye shadow that she herself could never get right. Expert highlights made her cheekbones look sharper, and her lips were stained a red that Anna would never have had the courage to try, but looked absolutely perfect on her.

"Nicola," she whispered, reaching out to touch the mirror. The woman in the glass copied her. "I look... I look..." She could feel her eyes sting, and she blinked furiously.

"No crying," Nicola said sternly. "You'll ruin all of my hard work. And you are already beautiful. This, this is just for fun. This makes you look *hot.*"

Anna laughed, and the tears vanished before anything could be smudged. "You're right. I *do* look hot." She had never been hot before. She reached over to give the other woman a hug.

Nicola accepted it, then pushed her away. "Go. You two need to leave soon if you're going to make your time. Your shoes and the wrap are right by the door. And make sure you order the caramel dessert they have there. It's amazing!"

Anna hurried back out into her bedroom and slipped into the shoes as she pulled the wrap around her. She knew she looked fantastic, and it made her feel... bold. Strong. *Confident.* She liked it.

Head held high and trying to look as though she knew how to walk in heels, she opened the door and stepped out.

Rhys was waiting in the entryway, and she was able to get a good look at him as she and Nicola approached. He was wearing dark slacks and a white dress shirt that went nicely with his dark hair and green eyes. He always looked beautiful, no matter what he was wearing, but Anna found herself enjoying the way the shirt clung to his skin, showing off a hint of the muscles that lay beneath.

He turned to look at her, and the expression on his face made her forget about how good he looked. Though his jaw didn't actually hit the floor, it came awfully close. And his eyes widened to the point she was afraid they might pop out of his head. She came to a stop just in front of him, enjoying the effect she was having on him.

"Anna," he breathed. "You look... Beautiful doesn't even come close." He reached out for her hand. She let him take it, and he lifted it to his lips. "I'm not so sure if I want to take you out looking like that. I'm going to have to fight off every man we run across."

"Probably some of the women, too," Nicola interjected. "Stop drooling, Rhys. You'll get it all over your shirt. Here." She handed Anna a small tube. "Lipstick. I'm sure Rhys will make sure most of it ends up on him before the night is even half over, so you'll need to refresh every once in a while."

Rhys let out an exasperated sigh, and Anna giggled.

"Now go. I don't want you to be late. You kids have fun. I'm not going to wait up. And don't forget, Anna. Order the caramel dessert. And if you want to bring one back for me, I won't complain."

Rhys had called a cab for them, and once they were safely tucked inside he made quick work of her lipstick. Neither of them could keep their hands off of each other. Anna was very thankful for the darkened partition between the front and the back seats. Still, she was sure the cabbie had gotten a good show. She didn't care.

As the cab pulled up to the restaurant, Anna reapplied her lipstick as Rhys wiped his face clean. Both were breathless and flushed, but she was happy to note that not a hair of hers was out of place. The industrial-strength hairspray Nicola had liberally applied was doing its job well.

She felt out of place as the black-tied host led them to their table, which was tucked into a quiet corner. It was fancier than any restaurant she had ever been in, and there were a lot of well-dressed people in there. There were not many tables, maybe fifty, and they were each placed by a large, picture window. The room was dark, with each table having several flickering imitation candles.

The window that their table was located at gave them a spectacular view of Big Ben. Anna was delighted. She had not had the chance to tour the famous clock tower yet, but she had seen it from time to time on her trips around the town. Abraham had promised to take her, but had died before he had been able to. She couldn't take her eyes off of it.

Rhys chuckled and reached across the table to touch her hand. "Hey. The clock's not going anywhere. You can stare at it all you want later. Let's order first, shall we?"

"Sorry," she blushed, picking up her menu. "It's just... That's *Big Ben!* It's like being close to a celebrity." She opened her menu, and sucked in a breath. "Rhys," she choked out. "This is..."

He threw his head back and laughed. It was full and rich and warmed Anna from her head to her toes.

150

The patrons at the tables closest to theirs looked at him, but he didn't pay any attention. "It's all right, Anna," he assured her, eyes glittering. "My family is very old. And, like I said, they were one of the founding knights. Money is not something we have to worry about." He tapped the back of her hand with one of his fingers. "I told you I wanted to do nice things for you."

She slowly closed her menu. Money might not be a problem for him, but, if her quick dollars-to-pounds calculations were correct, dinner would cost him more than she had made in a day back in the States. She wasn't used to having the funds to afford a place like this.

But she couldn't tell him that. He had obviously put a lot of thought into this, and he wanted to treat her to something special. If she refused, or didn't participate fully, it would upset him. So she turned her hand in order to thread her fingers through his. "You've been here before. Why don't you order for me?"

He arched an eyebrow at her. "You trust my judgment that well?"

"As long as it's not still alive, I'll eat it."

"All right. But if you don't like it, don't say I didn't warn you."

After her initial hesitation, Anna began to relax and enjoy herself. Much to her delight, Rhys seemed to be as at ease in a fancy restaurant as he was on the back of a motorcycle. She wasn't much of an alcohol drinker --- she had discovered in college that she was a lightweight --- but the wine Rhys ordered for them was crisp and light. He ordered an appetizer, then their entrees: a lamb dish for her, and some kind of fish for him. It was delicious.

The tables were small, and they took turns feeding one another. Rhys would steal kisses from her when he could. She blushed, aware that there were people staring at them, but she would be lying if she didn't admit that she was enjoying the attention. She also liked the idea that Rhys was letting others know that she belonged to him, and he belonged to her. She had never considered herself possessive --- quite the opposite, actually --- but some primitive part of her brain was shouting *Ha! He's mine and you can't have him!* every time she noticed someone's eyes on them.

She didn't have to remind him about dessert. He ordered two, one for them to share, and one to take back home. Nicola had been right. It was heavenly.

As they walked out of the restaurant, Anna let out a happy sigh and tucked herself under Rhys's arm. "Thank you. That was amazing."

He chuckled as he kissed the top of her head. "I'm glad you liked it. And it was amazing. *You're* amazing."

"And so unbelievably lucky."

He led her to a well-lit walkway that ran parallel to the Thames. They walked in companionable silence for a long moment. They crossed a small bridge that took them to the other side of the river, and Anna squealed in delight when she realized they were approaching the Tower of London. He pointed out the infamous Traitor's Gate, and promised her that he would take her to the Tower one day soon.

There were several other people strolling along the walkway. Anna didn't pay them any attention. She was too caught up in her enjoyment at being on an actual date with Rhys to worry about anyone else.

151

Which was why she was completely surprised when someone grabbed her arm and yanked her away from him.

She opened her mouth to let out a scream, but was stopped by something being pressed against her lower back. Even through the material of her dress, she could make out the distinctive shape and cold metal of a gun barrel.

"That's a good lass," crooned a voice in her ear, and she stiffened as she recognized Growly Voice. "You just be quiet now and no one has to get hurt."

She bit her lip and looked at Rhys, her eyes wide. He stood where she had left him, looking relaxed. But she knew differently. She could see the tightening of his mouth, and the way his eyes flashed. He was enraged.

"Now then." Growly Voice raised his voice so that Rhys could hear him. "We're all going to take a nice trip together. The boss wants to see you," he dipped his head at Rhys, "and we know you'll be more willing to cooperate if this one comes along. So let's just play nice and we can all go out for drinks later, eh?"

"Liar." Anna kept her voice quiet, but she was angry. No, she was *pissed*. Pissed because she was being used as a tool to hurt Rhys, and pissed because Thurston had managed to ruin her perfect date. "Thurston told me he wouldn't hurt me last time, and we know what happened then." Then, nastily, she asked "How's the nose?"

He let out a growl, and she felt a grim smile play across her face. *Point to me,* she thought. "Don't you worry your pretty little head. Boss will take good care of your boy toy there. And maybe I'll let him watch while I pay you back for breaking my nose."

She couldn't suppress the shudder that ran through her at his words, and she could feel real fear beginning to overtake her anger.

Rhys had heard their exchange, and his eyes narrowed at the other man. "Let her go," he said, his voice low and hard.

"I'm afraid you're in no position to be giving *me* orders, chap. I've got a gun poking into the lady's back, and all it will take is one slip of my finger and *pop!* She's dead. And, if you think you can bargain, forget it. Boss has already had a turn with her. We don't need her alive. We just need *you*. So it's in your best interest --- and hers --- to play nice."

She could hear the growl that rose from Rhys's throat, and saw him clench his fists. She couldn't help but notice that dark spots were appearing on the bandage that was wrapped around his palm. He had reopened his cuts from the day before.

For a moment, there was nothing. The three of them simply stood there as the other pedestrians flowed around them, unaware of what was happening. Anna found she was holding her breath, waiting for something, anything to happen.

Then, something caught Anna's eye. It was the bag containing Nicola's desert. It was flying out to Rhys's side, drawing her attention.

Apparently, it caught Growly Voice's attention, too. She felt him shift, and the press of the gun disappeared from her back as he aimed it at this new threat.

She never saw Rhys move. But he was suddenly there, pushing her down with one hand while the other slammed into the hand Growly Voice was using to hold the gun, forcing it up. A shot rang through the night, and someone screamed.

Anna was too stunned to move. Everything was happening so fast. But then someone was tugging at her, urging her away from Growly Voice. "Come on." Rhys's voice was breathless. "Run!"

She ran, letting him pull her along. When she stumbled over her heels, she kicked them off and kept running. She didn't care.

Behind her, she could hear someone swear. Then another shot rang out. Next to her, Rhys let out a grunt and stumbled. But before she could turn to him, she ran out of ground. She managed to let out a scream before plunging into the river, and the cold, dark waters of the Thames closed over her head.

Chapter Twenty-Four

Anna's parents had often joked that their daughter was part fish. She'd learned how to swim at an early age, taking to the water as though she belonged there. She had always enjoyed swimming. She wasn't an exceptionally strong or fast swimmer, but she was a *good* swimmer.

The cold of the water shocked her back into awareness, and she immediately opened her eyes, trying to get her bearings. She didn't know where she was, or where she had landed in relation to the walkway. She didn't even know if Rhys was still with her. But she knew that ---

Something zipped through the water in front of her. She couldn't make out what it was. Then another zipped by to her left. Then another one, this one just to her side. That was when she realized what she was seeing: bullets. Growly Voice was shooting into the water where he'd seen them disappear.

She immediately struck out, though she had no idea where she was going. She didn't care. She wanted to put as much distance between herself and Growly Voice as possible. She vaguely remembered watching a TV show that proved bullets were slowed by water, and she found herself fervently hoping that was the case as she continued swimming.

It was only when her lungs were near to bursting that she dared to surface, taking in a large gasp of air before sinking back into the water, only keeping her nose and eyes above the surface. She didn't want to give Growly Voice an easy target while she scanned her surroundings.

She had managed to swim about a third of the way out into the river, which put her at several feet from the shore. Looking up at the area where she had leapt from, she could see frantic movements. People were running. She could hear shouting. But she didn't hear any more gun shots, which was a relief.

She also didn't see Rhys. She remembered that he had been with her when she had fallen into the river. She also remembered hearing him grunt after the second shot was fired.

She looked around frantically. Had he been hit? Could he even swim? Where would he have gone? What if he was unconscious? Would she be able to find him before he drowned? What if ---

There!

A narrow ledge ran around the edge of the river. Under the pedestrian bridge that spanned the water, she could faintly make out a figure hauling themselves out of the water and onto the ledge. She wouldn't have even noticed him if not for the white shirt he wore briefly catching the light of one of the street lamps.

Anna gulped in a breath and slipped back under the water, making for the area where she had seen Rhys climb onto the river ledge. She hadn't heard any more shots, but she didn't want to risk Growly Voice being able to take pot shots at her. She had never had to swim in a dress before, and she found it restricted her movements to the point where she had to surface sooner than she wanted to.

But no bullets rained down around her, and it took only a few more strokes to reach the ledge under the bridge. She pulled herself up and reached out to the still form that lay on his face. There wasn't much light under the great stone span, but she could see a dark stain on the arm of the white shirt that couldn't be anything other than blood. She couldn't help but be afraid of what she would find. "Rhys?"

He was suddenly crouched on his heels, facing her. The suddenness of the movement startled her, and she let out a squeal and tried to jump back. She found herself flailing, and would have plunged back into the river if Rhys had not reached out to grab her, pulling her tight against him.

"Anna." His voice was rough, and he clutched at her hard enough to make her gasp for air. Then he let her go so that he could bring his hands to her face and peer at her, his eyes frantic as they roamed over her. "Are you all right? He didn't hit you, did he?"

"No. No, I'm fine. But, Rhys. You're bleeding."

He blinked, then looked down at his blood-soaked sleeve. "So I am," he murmured, as though he was surprised himself. "I'll just ---"

She grabbed the wrist of the sleeve and just pulled, ripping it all the way to the shoulder. He gave her an amused look, but she ignored him, focused on the area where the blood seemed to be coming from.

Even in the dim light, she could make out the long gash on the outside of his upper arm. Much to her relief, though, it didn't seem to be very deep, and it was the only wound she could see. "Just a scratch," he told her reassuringly.

"Still. We'd better get you to a hospital. Just to be sure."

"No." His voice was firm as he shook his head, sending water droplets flying in all directions. "No hospitals. We need to get out of here before the Met shows up. If Thurston is desperate enough to try a public kidnapping attempt on both of us, with a lot of witnesses, I don't have any doubts that he would try something at a Met station or a hospital. And there would be too many innocents there. We need to get home."

Anna sighed and raked a hand through her hair, sending a rivulet of water down the back of her neck. "That's going to be easier said than done, I'm afraid. Several people saw us jump into the water. I'm sure they've already called the police, and it won't be long until there are civilians down here looking for us."

He let out a curse. "Right. Let's head upstream. They will probably expect us to go downstream, especially if they think we were wounded and unable to swim. We'll stick to the shadows as much as we can. Hopefully, we can make it out of sight without being spotted. Then we can catch a cab and head back home."

"Catch a cab?" She raised an eyebrow. "Rhys, we're both soaking wet, and you're bleeding" Not only that, she had no doubt that she looked wild. Her hair was hanging in limp strands around her ears, and she could only imagine what the dip in the river had done to her makeup. "Also, I have no shoes."

He let out another curse, then sat back with a half-hearted grin. "Well, I guess we'll just have to figure something out then."

They stayed under the bridge for another long moment, listening to the shouts that rang out above them. From what they could tell, Rhys had been right: they seemed to be concentrating their search downriver of where the two had went in the water. When the shouting had died away, Rhys clutched Anna's hand and pulled her out from under the relative security of the bridge, running lightly along the ledge. He kept them crouched over and would pause whenever they reached a new patch of shadows.

155

Finally, they reached a ladder that led back up to the walkway they had jumped from. Rhys had tried to make Anna go first, but she refused. He had been shot in the arm. She wanted to be able to support him in case he couldn't use it to climb. He had sighed, but gave her a grin before scrambling up the ladder. Once at the top, they quickly hurried down the walkway until they could cross another bridge and be on the opposite side of the river from where the commotion was. Several people sent looks their way, but no one said anything.

Rhys was gripping her hand hard enough for it to hurt, but she didn't say anything to him. She knew he was angry, knew he would feel as though he'd put her into harm's way yet again, even though he had taken every precaution to keep them both safe. He needed to know that she was all right, just like he had the night before after his nightmare.

They waited until they could hear the faint wail of police sirens before hailing a cab. When the cabbie saw them he had started to drive away, until Rhys snarled at him. He still hadn't looked happy with them, so Anna promised that they would pay him double if he would take them to the Blackwood residence. He had turned cheerful after that.

Rhys was quiet during the entire ride, though he kept his tight grip on Anna's hand. He stared out of the window, his face turned away from her. But she could feel the waves of tension and anger coming off of him. She knew if she didn't do something soon, one of them was going to explode.

She let out a sigh and reached up with her free hand to touch his shoulder. "Rhys," she said softly. "Look at me. Please."

He did as she asked, his movements stiff. When he was facing her, he kept his eyes on her shoulder or on their hands, not meeting her gaze.

She grasped his chin and forced him to look up, tightening her grasp when he winced and tried to pull away. "Stop it," she said firmly. "This was not your fault. I won't let you feel guilty about anything."

He opened his mouth to argue, but she raised the hand that was holding his, silencing him. "I'm serious. You *cannot* live in a bubble all of the time. So what if Growly Voice showed up? You didn't know. It's not like you took me out tonight because you *planned* on this happening. You did everything you could to make sure we would be safe. So you have absolutely nothing to feel guilty for. And if you insist on feeling guilty anyways, I'll leave and go back to my flat. Because I won't put up with it. Got it?"

Rhys let out a sigh of frustration, but she could see one corner of his mouth turn up. "Growly Voice?"

"Hey, it works." She held his gaze, keeping her grip on his chin. "And don't try to change the subject. I will stick to my word. I don't care how great the sex is."

A choking sound came from the front of the cab, and the radio was suddenly turned up a notch.

Anna rolled her eyes, but kept her focus on Rhys. "Look," she said, her voice soft. "I know it's hard for you. I understand your need to protect, and its jus---"

"No, you don't." Rhys's voice was low, almost a growl. He reached up to remove her hand from his chin, and he now had both of her hands in his. But he was meeting her gaze head-on, and she almost wished he wasn't. His eyes were glittering with some unnamed emotion, and she had to fight not to shrink back from the intensity of it. "It isn't about me not being able to stop all of the bad guys. I know good and well that I can't stop all of them. I can't save everyone." She did flinch then, his emotion raw enough to

156

hurt. "But you are not everyone. I *love* you, Anna. I don't know how many times I have to say it before you *get* it. I have never once had someone like you, someone that changed all of the rules. You asked me to do this with you, and I am trying. But knowing that he had his hands on you, that he had a *gun* on you..." He stopped, his jaw clenching so tightly that he was unable to continue.

Her heart melted. At that moment, in the back of a London taxi, the last bit of wall she had built around her heart crumbled. All she could do was reach out to touch Rhys's face, to kiss him, to twine her arms around him. He pulled her closer, crushing her against him. His mouth was needy on hers, and she let him take what he needed. She could feel his arms trembling around her.

She pulled away so that she could lay her head in the hollow between his neck and shoulder, closing her eyes. "It's okay, Rhys," she whispered soothingly. "I'm not going anywhere. I'm right here. It's okay."

They stayed that way for a long moment, silent, until his arms stopped trembling. He never loosened his grip on her, but he let out a sigh and leaned his head back against the headrest, closing his eyes. "Why did you ask --- what was it? Growly Voice? --- about his nose?"

"Hmmm?"

"When he said he wouldn't hurt us, you called him a liar. Then you asked him how his nose was. He didn't seem to like that very much."

"Oh." She shifted a bit. For some reason, she blushed. "When Thurston kidnapped me, Growly Voice was holding my legs so that they could manhandle me into the van that Wyman was driving. I was fighting, and I managed to kick Growly Voice in the face. I think I broke his nose. I remember that I at least bloodied it."

Silence greeted her. Then she felt Rhys shaking. She began to get worried, wondering if his bullet wound was worse than she had originally thought. It wasn't until he threw his head back that she realized he was laughing. It was a full laugh, like the one he had let out at the restaurant earlier that evening. She felt her blush deepen.

When he had caught his breath, he leaned down to press his lips to the top of her head. "That's my girl," he said, his voice fiercely proud.

By the time they reached the Blackwood's home, Anna was miserable. The river had been cold, and London's ever-present dampness wasn't helping. Sometime during the cab ride, she had started shivering. Rhys had locked his arms around her tighter, trying to project some of his own warmth to her, but it didn't help. His own clothes were wet and cold as well.

She stood by Rhys as he paid the cab driver, hugging herself tightly. Her teeth were starting to chatter, and all she could think of was a long, hot shower and a warm sweatshirt.

"Get your girl in before she catches a cold," the driver said gruffly. "And don't worry about paying me extra. Sounds like you kids have a tough night. Go get changed and warmed up."

Rhys let out an exasperated sigh --- he had tried to insist on paying the cabbie for any damages their water-soaked clothes may have done to the upholstery --- but reached out a hand. "Thank you, sir. I'm going to make sure she gets taken care of."

The driver shook Rhys's hand, nodded at Anna, and drove off. Rhys put an arm back around her and led her to the door. "I wish I could carry you," he said grimly. "I know the ground must be cold on your feet."

"I'm fine," she said, leaning into him. "I used to run around barefoot in Tennessee. I promise you, my feet are the least of my worries. And I don't want you to hurt your arm any more than you already have."

Nicola was waiting by the door when they opened it, a huge grin on her face. She must have heard them talking outside. Well!" she said cheerily. "You two are home earlier than I thought. Do I need to..." Her voice trailed off as she took in their bedraggled appearance. "What the *hell?* Anna, go get in the shower before you freeze to death. Your lips are turning blue. Rhys, are you *bleeding?* Let me take a look at that arm. I'm going to go grab the first-aid kit. Go into the bathroom where Anna is going to take a shower. You need to get warmed up, too."

Anna didn't argue. She dashed into her bedroom and ran straight for the bathroom, where she turned on the shower to the hottest setting that she thought she could handle. Rhys followed her in, and, without a sound, began to unzip the back of her dress. She quickly shucked it off, followed by her bra and underwear, before stepping into the near-scalding water.

She gasped as the hot water assaulted her cold flesh, sending tiny pricks of pain all over her body. She braced herself against the wall, letting the water and the steam warm her until her legs quit trembling.

"Anna?' Even over the sound of the shower Rhys's voice was soft. And miserable. "I'm sorry our date got ruined. I wish... I wish I could have taken you out proper."

Anna let out a sigh and pulled the curtain back enough to scowl at him. "Rhys, it was perfect. Well, except for the whole bit about you getting shot and us jumping into a river. I had a fantastic time at the restaurant. I really did."

He looked so much like a little boy standing there that Anna had to fight the urge not to climb out of the shower and hug him. His hair had begun to dry and was curling around his ears. He had shoved his hands into his pants pockets and was looking down, a sad look on his face. It nearly broke her heart.

"Hey," she said softly. "It's okay. Really. We can go on more dates. I mean, you did promise to take me to the Tower. And I want to go to Big Ben, too. Ooooh, and the Palace! I want to watch a changing of the guard."

He looked up at her, a smile pulling at his lips. "You want to play tourist, huh?"

"Well, I'm not going to be a tourist if I have *you* taking me around now will I? It will be a fun date. Promise me you'll take me."

He sighed. "I'm not promising anything, Anna. Not until we find Thurston. I'll not risk you again."

She pouted. "Then promise you'll take me *after* we catch him. He can't hide forever. And once he's behind bars, you will take me out on a fun, touristy date. You can promise *that.*"

His smile widened. "Yes. I suppose I can."

She held up a finger and crooked at him. "Then come over here and seal it. Make it official."

His eyes changed as he walked forward to place his hands on either side of her face and kiss her. It was one of those deep, heated kiss that he had used the night before, and she found her knees go weak all over again. If she knew Nicola wouldn't be joining them in a moment, she would have pulled him into the shower with her.

She smiled at him as he pulled away from her, and he smiled in return. "It's a deal, then." She paused. "I have one more favor to ask of you."

He arched a brow. "Only one more?" His voice was low, almost a purr, and she reconsidered her idea of yanking him into the shower. Nicola could wait, damn it. But she knew his wound could not. "When Nicola is finished with you… I don't have any sweatshirts here, and I don't know if I'll ever get this cold out of my bones. I was wondering, do you have one I could wear?"

He was silent for a moment, watching her. Even when Nicola opened the door and stepped through he didn't move. "You want to wear something of mine?" His voice was thoughtful.

She nodded. "I do." Then she paused. "That is, if you don't mind. I know some guys have a hang-up about girls wearing their clothes, but I would really ---"

"Anna." He placed a finger across her lips, silencing her. "I would love for you to wear my clothes. I would love that very much." He leaned forward to kiss her again, and she could recognize his fierce joy in the kiss. She had felt it when he had kissed her in the hospital, and again last night.

Nicola cleared her throat. "If you two are *quite* finished, Rhys, sit on the loo so I can take a look."

Rhys winked at Anna, then did as he was told. She ducked back under the spray of the shower, letting hot water run down her back.

As Anna showered and Nicola tended to her brother's wound, Rhys explained what had happened, beginning when they left the restaurant. Nicola snorted when Rhys told her about Anna's nickname for the gunman, and about how she had taunted him. Nicola asked a few more questions, and Anna could hear Rhys hiss as she cleaned the gash across his arm.

"You're a lucky bastard," she told him. "It looks like it merely grazed you. It took a small chunk out of your arm, but the bullet burn is going to hurt worse than the wound itself. I'll wait and bandage it once you're out of the shower."

Anna heard the door open and close as Nicola left, then it was Rhys's turn to peek around the curtain. Anna watched as he started to say something, then suck in his breath when he saw her.

She couldn't help but smile. The fact that she of all people could have that effect on any man, much less this one, was empowering. "Care to join me?" she asked mildly. "There's plenty of room in here for both of us."

He swallowed. Hard. Her smile widened as his Adam's apple bobbed. "Sure," he said hoarsely. Then he was gone. A moment later he stepped into the shower, naked.

This time, it was Anna who sucked in her breath. While she had become quite acquainted with his body the night before, seeing him under the light was a different experience all together. And when the water began to stream down his torso, she found herself wanting to lick it off of his skin.

She shuddered, and it had nothing to do with the lingering cold.

He took a step forward at the same time he reached out to pull her to him. His mouth met hers again in that heated way that sent zings to all the right places in her body. He slowly shuffled them around so that he was standing directly under the shower spray and pushed her back against the wall, his hands flat on either side of her, caging in her in.

She felt a moan escape involuntarily from her mouth, and immediately kicked herself. They had just escaped yet another kidnapping attempt, Rhys had been shot, they had jumped into a river to escape, and yet here she was thinking about sex.

However, it would seem she wasn't the only one. "You know," Rhys murmured, leaning down to trace her collarbone with his nose. "I was really hoping I could make love to you tonight while you were wearing that dress. I suppose we're going to have to try something else."

He reached up to grasp one of her wrists and gently pulled her hand down to his waist, letting her fingers brush against his erection. She let out a slight gasp, then her fingers closed around him.

He let out a groan as he let go of her wrist and leaned forward to touch his forehead to hers. "Do you see what you do to me?"

She gently slid her hand up so that she could run her thumb across his tip. He shuddered. "I'm so sorry," she murmured. "I hate that I torture you so."

His eyes were full of smoky promise. "All I have to do is look at you," he said, voice husky. "Even before last night my body responded to you like this."

"Mmmm." She gently ran her hand up and down his length, enjoying the expressions that came over his face. Knowing that she had that kind of effect on him was a better intoxicant than any alcohol. "I bet you say that to all of the girls."

"No." It came out as a growl. "Only you, Anna. No one else."

"Good." She dropped to her knees.

He blinked down at her, a confused expression on his face. "Anna, what are you ----"

His words were cut off by a strangled cry as she took him into her mouth. One hand sank into her hair, the other shot out to brace against the wall. "Anna, stop. You don't have to do that."

She knew she didn't. She knew he would never ask it of her, even if he wanted it. And frankly, the idea used to nauseate her. But she wanted to do it to him, wanted to see what she could do to him. She remembered his mouth on her, the way it had made her feel. She wanted to do the same for him.

She wrapped her lips around him, keeping her hand around the base of his shaft as she began to slide him in and out of her mouth. Her tongue darted out to lick his satiny tip. The hand in her hair tightened, but she paid it no mind. Above her, he was making the most delicious noises.

Then she suddenly found herself upright, her back against the shower wall. Rhys was in front of her, eyes glazed. "Wrap your legs around me," he whispered hoarsely.

She did as he asked, her legs encircling his waist. He shifted, adjusting his grip on her, and then he was sliding into her, pulling her down until she was completely impaled

She couldn't help but moan. He filled her so completely. He wasn't so big that he stretched her to the point of pain. Rather, they fit together like a key in a lock. Like he was made for her.

He wasn't gentle, which was fine by Anna. She didn't want him to be. She tightened her legs around him as her backside slapped against the wall with the force of his thrusts. He bit her. She clawed at his back. Their kisses were bruising. He dug his fingers into her bottom, holding her against him as his pace quickened. She pulled his hair. And when their climaxes came, it was accompanied by growls and snarls instead of soft cries of pleasure.

When he finally pulled himself free and sat her on her feet, she had to hold on to him for support as her legs wobbled. He turned, reaching for the soap, and she winced at the long red lines that ran down his back. "Sorry," she said, feeling a blush spread across her face. "I, ah, guess I got carried away. I didn't mean to scratch you."

He grinned at her, all wolf. "Anna," he purred. "If that's what happens when you get 'carried away', then I need to make that happen more often. If it means having you turn into a wild woman when I'm in you, I'll happily be a walking bruise for the rest of my life."

They stayed in the shower until the water began to run cold. Rhys pulled out two large, fluffy towels so that they could dry one another off. Anna let out a growl when she saw the angry gash across his upper arm. She hated that he had earned yet another scar courtesy Graham Thurston.

Rhys wrapped one of the towels around his waist and moved towards the door. "I'll be right back. I'm going to go find you a sweatshirt. Unless I've warmed you up enough already." He leered at her.

She laughed and swatted at him. "You're horrible! Yes, I would very much like a sweatshirt. And hurry it up before I rip that towel off of you. You look good enough to eat."

Grinning, he left. She dropped her own towel to pull on a pair of sweat pants and a tank top. She had just begun running a brush through her tangled knots of hair when Rhys reappeared. He was in a pair of cotton pajama pants and a long-sleeved shirt. Anna thought he looked just as good as he had in dress clothes.

"Here," he said, coming over to stand next to her. "Lift your arms up."

She did as she was told, and he pulled a sweatshirt down over her head. It was several sizes too big for her, with the sleeves falling past her fingers, and the hem hitting her just above her knees. But it was warm and soft. 'Oxford Crew Club' was splashed across the chest. Anna could tell it had been worn often, and it smelled unmistakably of Rhys.

She hugged herself and smiled up at him. "Thank you," she said softly.

"Do you like it?" he murmured, running his hand own one sleeve. "It's my favorite sweatshirt. It was my father's."

Anna gasped. "Rhys," she choked. "This is… I can't…"

"Yes, you can," he said firmly. "You are my greatest treasure, Anna. And it means a lot to me to have you wear my second greatest treasure." He smiled. "Besides, I *like* seeing you in my clothes."

161

She touched the faded and worn lettering across the front of the sweatshirt. Unexpectedly, tears pricked at her eyes as she realized just what this small action meant to him... and to her.

"Hey," he said softly, reaching up to touch her face. "What is it? If it upsets you, then ---"

"No, no. Rhys, I am... Honored doesn't even come close." She smiled up at him. "Thank you. This... It really means a lot to me, too. You have no idea."

"I'm glad, because I want you to hang on to it for me, okay? Just for now." He kissed her before she could launch another protest. "Come on. Nicola called Finn while we were in the shower, and he's out there waiting for us."

Now that the adrenaline from the near-kidnapping had vanished, Anna was finding it difficult to stay awake. The fact that she was warm and the sweatshirt Rhys had given her was extra soft wasn't helping her in the least bit.

Finn was sitting in one of the chairs in the Blackwoods' living room, with Nicola sitting on one end of the sofa and Anna and Rhys sitting on the other end. Anna had her head on Rhys's shoulder. She was trying to follow the conversation in case she needed to add anything, but the sound of the other's voices turned into a dull murmur and she found her eyes closing against her will.

"Hey." Rhys nudged her with his shoulder, and she lifted her head, blinking her eyes. He was looking down at her with a soft smile. "Go to bed. You were starting to snore."

"At least I wasn't drooling," she grumbled, pushing at him. Then she let out a yawn. "Sorry," she apologized.

Finn laughed. "No need to apologize. You've had a long night. Rhys is right. You should just go to bed."

"Are you sure? Do you need anything else from me?"

He waved his hand dismissively. "I've gotten most of what I need from Rhys. And if I think of anything else later I can always call. Go ahead."

Anna let out a groan and pushed herself to her feet, ignoring the others as they resumed their conversation. She walked out of the living room but, instead of turning towards her bedroom, she made her way up the stairs and into Rhys's bedroom.

She crawled under the covers and pulled his pillow close to her. This was her sanctuary, this room that surrounded her with all things Rhys. Feeling safe and secure, she closed her eyes and drifted to sleep.

Chapter Twenty-Five

His arm was asleep.

That was the first thing that Rhys became aware of upon wakening. He lay on his side, one arm thrown across his eyes, the other one completely consumed by pins and needles.

He let out a sigh and tried to roll over, hoping to take some weight off of the deadened limb. However, he found that he was unable to move, thanks to something that was pinning his left side to the bed.

Slowly, he blinked open his eyes and craned his neck to see what was preventing him from moving.

The first thing he saw was blond hair. A *lot* of blond hair. And it was attached to a long, lean body that was pressed to his. One leg was draped over his, and an arm lay across his chest. The head of hair was pillowed on his shoulder, and his own arm was wrapped about a slim waist, explaining why he hadn't been able to move. And why his arm was asleep.

He blinked again, his sleep-addled brain trying to put a name to the person lying next to him.

Anna.

At that thought, a wide smile stretched across his face. She had chosen to sleep in his bed last night, instead of her own. He could remember stumbling into his room the night before after Finn had left and being surprised to find her there. The idea that she might want to sleep next to him had never even crossed his mind. He remembered the rush he had gotten at seeing her, but he had been so tired that he had simply fallen into bed next to her. Somehow, during the night, they had found each other. This pleased him greatly.

He reached over with his free hand to brush her hair away from her face, giving him an unobstructed view. Sleep softened her, making her look young... and vulnerable. Her lips were slightly parted as she breathed in and out in even measures. She hadn't managed to get all of her makeup off the night before, and there were still dark smudges around her eyes.

His smile grew to the point where it hurt, but he couldn't help it. She was beautiful.

As if sensing she was being watched, she let out a small sigh and her eyes fluttered open. She blinked for a moment, yawned, and turned to look at him. She blinked again as sleep fled from her eyes, and her own smile crossed her lips. "Good morning," she said groggily.

"Good morning, yourself," he responded, tucking her hair behind her ear. "Did you sleep well?"

"Mmmm." She rolled over onto her side, pulling him with her so that her back was pressed against his chest and he was able to free his tingling arm. "Having you here means my sleep was very well."

He chuckled as he buried his face into her hair, breathing in deeply. The hand that lay around her waist slipped under her sweatshirt just enough to rest on her stomach, allowing him the skin-to-skin contact that he craved. "I'm glad. I rather enjoy sleeping next to you, as well. Although, I have to say, waking up next to you is even better. I could get used to doing this every day."

"Me, too."

They lay that way for a long while, Rhys holding her tight against him. He had thought that she had fallen back asleep when she let out a sigh and began to slide away from him. "I really don't want to move," she said apologetically, "but if I don't go to the bathroom my bladder is going to burst."

He watched her move the covers aside before getting to her feet and walking towards the bathroom. He was more than pleased to see that she was still wearing his father's sweatshirt.

He could have leapt for joy when she asked if she could wear one of his shirts. He had always found the idea of a girl wearing something of his incredibly sexy, but he had never found a girl that he was willing to let have something that belonged to him. His inner caveman liked having Anna in his clothes because it was another way of marking her as his, but Rhys liked it because *she* wanted everyone to know that she was his.

As soon as she had asked, he knew he was going to give her his father's sweatshirt. As he had told Anna the night before, it was his greatest treasure. *Had* been, until she came along. After his father had died he had worn it for days on end, just needing something to make him feel as though his father was there with him. He hadn't even washed it for months afterwards, afraid that it would lose the smell of his father's cologne.

As time had gone on, he had worn the sweatshirt less and less as he learned to take comfort in the people around him instead of in the memory the shirt offered. Only when he had a deep, aching loneliness in his chest would he pull the shirt out and wear it again. He knew he would never have that feeling again, not with Anna. She filled in all of his empty places.

It obviously had meant a lot to her to realize just what he had given her. He knew she wouldn't just see it as a piece of clothing. He had given her something special. She already would love it because it was his, but she would treasure it knowing what it meant to Rhys.

Besides, he knew his father would like for Anna to have it. He would have liked Anna. He had once told Rhys in a stage-whisper to make sure and marry a blond because they were the most fun. He had given his son a wink while his wife --- who was very blond --- let out an exaggerated sigh and rolled her eyes. But she had been smiling.

The memory made Rhys smile. Yes, there was no doubt that his parents would have liked Anna very much. If for nothing more than the fact that she made their son deliriously happy.

"What are you smiling about?"

Rhys blinked, the sound of Anna's voice pulling him back to the present. He had been so lost in thought that he had never heard her return from the bathroom.

"Nothing much," he answered, reaching out to snag her wrist and pull her back down onto the bed with him. "I was thinking that my father would have liked having you wear his shirt. He had a thing for blonds."

She laughed as she fell against him. "I'm take it your mother was a blond?"

"Very. It was white blond. She often joked that Nic and I were proof of how stubborn my father was, since we both ended up looking like him. They could have been the poster couple for the 'opposites attract' theory."

She hesitated. "Do you think they would have liked me?"

"Absolutely. My father would have said you were too serious, though. Nic takes after him a lot that way. He was always laughing, even though he could be serious when he needed to. He used to boast that my mother never cracked a smile until she met him."

Anna snuggled up against him, pulling him back into their earlier spooning position. "I wish I could have met them," she said softly. "But I'm happy to know that you think they would have liked me."

"They would have loved you." He kissed the back of her shoulder. "Because *I* love you. They would have spoiled you rotten."

"Sounds like *my* parents. I know that if my mother ever meets you, you might run away screaming. She will adopt you in a second, and then start smothering you. My dad will try to be all manly and do men stuff with you to bond, but my mother is worse than a mother hen. Guess that's what happens when you only have one kid."

He paused at something she had said. "'If' I meet your mother? You don't want your parents to meet me?"

He tried to keep the hurt out of his voice, but she must have heard it. "It's not like that," she said quickly, rolling over to face him. "If it were up to me, I would take you back home with me and parade you in front of everyone I've ever met. But my family, well..." She cringed. "You would be bombarded by questions about marriage. And kids. I'm the only one left who's unmarried, and all of my aunts and cousins and a few uncles having been trying to fix that. And my mother is at the forefront of it all. Like I said, you would run away screaming."

He laughed, the hurt leaving as quickly as it had come. "Maybe we're beginning to learn the real reason why you moved to a different continent?"

"It sure helped make the choice a lot easier." She reached out to brush his hair from his eyes, and he caught her hand so he could bring it to his mouth for a kiss. "So. What is on the agenda for the day?"

'Well..." He rolled over until he was leaning over her, his toothpaste-ad grin in place. "I was thinking we could stay in bed all day. You know, we've earned a day of rest. Don't you think?"

"Mmmm. I'm sure 'resting' is what you have in mind."

He reached down to pull the sweatshirt over her head. "Of course. Why would you think anything else?"

She laughed as he leaned down to run his nose down her throat, wrapping her arms around him. "You know, if you keep this up you're going to tire of me soon."

He let out a growl as he moved to her collarbone. "Never," he said fiercely. "I could *never* tire of you. I can't get enough of you as it is." He planted a kiss in the hollow of her shoulder. "This is my favorite part of you. I think you should get my name tattooed there, mark it as mine."

"If you want me to get your name tattooed then you really are trying to get rid of me. Don't you know what happens when you get your significant other's name tattooed on your body? It's a curse."

"Well, considering the fact that I don't even want to let you out of my sight, I don't think we'll have to worry about that." He kissed her, and she felt her body tingle from head to toe.

"You know," she gasped when he pulled away, "I'm going to have to start working out if I'm to have even a chance of keeping up with you."

"Don't worry," he purred. "I can go slow." He reached down to grasp the hem of her tank top and was trying to tug it over her head when a knock came at the door.

"Rhys?" Nicola called out. "Are you awake? You have a phone call."

He let out a groan and closed his eyes, leaning his forehead against Anna's. "Of all the bad timing," he muttered. Louder, he said "Take a message. I'm busy."

There was a pause. Anna ran her hands under Rhys's shirt and up his chest, hoping that the other woman would take the hint and leave. But then Nicola's voice came through the door once more.

"I think you need to take this one, Rhys. It's Gabin LeBlanc."

Rhys moved so fast that Anna missed it. One minute he was hovering over her, the next he was opening the door to his bedroom and reaching for the phone. He took a deep breath and placed the handset to his ear. "This is Rhys Blackwood."

Anna propped herself up on her elbows so that she could watch him. She couldn't make out what was being said by the other party, but she could make out a deep, rumbling voice. A man's voice.

"Yes, sir." Rhys's voice was taut, formal. Anna had never heard him sound so nervous. "That is correct. We have had a few run-ins with Graham Thurston." He paused. "Yes. Yes, I understand. I think that's a wonderful idea." He paused again, and Anna could see his brows furrow together. "Sir? Are you sure that's --- " He turned to face Anna then, a deep frown on his face. "I understand. But I don't want to risk --- I know that we would all be able to protect her, but ---- It's not ---" He bit his lip, and she could see anger flash in his eyes. "Very well, sir. Two o'clock. We'll be there."

He ended the call and handed the phone back to Nicola, his face troubled. "Well?" his sister asked impatiently. "What did he want?"

Rhys let out a sigh and raked his hand through his hair, so Anna knew that, whatever had been said on the phone, he didn't like it. "He's heard about the rumors that the book was here, and he's heard about our run-ins with Graham Thurston. He wants to meet with us and the other London Templars to discuss it. And he wants me to bring Anna."

Both of Nicola's eyebrows shot up. "He wants to meet with *us? Today??*" Her hands rose and began patting at her hair absently. "But... What do I wear?!"

He gave her a grim smile. "I'm more worried about why he wants to meet Anna. I tried to tell him no, that it wasn't safe. But..." He spread his hands.

His sister gasped at this. "You tried to tell him *no?* Rhys! How could you??"

"Hello!" Anna called out. She was now sitting up on the edge of the bed and watching the siblings with curious eyes. "Would anyone care to tell me what's going on? Who was that on the phone? Why does he want to meet with you? And me?"

Rhys let out another sigh and pinched the bridge of his nose. Anna didn't think he looked particularly happy. "That was Gabin LeBlanc."

"I heard that part," she replied dryly. "Why is he important?"

"He's our Grandmaster," Nicola answered, her voice sounding a little breathless. "He's the leader of all of the Templars. *All* of us."

Anna waited. When neither Blackwood continued, she prompted. "And?"

"*And* he wants to meet with us. With *us!*" Nicola started patting her hair again.

This time it was Anna who sighed. Seeing Nicola turn into a… well, a *girl* was disturbing. "Okay. Let's try this again. Who is he, and why does he want to meet with me? I'm not a Templar."

"Exactly." Rhys leaned back against the wall, folding his arms across his chest. He looked relaxed, but Anna knew he was anything but. She could feel the waves of tension radiating off of him from two feet away. "LeBlanc lives in Avignon, France, the old seat of the Catholic Church. The Grandmaster is always French. The original nine knights were French, and so was the first Grandmaster. And so has every Grandmaster since then. Once a Templar has become Grandmaster, they don't leave France very often. Not unless they feel there is a problem that they need to deal with personally."

"Ah." Understanding dawned on Anna. "I guess he's not known for making social visits?"

"No. If he thinks this is bad enough for him to come to London…" Rhys trailed off.

"Then it's worse than we all thought," Anna finished, her voice grim. Then she paused before repeating her earlier statement. "But I'm not a Templar."

"And that is what is worrying me the most. He *never* gets involved with non-Templars, not even Scholars. He doesn't care for them. To him, non-Templars are non-entities. It's our job to protect you. If a large amount of people are hurt or killed, it's because of the knight, not the civilians involved." He shook his head. "I don't like the fact that he knows who you are. I don't want you on his radar at *all.*"

"Fine." She crossed her arms. "I won't go."

Nicola made a strangling noise at the back of her throat. Rhys shook his head. "I'm afraid it's not that simple. He's asked for you, and I have to bring you. Even if you protested, I'd have to bring you."

"Because he's what? Your *boss?*"

"More than that. I swore an oath to him, Anna. We all did. A blood oath. If I knowingly break it --- if I directly disobey one of his orders --- it could get… bad." His eyes begged her to understand.

She narrowed her eyes. "So there is going to be a group of people we don't know --- when there is a *traitor* somewhere in our midst --- and I don't get a say in the matter of my going because someone *asked* you to bring me? And you can't say no? Am I getting it right?"

Silence greeted her, giving her all the answer she needed.

She gritted her teeth. She had never seen either Blackwood this… compliant. Especially when it was clear Rhys didn't like the idea one bit. She already knew she wasn't going to like this Gabin LeBlanc. Blood oaths or not, he sounded like a bully.

"Very well then." She got to her feet and walked out of the bedroom, brushing past both of them. "I'll go get ready."

"Anna…" Rhys's voice was apologetic, but she brushed off the hand he placed on her shoulder and kept walking until she was down the stairs and in her own bedroom, the door shut firmly behind her.

She flopped down onto her bed, burying her face in her pillow. She knew she was pouting, but she felt she had earned it. Her date had been ruined the night before. And now her day with Rhys was being ruined. And there wasn't anything she could do about it.

Just one day, she thought. *I would just like to have one day where I get to spend time with Rhys with no interruptions. No one trying to kidnap us, and no mysterious Grandmasters showing up to snap their fingers. Is that really so much to ask?*

She lay there for a long moment, not moving. She considered going back to sleep. She had plenty of time to get ready. And she didn't want to deal with the Blackwoods right now. All she wanted to do was be alone and sulk.

Unfortunately, the house wasn't that big. And she couldn't avoid Rhys forever. So when he knocked on the door, she let out a sigh and rolled over, placing one arm over her eyes.

The door opened and Rhys peeked in. "Anna?" His voice sounded small, meek. "Nicola and I were going to order some Chinese food. Would you like something?"

"Mmmm." She didn't move.

She heard him let out a sigh, and then felt the bed shift as he sat down on the edge. "You're angry." He still had that tone in his voice, and it pricked Anna under her skin. She didn't like it. It didn't sound right.

She let out a sigh and reached up to find his shoulder and pull him back until he was sprawled out next to her. "I'm not mad at *you,*" she said, leaning her head against his arm. "I'm *mad* because every time we try to spend time together, someone interrupts us. And I don't like the way this French guy can just pull your strings like that."

Rhys shifted so that one of his arms was around her, and her head was resting on his chest. "Do you remember when you suggested that a Templar could be our traitor?" he asked, his chest rumbling under her ear.

"Yes. You said that it couldn't be."

"Right. And remember what I said about the last traitor we had?"

She frowned. "I was kind of drugged up at the time, but he's your boogeyman, right? I think you said they tell his story to scare all of you little Templars into behaving."

He chuckled and slid a hand over her hair. "Yes. That's the one." He paused. "Our blood oaths are not just words, Anna. They are binding, connecting every single Templar to the Grandmaster. If I were to disobey him, it could literally kill me. And not in a way that would leave a pretty corpse."

She frowned. "That sounds an awful lot like magic."

"It is a piece of Lost Knowledge. I don't know exactly how it works, but I'm not really eager to find out. I was told the boogeyman story, too. I was ten when I heard it the first time. I still remember it. If there is even a chance of that happening to me…" He shuddered. "No thank you."

Anna lifted her head so that she could look at him. "You really believe it, don't you? In these pieces of

Lost Knowledge that the Templars hide, what we would call magic."

His eyes were serious as they met hers. "Yes," he said firmly. Then he offered a smile. "Besides, it's only a meeting. I don't like it, but I can deal with it. It's not like he's asked to have sex with you."

She made a face. "And if he did?"

"Then I would at least insist he let me watch."

"*Rhys!*" She swatted at him. Laughing, he rolled off of her bed and dashed through her bedroom door, Anna close behind.

The meeting, as it turned out, was to take place in Temple Church. Anna found that rather fitting, as the Templars were the ones who had built it in the first place. It had been another place on her list to visit that she hadn't gotten around to yet. She was hoping that the excitement of being in such a historical place would cancel out the nervousness she felt at meeting a large group of strangers.

Rhys stood by her, his fingers lightly laced through hers. He was trying to appear casual, but she watched as he cast his eyes warily around, looking out for any potential threats. Nicola stood on her other side, nearly vibrating with nervous energy. Anna was glad for both of them. Even though she knew they were both feeling off, they wouldn't let anything happen to her. Not if they could help it.

And it was that reason --- and Rhys's fear that something may happen to him if he didn't bring her to his mysterious Grandmaster --- that kept her from running out of the church doors. Instead, she let Rhys lead her further inside. She felt her heart rate speed up as they moved further away from the doors, and she found herself gripping his hand even tighter.

"It's all right," he murmured to her. But he squeezed her hand back just as tight, and she wondered if he was trying to reassure her or himself.

"There's the man of the hour!" boomed a cheerful voice from somewhere up ahead. "I was beginning to wonder if you were going to show your ugly mug around here any time soon. At least you were kind enough to bring your hot sister."

Rhys's face split into a wide grin at the voice, and it grew even wider when another man appeared. "Jack, you bastard. It's good to see you, too."

The two embraced each other in that manly, back-pounding way that longtime friends often did. Anna stepped back next to Nicola so that she could study the other man. He was close to Rhys's age, she guessed, with sandy colored hair and brown eyes.

Rhys let the other man go and placed a hand at the small of Anna's back. "Anna, this is Jack Pennington, an old friend of mine. We grew up together. Jack, this is my girlfriend, Anna."

Anna immediately warmed. That was the first time Rhys had claimed her in front of someone she didn't know, and it pleased her to no end. "Pleased to meet you," she said, holding out her hand.

Still grinning, Jack took her hand and raised it to his lips. "I can assure you, the pleasure is all mine." He looked at Rhys, his eyes glittering. "Careful, Blackwood. I may just steal her away from you."

Rhys answered with a wolfish smile, and Anna could feel his hand press deeper into her back. "I'd like to see you try."

Jack threw his head back and laughed, the sound echoing off of the stone walls. "Ah, I'm glad to see you finally caught a lady that can put up with you. It doesn't hurt that she's easy on the eyes." He waggled his eyebrows. "Speaking of easy on the eyes... How are you doing, my fair Nicola?"

Nicola sighed dramatically. "Oh, you know. The usual. Putting up with this lump, trying to solve the mysteries of the human mind, and looking for a smokin' hot girlfriend of my own."

"Mmmm. I know. The lack of smokin' hot girls in this world is tragic."

Nicola grinned at him. She opened her mouth to say something else, but another voice floated to them, this one decidedly female.

"Ah. *There* you are. I thought I heard the sound of your voice."

Anna had been too busy concentrating on Jack that she hadn't noticed anyone else approaching them. But she couldn't miss the way all three of her companions stiffened at the sound of the new voice, and the way Rhys pulled her closer to him.

The woman who joined them was beautiful. Actually, Anna thought *beautiful* was too light a word. This woman could have easily been a supermodel. She was tall and willowy, managing to look fragile at the same time she literally glowed with sex appeal. She had rich brown hair that fell into envious curls around her shoulders. She was wearing jeans and a tight t-shirt that showed off her curves and rose up just enough to show a strip of tanned skin between the waistband of her jeans and the hem of her shirt.

Anna suddenly felt very, very out of place. For some reason, this woman made her want to turn and run worse than the idea of meeting their Grandmaster did.

The newcomer came to a stop just in front of them. She placed her hands on her hips and looked directly at Rhys, her green eyes smoldering. "Hello, Rhys," she purred. "It's been a while."

Rhys's earlier grin had faded, replaced by a polite smile. "Lauren," he said smoothly. "How nice to see you again." He used his free hand to gesture at Anna while the hand on her back curled possessively. "I'd like to introduce you to my girlfriend, Anna. Anna, this is Lauren Potter."

Anna smiled and held out a hand. "Hello. It's nice to meet you."

The other woman didn't move to take Anna's hand. Instead, she raked her eyes up and down the length of Anna's body, and Anna could almost see her mentally comparing the two of them. She could also see the smile that crossed Lauren's mouth when Lauren realized that she came out on top. "Ah, yes. The little librarian that has the Grandmaster in such a kerfuffle. Charmed, I'm sure."

Jack frowned. "Lauren," he said sharply.

But she ignored him, her eyes already back on Rhys. "You should call me," she said, her voice husky. "We haven't seen each other in some time. It would be fun to catch up. I could make it worth your time."

Anna narrowed her eyes. Was this woman actually *propositioning* Rhys? After he had just introduced Anna as his girlfriend? *Of all the cheek...*

"I don't think so." Rhys's voice remained polite, but Anna could feel his body tense in anger. He slid his hand around her waist to clutch at her, and it made her feel much better.

Lauren pouted at him. "Rhys, I'm hurt! We used to have good times together. I'm sure you're having fun with... " Her hand fluttered at Anna. "With *her*. But let's face it. Not a lot of women can keep up with you. And you know well and good that I can." She licked her lips.

Anna felt herself shrink back at those words. She herself had been thinking the very same thing this morning. But she'd be damned if some bimbo was going to come slinking up and bat her eyelashes at him while she was standing right there. So she took a step forward and cleared her throat.

"Excuse me," she said politely when everyone had turned to look at her. She still held a smile on her face, even though she was sure it was more of a grimace. "First of all, I am standing right here. If you are going to insult me, please have the balls to do it to my face. Second, I can assure you I am more than capable of 'keeping up' with Rhys." She bared her teeth at the other woman. "Which is probably one of the reasons why I woke up in his bed this morning and you didn't."

Silence fell on the group. Anna watched with satisfaction as color rushed into the other woman's cheeks as Lauren finally turned to face her. Anna crossed her arms over her chest and lifted an eyebrow, waiting for the other woman to respond.

She didn't. Instead, she turned back to Rhys. "Just remember what I said," she muttered, her hands balling into fists. "My offer still stands." Then she turned and stalked away from them, head held high and hips swishing.

Anna blew out a long breath as she watched Lauren's retreat. "You sure do know the most interesting people," she muttered.

Jack was suddenly howling with laughter. Anna blinked at him in surprise as he leaned over, hands on his knees, tears leaking from the corners of his eyes. "That was... I have never seen..." He reached up to swipe at his eyes, his shoulders still shaking with mirth. "Ah, Rhys. You better hold on to that firecracker. If you don't, I really might steal her."

Rhys was looking at Anna with something akin to awe in his eyes. "Don't worry," he murmured. "I don't think you have to worry."

Nicola made a face. "Lauren is such a cunt," she said with feeling, causing Anna to gasp in shock. Nicola could be serious when she needed to be, but Anna had never heard her use language like that with such vehemence. "I can't believe she just did that."

"Yes, well. What did you expect?" Jack shrugged. "Some people never change. Especially self-centered, shallow people." He sighed. "I guess we should head on in. Pretty much everyone is here. We're still waiting on the Grandmaster and a few others, but they should be here any minute."

"You two go ahead," Rhys said, his arm circling around Anna's waist once more. "We'll join you in a moment."

Jack nodded, a smile tugging his lips upward. Anna got the impression that he smiled a lot. Then he turned to Nicola and made an elegant bow, offering his arm. "My lady, it would do me the greatest honor if you would grace the arm of this oh-so humble man."

"Humble, my arse," she muttered. But she was grinning as she linked her arm through his. They immediately started chatting as they headed off in the same direction as Lauren.

Anna was watching them go, but found herself being pulled off to the side by Rhys. She let him lead her to a corner of the room, sheltered by a large column and hidden away from view. "What are you ---"

He cut her off by pressing his mouth to hers. She blinked, his kiss totally taking her by surprise. But then those familiar tingles started arcing all over her body, and she closed her eyes and kissed him back. His hands came up to cup her face, and his body pressed against hers. Before she knew it, she could feel the wall at her back, and his mouth had moved to her throat.

She sighed and draped her arms around his neck. "What's gotten into you?" she asked. But she couldn't help titling her head back to give him better access.

"Are you kidding me?" He traced kisses along her jaw before skimming his nose down her neck. "The way you handled Lauren, the way you claimed me as *yours* in front of her..." His hands slid down to grasp her hips. "If we didn't have to go to this meeting, I would find an empty closet to drag you into right now."

"Mmmm." She closed her eyes. "So me standing up to jealous ex-girlfriends gets you excited, does it? How many more of those do you have lurking around?"

He sighed and pulled away, and Anna instantly regretted saying those words. He rested his forehead against hers. "I never thought she would speak to me, else I would have warned you. Lauren was... a mistake. I was young and stupid and she was beautiful."

"Still is."

He smiled, but there was no humor. "Only on the outside. I thought I loved her once. I thought she loved *me*. I mean, don't get me wrong. Our relationship was very physical, and that was the most important aspect for both of us at the time. But I thought there was something else there, too. Something deeper."

"But..."

Rhys sighed and pushed a hand through his hair. "Then I went to Prague," he said grimly. "And when I came back... Well, you know." He gestured at himself. "She made it clear that my body no longer suited her. And that was when I realized that there had never been anything else. At least, not for her."

Anna stood there, staring at him. She was looking at him, but she was seeing something different. She remembered the night they had first made love, his hesitation at taking off his shirt. She remembered how he'd pulled away when she touched the scars that marred him. Most of all, she remembered the haunted look in his eyes as he waited for her reaction.

He had thought she would be disgusted, that she wouldn't want to touch him. She could tell that he didn't think he deserved to be touched, that he was somehow disfigured. She had simply thought it was because of the scars themselves. But now, now she knew it had been because of another person telling him that he was unworthy. And that person was going to be sitting in the same room as Anna.

She let out a low growl, her vision going red. "That *bitch!*" she spat out. "Just wait until I get my hands on her. I'll make her wish that she had never ---"

"Anna!" Rhys had his hands on her face again, forcing her to look at him. "Don't stoop to her level.

You're right. She's just jealous. I'm sure she thought no one would ever want to be with me. Hell, *I* didn't think anyone would ever want to be with me. Seeing me with someone else must be driving her crazy. But there is nothing to worry about. I don't want anything to do with her." He trailed a finger down her cheek. "I only want you."

She was nearly vibrating with anger. "I don't care," she snarled. "She *hurt* you, Rhys. She left scars on you just as much as Thurston did. I want to rip her throat out."

He blinked at her, then he was laughing. It was his full-bodied laugh that Anna loved so much, and she was glad to hear it, even if she was still enraged. "I love you," he murmured, sliding his arms around her and pulling her tight against him. "Thank you for standing up for me. And thank you for loving me for who I am."

She sighed as she wrapped her arms around him. "I do love you. So much. And I can't stand the fact that she hurt you. And then to expect you to just jump back into bed with her because she threw you a crumb…. Ooooh. I *hate* women like that."

He chuckled as he pressed his lips to her forehead. "Don't worry. I don't think we have to worry about her anymore, not after you showed her up. I don't think anyone has ever done that before. She's not going to have a clue how to handle it."

"As long as she stays away from you," Anna said firmly. "If she tries anything else, I will punch her."

He kissed her again. "You're amazing," he whispered. "And you're all mine." Another kiss, then he was sighing and pulling her back out from the corner. "Come on. Let's go get this over with so I can get you home alone."

Anna had never been so nervous in her life.

She was sitting in the church's small Chapel of St. Anne, where the pews had been pushed aside to allow for several folding chairs to be placed in a circle. Rhys sat to her left, holding a quiet conversation with Jack. His hand rested on her thigh, and she had no doubt he could feel her nervous tension. Nicola, seated to her left, was also chatting with the person seated next to her. Anna let her eyes roam over the small room, looking everywhere she could to avoid Lauren's eyes. The other woman was sitting on the other side of the circle of chairs, but Anna could feel her eyes on her like twin lasers, hot and angry.

There were seventeen knights that worked in and around London, she had discovered. She was surprised by the wide range of people that were gathered in the room with her: there were old men and women, as well as young. The hum of several conversations taking place at once told her that there were several different accents as well. She could make out a thick Irish brogue from somewhere to her right, and a light, female voice from across the room was unmistakably Scottish.

She wished she could sink into the floor. She felt very, very out of place.

The door to the chapel opened then, and a hush fell across the assembled group. Then, as if following an unspoken rule, everyone rose to their feet. Anna followed, if nothing more than to avoid drawing attention to herself.

The man that entered didn't *look* very remarkable. He was older, perhaps in his late fifties, but he carried it well. He had silver hair and bright blue eyes that Anna doubted missed anything. He wore gray slacks and a white dress shirt that looked good against his tan skin.

But anyone looking at him would remember him. It was the way he *moved*. He carried a sense of Power about him that even Anna could feel. His strides were measured and long as he walked towards an empty chair He was graceful, and Anna was sharply reminded of the way tigers moved. She had no doubt whatsoever that this man was the Grandmaster.

He stood in front of his chair, looking out at the others. After a moment he nodded before sitting, and everyone else followed. "Thank you all for coming." His voice was soft, but, like his movements, carried Power. He was used to giving orders, and used to being obeyed. And his words were flavored with a light French accent. "Especially as this was such short notice. But I'm afraid we have a serious threat in your city, and it needs to be dealt with. Quickly." His eyes swept around the circle until they came to rest on Rhys. Anna could feel his hand squeeze her thigh. "Rhys, would you mind explaining what has been happening?"

Rhys let out a deep breath before launching into the story, beginning with Abraham's death and ending with the previous night's attempted kidnapping. He told them about the book, about what Finn had learned from the fake inspector, and about their realization that there was a traitor feeding information to Thurston. He told them about Anna's kidnapping, and how Thurston had planned to kill her. He told them about Graham, about how he had once been a Scholar who had decided to use the information he had learned from David for profit, and how he had killed before.

When he had finished, the Grandmaster gave a nod. "Thank you, Rhys. Now that you all have heard the details, we need to work together to decide how we are going to handle this threat." His blue eyes landed on Anna, and she had to fight not to wince away. "The first order of business is to make sure Miss Miller is safely out of harm's way. I will arrange to have her flown back to America as soon as we are finished here. She can return once Graham Thurston had been dealt with." Then his eyes had moved on and he was continuing to discuss what steps needed to be taken.

Anna blinked at him. That was *it*? He was just going to dismiss her like that? Like she wasn't even there? Before she knew what she was doing, she was standing. "Excuse me!" she called out. "I have a few issues with your plan."

Gabin LeBlanc turned back to her, his eyes narrowed. "I'm afraid you do not get a say in this matter." His voice was low and dangerous. If Anna had been an animal, she would have tucked her tail between her legs and scampered away.

Instead, she swallowed. "I'm afraid you are incorrect," she responded, hoping her voice didn't sound as shaky as she felt. "I am not one of your knights. Therefore, you have no claim over me, no right to dictate my actions. Furthermore, I have already sacrificed quite a bit. I have lost my mentor. I was kidnapped and tortured. I have shed *blood* for this. I will *not* be shipped off so the 'big boys' can handle things. I am staying right here, whether you like it or not." Just so he understood how serious she was, she crossed her arms over her chest and tried to look menacing.

Silence fell over the room. It was a heavy, pregnant silence, like the kind that came just before a storm. Anna could feel the eyes of every person in that room locked on to her as they waited for their Grandmaster to reprimand her. She did her best to ignore them, keeping her own gaze locked with that of LeBlanc. She knew he couldn't do anything to Rhys. Rhys had not violated any orders. But that didn't mean LeBlanc couldn't punish her somehow.

Suddenly, LeBlanc threw back his head and laughed. It reminded her of the laugh Jack had let out earlier when she had stood down Lauren. The Frenchman even slapped a hand on his knee.

Anna blinked at him, confused. She thought he would be angry. He didn't seem like the type who let others disobey him, especially not in front of his subordinates. It could make him appear weak. So why was he laughing? Unless she had somehow done something that would allow him to punish her. And maybe Rhys and Nicola, too. That thought made her sick.

But when LeBlanc finally lifted his eyes to meet hers again, they were full of laughter. A wide grin stretched across his face. "Ah, Miss Miller. It has been a long time since someone stood up to me. I must admit, it is rather refreshing. And I am glad to see that your ordeal has not lessened your gumption. Good. I was hoping you were not the type to go run and hide when things did not go well."

She blinked again. "Wait," she asked, her voice sounding small. "That was... what? A *test?*"

"*Oui.* This is why I had you attend as well." His smile faded. "I am afraid we are going to need the assistance of the Scholars in this matter, and, as Rhys pointed out, we may not be able to trust them entirely. However, we know *you* are not the traitor, so you are the best candidate we have. I had to make sure you could handle it, though. But I should have known. If you have not left yet, then you are not going to scare easily." He gave her a slight nod of respect.

Anna's breath left her in a whoosh, and she fell back onto her seat. Her head was spinning, and she missed what LeBlanc said next as she tried to understand what had just taken place. Rhys reached over to take her hand. When she turned to him, he was grinning fiercely at her, pride evident in his eyes. He lifted her hand to his lips and kissed every finger before dropping their joined hands to his lap, still grinning. She managed a weak smile, feeling dazed.

She didn't pay much attention to what was being said. She knew she wouldn't understand it all anyways. But when she felt Rhys shift in his seat next to her, she paid attention. "We already know Thurston is after me," he was saying grimly. "His henchman said as much last night. I'm his best bet at finding this book now. He is convinced it is at the Bradley, even though there has been no further evidence to prove this. Abraham is dead, and he has already tortured Anna. I was Abraham's son, for all intents and purposes, and am in a relationship with Anna. He will think that either one of them would have told me about the book."

Anna narrowed her eyes at him. "Rhys..." she said in a warning tone.

He turned to her and flashed her a smile before slightly shaking his head. "Don't worry," he murmured, giving her hand a reassuring squeeze. "I remember my promise. We're trying to figure out what Thurston's next move will be. He's bound to come after me again. We're just going to have to cut him off at the pass."

"Do you think he will come after you himself?" That was LeBlanc. He was slouched in his chair, looking thoughtful.

"I do," was Rhys's reply. "He's lost two of his key players. And one of his henchman has already failed. He won't have much of a choice." He gestured to Anna. "That was also the case with Anna's abduction. Everyone else had already failed to get the information needed, so he felt he had to step in and do it himself."

"I see. And Thurston is familiar with the Templars. It stands to reason that he will know who all of you are, so merely adding extra guards won't do much good."

"No, sir. Except maybe to cause more people unnecessary harm."

"I agree." The Frenchman's eyes glanced around the circle. "Does anyone else have any ideas? I will not risk any of you without reason. That includes you, Miss Miller. We *will* stop this man, and I will not let him hurt Rhys if there is anything I can do about it. We need to find the best way to lure Thurston in where we can take him under our own terms that will be the least risky."

Anna felt better upon hearing the sincerity in the man's voice. He wasn't going to just throw Rhys to the wolves in order to capture Graham. He wanted to keep Rhys safe, too. She felt her opinion of him rise.

The next few hours was spent throwing ideas around as to the best way to handle Thurston. Anna was impressed by the range of talents in the room. There were a few knights who were in the military, even one who was MI6. There was a policeman as well, and they all were offering their services to guard Rhys while remaining out of sight in hopes of luring Graham in.

When the meeting was finally adjourned, she couldn't help but feel better. If anyone could catch Graham Thurston, it was the men and women in this room.

She stood and stretched, wincing as she realized just how numb her bottom had become. She stood for a moment, letting the room empty out around her while she waited for feeling to return to her legs.

"Miss Miller?" LeBlanc's voice skittered across her conscious, and she turned to see he was still seated, but his blue eyes were drilling into her. "May I have a word with you please?"

She frowned. Hadn't he already got what he wanted out of her? "Sure," she said with a shrug.

Rhys took up position next to her, his hand finding its normal place on the small of her back.

LeBlanc smiled at that. "Alone, if you please." He held up a hand before Rhys could protest. "I'll do no harm to her, Rhys. Nor will I let any outside harm come to her. I only wish to speak with her. On my honor."

Rhys frowned. Anna could practically see his mind warring with itself over what to do. On one hand, Gabin was his Grandmaster. Even though the Frenchman had not given Rhys a direct order, Rhys still did not want to refuse him. But he didn't want to leave Anna alone, either. Not even for a moment.

"I'll be all right," she murmured, not wanting him to get in any trouble. She bared her teeth at the Frenchman. "I'm under no oath to obey him. If he tries anything, I know where to kick."

In response, the older man grinned. "She does have a point. And she's already demonstrated that she is not afraid to use her immunity to me to her advantage. I don't believe you have anything to fear."

Rhys let out a sigh of defeat, his shoulders slumping. "I'll go wait outside," he said softly to Anna. His eyes glittered with worry. "If you need me, just yell. Okay?"

She nodded. "I will. Promise."

Rhys leaned in to kiss her, not caring that they had an audience. When they pulled away, he gave a curt nod to LeBlanc before turning on his heel and walking out of the chapel doors.

The Frenchman watched him go with a fond smile on his face. "Rhys is a good man," he said softly.

"You don't even know the half of it," Anna snapped, crossing her arms over her chest.

He turned his eyes to her, and his smile widened. "You don't like me very much, do you?"

"No. I don't like this hold you have over Rhys, how you can make him do whatever you want, even if he doesn't want to."

Gabin let out a sigh and ran his hand through his hair. Anna couldn't help but note how much it made him look like an older version of Rhys. "Every knight is sworn to me once they turn eighteen. The power that gives me does have its... advantages. But I don't like to use it. I would much rather have them obey me out of loyalty and respect than because they *have* to. However, I *will* use it if I need to. We are talking about people's lives, here."

She lifted one shoulder in a shrug. "Doesn't mean I have to like it. Or you."

He snorted. "No. I suppose it doesn't. Have you had a chance to look at the Round yet?"

Anna frowned. "The Round? You mean, the ambulatory?"

"Yes. Where the effigies lie." He gestured her towards the door. "Please. Walk with me."

The church was eerily deserted when they emerged from the chapel, which struck Anna as odd. It was Saturday evening, and she would have expected tourists to be streaming in. Come to think of it, she had not seen anyone other than the knights when they had first entered. She knew she shouldn't be surprised. After all, she was currently standing next to the leader of the organization responsible for the church's construction. It would make sense that the Master of the Temple would make sure it was empty so that the Templars could conduct their business without arousing suspicion.

Gabin led her to where four stone effigies lay in repose on the floor of the church. "I always enjoy coming here," he said softly. "Seeing them reminds me of why I do what I do. It's not always easy, especially when I know I have to put one of my people in danger. But the Marshal and his sons help me regain my focus and resolve."

Anna had seen many pictures of the effigies, but seeing them in person was not as awe-inspiring as she would have thought. First of all, their eyes were open, which unnerved her much more than she was willing to admit. Three of them held drawn swords, looking as though they would climb up off the floor at any moment to defend their father. It was that image, as well as the somber thought that the mortal remains of these men lay beneath her feet, that caused Anna to shiver.

Her companion let out a sigh and leaned against one of the pillars, his arms crossed across his chest. "I seem to find myself in a somewhat embarrassing position," he told her grimly. "And, as much as I hate to admit it, I need your help."

Anna's eyes went wide. "*My* help?" she squeaked. "But you don't like Scholars!" She winced as soon as the words left her mouth.

But he just smiled. "You are your colleagues are vital to us," he said. "I am very thankful for the skills that you provide. However, I have my own people to take care of. The knights are my priority. I cannot afford to worry about them *and* the Scholars as well." His smile faded. "And, it seems, that has come back to, what is the expression? Bite me in the arse. I never would have thought of a Scholar betraying us. I perhaps underestimated your lot, thinking that you were all only a bunch of academics and could do nothing to hurt us."

Anna was silent. She got the impression that the Frenchman didn't admit to flaws very often, and she was more than happy to let him squirm through it.

"I am hoping that I can remedy this, with your help." His eyes locked on to hers. "I need someone to keep me up to date on what the Scholars are doing, any rumors or gossip or information that could impact the knights. I need someone I can trust. I need *you*, Anna."

She blew out a breath. "You want me to be a *spy?*"

He waved his hand dismissively. "Not a spy, per se. You'll be my eyes and ears. Someone who can keep me informed. I can't do it myself." He suddenly gave her a wolfish smile. "And I know that you won't betray the knights, not as long as Rhys is involved."

He was right about that. She would *never* do anything that could cause Rhys harm. But still... She shrugged. "Why me? I've only just joined the Scholars. I haven't even really done anything... Scholarly yet. Wouldn't someone who was more entrenched be better?"

He shook his head. "Anyone who has been a Scholar for some time will be more likely to let their sense of loyalty outweigh the need to keep me informed. You are young, and you are new."

"Meaning I'm someone you can mold however you want," she replied dryly.

"Yes," he said, unapologetically. "I also know that if I recruit you now, I will have someone on the inside for many years. Hopefully, we will never find ourselves in a situation like this again."

"What if Rhys and I break up?"

Gabin smiled at her, a *real* smile that reached his eyes. "I've seen the way he looks at you, and you at him," he said softly. "It's not a look one sees often, and you don't forget it when you have. I don't think I have to worry about that."

For some reason, his answer made Anna blush.

He let out a sigh and pushed away from the column he was leaning against. "I am not asking you to betray anyone, Anna. I will not put you in any danger. First of all, that is not what I am wanting. Second, Rhys would kill me, oath be damned. All I ask is that you send me regular updates on anything that you are hearing about. No one else needs to know about this."

"Can I tell Rhys?" She wouldn't be able to keep anything from him.

"Yes. And Nicola, too. But no one else. I can give you my private number and email address so that you can contact me directly." He tilted his head to the side. "Do we have a deal?"

She thought about it. He wasn't asking her to do anything that would get her in trouble. He was only asking to keep him informed. And it could help save lives, help keep the knights safe. She couldn't do much, but she could do that.

She walked over to stand above the stone effigy of William the Marshal and held out her hand. Gabin walked to the other side of the effigy and took her hand in his, giving it a firm shake. She felt the eyes of the effigy looking up at her, and fervently hoped that the old knight approved.

When she opened the door of the church, she found both Blkacwoods waiting for her. Nicola was leaning against the building, while Rhys was pacing back and forth. He immediately leapt to her side, his eyes worried.

"Everything all right?" he asked her. "What was that all about?"

She let out a sigh, still feeling slightly dazed over the day's events. "I'm not really sure," she murmured. "I'll tell you about it on the way home."

Chapter Twenty-Six

The next morning, Anna found a note in the kitchen when she went looking for breakfast. It was from Nicola. *I'm going to be out all day,* it read. *I'll bring something home for dinner. NO SEX ON MY BED!*

Anna couldn't help but laugh, at the same time feeling deeply touched. She had no doubt that Nicola had left so that Anna and Rhys could finally have time together on their own.

"What's so funny?" Rhys asked as he came to stand behind her, wrapping his arms about her waist.

"This," Anna replied handing him the note. "I love your sister."

Rhys read the brief note, grinning as he got to the last line. "She asked me last night if she needed to make herself scarce today."

"Well, it was really nice of her." Especially after Anna had been so upset yesterday at having her time with Rhys interrupted.

"I agree." Rhys spun Anna to face him and lifted her, causing her to squeal, before sitting her on the counter. He nudged her legs apart so he could stand between them, grinning up at her, green eyes sparkling. "And I think we should take advantage of every moment she's given us."

Anna couldn't agree more.

The next few days passed as close to normal as any day had since the night Abraham had died. Rhys took her to work, she spent her day at the library, and he picked her up. In the evenings, the Blackwood siblings would tell her about any new information they had learned during the day. Both of them assured her that there were other knights keeping an eye out for Rhys, even though Anna hadn't seen any. But she felt better knowing that someone was watching over him.

And the nights…. were magical. She had abandoned sleeping in her own room, preferring to sleep with Rhys. Some nights they made love, some nights they simply held each other while watching TV. Anna didn't care. For her, all that mattered was that he was there when she fell asleep at night, and when she awoke the next morning. Despite everything happening around her, she was deliriously happy.

On Thursday, she finished the monk's journal. She sat for a long while, staring at the last page, feeling a strange sense of sadness. She had spent several months pouring over this man's life, living each day with him, sharing his joys and sorrows. She wondered why he had stopped writing, if he had died or had moved on to another book or simply ceased tracking his daily activities. Reverently closing the cracked leather cover made her feel like she was saying goodbye to a dear friend.

She sat back with a sigh, closing her eyes. She still had plenty to do. She had to type up her translation of the journal, then she could start cross-referencing. But she needed a moment. She couldn't just reach the end of the monk's story and then immediately ----

Her cell phone suddenly let out an angry buzz. Frowning, she opened her eyes and reached for it. No one ever called her or texted her while she was at work. Everyone knew to call her work phone.

It was a text message from Rhys. Anna couldn't stop a goofy grin from crossing her face as she checked it. Rhys rarely sent texts. He said it was impersonal. Whenever he did, it was usually some small thing that would be sent in order to brighten her day.

This, however, wasn't romantic. *Something has come up,* it read. *Do you think Maggie can give you a ride home?*

Anna frowned, suddenly feeling unsettled. *Is everything all right?* she responded.

A moment passed before the phone buzzed again. *Yes. And I hope to be home by the time you get there. But I don't want to leave you alone at the library.*

I'm sure she won't mind. If nothing else, I can take the train.

No. His reply was almost immediate. *If Maggie can't bring you home, I'll find someone to come and pick you up.*

Let me go ask. Anna stood and walked the short distance down the hallway to Maggie's office. "Maggie?" she called out, peeking around the doorframe.

The head librarian was sitting behind her desk, frowning thoughtfully at her computer screen. She didn't notice Anna. It took the younger woman calling out her name twice more, each time in a louder voice, before Maggie noticed her.

"I'm sorry, dear," she said apologetically, removing her glasses to rub at her eyes. "I am absolutely appalled by the grammar some of these younger librarians use. I am so glad you actually spell out words instead of using that awful text lingo. What can I help you with?"

Anna couldn't help but wince in sympathy. That was one of her biggest pet peeves as well. "Could you possibly give me a ride to the Blackwoods' after work? Rhys said something has come up, and he won't be able to come and get me. I offered to take the train, but...."

"I'll be happy to take you home. If you took the tube Rhys would have both of our hides." Maggie grinned. She knew how protective Rhys was when it came to Anna. "I happen to like mine just where it is, thank you very much."

Anna grinned in return. "Thanks, Maggie. I'll owe you lunch."

The older woman waved a hand in dismissal. "No worries." Then she brightened. "Actually, I have a way for you to pay me back. How about you try to decipher these emails for me before I throw something?"

By the end of the day, Anna was feeling pretty cranky as well. Maggie was right. No matter how old, a librarian should know better than to use text lingo in a professional email. The two women spent the entire ride to the Blackwood residence rallying against the evils of the modern age and the woeful lack of writing skills prevalent in the younger generation. Once again, Anna was extremely thankful she had decided to not be a teacher.

She let out the breath she hadn't realized she'd been holding when they reached the Blackwoods' home and Rhys's car was parked in the driveway. He had told her not to worry, that everything was under control, but that hadn't stopped her. Especially since he never told her what had happened. He had

181

promised he would tell her that evening.

"I appreciate the ride," she said as she prepared to climb out of Maggie's car.

"And I appreciate you handling those emails for me," the older woman said with a grin. "I'm pretty sure I got the better end of the deal. You tell Rhys he can let me drive you home anytime he wants."

Anna laughed. "I'll be sure to let him know." She stood in the driveway and waved goodbye until Maggie's taillights disappeared. Then she turned and walked into the house. "Rhys?" she called out, letting the strap of her purse slide off of her shoulder. "I'm home. Is everything---"

Something moved in her periphery. Before she could turn to see what it was, however, a large hand clamped down over her mouth and an arm snaked around her chest, pinning her arms to her side.

She immediately began to struggle, twisting violently in the grasp of her captor. She tried to bite the hand that covered her mouth, but whoever was holding her was clenching her jaw, leaving her unable to move.

A chuckle floated down to her. "Did you think that I would let you do that to me twice?" came a cultured male voice. "I learned my lesson the last time."

Anna let out an involuntary whimper.

It was Graham Thurston who held her.

"That's a good girl," he purred as fear stopped her struggling. "Now, then. We are going to go into the kitchen and have a nice, civilized chat." He let go of her, but before she could even think about moving, his hand was in her hair, twisting it around his fist and pulling at it painfully. Anna let out a cry and reached up to grip his hand, trying to take some of the pressure off of her scalp. When he tugged her into motion, she had no choice but to follow.

He pulled her to the kitchen, the pain making in her eyes water. But as soon as they stepped into the brightly lit kitchen, her own pain was immediately forgotten.

Rhys was there. He was sitting in a chair, his hands tied behind his back. He was gagged, and blood ran freely from his head. His eyes, when they met hers, were clouded and full of pain.

"*Rhys!*" She pulled against Thurston's grip, not caring about the pain. When he let her go, she stumbled forward, dropping to her knees in front of Rhys. Her hands went to the strip of cloth that Graham had used as a gag, pulling it free. "Rhys. Are you all right?"

His breathing was ragged, and she was alarmed to see more blood on his shirt and jeans. "Anna," he rasped. "So sorry. That text... He said he was..." He dropped his head and closed his eyes.

She understood. The text had come from Thurston using Rhys's phone. She felt a flash of anger pass through her. How long had the former Scholar been there, hurting the man she loved?

"Shhh." She reached up to find the wide gash on the top of his head, the source of the blood that was flowing freely down his face, and pressed the cloth against it. He hissed. "It's okay. I need you to look at me, okay? Rhys?"

"I'm fairly certain he has a concussion," came Graham's voice from behind her, carrying a hint of amusement. "He was unconscious for quite a while. I was beginning to wonder if I had hit him too hard."

But he recognized you, which means he should be just fine."

Anna turned just enough to glare at the other man, keeping the cloth pressed tight against Rhys's head wound. "What do you want?" she snapped.

He spread his hands. "Why, I only want to talk. I need to find my book, and your young knight is going to tell me where it is."

"He doesn't know where it is, either," she spat, turning her back on Thurston once more. Her free hand went up to gently touch Rhys's cheek. "Rhys?" she said softly. "Listen to me, okay? I need you to ---"

Suddenly, a hand was back in her hair, dragging her backwards. She let out a shriek, her hands coming up to scrabble at the arm that held her. She heard Rhys let out a cry, but she was too busy trying to keep her scalp from being ripped off. She felt herself being lifted by nothing but her hair, causing her to let out a cry of pain, before she was thrown into a second chair, one she hadn't noticed when she had entered the kitchen. She sat there for a moment, gasping as the pain slowly faded.

"Wrong answer." Graham's voice was a low purr, and it was right at her ear. She tried to jerk away, but her movements were halted by the very sharp knife he was suddenly pressing into her neck. "I'm willing to bet that he knows *exactly* where it is. And he is going to tell me. Or he is going to watch as I slice you to ribbons." He moved his mouth closer to her ear and dropped his voice to a whisper. "I was only playing with you last time. You have no idea of what I am capable of."

She shuddered. She didn't doubt him.

"Let her go," Rhys called out in a rough voice. "If you hurt her, so help me God..."

"Come now, Mr. Blackwood. There is no need for threats. All you have to do is tell me where my book is and there will be no need for me to hurt her."

A low growl rose from Rhys's throat. He had lifted his head and was glaring across the kitchen at Thurston, even though it was obviously difficult for him. "I don't know where the damn book is! I didn't even know about the book until a few days before you had Abraham killed. You probably know more about the book than I do!"

"Ah, now. I do find that hard to believe." The knife at Anna's throat begin to slide downward, and she took a deep breath, holding it as the knife trailed down her throat, leaving a thin ribbon of blood in its wake. "Did you know that when I was seducing your Anna I had wondered what it would be like to take her? She was so innocent, so sweet. And she trusted me implicitly. After I realized what she meant to you, I regretted not doing it." The knife began to make its way across the swell of her breasts. "Perhaps I should remedy that. Right here, so you can watch." He licked his lips.

"I don't know!" Rhys's face was turning red, and Anna could see him struggling against his bonds. "There is nothing else I can tell you. *Now let her go!*"

"I don't think so." The knife was suddenly gone from Anna's chest. Without so much as blinking, Thurston grasped the hilt and drove it into Anna's thigh with as much force as he could generate.

Anna stared at it. Part of her wanted to reach for it and pull it out of her leg, but her practical side told her that it was better to leave it in so that she didn't bleed to death. She had seen that on TV. She was vaguely aware of someone screaming. It took her a moment to realize it was her.

"Anna!" Rhys's face was contorted in agony. "I'll kill you, Thurston. Do you hear me? *I'll kill you!*"

The other man only smiled coldly. Then he reached behind him and pulled out Rhys's handgun and pointed it at Anna. "I don't think so," he said, his voice quiet.

A hush fell over the room, broken only by Rhys's ragged breathing and Anna's whimpers. The two men stared at each other, while Anna gripped the arms of the chair and tried to keep herself from passing out. She knew she had to stay conscious. If she fainted, she wouldn't be able to defend herself. Graham would kill her, possibly rape her, and he would make Rhys watch. She couldn't let that happen.

"I don't need her for anything," Thurston said, his voice hardened steel. "If you don't want to cooperate, I will kill her. I'll have my way with her first, then kill her. Slowly. And I'll make you watch every second of it. So tell me what I need to know, else you will be signing her death warrant."

Rhys let out a snarl. "I *am* telling you. You just don't want to hear it. Abraham never told me where the book was."

The hammer was pulled back on the gun. "Then why did Abraham get you involved? He wouldn't have called in the knights unless he had something to protect."

"He *did* have something to protect: Anna. He had been told about the letter in Turkey, and he was afraid that someone might come to the Bradley looking for the book. He hadn't even told Anna about the Scholars yet. So he asked me to come by and pretend to be a patron, to get to know her and stay close to her so that I could protect her if I had to."

"Did he tell you if the book was there?"

"No. He didn't tell me anything else about the book. He only said that he was worried about someone coming after Anna and wanted me to look after her. That was it. I had just gone to the library to meet her when you sent your goons in and they killed Abraham."

Thurston was silent, mulling over what Rhys had said. Anna tried to get her breathing under control. She was now aware of the pain in her leg, and it was throbbing. But she couldn't take her eyes off of the gun that was only inches away from her.

Finally, Graham let out a heavy sigh. "You're lying," he said simply before pulling the trigger.

The sound of the shot echoed loudly in the enclosed room. A hot, searing pain tore through Anna's shoulder, and she screamed. She had never screamed so loud in her life, and her throat was burning from the force of it. But even that was nearly drowned out by the loud howl that came from Rhys.

"Anna!"

I'm going to die, the part of her that could still form coherent thought said. And she believed it. Graham was insane. There was no denying it. He would never believe that Rhys didn't know where the book was. And he would keep hurting her just to torture Rhys.

A tear leaked from the corner of her eye. She didn't want to hurt Rhys. But there was nothing she could do. Graham would ----

Suddenly, Rhys let out a scream of his own. As Anna watched, her vision swirling, he managed to stand, hunched over with the chair on his back. She thought he looked like a turtle. Letting out another battle cry, he managed to scurry forward, using the chair's weight to propel himself. Then he was crashing into the other man, sending them both flying into the wall.

Anna heard a loud *crunch,* and tried to turn to see what was happening. But moving sent a fresh wave of pain from both her shoulder and her leg, and she found herself on the verge of passing out. Behind her, she could hear Thurston swearing, and she knew she had to do something.

Something glinted to her right. Turning slowly, she saw Rhys's gun lying on the floor. Her eyes widened as she realized Graham must have dropped it when Rhys hit him. It lay two feet away, but it might as well have been two miles.

Sickening thuds arose from behind her, and Graham's voice was snarling curses. She didn't have to look to know that he was beating Rhys, who was still bound.

Move! her brain shouted at her. *Move, or he's going to kill Rhys!*

She wouldn't let that happen. Not while she still had breath. So she moved to the end of the chair and slid to the floor.

That movement sent her reeling, and she had to close her eyes and grit her teeth as the nausea passed through her. She heard a distinct crunching noise, then the unmistakable sound of Rhys screaming. She bit her lip so hard she tasted blood and focused on that pain, pushing the rest of it to the back of her mind. She crawled forward, staying on her side so that she didn't jostle the knife that was still in her thigh. She reached out, using her one good arm to pull herself forward, then using her good leg to push.

It seemed to take an eternity, but she finally found the cool metal of the gun beneath her fingertips.

A surge of hope passed through her. She gripped the gun and turned back to where Graham was hunched over Rhys, kicking at the bound man. She pulled herself up to a sitting position and raised the gun. "Thurston!" she called out.

He stopped and turned to her. When he saw what she held, he sneered. "Are you going to shoot me, little girl? Look at you. You can't even hold it still. Do you really think ---"

She pulled the trigger.

Her first shot was off, hitting him on the top of his left shoulder. So she adjusted the way her father had taught her and pulled the trigger again before her target could move. This time, a bloom of red appeared in the center of his chest.

Graham stopped and looked down, his eyes going wide in surprise. He opened his mouth, as though to say something, but Anna never gave him the chance. She raised the gun a little higher and pulled the trigger a third time. This time, it hit him in the eye.

Graham Thurston dropped to the ground without a sound.

Anna held on to the gun for another moment, keeping it trained on the prone figure, just in case he moved. Finally, she realized that he wasn't going to be getting up again. The gun fell from her suddenly nerveless fingers, and she fell into darkness.

Chapter Twenty-Seven

Anna had never been so bored in her life.

She lay on her bed in the Blackwoods' home, her wounded leg propped up on a stack of pillows, her arm strapped firmly to her torso. The remote for the TV lay on the nightstand, and a stack of books and crossword puzzles rose almost to the height of the bed. But she had already worked several of the puzzles, couldn't concentrate enough on the books, and couldn't find anything to watch on TV.

She let out a frustrated sigh and turned to look at the clock on the nightstand. It would be another two hours before she would be allowed to take her pain medication again, two more hours until she could drop into deep, dreamless sleep. Until then, she would have to find something to keep her occupied.

A knock came at the door, and she brightened. Nicola must be coming to check on her, which meant that Anna could get the other woman to help her up so that she could at least walk around a bit. "Come in!" she called, carefully scooting back on her pillows.

The door opened, and Anna's heart dropped. It was Nicola, but she wasn't alone. She had her shoulder under Rhys's arm, supporting him into the room.

She instantly dropped her eyes, training them on the TV, not looking at him. She couldn't. It hurt too much.

"Here you are," he said, his voice rough. "Nic said you were here, but I was beginning to wonder if you had left without saying goodbye."

"What are you doing up?" she asked softly. "You should be in bed. Nicola ---"

"There is a bed right here," he interrupted. "And there is plenty of room for both of us, if you will scoot over. Remember?"

She didn't answer. Nor did she move.

He sighed. "Anna, if you don't move, Nicola will move you herself. I'm not leaving. It's your choice."

She still didn't move.

He shrugged. "Fine. Have it your way, then." He turned to his sister. "If you would be so kind…"

"Fine!" Anna said hurriedly. "I'll move. Just… You'll have to give me a minute."

While she was extremely thankful that Thurston had shot her in her left shoulder instead of her right, it made moving to the left a bit tricky. She moved her left leg, the one that was uninjured, to hook it over the side of the bed and anchor herself. Then she lifted her body, using her good arm to push herself to the left. She was able to move several inches over, giving Rhys enough room to lie down next to her. It also left her exhausted.

Nicola gently lowered Rhys onto the edge of the bed and, and Anna winced at the sounds of pain he was trying to cover up. "You shouldn't be moving so much," she snapped at him. "What were you thinking, Nicola? He needs to rest!"

The other woman fixed her with a stare. "You know as well as I do that he doesn't listen to reason. He told me I could either help him down here or he would crawl." She walked back to the door. "Now, you kids play nice. Yell if you need anything."

Then she was gone.

Rhys stretched himself out on the bed, letting out a sigh of relief as the movement eased the pain from his broken ribs. He slid closer to her until he was only an inch or so away, and held out his arm, inviting her to move into him.

But she stayed where she was, keeping her eyes away from him. "I don't want to hurt you," she murmured.

"Anna, please." His voice was filled with pain, and not the physical kind. "I need you."

She closed her eyes and turned her head away. She should have known he would use her own words against her. It wasn't fair, but it worked. She moved to her right until she could carefully pillow her head on his shoulder.

His arm tightened around her, his hand resting on her waist, and he let out a contented sigh. "There," he murmured. "That's better. Now, let's talk about why you've been avoiding me."

She felt herself stiffen. "What do you mean? I haven't been avoiding you." But the lie sounded weak, even to her.

Rhys chuckled. "Anna, I know avoidance when I see it. Nic told me you've been asking after me, but that you refuse to come see me. She said you make up an excuse every time she offered to bring you to the hospital or up to my room. And I know you can move around." He nodded over her head. She knew what he was referring to: a single crutch and a hospital-issued wheelchair. "So the reason you haven't come to see me is because you don't want to."

The accusation in his voice stung worse than the knife wound in her leg. "Rhys, I..." She tried to come up with a reason, but nothing was coming to mind that wouldn't sound like the lie it was.

"What is it, Anna?" His voice sounded agonized, making Anna's heart ache. "Is it because of what happened to you? I am sorry. I know I promised to protect you, and I failed. I let you down." He paused. "If... If you want to go back to America, I won't blame you. I won't even try to stop you." His voice had dropped into a tortured whisper.

She blinked, looking up at him for the first time.

His face was nothing but one gigantic bruise. Graham had broken his nose, and Rhys's left eye was still swollen shut. The gash in his head had required several stitches, and he had indeed suffered a concussion. In addition, he had suffered a broken wrist, several broken ribs, and a punctured lung. Nicola had assured her that he was okay, but seeing him so battered made Anna want to cry.

And he thinks it's his fault I don't want to see him!

"Rhys, no." She lifted her good hand so that she could touch his face, but then dropped it when she realized there was nowhere on his face that wasn't bruised. "I'm not going back to America. I'm not leaving you."

There was a pause, then she felt his body sag in relief as a breath of air escaped him with a hiss. "Then what is it?" he asked, his voice full of desperation. "Why are you avoiding me? Tell me what's wrong so I can make it better."

She drew up, trying to make herself as small as possible. "You can't," she said miserably. "No one can. You should just... stay away from me."

He growled. "Now why the hell would I want to do that? I *love* you, Anna. That hasn't changed. I have been so..."

He trailed off, and Anna cringed. Rhys wasn't stupid. She knew he would realize what she was talking about. And when he did, he would leave her. She knew it.

"Oh, Anna." His voice was barely more than a whisper. "Sweetheart, no."

She closed her eyes, feeling the hot prick of tears form behind her eyes. *This is it,* she thought. She waited for the blow to fall.

He tightened his arm, trying to pull her closer. He turned his head to the side so that he could gently bury his nose in her hair. "You did what you had to do," he whispered. "No one blames you."

"But I *killed* a man!" she cried out, finally giving voice to the fear that had kept her away from him ever since that fateful night. "I'm a murderer. A *monster!*" Tears were pouring down her cheeks. "I'm no better than *he* was."

"No. You're *not* a monster. And you're not a murderer." His voice was firm. "Anna, he was going to kill you. He was going to *rape* you. And he would have killed me, too." She could feel him smile. "He almost did."

"I *know!*" she wailed, hunching even further into herself. "I couldn't stop him. He still hurt you. And then I killed him. I could have wounded him. But I shot him three times. I didn't have to." Now that the words were coming out, she couldn't stop them. "I thought you were dead. I thought I was too late. And I still killed him. And I was *happy* about it!"

Rhys fell silent, and she waited for him to move away from her, waited to hear him say the words she had been dreading since she had awoken in the hospital nearly two weeks ago. *I'm sorry,* she had imagined him saying. *But I have to leave. I can't be with you. I just... can't. Not anymore.*

Finally, he spoke. "Do you know," he said, his voice soft, "that when I heard those shots I thought he had shot you again? I don't know how I was still conscious, but I was, and I realized that he had stopped. That he wasn't still beating me. I thought that he had turned his attention back to you, knowing that I couldn't go anywhere. When I heard that gun go off..." She felt a shudder go through his body. "I thought I had lost you. I thought that he had taken you away from me, that I hadn't been able to keep you safe. All I could think in those first few moments was that I was going to kill him. That I was going to kill him slowly. That I was going to inflict as much pain on him as I could before I ended him. That anger is what kept me alive. It wasn't until I woke up in the hospital that Nicola told me you were alive. And that Thurston was dead." His voice caught. "When she told me that... I have never been so happy in my life."

Anna turned her face so that she could press it into his side. Even though she thought she was a monster, she craved his familiar touch and scent. She needed him, even though she wanted to push away from him at the same time. She didn't deserve him. Not anymore.

The hand at her waist began to move up and down her side in a soothing gesture. "I wish you didn't have to carry this burden. I wish I could have been the one to kill him instead. But you didn't murder him. You saved my life, Anna. More importantly, you saved *your* life. I respect you for that. And I still love you. Nothing, and I mean *nothing* can change that. Do you understand me? *I love you."*

She wept then, giving in to all of the pain and sorrow and anxiety that the last few weeks had brought. She had almost lost him, had almost been too late. A few more minutes and Graham would have left irreparable damage. As it was, Rhys had had to stay in the hospital for a week and a half after she had been released. And then she had been so afraid that he wouldn't want her any more, not after he finally realized just what she had done, that she wouldn't let herself go see him, as much as she wanted to.

Rhys continued to comfort her as best as he could. "I know," he whispered. "I know you feel... dirty. Contaminated. Like you are someone who deserves to be shunned." Then his voice turned firm. "But you are *not* a monster. Thurston was the monster. He had killed before. He killed Bella. He nearly killed me. He had *Abraham* killed. And who knows how many others he's killed along the way, either by his own hands or at his instructions. And if you hadn't have stopped him, he would have killed both of us. Then he would have killed others. I refuse to let you feel like you are less of a person because of *him*. He's *gone,* Anna. It's over. He can't hurt either of us anymore. Nor will he ever be able to hurt anyone else. And it's thanks to you."

She pressed herself closer to him. If her arm hadn't been strapped to her, she would have thrown it around him, holding him to her. But she took what she could, taking strength from him, letting his love and acceptance surround her. "I love you," she hiccupped, her voice muffled.

She felt him sigh as he pressed a trembling to kiss to the top of her head. "We're together," he whispered. "Everything is going to be okay."

Epilogue

Anna inhaled deeply as she pulled out the pan of spaghetti, breathing in the familiar aroma. She carefully sat the pan on top of the stove before inserting a second pan, this one covered with slices of garlic bread, into the oven. The smells reminded her of home, and she felt a slight twinge of homesickness. But then it was gone, and she closed the oven door.

It felt odd to be back in her own flat. She had been here so little over the past two months that nothing about it seemed familiar. Worst of all, it didn't have anything of Rhys's in it, which made her feel jumpy and paranoid. She wore his sweatshirt, breathing in his scent, giving her the only feelings of safety that she could manage.

It had been several days since she had last seen him, and she missed him far more than she was willing to admit. She was still coming to terms with the fact that she had taken the life of another human being, and after the third night of Rhys waking her from a nightmare, she had refused to sleep next to him until she had gotten herself under control. He was still healing. He needed rest.

Nicola had referred Anna to one of her colleagues, who had immediately suggested she get out of the Blackwoods' house. After all, that was where she had killed Graham. It made sense that being there was playing havoc with her mind, which was already saturated with guilt. So she had packed up her things and went back to her own flat. The nightmares had gotten better. She wasn't having them every night now. But maybe that was because she rarely slept through the night now that she was alone.

Rhys and Nicola had been very busy. Now that Graham was dead, the man they had known as Inspector Pelley had opened up and confessed everything, including the names of the two henchmen, the ones who had killed Abraham and helped to kidnap her. The Blackwood siblings were working with Finn to track the two men down and arrest them. They were also looking into Graham's personal papers, hoping to discover the name of the traitor who had been feeding them information. The last time Anna had spoken to Rhys, they had several boxes of records to go through.

She had not been charged with anything. Her shooting of Graham had clearly been self-defense. The police officers who had questioned her had told her that she had done the right thing. It was obvious from the injuries both she and Rhys had suffered that he would have killed them if she hadn't killed him first. Hearing the police tell her she wasn't guilty made her feel better.

She didn't remember anything after passing out on the floor of the Blackwood' kitchen. Later, Nicola had told her that one of the other knights who had been set to watch Rhys had been alarmed because he hadn't heard from Rhys for several hours. When he came by the house to check on his charge, he had found the three of them and called for an ambulance. Gabin Le Blanc had come by the hospital to apologize profusely and to check on both of them several times.

She had gone back to work, once more taking the Underground to and from the library. Sarah had once again become her friend, hoping for a bit of gossip. This time, Anna didn't bother to share. And when Maggie had firmly told the older librarian to leave Anna alone or else, Anna was relieved. She was glad to be back at work. It gave her something to concentrate on other than the vision of Graham dropping to the ground with a bullet through his eye. And it didn't hurt that she had a large and brilliant bouquet of flowers on her desk, most of them daises, sent by Rhys. The card he had attached to the flowers said he wanted her to have something that would make her smile and think of him.

Tonight, though, Rhys would be coming over. She was nervous, though she had no idea why. She knew everything was okay between them. He didn't see her any differently than he had before she had killed Graham. He told her he was worried about her, but he hadn't crowded her. Instead, he had given her the space she needed to work through her guilt. She loved him all the more for it.

If she wanted to be honest with herself, she was nervous about the fact that they would finally be able to be a 'normal' couple. Everything they had done so far had been dictated by Graham Thurston. They had spent so much time worrying about him and his cronies that she found the idea that they could do whatever they wanted when they wanted odd. She was also afraid that it would give Rhys time to see her in a normal light, and that he would find her wanting.

Before she could let herself get mired in that depressing thought, the doorbell rang. She quickly hurried through the kitchen and into the living room, smoothing down her shirt as she peeked out through the peephole in the door.

Rhys was standing outside.

She wiped her suddenly sweaty palms on her jeans and opened the door. "Hi," she said softly.

He looked... *amazing,* her brain finished for her. The bruises on his face had faded, and only a faint yellow smudge around his left eye was left. His nose was now slightly crooked, but it didn't detract from his attractiveness at all. The doctors had said he was healing very well, and would be back to normal in no time.

She felt her lips tug up in a smile. It was good to see him looking like himself again.

"Hi, yourself," he replied. He tilted his head to the side. "What are you smiling about?"

"Nothing." She stepped aside. "Come on in. Dinner's almost ready."

She waited until he had stepped past her before shutting the door. She turned to walk back towards the kitchen, but found herself caught up in a powerful embrace. Rhys clutched her tight against him as his mouth crashed down onto hers in a desperate kiss.

She was caught off-guard by the sudden movement and by the deep emotions that she felt sweeping through him. She grasped his forearms, her knees suddenly refusing to support her. Only his strong arms around her waist kept her from falling into the floor in a boneless heap.

She let out a gasp as he pulled away. "Don't let go," she whispered, clutching tightly to him.

"Never," he growled, his eyes flashing. Then he was kissing her again.

When they broke apart once more, Anna was absolutely breathless. It didn't help that Rhys had lowered his head to nuzzle her neck. "Stop," she told him, pushing at him. But her efforts were only half-hearted. "I need to get the bread out of the oven before it burns."

He let out a disappointed sigh, but let her go. Feeling flushed, she hurried back into the kitchen to pull the garlic bread out of the oven.

Rhys had followed her. "You didn't have to do all of this for me," he said quietly, though she could hear the pleasure in his voice.

She shrugged. "I thought it would be nice. You know, cook us a real dinner. Then we could just stay in all night." She turned and offered him a grin. "Besides, you haven't actually tasted my cooking yet. You may not be thanking me once you eat."

He laughed, and she felt her smile widen. It felt as though it had been forever since she had heard that sound. "I'm sure it will be fine," he said, eyes twinkling. "It smells divine. But there's something I need to do first." He held out his hand.

She frowned, but reached out to place her hand in his. "What is it?"

"You'll see." He pulled her into her small living room and sat on the couch. Before she could say anything, he was tugging her down onto his lap. He reached into the back pocket of his jeans and pulled out an envelope, which he handed to her. "Here. This is for you."

Puzzled, she took it. "What is it?"

"Open it and see."

Anna ran a nail under the flap of the envelope and pulled it apart. Reaching in, she pulled out several strips of paper. *Tickets,* she realized after a moment. And not just any tickets. Two of them bore the familiar picture of Big Ben, and two of them were for the Tower of London.

She blinked at them. "Rhys…"

"I made you a promise, didn't I?" He rested his chin on her shoulder. "Thurston is dead. He can't bother us anymore. So I can finally take you on that date that you asked for. I thought we could go tomorrow. We'll hit Big Ben first. It's really beautiful in the ---"

He was cut off as Anna threw her arms around him, squeezing him tight. "You remembered," she whispered, her voice suddenly thick.

He chuckled as he hugged her back. "Of course I did." He pulled away so that he could cup her face in his hands. "I like spoiling my girlfriend, and she wants to go on this crazy, touristy date. So that's what I'm going to do."

She laughed, feeling all of her worries and doubt about her relationship with him evaporate. "I love you, Rhys Blackwood."

"And I love you." Suddenly, he got to his feet, holding her in his arms. Before she could say anything, he was striding towards her bedroom.

She let out a squeal, but was still laughing. "Hey. Dinner's going to get cold!"

He gave her that toothpaste-ad grin, and her heart flip-flopped. "Dinner can wait."

Made in the USA
Lexington, KY
05 April 2015